Pilgrims of Promise

THE JOURNEY OF SOULS
SERIES

Pilgrims of Promise

C.D. BAKER

RIVEROAK®
Good News in Fiction

COOK COMMUNICATIONS MINISTRIES
Colorado Springs, Colorado • Paris, Ontario
KINGSWAY COMMUNICATIONS LTD
Eastbourne, England

RiverOak® is an imprint of
Cook Communications Ministries, Colorado Springs, CO 80918
Cook Communications, Paris, Ontario
Kingsway Communications, Eastbourne, England

PILGRIMS OF PROMISE
© 2005 by C. D. Baker

This story is a work of fiction. All characters and events are the
product of the author's imagination. Any resemblance to any person, living or dead, is coincidental.

Cover Design and Photo Illustration: Terry Dugan Design
Map by dlp Studios, Colorado

First Printing, 2005
Printed in the United States of America
1 2 3 4 5 6 7 8 9 10 Printing/Year 09 08 07 06 05

**Published in association with the literary agency of
Alive Communications, 7680 Goddard Street, Ste. 200,
Colorado Springs, CO 80920.**

Unless otherwise noted, Scripture quotations are taken from the
HOLY BIBLE, NEW INTERNATIONAL VERSION®. Copyright ©
1973, 1978, 1984 International Bible Society. Used by permission
of Zondervan. All rights reserved. Scripture quotations marked NKJV
are taken from the New King James Version®. Copyright © 1982 by
Thomas Nelson, Inc. Used by permission. All rights reserved. Scripture quotations marked KJV are from the King James Version of the
Bible.

ISBN: 1-589190149

*To those glad hearts redeemed
to their adoption*

*Editor's note: Please find at the back of this book
powerful discussion questions for group or personal
study (Readers' Guide, p. 481), as well as a helpful
glossary (p. 495) for clarification of terminology and
historical information.*

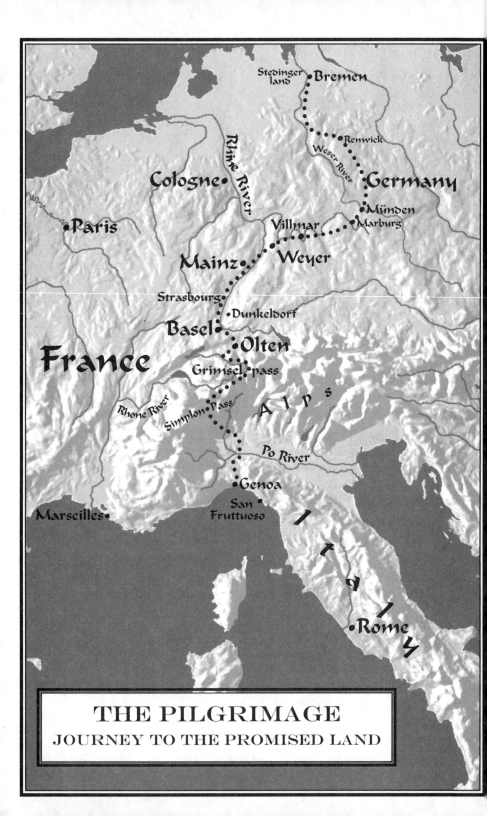

THE PILGRIMAGE
JOURNEY TO THE PROMISED LAND

ACKNOWLEDGMENTS

This book is the third volume in a series that has taken ten years to write. It is, therefore, a fortunate repetition for me to extend thanks to my wife, Susan, for her remarkable contributions of patience and grace. She has been a delightful research companion and a supportive critic. Without her I would have had no compass for this journey.

I must also applaud my circle of draft critics for their generous support of this project, particularly Dr. Father Rock Schuler, Mr. Edward Englert, Rev. Matthew Colflesh, Mrs. Karen Buck, Mr. David Baker III, and Mr. and Mrs. Charles and Elizabeth Baker.

To my agent, Lee Hough, another hearty thanks. He has been a faithful advocate and friend. Craig Bubeck and his editorial team at RiverOak cannot go unmentioned. They and their marketing associates deserve recognition for their outstanding professional oversight. My German instructors, Joseph and Elizabeth Christ, have provided enthusiastic support and helpful guidance.

Again I extend my deep appreciation to the Roths, Wickers, Klums, and Lauxes of Weyer, Germany. They endured many selfless hours by foot, car, train, and plane teaching me much about their homeland. Their contribution to my work is incalculable.

Many other kind persons throughout Germany, Switzerland, and Italy helped my research in innumerable ways.

In Germany I was ably assisted by Ms. Saskia Langkau of Münden, Mr. Eberhard Wigro of St. Boniface's Church in Hameln, and particularly by the Rev. Peter Meinert of St. Gallus Church in Altenesch. To these and to all the unnamed curators, passersby, hosts, and helpful guides who provided assistance, I offer my sincerest thanks.

Finally, allow me to express my gratitude to God for His goodness to this struggling writer. His hand has been clearly present from the outset, and I pray my work may bring Him at least a portion of the honor He alone is due.

INTRODUCTION

The councils of Christendom's kings fell silent and the halls of her mighty knights were stilled. By the solemn prayers of Hallowmas in the year 1212, news of the failed Children's Crusade had been whispered along the winding byways of Europe and filled countless hearts with grief. From the pope's lavish palace to the damp recesses of far-flung parish churches, a collective groan was lifted to heaven.

The records tell us that a frustrated Pope Innocent III soon scolded Europe's knights for hiding within their castles while leaving the children of Christendom to serve the holy cause in their stead. It was a complaint that more likely caused harm to his crusading vision than it did to inspire his princes. His successor, Gregory IX, elected in 1227, would offer a more fitting tribute to the young crusaders. He erected the Chapel of New Innocents in memory of those children who drowned by shipwreck. Its ruins can still be found on the sunny island of San Pietro, which lies in the crystal-blue waters of the Mediterranean Sea near the coast of Sardinia.

Other facts appear in the chronicles of at least four credible witnesses. The annals of Brother Alberic of Trois Fontaines, Brother Godfrey of St. Pantaleon, Bishop Sicard of Cremona, and one M. Paris are supported by oral tradition and the later writings of Roger Bacon. Accordingly, we have learned that many adults chose to blame the surviving children for the failure of the crusade rather than face their own complicity in the matter. They accused them as having failed in their faith and, consequently, subjected the helpless lambs who ventured home to the most vile acts of human imagination.

Despite the incredulous imputation of blame by many adults, villages and towns across Germany and France were also filled with anguished parents who rued the day that their beloved sons and daughters had taken the Cross for such a hopeless and ill-reasoned cause. An angry mob gathered in the city of Cologne, where Nicholas—the German crusade's self-proclaimed boy prophet—had previously excited the imagination of many. Venting their fury, enraged men dragged Nicholas's father from his house and hanged him. Nicholas himself was never found. He quickly became a character of legend, some believing that he was sold into slavery in North Africa only to escape and eventually take arms against Islam in the Fifth Crusade. His twelve-year-old French counterpart, Stephan, vanished from history's record altogether.

Despite the disquieting loss of legions of children to misplaced devotion and the discontent of the masses yet yoked to bondage, the stubborn grip of an aging order held Christendom fast. The lords attached themselves greedily to the determined cause of popes who sanctioned several more crusades. These failed efforts would be pitiful shadows of the mighty First Crusade. Far from defending brothers in Christ from the cruel expansionist swords of Islam, they degenerated into little more than pillaging adventures that resulted only in furthering the cause of hatred.

By the close of the thirteenth century, interest in Rome's old crusading vision had finally waned beyond revival, and the pleas of exasperated popes went unheeded. Many had become weary of bloodshed, corruption, and tyranny. The embarrassment of the Children's Crusade had ignited a simmering dissatisfaction that, fueled by Europe's exhaustion, ultimately contributed to the end of the crusading era.

A new vision of the future was arising, and its messengers would be quite different from those of the past. Devout monks, restive poets, courageous scholars, and defiant peasants—motivated by the insufferable errors of their world—would put feet to change.

Against the abuses of Roman authority—no doubt *because* of them—a contrasting way of faith began to emerge. Christian men and women such as St. Francis and St. Clare of Assisi began to proclaim the Christ of the Gospels. Denying themselves, Francis and Clare carried words of love and compassion out of the monasteries and directly to the weary people of Italy. Their words and those of others would spread and gradually awaken the hearts of Christendom's long-suffering folk. Their legacy would warm the soul of Christian Europe in powerful ways.

While such matters stirred, the political power of the Roman Church weakened, and the slow rise of nation-states began. However, it would not be enough for power to simply slide from pontiff to king. The age that had gone before would simply not allow it. The people had borne the weight of oppression for so long that it had made them muscular, and truth had invigorated their spirit. The natural consequence of truth, of course, is the rise of liberty. Political institutions formed that recognized the divine rights of both kings *and* persons. It was *Magna Carta*—guided by the enlightened hand of Archbishop Stephan Langton and escorted to the future by the "Flower of Chivalry," Sir William Marshall—that laid a framework for the liberties of the English-speaking world.

The world of this story was at the beginning of all these things, when an old age was sputtering in its death rattle and the faint heartbeat of another life had begun. The disquieting events of the Children's Crusade became joined to centuries of hardship as more kindling for the fires of liberation. Like dough broken and pounded by the baker's hand, the lives of many had been kneaded and pressed so that another era might finally rise fresh and fragrant. Those who had endured the troubles of the past had suffered along their way, but their tears of sorrow had swelled the river of promise where currents of truth would lead others to new life.

So, now come, join our brave companions one more time. They have struggled to overcome great things, but their journey has not yet ended. Like the world around them, theirs is a season of change, a destiny of new beginnings, a time to lay hold of that which they have become.

Nova Vita

Chapter One

SCARS OF MERCY

here are moments in the times of men when the hearts of angels fail, and their legions join with breathless mortals to plead before the throne of grace. And in this sacred pause, it is as though all the world lies in wait for mercies to rain from heaven, for the mighty hand of God to stay contrary winds, and for a troubled few to find deliverance in the triumphant herald of a kindly Providence.

It was a moment such as this, on the twenty-eighth day of September in the year of our Lord 1212, when the sun shone brightly over the salt-splashed rocks of Genoa's jetty. Far above the few stray clouds, beyond the yellow star, a host of heavenly beings looked on as their fellow warriors battled the servants of evil to save the lifeblood of one and the spirit of another.

Below, atop the jagged black rocks, a weary and frightened old man begged his God to deliver them from the day's sorrow, while another stood in the pounding surf with his face uplifted, abandoning all ways except the way of faith.

"Help!" cried the desperate, shrill voices of a company of children floundering in the sea. "Help us!"

Pieter tore his attention from the plummeting body of young Wil and cast his gaze across the water at the flailing arms of his precious ones. The old man roared to the anxious cluster of children standing slack jawed by his side.

"Everyone! All who can swim, go! Save these as you can!"

Without hesitation, the brave young lads and maidens clambered down the dark rocks and plunged into the water. As the relentless waves pushed them backward again and again, they coughed and sputtered their way from the jetty's safe edge to depths where bare toes could no longer bounce upon the sea's gravel bed. Those who were able swam awkwardly toward the frantic, grasping hands of their floundering comrades.

Bellowing cries of anguish, Heinrich could do no more than rock forward and back again, pleading with his God, the angels, Mother Mary, and all the saints gone before to give strength to these failing children—and to spare his beloved sons. He fixed his eye on the spot where he had seen Wil enter the sea after leaping from the cursed, wicked ship of devils. *Does he still live, or is he lost?* He scanned the bobbing heads between the jetty and the vessel for a glimpse of red hair. "Oh, that Karl is among them!" he cried.

Many of the child crusaders who had jumped ship took hold of an assortment of debris that they had wisely thrown overboard. These fortunate ones clung desperately to their dubious crafts and slowly, so terribly slowly, struggled closer to the waiting jetty and the anxious hands stretched toward them.

Pieter stumbled about the rocks, rushing in and out of the water with one sputtering child after another in his grasp. Heinrich, too, dragged coughing crusaders to safety, all the while shouting for his children. He ran from one child to the next, lifting chins and turning faces. He did not find either lad.

He looked up into the sky, brokenhearted and desperate—all hope was fast fading. Then the voice of a young woman reached his ear. "Sir Friend, he shall live."

For a moment Heinrich said nothing. He closed his eye in disbelief and then opened it in faith. "Aye, girl, so he shall!" The man stood upright and boldly rushed once more to the water's edge. There, joined by Pieter, dripping Solomon, and a growing host of believers, Heinrich faced the blue water of the rolling sea.

A gull called overhead, and then another echoed the lonely call as a wave splashed loudly to one side. For a quiet moment all watched in utter silence, until Heinrich cried the sound of heaven's joy. "There! There is my son!"

In an instant, a flock of pointing fingers gestured excitedly toward the golden head of Wil, half-submerged, yet clearly visible in the roll of the sea. As though with one voice, Heinrich and Pieter shouted for swimmers to race out with what flotsam had washed ashore. The lad's father could barely restrain himself as he splashed into the surf, urging Rudolf, Paul, Helmut, and an exhausted, though bravely determined, Otto to the rescue. The four paddled furiously toward their friend.

Pieter joined Heinrich, and both men stood chest deep in water, shouting encouragement to the brave crusaders. Little Heinz plunged into the water followed by Frieda, her sister Gertrude, and nearly a dozen others. Poor Heinrich cursed his missing arm as he stared helplessly at the flotilla of swimmers challenging the sea to save his son. He watched breathlessly as Wil's head rose in the swells, and with each roll his pounding heart leapt for joy. For a moment the lad disappeared from sight in the troughs, and the man's mind flew to Karl. "Pieter," he said anxiously, "what about my Karl?"

Pieter pursed his lips. "Pray for Wil, my son. We'll speak of Karl soon enough."

The answer chilled Heinrich, but before he could reply, desperate cries from the water drew his attention. He craned his neck but saw little more than furious splashing and lurching bodies. "Trouble, Pieter!"

The old man nodded. "What I would give for the strength of my youth!"

The children standing on the jetty watched nervously as their fellows floundered in the deep waters. From their vantage point, the scene near Wil had become chaotic. Most of the swimmers had turned back and were now crawling against the current toward the safety of the black rocks. However, it seemed as though Wil had somehow been snatched from the water and laid atop a floating litter.

Finally, the first swimmers returned and were pulled from the sea by the hands of their fellows. Others came behind, most coughing, gasping for air, and some in tears. Frieda staggered onto the shore wailing in grief. Her hair hung in dripping strands across her heaving shoulders, and her eyes were wide with terror. Heinrich and Pieter ran to her as Heinz collapsed at her feet.

"Gertrude!" she shrieked. "My sister!"

Pieter placed his arm around her, and she fell into his embrace sobbing and trembling. Dripping wet and gasping for breath, Heinz turned a sad face to Heinrich. "Gertrude … drowned."

Heinrich paled. "I remember her."

The young boy nodded. "We got near … Wil … and she just … sank."

Heinrich turned a quick, though compassionate, glance toward Frieda before hurrying back to the water's edge. Coming toward him, ever so slowly, was Wil, guided by four rescuers. He had been balanced facedown along a plank. His limbs dangled limply over the sides, and he was close enough now for Heinrich to see swirls of blood around the satchel still slung across his shoulder. "Pieter! Come quickly!"

The man gave Frieda a tender squeeze and then made his way for the surf, where he waited alongside the anxious baker.

"See … there is blood in the water."

Pieter nodded. "With that much, 'tis a good chance he's alive, though perhaps not for long. He must be badly cut. I'll need thread, wax, and a good needle." He thought for a moment, then summoned little Heinz, Ava, and another strapping lad. "You three, hear me well. Run as fast as your legs will carry you to the sailmaker's shop along that path, right over there. Tell him we need a roll of thin thread, a candle, some sailcloth, and a stitching needle. Tell him we'll pay later, but you must hurry! 'Tis most urgent."

Heinz narrowed his squinty eyes. "And if he won't give 'em up, or if he isn't there?"

Without a blink the priest replied, "Then take what we need and run like the wind!"

The three sprinted away as Pieter splashed behind Heinrich into deeper water, where they awaited the four exhausted lads slowly lurching toward them. "Good men!" cried Heinrich. "A little farther now ... just a bit more!"

Straining forward, Heinrich and Pieter stretched out their hands. At last, Heinrich laid his thick fingers on the arm of Otto and pulled him toward shore. Pieter grabbed hold of Rudolf and the group rolled forward in a gentle swell. Falling, stumbling, and tripping about the wet rocks, all hands seized Wil's body and slid him off the board and into a cumbersome six-way embrace as they struggled to carry him to the flat boulder Pieter had so calmly sat upon that very morning. "Methinks he's nearly dead!" cried Otto.

"Quickly, let me see him!" ordered Pieter impatiently. He and Heinrich rolled the motionless lad to his back and looked him over hopefully. But, alas, none saw any signs of life. His color was drained, his skin ghostly white, and his lips faded purple. His limbs and torso had been sliced into red ribbons; a long gash split his left cheek. Heinrich looked to Pieter with a forlorn, despairing face and silently implored the old priest to do something.

Pieter stared at the face of his beloved young friend and wanted to weep. A breeze tousled his hair and seemed to carry a message to him. He suddenly looked up, for he thought he could hear Karl's voice whispering to him, "But there *are* miracles, Pieter." The old man nodded to the unseen face and, to the astonishment of the others, answered out loud. "Aye, lad, there are miracles indeed!" He abruptly bent low to lay his head on Wil's chest, then rolled the lad on his belly and pressed hard on his back.

"What—?"

"Not now, Heinrich!"

Water suddenly gushed from the boy's lungs as Pieter pressed firmly. He quickly folded Wil's hands under his face and alternated pulls on his bent elbows with pushes on his back. The children stared dumfounded as the man kept pressing and pulling, pulling and pressing, all the while pleading with heaven for mercy. Some thought he had surely gone mad.

At last, blood began to ooze more generously from the lad's wounds, and Pieter shouted for joy. The children now believed he had truly lost his mind. He rolled Wil to his back and listened to a heart beating very, very weakly. "God be praised!" shouted the old man. "Now, where's m'thread?"

At that moment, all heads spun about to see three of their fellows sprinting wildly across the rocks, racing away from a shouting guildsman chasing them with a brandished knife. At once Heinrich jumped to his feet and drew his dagger. He moved toward the man as the imps scampered past him with a handful of supplies.

"Father Pieter!" cried Ava as she fell at the priest's feet panting. She proudly opened her palm and presented Pieter with two thin needles, both slightly arced.

"Perfect!" cried Pieter.

Heinz arrived next with a ball of thread and a smile as wide as the blue horizon. "Thread!" he boasted.

"Aye, lad, well done!"

The third comrade presented a stout candle and an armload of cloth. He handed Pieter his treasure with a nervous glance backward.

Meanwhile, Heinrich held the cursing sailmaker at bay with the point of his long dagger. "Hear me, whether you understand me or not!"

The man growled. "*Ladro!*"

Heinrich nodded. "Aye, take this." He tilted his head toward his satchel and motioned for the man to back away. When the man had taken several steps backward, Heinrich put the dagger in his teeth and plunged his hand into his coin pouch. He produced five silver pennies and tossed them to the grumbling fellow.

The sailmaker picked up his pennies and narrowed his gaze at the broad-shouldered, shaggy German's menacing appearance and glistening dagger. Deciding he'd be better off not pressing the matter, he turned away, leaving a string of blasphemies in his wake.

By now Pieter was working furiously over the unconscious Wil. Surrounded by nearly two score of gawking onlookers, he barked orders to many. "You boys ... build us a fire there." He tossed his head toward an empty field about two bowshots south. "You four, tear this cloth into strips. You, Otto!"

"Aye, sir."

"Scour the shore for anything we might use for a night's camp; then take a counting of our company."

Heinrich hurried to Pieter's side. "Shall he live?"

The old man looked up with a resolute expression. "*Ja!* Somehow I can *feel* it! Now help me press cloth into these wounds till I sew them."

The baker nodded and took hold of a handful of bandages that he pressed firmly on Wil's most severe wounds. "Ah, dear boy, you must fight!" He turned toward Pieter, whose fingers were nimbly dragging thread across the wax candles. "I've not yet seen Karl. I fear the worst."

Pieter looked up sadly. "I've not time now, Heinrich. We must save this one." The old man wondered why Heinrich made no query of Maria.

❧

It was two hours of careful stitching before Pieter released a heavy sigh. Wil had narrowly escaped the attempted butchery of the *San Marco*'s evil crew, but whether he'd survive his wounds was yet to be known. The late September sky was darkening quickly, and word of the crusaders' presence had drawn s more children to the southern end of Genoa where Pieter's camp was now forming around a large driftwood fire. Wil was carried carefully to the fire's edge, and Pieter attended him anxiously with Heinrich close by his side.

Though Wil's future still teetered in the balance of destiny, Otto bore despairing news of the others. Four fellow crusaders had perished, including Gertrude and Conrad, whose bodies had washed ashore with the evening tide. According to Otto's count, of those who had followed Wil into Genoa, only eleven had survived. But now, this company added to the other young crusaders numbered more than three score and was growing.

Searching the young faces by firelight for any sign of

Karl, Heinrich had come to his own conclusions when he confronted Pieter once more. "Father, I beg you. Tell me of Karl." Etched in shadow, Heinrich's face was drawn in grief.

Pieter nodded and bathed Wil's bandaged wounds with another cup of salt water.

"Did you hear me, Pieter?"

"*Ja*, my friend." The priest stood, took a long, trembling breath, and faced the anxious man tenderly. "Dear Friend, your good son is with the angels."

Heinrich closed his eye and struggled to breathe. He groaned, then staggered backward with an anguished cry. Pieter stretched a tender hand toward the grief-stricken wretch and prayed for him quietly. "And Maria was left with the good brothers in Arona."

The baker mumbled a few incoherent words, then retreated into the darkness, sobbing. He left the light of the campfire far behind as he hurried angrily along the turbulent shoreline. Alone under a magnificent night's sky, he paused to stare at the silvery silk of the water's surface as his gaze blurred behind a curtain of tears.

His mind carried him to happier days in Weyer, times when hope had not yet faded. He could feel his little boy crawling up on his lap and wished only that he might wrap two arms around him once again. He could see his beloved Karl romping about Weyer, wrestling with his brother in the tall grass of summers past, selling bread along the Münster road, and bidding him a sad farewell. He drew some comfort from the happy images and even smiled sadly. But this was a loss he could not bear, and the man collapsed to the ground in despair as the sea rumbled and hissed at him from the crevices of the rocks.

In the whispers of the surf, he heard Emma's voice again, and in the deeper tones he heard the gentle words of Brother Lukas. He set his jaw, turned his face, and looked far up into the sky, past the merciful moon and beyond the twinkling of kindly stars. His throat swelled as he thought of Karl smiling from above, free to laugh, free to sing, free to dance in the gardens of heaven.

~

At dawn's first light, the currents of melancholy, exhaustion, hunger, and privation swept over Heinrich and Pieter like a rush of unwelcome waters. Wil was sleeping restlessly in a state of fever while a host of children milled about the field without food, proper clothing, or purpose. Their want was now a burden stacked atop the broad shoulders of Heinrich and leaning upon the clever craft of Pieter.

Heinrich had returned to Wil's side in the dark hours before dawn, still grieving in unspeakable agony, yet so thoroughly exhausted that his heart was fast becoming numb. Poor Frieda had spent the night in silent vigil by the shrouded corpses of her sister, Gertrude, and her friend Conrad. The whole of the camp had grown larger through the night, and Otto stumbled to Pieter's side with a dutiful report.

"Our numbers now are four score and six," he mumbled.

Pieter wanted to weep, but he clenched his jaw and looked about thoughtfully. *Four score and six; no food, no shelter, no medicine for Wil. Me, a useless old man; the baker, broken in grief; they, an ever-growing flock of starving castaways. What can I do?* He squeezed his crook hard and looked to heaven. "O my God, give me strength." Finally, he took a deep breath to call for all to join him by a nearby cypress tree.

As a large company followed the white-headed man and his shaggy dog, he bade any hands willing to begin scooping four graves. In good time the graves were dug and a pile of rocks collected. Then all fell silent as Otto led those bearing the remains of Gertrude, Conrad, and two unnamed souls toward them.

Each shrouded body was laid gently in its grave midst muffled sobs and tears. Frieda knelt by her sister's body, while Otto and Heinz remained steadfast alongside their comrade Conrad. Pieter leaned hard on his staff and raised his arms over the assembly of lost crusaders. "I am Pieter, once monk, now priest to all in need. Bless you all in the name of our Lord." He then lifted his eyes to heaven. "*In nomine Patris, et Filii, et Spiritus Sancti...*" He proceeded to pray for the souls now departed, for those yet in peril, and for the hearts of grieving parents in so many faraway places. He blessed the brave ones gathered near, urged God's judgment on those who would cause His lambs more harm, and finished his prayer with a verse from the Thirty-Fourth Psalm: "I will bless the Lord at all times, His praise shall be always in my mouth."

The bodies were reverently covered with dirt; their shallow graves then mounded with small rocks and stones. Four crosses were offered by four crusaders and were set securely above each head. Lying in their graves facing east, toward the Jerusalem they had not seen, the four were then left to wait for the resurrection to come.

It was midmorning when tears had dried and huddles of hapless children began to form. It was then that Heinrich emerged from his own grief to join Pieter. He squared his shoulders and lifted his chin. "Pieter, I shall carry m'loss always. But now we must find a way to help these others. We've need for a plan."

Pieter stared at the red-eyed man with admiration. *One eyed, one armed, scarred in body and in soul, yet thinking of others.* Encouraged and inspired, the priest welcomed his new friend into his embrace. "Heinrich, Heinrich, my son ... may God's blessings be upon you." He took a deep breath and faced the throng of tattered children. "Heinrich, our God is a God of scars. Wounded people serve others well."

"Then these poor wretches ought bring joy to many."

Pieter chuckled. "I was thinking of *you!*"

The children were stirring amongst themselves. Many wished to go home. Others were more defiant. "We'll not fail in this!" shouted one. "I say we press on, on to Jerusalem!"

"Aye!" cried another. Fists were raised into the air, and a weak hurrah was sounded.

Paul, a quiet lad from Cologne who had taken Gertrude's place on the *San Marco*, stepped forward with a number of boys at either side. "Sirs, a word?"

The two men stood and greeted the young man. He seemed to be about Wil's age, calm and resolute. "I've traveled with my comrades from Cologne. We followed Nicholas's column along the west bank of the Rhine from Mainz, but we fell behind in the great mountains somewhere in France. Now we've word that Nicholas did not board a ship at all but is marching to Rome with many of our fellows."

Pieter grumbled.

"I've met with m'own company, and many wish to follow. The Holy Father shall set all this to right."

In a single voice, Pieter and Heinrich objected loudly.

The lad was undaunted. "No, sirs. We shall press on."

Pieter sighed. It would mean fewer mouths to feed and care for, yet his heart ached for them. "How many would you take?"

"We took a counting. About half say they'll join us, including some of yours."

Pieter was alarmed. "Some of mine?"

"Aye, Father." Paul pointed to a small knot of children standing proud and erect, determined to continue their quest. The priest's throat swelled. "Ah, Leo and Oswald, little Pepin and Edel ..." He sighed and turned to Paul. "Good lad, you are needed here with us. We need your help."

Paul smiled, aware of the ploy. He answered firmly. "Thanks be to you, Father Pieter. Your heart is good, but we've our duty and you'll not dissuade us. We leave for Rome on the morrow, and in the meanwhile we shall find food enough for all and what medicines you need."

Heinrich had said nothing. He looked about the haggard young crusaders with a mixture of admiration and dread. Looking upon each face, he wondered about the broken hearts of countless mothers in villages all across Christendom.

Too weary to contrive any clever schemes of dissuasion, Pieter yielded. "Then I've need of the following: bayberry bark ... ground or whole, leaves of sage, willow bark in any form, chickweed, and comfrey root in a heavy quantity. Now might I ask how you propose to acquire these things?"

Paul shuffled awkwardly on his feet. "Sir, this city's done naught but harm us. We think it ought offer what we've need of."

"So you're going to steal it." Pieter's face darkened ominously.

"Aye, Father."

The priest and Heinrich looked at each other for a long moment, then at the growing host of hungry faces. Heinrich was about to reach for the gold of Anoush still riding in his satchel when Pieter answered. "God's will be done."

Heinrich was surprised, and even Paul raised his brows in surprise. "But …"

"Hold your tongues; I'm too weary to argue about it." He whispered to Heinrich, "No amount of money in any of our purses could buy enough of what is needed."

Pieter turned back to Paul. "A man has a right to keep what is his, that is true enough, so long as none in his view is starving. Look about you. These innocents have been beaten and worse, cast out like so much rubbish by Liguria's most wealthy families. I need say no more."

Paul agreed knowingly. "My spies tell me that for now the city's glad we've moved beyond. We've spread the word that we're off to Rome."

Pieter nodded and then faced the sky and drew warm air through his nose. "We must speak with those who will not follow you, Paul. 'Tis too late for them to cross the Alps, and we cannot travel far with Wil. Yet we also must not stay here much longer."

"Can y'not delay one more day? We must allow Wil a little longer to heal and give ourselves time for a plan."

Paul wrinkled his nose. "Aye, perhaps. But we must be off soon."

"Thank you," answered Pieter. He beckoned Heinrich follow him away from the others, where they spent the next hour discussing their plight. They considered their numbers, the risks and advantages, as well as the season.

"Now, Friend, 'tis plain to me it is far too late to begin a march home," said Pieter.

The baker nodded. "And Wil cannot travel for some time."

Pieter sat thoughtfully. "Well, he cannot travel very far, but we must leave this place. The salt water is good for his wounds, but I fear for him if we stay here. With good herbs and some nourishment the lad may have a chance."

"So we need to find shelter for these many children, no doubt until Holy Week or beyond."

"Aye. And we've the little matter of feeding them ... nearly a hundred souls. The olive harvest is yet weeks away, and I've little faith in either the folk or the churchmen here in Genoa."

Soon after the bells of terce, Paul reported to Pieter and Heinrich that he had divided the camp between those who would follow him to Rome and those who would not. "My group is over there. We'll be returning to the city for another day's begging." Turning away, he hurried to the head of a line of some three score threadbare, bony urchins on bare feet. Wooden crosses were still tucked in each belt, and heads were held high.

Pieter sighed, then called for those from his original company who intended to remain with him. As the three gathered, he introduced them to Heinrich. "This little scamp is Heinz. Neither he nor I remember when he joined us, but he has been a worthy crusader. The children often call him 'Elfman.'" Pieter looked affectionately at the impish boy of about nine. He was a winsome lad with squinty eyes and an upturned nose.

Heinrich smiled and clasped his hand. "You've the look of a clever elf!" he chuckled.

Pieter smiled and turned to Heinrich. "Now surely you must know Otto?"

Heinrich turned toward the stout lad and studied him carefully. The boy was about Karl's age, thirteen. He was sandy haired, green eyed, and freckled. "Ah, you'd be from Weyer, the new miller's son!" He laid his hand on his shoulder and squeezed it with affection. "I remember your father and, as I think of it, even you. You were quite a bit smaller in those times!"

Otto smiled. "*Ja, Herr* Heinrich. M'papa spoke oft of you and your bakery. He said you made the best bread in all the empire!"

Heinrich laughed. "Finally, a miller who'd be a truthful

man! We needs talk of Weyer some."

"Otto lost his brother Lothar along the way."

The lad hung his head. "I carried his cross with me all the way to the *San Marco,* but I lost it in the sea."

"Ah," answered Heinrich sympathetically. "And what of your own cross?"

"I left it at Lothar's grave in Dunkeldorf."

Grumbles followed the word *Dunkeldorf.*

"And my cross is lost, too," added Frieda.

All eyes turned toward the young woman of nearly seventeen. She was still grieving her sister's death, yet bore her sadness with remarkable dignity. "I lost it in the sea as well, Otto."

"It was made for you by Wil," added Pieter.

"Yes. He made them for us at … at …"

"Ah, Heinrich, do you remember Frieda?" Pieter interrupted.

The man nodded. He remembered her from Basel because he had so feared for her there. "Indeed." He bowed politely. "You were about to say where Wil made the cross for you?"

Frieda hesitated and cast a quick glance at Pieter. He shrugged slightly and nodded.

"I … I set my first cross on Karl's grave."

Heinrich stiffened and a lump filled his throat. "I see. And did Wil leave his there as well?"

"Nay, sir. He had never carried a cross till then."

Heinrich thought for a moment, then looked about the little group. "So it seems you have carried one another's crosses like good Christians ought."

Pieter smiled kindly at his children. "Aye, Heinrich, 'tis so. They surely have!"

"And may I ask who has Karl's cross?"

The three stared at one another before Otto finally answered. "Karl set his first cross on Georg's grave."

"Who was Georg?"

"The fat fellow. Do you remember him?"

Heinrich nodded. "Ah, yes, I do. He had a kindly face. I remember him from Basel's dock."

Pieter bit his lip. "He saved Karl's life along the way."

The baker said nothing.

Otto continued. "Karl then carried Georg's cross and left it with his sister, Maria, at the cloister. Then he took your daughter's until he died; now Pieter has it."

Heinrich turned to Pieter blank faced. "I have no daughter on this earth."

The group darkened. "She is alive, sir! You needs believe it!" cried Heinz.

The poor man was completely confused. "I ... I had a daughter born very many years ago. Her name was Margaretha, but she died soon after her birth."

"But Maria is Wil and Karl's sister!"

Heinrich sat down stiffly and shook his head. "If so, my friends, I am sorry for it. I am not her father."

Pieter's mind was racing. "When did you leave your village?"

"Six years ago, almost to the day."

"Pieter," blurted Otto awkwardly, "do you still have Maria's cross?"

"Aye, lad," answered the old man slowly. "Now, enough of this." He cast a troubled glance at Heinrich. "When Paul's company returns, we must speak with them once more. I fear Rome shall not welcome them gladly."

Heinz shook his head. "They'd be a stubborn lot. I've talked to many, and they've set their minds."

Pieter sighed. "I fear so. I admire their resolution, but without wisdom, even that is vanity. I fear they see only failure in their crusade, not the wonder of lessons learned." He laid a kind hand on Heinz's shoulder. "Know this, boy. Fixing your eyes on failure is like staring into a chasm; it draws you to disaster."

Chapter Two

SUFFER THE CHILDREN

In the early evening, Paul and his crusaders returned to camp with a few baskets half-filled with a scanty selection of alms. They carefully divided stale bread, a pail of old olives, a few large fish gnawed by the cats of the fish market, a dozen citrus fruits, a few strings of garlic, some onions, and handfuls of sundry vegetables.

"Pieter, the city is completely wretched; it has only two good souls," declared Paul angrily. "The *podesta* ordered the beating of three of mine by the *Porta del Vacca*. Two kindly nuns had pity and took them in. They gave us the herbs you asked for. Use them well, for the cost was high." He handed Pieter a basket of corked clay jars.

"I tell you, Father, tomorrow night I shall take great joy in pilfering this place as it rightly deserves." He set his jaw hard and squeezed his fists. "My lads spied the place today, and we know what can be taken with ease. Inside the walls are palaces aplenty!"

Indeed, the free city of Genoa boasted the marble facades of its wealth. Since the days of Rome it had been home to successful traders, but since the great Crusades, Genoa had become one of the mightiest seafaring cities on the earth. Her ships protected cargoes throughout all the Mediterranean, and her mighty armies clashed with the Saracen in far-distant places. Having earned her freedom from the emperor years before, she now crowned her streets with the splendor of her riches.

The mountains that rose steeply from the sea were dotted with castle fortresses and church spires. Gracious gardens, vineyards, and olive groves filled courtyards and grand piazzas. In a large arc around the deep blue harbor, Genoa's villas proudly vaunted the hoarded wealth of the centuries. Within her rambling stone walls echoed the music of the money changer and the haughty laughter of great gain.

Pieter received the herbs with a cry of joy. "Well done, dear boy! Thanks be to God for those blessed nuns!" He ran toward Wil while shouting for Heinrich. He fell next to the boy's side and began digging through the basket like a child with new toys. "Ah, *ja!* Bayberry bark and willow, sage ... yes, yes ... and chickweed, and, and ... aha! Comfrey!"

Rudolf, the lad from Liestal, leaned over Pieter's shoulder. "May I help, Father?"

"Eh?" Pieter turned about and gawked at the pleasant fourteen-year-old for a moment. "What was that?"

"May I help?"

"Ah, of course. Yes, Rudolf, indeed. Go fetch me some fresh water and three small pails."

The boy sprinted away.

Another lad, Helmut, stepped close. He was about the same age as Rudolf, wore his sandy hair long like Wil, and turned his light blue eyes on Pieter with an earnest interest. "And me?"

Pieter smiled. "You are ..."

"Helmut, Father, of parts near Bremen."

"Helmut, yes, of course. I need a fire within two narrow rows of rocks built close enough to set m'pans on."

"Aye, sir."

Heinrich was kneeling by Wil's side, bathing his wounds in salt water again. He stroked the lad's face and wiped the sweat off his brow. "He's no worse."

"No worse, some better, methinks," answered Pieter.

Heinrich scratched his head and peered into Pieter's basket. "You'll be making a poultice of the comfrey?"

Pieter brightened. "*Ja!* You've some knowledge?"

"Just a bit gleaned from an old monk."

"Good. The chickweed makes a good ointment for the wounds as well. I'll apply the poultice by day and leave the chickweed to work through the night."

"And an infusion for the fever?"

"Aye, if he'll swallow. The bayberry bark is best, but I'll add the leaves of sage ... here, can you smell them?" He withdrew a pinch of brown grindings from one of the jars and held them to Heinrich's nose.

"Yes, that smell reminds me of home. I believe the willow bark can be used for the wounds as well. It has tannins."

"Hmm. Good idea," answered Pieter. "I'll use it to make a warm saltwater wash. The willow also goes into the infusion for fever."

Frieda came to their side and knelt by Wil. She took a rag from Heinrich's hand and gently dabbed Wil's face and neck. "I should think all his bandages need changing by now, Pieter," she said slowly.

The priest nodded and laid a gentle hand on her shoulder. "I am so sorry, my dear. Gertrude was a dear maiden."

Frieda nodded and smiled sadly. "Thank you, Father Pieter. She loved you as well. But now we need tend the living, don't we?"

Pieter said nothing as the girl began to gently unwind the lad's wraps. She had braided her blonde hair to keep it from falling into her face as she bent over Wil. Her brown eyes were now clear and wide, fixed on her purpose. She handed the stained bandages to others for washing in the sea and worked with Pieter to clean and tend the wounds with comfrey poultices.

By nightfall, Wil's fever began to break, and the young man tossed uncomfortably on his bed of leaves. But within a few hours he became more peaceful, even serene. Then, at long last, Wilhelm of Weyer opened his eyes and smiled weakly, for there, gazing down at him with warmth and abounding affection, was the firelit face of a very glad-hearted Frieda.

ॐ

Heinrich wept for joy with the news of Wil's awakening. He ran to the young man's side and sat close by him, resting one hand lightly on the lad's shoulder. He wiped his eye and smiled broadly. "Wil, 'tis so very good to see you!"

Wil stared blankly. In the firelight Heinrich looked menacing and unfamiliar. His beard was long and his hair wild. With a patch on one eye and one arm missing, the man looked like no one he had ever known. He nodded warily.

Frieda laughed. "Wil, 'tis Friend ... the one who saved us in Basel!"

A small light of recognition entered Wil's expression. "*Ja,*" he whispered in a weak voice. "Now I remember."

Heinrich's heart fluttered. *It is time,* he thought, *time to reveal my identity.* His mouth went dry and his tongue thickened, filling his mouth like heavy porridge. His mind raced and his heart pounded. *Dare I do this? Will he forgive me? Should he forgive me?* He drew a deep breath and leaned close. Barely able to form words, the shaking man spoke in a nervous rush. "Wil, dear lad. Please look at me. I am ... I am your father."

Wil's eyes narrowed and his brow furrowed. He pursed his lips and looked away.

His stricken father closed his eye and nodded, then bravely stood and stared helplessly at his son. Wil refused to speak. His face remained hard and his expression distant— fixed on some faraway view like the sightless gargoyles of unreachable heights. Heinrich drew a deep breath and stepped back in defeat. No long-sword in all Christendom could have pierced his heart more deeply, nor cloven it so completely as that bitter moment. He wanted to run.

Frieda took his elbow. "*Herr* Heinrich, he's weak and confused," she whispered.

The baker shook his head. "And with every right to anger, dear girl. Every right indeed."

The two faced each other for a long, silent moment before Heinrich finally turned to find solace in the solitude of the night. Frieda watched him trudge away, and her own heart ached. *He will forgive you,* she thought. *I know that he surely will.*

By now Pieter had heard the good news and came hurrying to Wil's side. "Ha! What a fright you gave us, lad!" he cried. "We thought you might be finished."

Wil offered a weak smile and nodded. "Me, too," he whispered.

Solomon licked the lad's face lightly. The dog's eyes flickered bright and cheery in the light of the crackling fire. Wil chuckled, though a bit painfully.

"Now, Solomon! Leave him be." Pieter pushed his faithful companion away playfully, then gave thanks over Wil with a prayer of praise. "My God, I love You above all things, with my whole heart and soul...." By the time he had finished, Wil had fallen fast asleep. The old man laughed quietly and lovingly wiped the young man's forehead with a damp cloth. "God be praised, God be praised!" He then reached for the cross of Maria that he had vowed to return and laid it by the lad's head. "May God's mercies be upon you both."

A cloud-filled sky obscured the stars, and the far edges of the crusaders' camp were shrouded in blackness. The children huddled around several small fires to keep warm. Pieter was handed a small bit of salted fish, and he worked hard to mash it between his gums. His single tooth always made salted meats a challenge, but he was grateful for the struggle!

He beckoned for Heinrich to come near, and the two huddled quietly in conversation. Paul had agreed to postpone his departure for one more day. Pieter disclosed his immediate plan to move the company to a nearby monastery that he knew. Satisfied, Heinrich agreed, though they both wished they had more time before moving Wil. "There's to be no changing Paul's mind," grumbled Pieter. "I can see it in his eyes."

"Aye. And once the city's looted, the guard will hang any they catch."

The priest nodded. "We must be as far away as we can by dawn's light. Pray for another miracle on the morrow."

Heinrich nodded. He had learned that miracles were rare but not impossible.

"My friend, what are we to do when the passes are melted?"

The baker sat quietly, scratching his finger aimlessly on the ground. "I've thought of little else other than returning to m'boys."

Pieter waited.

"I ... I suppose when the lad's able, we shall go home, home to Weyer. 'Tis where we belong."

Neither spoke until Pieter offered carefully measured words. "My friend, I know but a little of your story, but methinks you're not the same man who left Weyer those years past."

Heinrich nodded. He knew the man spoke true. "And what of it?"

"Forgive me, but were you not a bound man?"

"I *am* a bound man." The words sickened him. His stomach twisted and his mind raced. *A bound man? Servile? To whom? Who has the right to bind me?* The man clenched his jaw.

Pieter hesitated, then asked, "By faith, Heinrich, is Weyer truly where you belong?"

The man was not prepared for such a question. "Of course!" he blurted. "I am Heinrich *of Weyer!* I was born to men bound there since before time was counted. I was baptized in the Church; I've m'bakery, m'half-hide ... and m'wife." His voice sounded suddenly urgent, as if he was straining to argue the case to himself.

Wisely, Pieter remained quiet and listened to the man repeat all the ways in which Weyer claimed him. He learned of the cause and the code, of uncles and friendships, of Emma and Lukas, Richard and Ingly. He heard of harvests and feasts, sacred days and gardens—of butterflies and the Magi; of the bubbling Laubusbach and wending rye. It was a blend of things good and things evil, happy and sad; in short, a harvest of things familiar.

Finally the baker finished. "So, Father, I shall take my son home to his mother ... to Weyer."

Pieter nodded and held his thoughts as he looked about

the milling children. "So what of these?"

Heinrich stared at them sadly. "We ought to ask them."

"Indeed."

The two men stood and summoned those who had chosen not to follow Paul to Rome. The children came willingly and gathered at their feet. Both men had earned their trust—Heinrich several nights before when he protected so many, Pieter by his clergyman's robe and his unmistakable wealth of wisdom. As the children waited patiently, Solomon trotted among them and happily accepted their proffered affection.

Yielding to Pieter, Heinrich stepped to one side and carefully studied the faces of those assembled. They were a diverse group of boys and maidens from ages five to sixteen. All were thin, and all were weary.

"My blessed faithful innocents," began the priest, "God be praised for each one of you. Tomorrow is our last in Genoa, for we must find a safer refuge for a season. But when the winter passes, *Herr* Heinrich and I need to know how to serve you."

The group began whispering. After a brief delay, a squeaky voice offered the obvious. "I should like very much to go home."

The children murmured more loudly.

Pieter nodded. "Where is home, children? Where do you belong?" The names of dozens of places drifted forward. Heidelberg and Worms, Cologne, Mainz, Strasbourg, and Bonn … Freiburg and Basel, Zurich, and St. Gall. The crusaders offered the names of villages and hamlets from Swabia and Franconia, the valleys of the Alps and the flatlands of Saxony.

A small girl stood. Heinrich thought her to be no more than six or seven. She walked to Pieter and tugged on his sleeve. He bent low to hear her whisper sadly, "I'm afraid to go home."

Before Pieter could answer, another child cried from the edge of the campfire, "I cannot go home."

"Why not, boy?"

"I'll be beaten, now more'n ever. I've failed."

Pieter's face tightened as a chorus of others agreed. "Tell me how you've failed."

Answers, heretofore repressed, now came quickly. They erupted from aching hearts that had been locked by shame and confusion. "We did not reach the Holy Land, and so we failed God"; "My faith failed me ... methinks God must hate me now"; "I was afraid"; "I stole things"; "I cursed Mother Mary" ... On and on they listed their failings. Their poor little hearts emptied themselves of guilt like the spewing of poison from the mouth of a serpent.

Heinrich listened silently and understood. He saw his own painful emotions reflected in the contorted, woeful faces of these children and wished they all might be set free. He looked toward the wise old man and waited for his answer.

At last a weeping Pieter turned to Heinrich and said quietly, "Guilt sprouts where shame is planted."

He wiped his eyes and faced his children. "Oh, my blessed lambs. Fear not, you have *not* failed. You have walked with angels; you have trod on holy ground. Faith is not proven by things attained, but by walking in love.

"Oh, my children, my tender hearts, I see love abounding all around me! Look at you, each one. There." He pointed. "One holds another's hand. And there. There one wipes another's tear. You, little ones, have borne one another's burdens. You have been sisters and brothers, protectors and comforters to those who have shared your journey.

"Have you failed? No, most certainly not! Have you suffered? Indeed, and much. But know this: suffering is the path to faith and the doorway to compassion. Your suffering has made your faith stronger because you've learned to depend on love; it has softened your hearts toward one another because you've learned to feel pain. Sons and daughters of God, be proud of who you have become!"

The children sat spellbound, as did Heinrich. Shivers tingled his spine, and he suddenly wanted to cry out for joy. Pieter had given him hope again—hope to believe.

Lying on his pallet near the fire, Wil heard the message too. His heart was touched in deep places, and a lump filled his throat. Frieda took his hand and smiled.

Pieter leaned on his staff wearily. His face was yellowed in the firelight and etched deeply by flickering shadows. Finally he nodded. "So, my precious ones, what do we do?"

The circle remained quiet, and the old man prayed silently. It was not long before it became clear to him that he, Heinrich, and Wil had been called to redeem the journey of suffering that all had endured; it would be their sacred duty to shepherd these lost lambs to a place of safe-keeping. He beckoned the baker to his side and spoke to him quietly for a few moments. Heinrich nodded and clasped Pieter's hand. Then the pair faced the young crusaders once more.

"Listen, children, listen well," cried Pieter. "We shall pray for God's grace to protect you and guide you, to teach you, and to feed you in body and spirit. In the end, we may not take you home, but it is our humble prayer that we shall deliver you to the place where you belong."

The children were silent and suddenly content. A voice cried out, "God bless you, Father!" Soon the whole of them crowded around their guardians and rejoiced. Hope was sprouting where trust had been planted.

æ

Later the same night, Pieter wandered between the two separate camps that were assembled by the sea. While walking about, however, he caught sight of three figures standing quite still at the farthest reach of firelight. Each was wearing a hood over his head, and the figure in the center stood the height of a man; the other two were much smaller. The priest watched for several moments until the trio shuffled to the margins of another campfire, then another. He narrowed his gaze and moved beyond the reach of any light to draw closer.

The three skulked suspiciously near Wil's litter and toward Frieda sitting nearby. Pieter followed, but the cheery voice of Ava distracted the priest for a costly moment. She had screamed loudly as some boys tickled her. Pieter turned his face back to the place where the three had been standing, only to find them gone.

The priest hurried forward and arrived at Frieda's side. "Did you see them?"

"Who?"

"Three shadows under hood."

Frieda looked about. "No."

Pieter made a hasty circle of the whole field, driving his staff hard into the stony soil. "They must be here!" he grumbled. But, alas, they were not to be found. The old man sought Paul and upon finding him, drew him aside. "Listen, lad. Methinks spies have been about the camp. Have y'seen three figures under hood?"

Paul looked about carefully. "*Ja.* One of m'lads said he thought he saw three moving in the shadows like they didn't belong. He followed them, but they disappeared."

Pieter took a deep breath. "*Ja,* 'tis spies. I can feel it. Now listen to me. Your plan for tomorrow night must be changed. They'll surely report what they've heard to the city guard, and there will surely be an ambush."

Paul's face tightened. "No, Father. We've delayed long enough. Tomorrow we beg, tomorrow night we steal. Besides, we kept our talk in whispers."

Pieter yielded. "Then, at prime I'll lead my column into the city along with yours. I will try to meet with the *podesta* or his magistrate. If I get the ear of one of them, we might be given provisions enough. If I'm refused, I'll preach in the squares until the stones cry out for mercy."

"You seem uncertain," said Paul.

Pieter nodded. "'Tis true, I am. This city has a chill about it; it lacks the joy of goodwill. Wealth has turned the people inward. But I should not be surprised; greed is oft found in proportion to gain. My hope, however, is in this other sad truth: that oft the promises of a priest will do more to prompt alms than a hungry child's face."

❧

At first light, the camp assembled for a final day's begging. Pieter rose and scanned the milling throng with Heinrich standing near. "There, Ava, and there, my own Heinz and those over there and these." He pointed to this one and called to another and soon gathered a score of bony urchins around him. He laid his hands on Ava and Heinz with a chuckle. "Who could deny either of you?"

Indeed, only the hardest of hearts could resist their delightful charms. Ava, a tiny, feisty girl of seven captured all with the twinkle in her devilish green eyes. She with the elfish Heinz would make a memorable pair, particularly when joined with their snaggletoothed, spindly companion! The old priest called for Solomon and laid hold of his staff as he turned to Heinrich. "Pity for these, charity for me ... 'tis my hope for Genoa! I do pray, baker, that we return with a whole caravan of Christian kindness in tow! Now, children, follow me!"

Heinrich watched with some amusement as Pieter's company hurried through the field and to the roadway beyond. Pieter's rolling gait reminded him of a lame ox he had once plowed behind, and he laughed out loud. A breeze toyed with the old man's wispy white hair and bent his beard sideways. The baker smiled and remembered stories of Moses. Perhaps the old Hebrew had returned to the earth!

The baker returned to his son's side, where he sat by Frieda for nearly an hour. Wil awakened from time to time, took sips of water drawn from a nearby well, and then returned to sleep. Frieda had kept a faithful vigil, changing the lad's poultices regularly and washing his wounds in salt water. Pieter had instructed her to let the sun shine on the wounds for short spells, and so she obeyed. The young woman had been softened by many sorrows and now served others gladly.

Wil had endured so very much as well, and he had endured it in a matter befitting one saved through blood and water, being healed by salt and light. The ghosts of past shame and failure were fast fading into his fever's dreams, rendered weak by others' love and soon to drift to the margins of his memory. But sadly, some old hurts had not yet been healed, and the lad was not able to turn a kindly eye toward his contrite father.

Heinrich stood and sighed. His failings had made him a wiser, though sadder, man. His heart, exposed through

time to the frailty of others and of himself, was often heavy
with the felt knowledge of a world gone mad. Such sadness,
Brother Lukas had once told him, was the cost of wisdom.

"He's doing some better, *Herr* Heinrich," said Frieda
softly.

The man nodded. "You are his angel of mercy, m'dear.
Thank you for your good care of him." He turned and
walked toward the comforting sounds of the surf. He
looked thoughtfully across the deep blue and drew a long
breath through his nose. The sun felt warm, the air delightful. Finally, the weary baker looked up and stared at the
puffed white clouds hovering high above. His eye moved
from one to another, tracing their shapes. At last he smiled.
A plump one near the horizon had made him remember
someone very dear.

૱

Pieter and his company followed the harbor road as it arced
its way along the water's edge. Back toward the city they
marched, past the jetty of death and deliverance, past the
brawling tavern, the sailmaker's shop, along the wharves
and the wall until they stood staring hopefully at the twin,
cylindrical stone towers of the eastern gate, the *Porta
Soprana*. Pieter winked at his companions and joined a
throng of well-dressed merchantmen, coarse teamsters
and their wagons, and a colorful procession of nobles,
men-at-arms, and seamen funneling through the sixty-
year-old portal. As they passed by, Pieter's eyes fell upon
an inscription: "If you come peacefully, you may touch
these gates; if you come in war, you will leave defeated." The
old man grinned and dragged his hands along the rough
stone. "I'm not sure yet!" he mused.

Inside the city's four hundred-year-old walls the group
paused to stare. Otto called from the rear of the group, "It
stinks like Basel!"

"Aye! What city doesn't?" answered Pieter with a laugh.
The ancient city reeked of human waste and manure, of
urine and garbage. But despite its terrible odor, wealth had
begun to reshape the bawdy port. Competing with Venice
and with Pisa, the Genoese had pilfered the Christian East

as well as the coffers of Islam during various crusades. Their first patron saint, St. George, had been joined by St. John the Baptist, St. Lawrence, and the Virgin Mary in the city's protection, and these new saintly alliances seemed to have provided every advantage to its residents. The old city of fieldstone and timber had fast given way to marble from Carrara and Promontorio. Master masons from Milan, sculptors, painters, and architects from Byzantium had joined with the finest Genoese craftsmen to form powerful guilds that had reborn the city as a vital, artistic jewel of the Christian Mediterranean.

Pieter and his companions wasted no time in searching for city officials. The priest hoped to have an audience with the governor—the *podesta*. What he could not have known was that the Brescian-born governor, Manegoldo of Tettoccio, was unpopular enough already and had no tolerance for the stray waifs annoying his city.

"Children, get in good order!" snapped Pieter. With his threadbare crusaders in queue and Solomon trotting at his side, he began approaching numbers of guards, strolling men-at-arms, and other minor officials. "*Si, si,* I understand," pleaded the old man, "but we must be taken to the *podesta* or a magistrate ... perhaps the captain of the city guard?"

Again and again his pleas were met with scoffs and threats and even one awful wad of spittle in the face. Discouraged, Pieter climbed the hills of the city until he finally led his trudging company to the gates of the governor's palace. He had barely opened his mouth before lowered lances chased him away. Returned to the streets, Pieter pointed to a wall. "See, there? A fresco of incredible value! Yet they will not spare a pittance in charity."

"Should we forgive them, Father?" cried a voice.

The old man spat. *Reproved by a child!* he said to himself. He leaned on his staff and faced his column. "What say you?"

The children shrugged, most wrinkling their noses.

"Our Lord said, 'Forgive us our trespasses as we forgive those who trespass against us.' Think about that in this place." He turned and whispered to Solomon, "And if they can forgive the devils, I hope they teach me how!"

Thoroughly discouraged, Pieter led his weary children on a wandering trail through the alleys and byways of Genoa. Eventually the frustrated crusaders became utterly lost among the arcades and markets, the courtyards and gardens of the city. They tramped through the neighborhoods of the nobles, past marble portals, lovely colonnades, and arched windows of colored glass. They trudged by fountains and into a spectacular piazza where Pieter finally paused to preach.

A growing group of curious onlookers listened to the old man crow in his poor Italian, pleading with them to offer one last gesture of Christian virtue for the welfare of the little ones. He preached of the compassion of Jesus, the love of Mary, the faithfulness of the saints, and the hope of the angels. He promised them that he would lead his broken lambs far away, that the foreign children would "no longer stain the beauty of fair Genoa with their wretched presence"—if only some could fill their baskets and their opened palms with pennies or scraps of food or even rags for their bleeding feet.

With arms spread wide and his face tilted toward heaven, the old man begged the gathered citizens on behalf of his starving waifs. He entreated, he implored, he beseeched, coaxed, petitioned, and finally fell to his knees weeping in a final, desperate supplication.

He then fell silent, exhausted and without words.

The audience murmured, then tittered, and then returned to the tables of wine, cheese, and fruits scattered about the piazza, a few tossing pennies for the pleasure of seeing the desperate children scramble for them. Pieter stood quietly and finally gathered his little ones. "Come, my lambs, follow me." The old priest smiled at his flock and took his position at the fore of their column. With a firm grip on his staff, he lifted his head proudly and led his young crusaders through the square, elbowing his way past ample women adorned in all their finery, past protesting gentlemen in velvet doublets, and past gaping churchmen boasting fine vestments.

With little more than a shilling for their troubles, the company stumbled upon a kindly cluster of nuns who pointed them to the monastery of St. Andrea, where they fared a little better, leaving with baskets now half-filled with bread and some cheese.

Croaking like a veteran beggar, Pieter strained through the narrow streets of the city, passing by countless ruins of imperial Rome, along the crowded edges of piazzas and under the watch of the city's many towers. He scolded one of his young boys for pilfering a blind man's basket but ignored the quick hands of a little girl who plucked a lemon from a passing cart.

Pieter's crusaders passed the palaces of noble families with names such as Alessi, del Popolo, Sale, and De Martini. Begging as they went, they marched through the rutted streets along the ancient wall until they arrived at the city's cathedral—the Cattedrale di S. Lorenzo— where they paused to gawk. "Inside, children, are the wonders of conquest. I am told it is filled with gold and silver chalices, jewel-studded crosses, the finest vestments, and breathtaking reliefs. Crusaders have filled its reliquaries with miracle-working icons, including the ashes of St. John the Baptist. Humph, pity to have all that yet no food for the poor."

Turned away by an impatient clerk, the discouraged crusaders finally made their way to the shade of a squat tree. A wealthy woman strutted past and tossed a penny with her nose lifted high. Pieter caught the coin and called after her, "*Danke!*" The word prompted a loud "humph."

"Papa Pieter, why won't any help us?" asked Ava.

Pieter shrugged. "I feared it would be so. Look at us. Our skin is pink, our tongue is different. Look at our clothes.... We are poor and dirty. We come here uninvited, unwelcome. We do not belong."

Chapter Three

THE SEARCH FOR EDEN'S GATE

H ow is he?" asked Heinrich as he crouched by Frieda's side.

"Somewhat better. He was awake until moments ago. I told him of all that has happened."

Heinrich nodded and lightly touched Wil's face. "Seems the fever's broken."

"*Ja*, but we must allow the wounds to dry."

The man studied Wil's bandages and lifted a few to check his stitched wounds. "The red worries me some."

Frieda nodded. "The deep cut along his belly is the worst. It gives pus and the redness has spread."

Heinrich gently lifted the bandage off the lad's left cheek. "He'll have a scar from nearly eye bone to chin."

"There is no better scar in all Christendom, m'lord. 'Twas earned in saving others, and I'll see it always as his mark of honor."

"Ah, my dear. Well said. The boy has the heart of a knight."

At that moment Otto appeared with a couple of younger boys. They were the first of Pieter's column to return from the city, and they dumped a pitiful collection of crusts, garlics, cracked eggs, and onions on the ground. "They deserve to be robbed," he grumbled.

As the rest of the crusaders returned to camp, the bells of the city pealed loudly, announcing the prayers of nones.

The children had been given little, though the monasteries had provided what they could. Soon the day's collections were combined, and after a few words of thanksgiving, Pieter, Paul, and Heinrich summoned eager hands to begin the distribution.

By compline, what had been gathered was eaten, a few pennies counted, and feet were wrapped in the city's rags. Pieter made one final attempt to dissuade Paul from either his plot to rob the city that night or to take his crusade to Rome. Failing once more, he returned to Heinrich, and the two men surveyed their new company.

Forty children had chosen to follow Pieter and Heinrich. Most of the children were younger, as the majority of older ones had chosen to follow Paul. They were small and bony, and though a fortunate few wore shoes, none carried a blanket. About a third of the group were girls of varying ages, most being under twelve. Their ankle-length gowns were torn and tattered, their hair tied with weedy vines or loosely braided.

Heinrich looked about his group. "You, lad, your name again?"

A broad-faced boy of nearly fifteen stepped forward. "I am Rudolf of parts by Liestal."

Heinrich nodded. The fellow seemed pleasant enough, respectful and proud. "It was your parents who gave help to Wil's company in the mountains of the north?"

"*Ja.*"

The two chatted for a few moments before Heinrich said, "You'll be a captain." The man called another forward. "And your name, lad?"

"I am Helmut from parts near Bremen." The narrow-faced boy was about the same age as Rudolf.

"Bremen?" The familiar name caused Heinrich's face to tighten. "You live far to the east to join the crusade in Cologne."

"*Ja*, sir. My father is a free merchant in the lands of Lord Ohrsbach. He took me to the fair in Cologne when Nicholas was preaching of crusade."

The baker nodded. "I see. Very well then. You're to be

the other captain."

Heinrich raised his hand over the quieting assembly. "Hear me, all of you. We shall divide you into two groups of twenty. Each group will report to one captain. Over the captains is Otto, whom we shall call 'Master,' and over Otto is Wil, Father Pieter, and m'self. When Wil is healed, he shall be your leader, while Father Pieter and me will be his counselors. Is that understood?"

The children whispered amongst themselves. Most thought it a reasonable order of things. What Pieter lacked in menace, Heinrich had; what Heinrich lacked in wit, Pieter had. Wil, of course, was one of *them* and, as such, their true leader.

"Master Otto!" called Heinrich. "See that the groups are arranged. Keep the girls and little ones divided evenly."

The thirteen-year-old puffed his chest. *Master!* he said to himself. *I like the sound of that!*

Pieter drew Heinrich aside. "'Tis time we were leaving. Paul will not be dissuaded, and his group will enter the city about an hour past compline. If my memory holds, the monastery I spoke of is about six leagues south. With this bunch I fear it is a three-day march."

"You think Wil can travel safely?"

"I do. His litter is sturdy."

"And what about food along the way?"

"I've no idea. We'll pray for mercy."

Heinrich sighed. "Forty of us and barely more than a turnip or a pea! I've some gold that should help and some silver pennies."

"*Ja*, my son. But we must not forget we've a long journey north when winter's past. We should use your gold coins sparingly. How many have you?"

The two walked out of view, where Heinrich reached into his badly worn satchel and retrieved the pouch once presented by the old tinker of Salzburg—the gift from poor Dietmar of Gratz. He lifted it and handed it to Pieter.

As the priest untied the bag, he stared inside and informed Heinrich that the coins were likely minted in Sicily. "Ducats ... they're precious and valued all over Christendom."

"Aye." Heinrich picked one out and set it aside. "I've a special use for this one," he said. He then grabbed a handful and began dropping them one at a time into Pieter's joined palms. As they fell, each counted coin clinked atop the others like the sound of rain on thirsty ground, and when the counting was done, the two men looked at one another in astonishment.

"Amazing!"

"Unbelievable!"

"How can it be so?"

"Forty!" exclaimed Heinrich.

Pieter grinned. "Ah, the angels are surely with us. One gold coin for each child! God be praised!"

The pair returned to their company and immediately disclosed the plan to leave within the hour and to travel by night until they were beyond the wrath of Genoa. Surprised, the children were immediately anxious. Travel by night was a fearsome thing. Evil was known to lurk in darkness—highwaymen, wicked villains, beasts, spirits, and dreaded creatures of legend. They might become lost to wander endlessly in the mountains rising steeply from the sea. Or they might stumble upon some unseen precipice, only to fall into the merciless black waters below. "Pieter," said Otto, "surely not by night."

The priest understood, as did Heinrich. The baker, too, had ventured out in darkness along some fearsome trails. He thought of the Bohemian swamp and shuddered. Pieter nodded. "*Ja*, but know this: your enemies fear as well. You've suffered far more than they, and your sufferings have made you stronger than them all."

"But you've not yet said where we'll be going?" Otto asked.

"We've spies about, Otto, so I cannot say. I ask that you trust *Herr* Heinrich and m'self until we've begun our journey."

Still worried, the lad nonetheless agreed.

"Good. Now we must make ready. Have you organized the groups according to Heinrich's plan?"

"*Ja.*"

"Have we any sort of buckets or flasks?"

"We've a few things among us," answered Helmut. "A few pots, some clay jars, and the like."

"It will have to do." Heinrich cast a worried eye at Paul's group now assembled and receiving instructions from their commanders. *Brave lads, all ... and maids as well,* he thought. *If they only knew what sorrows are waiting in Rome.* He shook his shaggy head and walked toward them.

Paul turned to greet the man. "Godspeed to you and yours, *Herr* Heinrich."

"And to you, son." The man studied three rows of about twenty crusaders each. Most still carried wooden crosses stuffed defiantly in their belts. Their breasts still boasted embroidered red crosses—faded and tattered though they were. "Is there to be no changing your mind on this?"

"Nay, m'lord. We are fixed to do what we must to save our crusade."

"You truly believe the pope will give you guidance?"

Paul nodded confidently. "He shall equip us to carry on our crusade."

Heinrich sighed sadly. "Each of your followers has been offered a fair chance to join with us?"

"Aye."

"And none of yours wishes to refuse your night's raid on the city?"

"Aye."

Heinrich looked at Paul's gathering comrades quietly. *Brave, but so foolish,* he thought. Realizing he could not stop them, he relented. "Well then, walk with me for a moment." He led Paul a short distance from all the others and extended his hand. In the center of his palm was a gold coin. "Take this, my son. Take it to Rome. Find the church called *Santa Maria in Domnica,* and there you must give it to Sister Anoush. Tell her of me; tell her I've sent you. Tell her 'the worm is no more.' She will help you in ways beyond what the mere value of this gold could ever do."

Puzzled but grateful, Paul received the coin and closed

his fingers around it tightly. He looked into Heinrich's face with sincere gratitude and nodded.

Each camp reviewed its particular plan one final time. For Paul, the strategy of the night's robbery was complicated and perilous. He had decided to send seven groups of five through the gates along the northern arc of the city wall, the rest in trios through the carefully guarded southern gates. He had assigned most to the neighborhoods of the wealthy, though his group was intending to pilfer the Commenda—the hospice for travelers en route to Palestine. After the raid, they'd make their way quickly southward in hopes of eventually gaining an audience with the pope in his Lateran Palace.

Meanwhile, Pieter's captains checked their commands carefully to be sure all were accounted for and what few possessions they had were not forgotten. Frieda changed Wil's bandages before others tied the young man securely to his litter. Pieter prayed for his new flock, then for Paul's, pleading in grave tones for the safety of both and a happy end to their suffering.

Then, as the bells of compline prayers began to echo over the rooftops of Genoa, the two bands of crusaders bade their reluctant farewell. With tears, both companies embraced and wished one another Godspeed. They now suffered that painful moment when friendships lose their breath to become mere memories, when the sharing of life ends and reminiscing begins. For these veterans of hardship, purposes were no longer held in common, and new paths would lead them to different places. So while one was yet called "crusader," the other would now be called "pilgrim." And with that simple change in title, that subtle shift in name, destinies would be forever divided. They would never meet again.

≈

Night fell quickly as Wil's company hurried away from Genoa. As fearsome as the darkness was, however, it did not quench the relief felt by leaving the unfriendly city behind.

The road was narrow but remarkably free from ruts. It

had been cut through the mountains by the Roman legions centuries before and followed the arching Ligurian coastline from Genoa to all parts south. The forty pilgrims could not see it, but just two rods beyond the road's shoulder were steep slopes and stark cliffs dropping to the rock-edged sea. It was enough that they could hear the menacing rumbling far below.

Pieter had not yet disclosed his destination to any but Heinrich. He had been nagged by a sense of watching eyes since he had spotted the hooded figures in the shadows the night prior. He had felt them while begging in Genoa and said nothing; he had felt them upon his return. He had felt them again as the camps divided and felt them even now, deep in the darkness and more than a league from the city. Consequently, he had been reluctant to share his plan out loud or to even pass it secretly among the many wagging tongues of his flock. *Spies? Highwaymen? Spirits? I know not, but I sense they are very real!* he said to himself.

At long last, however, it was necessary to rest, if only briefly. Heinrich, Otto, Rudolf, and Helmut had been carrying Wil's litter since they had left camp, and their arms ached. Wil had remained awake through most of the journey, doing his best not to reveal the pain each stumbling foot brought to his wounded body. The smallest children were exhausted, though not a single one complained.

The left shoulder of the roadway was narrow and etched tightly into the steep, pine-covered mountains rising sharply alongside it. Pieter was now anxious, for being bordered on one side by the mountain and the other by seacliffs made his company vulnerable to any pursuit by Genoese men-at-arms. Fearing that the wrath of the *podesta* might have already been kindled by Paul's ill-timed raid, he counseled Heinrich to hurry the travelers along. "We must find rest *away* from the road. Pray we find a break in this eternal wall of mountains!"

"How far have we come?"

Pieter answered in a whisper. "From camp I reckoned us to be about five or six leagues away. With Wil and the condition of the children, I fear we'll do little more than two leagues a day. We need to find refuge off the road and travel only by night."

Heinrich nodded and returned to Wil's litter. He put a firm hand on its handle. "Up, lads," he said. "We've a bit farther to go."

The company stumbled along in the darkness as a cool mist added yet more misery. Unseen clouds then released gentle showers of rain. It was another hour before Pieter finally found a wide clearing to his left. Hoping to have found a pathway of sorts, he fumbled through wet pine boughs and tripped along rocks as he followed a ravine away from the road. "Come, children!" he urged.

Stumbling and falling, they pressed their way deeper into a dripping blackness that finally blinded them. "Enough!" cried Heinrich from the middle of the column. "Pieter, enough. We've nearly dropped Wil a dozen times, and none can see."

The old man's voice came from somewhere ahead. "*Ja.* I fear I can see nothing more. Here we shall rest."

Wet and shivering, the pilgrims searched for one another with groping hands. Finally they formed a tight huddle in the base of the ravine where they lay until a gray dawn wakened them from their uncomfortable slumber. Groggy and miserable, they said little as they waited for Heinrich and Pieter to command them. Not far from their hideout they could hear the rumble of carts and horses along the roadway. "Dare we venture out?" queried Heinrich.

The old priest wasn't sure. "We've probably four leagues to travel or more. At night we might travel a league, maybe two. We could travel farther by day, but I fear the provost guard may be about."

Heinrich grumbled. "Well then, it seems wise to hide by day. If we move deeper into the mountains, we might build a fire until dusk."

"And food?"

"We've none."

"Water we can collect from puddles."

"Aye, priest. A plan a day is all we need."

The two agreed quietly, and soon the column was picking

its way carefully through the heavy brush of the deepening ravine, eventually emerging into a wide grassy glade dotted with hornbeam, wild nut trees, and pines. "Ha, look!" laughed Pieter joyfully. "Almond trees and chestnuts ... pinecones all over the ground. Otto, the almonds should be ripe for shaking. Send one tithing to gather what they will; then break them open with rocks. But hear me now—let no one eat the bitters. Just a few will poison you."

"And the chestnuts?" asked Frieda.

"Yes, my dear. We are a bit early for them, but let's give them a go. Break the husks and we'll roast them."

Heinrich checked on Wil, who was lying uncomfortably on his litter. The young man's wounds needed dressing and he was thirsty. "Frieda, we need fresh bandages."

"Aye, sir. So I've seen. I've m'bucket to gather water, and you can help with the compresses."

"And, Otto," called Heinrich, "send the others to find dry wood. I'll flint a fire there, atop that rock."

So with many hands scattered across the soggy forest floor, the company quickly gathered pine nuts and almonds, chestnuts and even great handsful of mushrooms. To the delight of all, by midmorning a smoky fire was snapping cheerfully, and pots were boiling with a bounty of what treasures the Ligurian woodland offered. The day was still heavy, however; an eastern wind had brought dark clouds and more showers.

Wil was soon helped to his feet, a remarkable event considering the wounds he had suffered just days before. He leaned against a stubby, silver-leafed almond tree and smiled at his cheering comrades. "Soon, my friends, I shall lead you on m'legs!"

Frieda stood watchfully by his side and steadied him as he sat near the fire. His wounds had been bathed and his bandages replaced. Grimacing from time to time, the young man was truly grateful to be alive and had spent many an hour reflecting on his miraculous salvation. An occasional wistful glance from his father was the one troubling circumstance that weighed heavily on him, however, and he turned his face away.

By late afternoon, Heinrich felt uneasy for other reasons. He walked slowly to Pieter and bent low to his ear. "I feel someone watching us."

"*Ja.* Me as well."

"I fear we've been followed."

Pieter nodded. "Solomon's ears have been up and his snout lifted all the day long."

Heinrich fingered the bone handle of his dagger and leaned closer. "I'll make a wide circle."

The old priest drew an anxious breath. "Take another with you."

Heinrich hesitated, then agreed. "Who?"

"Heinz. He's the nose of a fox and is quicker than all the rest."

Without another word the baker casually edged Heinz to the margins of the camp. Then, like shadows under light, they vanished.

As a diversion, Pieter gathered his company and circled them close to the fire, where he began to spin them tales of old. Like he had done so often before, he thrust his staff into the air as if he were St. George slaying the dragon or the mighty Hermann, chief of the Germans who slaughtered the legionnaires of Rome. He stirred cherished memories of their homelands as he whispered of woodland sprites and elfish kings. When he spoke of the Saracens, the whole of the company stood and jeered; when he spoke of the Templars, they cheered and hurrahed! He made them weep for the hideous drowning of fair Minna and cringe at the nature-spirits hiding in the mists of the fateful Rhine.

Meanwhile, Heinrich and Heinz crept carefully across the needled carpet. Crouching under a dripping canopy of knotty branches, the baker peered into the brushy woodland. "Do you see anything?"

Heinz shook his head, then cocked it. "There!" he whispered.

Heinrich had heard it as well. A snap, then a rustle. He gripped his dagger firmly and moved forward. Step by step, the pair inched its way across the ravine. They stopped again as Heinz lifted his finger. "There." He pointed slowly.

Heinrich's eye followed it into a grove of pines where three hooded figures were squatting close together, facing the smoke of the camp. They appeared to be straining to listen, fixed on something. The baker's heart beat more quickly. He turned to Heinz and whispered. "Boy, hold fast." Silently and slowly, he crept toward the figures. As he drew closer, his mouth dried and his breathing quickened. A jay chattered nearby and a dove cooed. A squirrel rustled to one side, some unseen creature to the other. The man held still, then moved again, slowly through a bed of wet ferns to the cover of a low clump of myrtle.

The three spies had not heard a sound and surely had not anticipated Heinrich's flanking maneuver, but one suddenly stood and nervously turned his head from one side to the other. Perhaps he had realized that the burly, one-armed man was missing. Perhaps he sensed eyes now fixed on him.

Heinrich stopped and crouched yet lower as the figure spun abruptly in his direction. The baker's view was partially obscured by wild shrubs, but he was able to see that the face was young. The other two now stood, and all three drew short-swords from within their capes.

The dull silver frightened Heinz, who had been watching from a tangle of leafy saplings a safe distance away. He wanted to run, to sprint wildly away, but he held fast. His eyes darted from the three to Heinrich and back again, and they stretched wide when the baker began to move forward.

The man's jaw was set. He had faced more danger in his day than three slender youths, armed or not. He left his low cover and slid his booted feet quietly along the wet woodland floor, pausing only when eyes swept toward him. Closer he moved, then closer still. The heavens abruptly opened, and a heavy rain shower began to fall loudly through the trees. Like a veteran warrior, Heinrich seized the moment and rushed forward. "Ho there!" he cried with a menacing tone. "Hold fast!"

The startled spies whirled about.

"Your names!" shouted the baker as he approached.

For a moment, the three stood slack jawed as the shaggy

Teuton strode ever closer. Then, as if suddenly awakened from a trance, two sprinted in different directions, leaving their leader behind.

The flash of the figure's drawn sword changed everything. Heinrich snarled and clutched his dagger. With a shout, he charged forward as the youth planted his feet and crouched, sword at the ready.

Then, when Heinrich's hard-set face was plain to see, the lad lunged forward. The heavy-limbed man dodged the youth's sword with surprising skill and countered with a vicious swipe at his head, slicing the hood along the ear. With a loud cry, the spy stumbled backward, only to lunge again. His sword missed its mark, and Heinrich countered with another savage swipe. The youth's agile frame quickly veered, barely avoiding the severing of his throat, but it was enough for him. He turned on his heels and bounded away.

With the spies having disappeared in the misty cover of the forest, Heinz ran to Heinrich's side. "*Herr* Heinrich!"

"Aye, lad. All's well."

Heinz was shaking. "God be praised, I wasn't so sure you'd—"

"Eh? You thought me no match for three?" Heinrich winked. "Well, perhaps you're right, but we've lived to see another day!" He looked at his dagger and saw a line of deep red along its edge. He wiped it on his leggings and looked into the forest. "That should send him running."

The pair returned to the camp, which was now completely silent. "*Alles klar,*" announced Heinrich.

A cheer rose up as Frieda ran to Heinrich's side. "We heard the shouts in the wood!"

"*Ja,* girl. We'd spies on the hillside there." He pointed vaguely.

"Did you have a look?" asked the priest.

"There were three, but I only saw the face of one. It was somewhat familiar to me, though ..."

"Perhaps the same three as I saw," muttered Pieter.

"He was young, near Wil's age, and dark eyed, but 'tis all I can recall. I wounded him in the ear or side of the head."

"Enough to send him back to Genoa?"

Heinrich shrugged. "We can hope."

Pieter leaned on his staff and called for Solomon. The dog had given chase and disappeared into the mountain. "Otto, call your captains. We leave at once."

à·

Dusk was short lived and night fell quickly. To the delight of all, Solomon had returned with a mouthful of brown wool— either from someone's leggings or sleeve. "A fine loom," observed Frieda. "Expensive."

It had been decided that Heinrich would provide a rear guard by taking a position about a bowshot behind the column with Solomon. From there they might better know if any were following.

The rain eased, and the pilgrims traveled through the night without incident. The following day brought welcome sunshine and the safety of another small clearing in a brushy hollow, where the children found an ample supply of mushrooms and a few snails. Pieter's plan was for them to leave that afternoon on a circuitous route. "Children," he began quietly, "come close. I am leading you to a sanctuary where I believe we shall all be safe. It can only be found by boat or by a small footpath marked by a cross etched into a gray boulder under an ancient olive tree. Very few know of it; even fewer care to make the journey.

"The path begins about half a league beyond the fortress of the Dragonslayer."

All chins dropped. "Dragonslayer?"

Frieda's large brown eyes were as wide as Pieter had ever seen, and he laughed. "*Ja.* The folk nearby call it 'Dragonara.' I remember it as a little redoubt atop a rocky cape. I'm told the lords of Genoa are building a castle there now."

"Why the name?" asked a voice.

"Ah, it is named after the blessed St. George, the Dragonslayer of old. But we'll save the story for later. For now, listen. The castle and the village lie along this same sea road. I fear the garrison must be alerted by now, so we must pass wide in daylight ... through the mountains. Then we must circle back to the edge of the road again not far past the village. There we'll hide until first light on the morrow, then hurry for the marker."

The company grumbled. A march through the mountains would be difficult, even in daylight. Their feet were bleeding, and they were wet and cold. Finally, Wil called from his litter, "Hear me, all of you. Trust him. It is the only way."

The words of their wounded hero comforted the weary pilgrims, and after an hour's rest, Pieter raised his staff. "Follow me!" he cried.

ॐ

True to his plan, Pieter and his company marched into the mountains east of the roadway, then southward until angling back to the sounds of the sea once more. Shortly before dusk they arrived just south of Dragonara, where they could hear the surf crashing against a wall of rocks. "Ah, good," cried the old man. "We're very close now!" They hid in the brush off the roadway for the night and emerged from their woody cover at the first light of dawn.

As soon as he could see his feet, Pieter burst on to the road with a youthful stride and a happy smile, leading his column in search for the hoped-for footpath. Eventually, the old man slowed his pace as he scanned every rod of the shoulder for the obscure signpost. At last he stopped and raised his hands. "Here! God be praised! Look!" Just as he remembered, a gnarly olive tree stooped over a gray boulder. The rock had been carved centuries before, probably when the remote church was first built to serve some humble community now long forgotten. Barely visible on the boulder's face was an etched cross.

The column quickly turned off the road and entered the narrow footpath in single file. Judging by the undergrowth, it seemed the path was rarely used. The forest pressed tightly on both sides, leaving a corridor no wider than a small man's shoulders. Cutting thorns and brambles crowded the way, a certain obstacle for the merely curious. "The monks prefer to travel by boat," offered Pieter. A chorus of understanding answered.

For two hours the children followed the old priest along

the meandering footpath. Most grew discouraged, especially when the trail began to fall through steep ravines and then climb over stony knolls.

The sun was now high overhead, and what sky could be seen was blue. The forest's green was stale, of course, a thing natural to the season. Wood thrush fluted their throaty song from time to time, and a few warblers added music to the woodland. But, despite their pleasant sounds, Heinrich thought the mountainside to be rather plain and lacking in beauty.

The baker remembered climbing the Appenines weeks before and wishing for all the world that he could be returned to the heavy oak and massive beech of the noble forests of the northland. Here it was only softwoods and stubby maples, tangles of small-leafed brush and useless stands of scrubby pines.

The pilgrims pressed on, dragging themselves along the tight pathway in and out of the shadows of the wood. They had climbed steeply for a considerable distance and had begun a partial descent, when Pieter raced ahead. He turned and raised his staff. "Come, my blessed ones!"

The company followed him onto a sunny outcropping, where they gaped in awe at the splendid scene below. There, at the end of their sharply descending trail, was a simple jewel placed by the angels neatly at the edge of a crystal sea. Astonished, the column stared at the little paradise tucked safely away from the perils of a broken world. Below them were the old white buildings and impeccable gardens of the monastery of San Fruttuoso.

The complex had been built at the end of a narrow bay shaped like a blue finger that probed deeply into the green mountains. From high above, a sandy shoreline looked like a narrow white ribbon rimmed with palms and umbrella pines. On one shore stood a simple church and the monks' cloister that were set a comfortable walk from the water's edge. Directly across was an arched arcade that served as the monks' boathouse. The water was clear and inviting. A more welcoming haven none had ever seen.

Pieter then pointed the pilgrims' attention to the larger

view. The bay gradually widened in the distance until it finally yielded to the great sea that marked the horizon with a subtle blue line. Its waters were beautiful and shimmered blue-green, hemmed on three sides by steep, rugged mountains covered in pines, softwoods, and heavy shrubs and scarred with stark cliffs and crags.

The children's gazes remained fixed on the wondrous scene for long, dreamy moments, and they smiled. A pleasant scent from a landscape of hidden shrubs filled the nostrils of the forty glad-hearted travelers. The terrors of a lost crusade were briefly forgotten. The hypnotic cry of soaring gulls and the hush of distant surf softened the heartaches of comrades lost and of broken dreams. The sight before them was a healing balm, a gift from heaven to little ones who so desperately needed a Sabbath rest. Heinrich and Pieter gazed about their tattered column with the joy of good shepherds. They now hoped the brethren below would be as charitable as the wondrous vision might suggest.

In the meantime, Wil had been helped up from his litter by Frieda, and he stared at the panorama quietly as she lightly supported him. The aroma of fragrant flora mixed well with the scent of the sea, and he inhaled deeply. The warmth of Frieda's body faintly heating his own made his blood swim with joy. His belly fluttered and his skin tingled. Yet, despite the power of that moment, a haunting memory suddenly stole the young man's thoughts, and his eyes began to sting. He shifted uncomfortably, then turned to Frieda, and took her tenderly by the hand. His tongue felt thick and heavy, his throat numb. He hesitated, but as he looked into her face, all fear fell away and his spirit was emboldened. "I must ask you again to forgive my betrayal," he whispered. "I am proud to stand here with you."

The young woman bit her lip and nodded. They were words she had hoped to hear. Without a moment's hesitation, she lifted Wil's hand to her lips and kissed it softly. "I have already forgiven you, Wil. I surely have."

Wil smiled. His eyes, so often fired, were now limpid

his wounds. Heinrich, Frieda, Pieter, and Otto hovered nearby, offering bits of history as to the lad's condition over the past days. Wil grimaced a bit, then smiled at Frieda as the nimble fingers of the monks lightly ran along his many stripes. They mumbled and nodded, shrugged and wrinkled their noses until the infirmer turned to Pieter. "You've done well!"

The old man nodded and tilted his head toward Frieda. "*We've* done well."

"With permission, we would like to treat him with our own herbs and methods. We would like to start by laying him on that reed bed without bandages so that the wounds may dry. Later, we may soak him in the bay for an hour a day."

"The salt."

"*Si, Pater.* The salt and the sunlight. The water is as clean as any on the earth. It shall heal him like no other balm. In the night we shall wrap him in fresh compresses soaked in our own herbs. For most of the day we need to leave his wounds dry in the shade. In the meanwhile, he needs much citrus and vegetables. We abound in lemons and have a few struggling citron groves. Our gardens yield every green thing one might want.

"In any case, the lad is keen eyed and strong. His fever's nearly gone and his mind is clear. I've great hope for him."

Heinrich wiped his eye and nodded gratefully. "He's m'son…. Pieter, tell them he's m'son."

☙

It was true that Eden's gates had been long since barred, but the pilgrims agreed that no place on the earth could have served as a better reminder of what had been lost to man's sin. "A taste of what's to come, my children," said Pieter cheerfully on the second day. "These men of God have shared their food, their shelter, their kindness. They give us charity beyond what we deserve. It humbles me."

Indeed, Brother Patroclus had provided more food than any had seen since their failed crusade had begun and most likely more than any had enjoyed in all their young lives. He provided them a dormitory once used as a temporary garrison in the wars against invading Muslims and was already busy having his monks gather ells of their own black cloth for the sewing of new clothing for all.

For the next week, Wil's company rested comfortably under the swaying palms. They swam naked in the clean waters of the bay, explored the groves of lemons and olives that were planted deep in hidden clearings, and began to explore the monks' boats. The place was a place of healing—of new beginnings. In just these few days, the bellies of all were already beginning to swell and faces fill. Soon ribs would disappear, and black rings would vanish from under sparkling eyes.

By the end of the month, many were boasting new clothing, caring little that it was only black. Sandals would come later, but few minded. The superior had discussed the general situation at some length with Heinrich and Pieter and had generously offered to care for the children until the season was right for travel. "Truth be told, my friends," Patroclus said, "we could surely use their hands about the place. The lemons are ready again, grapes need harvesting for wine, the olives are soon ripe, fish need to be netted, wheat needs threshing, pigs need to be slaughtered—"

Pieter beamed. "God bless you, brother, God bless you indeed!"

Patroclus bowed. "We monks claim we are here to serve, yet I fear we have hidden ourselves from the world. There is one Francis of Assisi of whom I have heard. He thinks we ought to venture forth and serve the needy where they are. It is a teaching that intrigues me."

Brother Stefano translated for Heinrich, who immediately thought of Brother Lukas in faraway Villmar. The baker nodded approvingly.

"So," Patroclus continued, "it is good for us to serve these children as we may. We are happy for them to remain with us until you are ready to lead them away."

Heinrich and Pieter clasped the man's hand and thanked him again. A voice interrupted the meeting, the voice of a very old man who had spent the past weeks studying Pieter from a distance. "Peace be unto you," he said with a weak grin.

The four turned and received old Brother Nectarios. He was nearly as old as Pieter. "You were here once!" he said as he pointed to Pieter. "Smile for me."

Pieter was confused.

"*Si*, smile for me, please."

The priest shrugged and offered a halfhearted smile.

"*Si, si!* Ha! I remember you, and so do some others. 'Twas nearly twenty years ago. I remember, for I had just arrived myself."

Pieter nodded. "I was here long ago. I remember it well."

Old Nectarios threw back his head and roared. "You came here with four teeth and left with one!"

Pieter raised his brows, then chuckled. "Aye, old brother. I am not proud of that moment. I thought to keep it a secret!" The priest turned to Heinrich. "*Ja.* I wandered here for a forgotten cause and was kindly invited to share in a barrel of red wine brought from Rome by some clerk sitting at the head of the table. When asked my opinion of the wine, I unwisely complained that it was rather sour to my taste. 'Leathery vinegar' I believe is what I said. Well, having spent most of his time in Rome, the clerk was unaccustomed to truth, and before I knew it, we were quarreling loudly.

"Our quarrel quickly divided the brethren into two groups. It seems some of them had a liking for the pie-faced oaf, others not. We all began shouting, but when I cried out that his breath was so foul, it could turn gold into acorns, he threw a fish at me! So it began. First a fish, then a few flasks, a tankard or two, then fists. It went poorly for the dolt, and he returned to Rome with a crooked nose. But the pleasure of his beating cost me three of m'teeth!"

࿇

All Saints' Day was greeted with a gentle shower. The rain dimpled the inlet's water softly, and Wil's company gathered within the dormitory. Otto had counted heads with his captains and reported to Heinrich that all was in order. Frieda reported that Wil's health was greatly improved, and all cheered. It was then that Pieter made a startling announcement.

"I've a heavy burden on m'heart, as does Wil. He's whispered it to me on the journey from Genoa. His sister, Maria, was one of our company on crusade. She was sick and near death, left in the care of Benedictines near Arona, along the Lago Maggiore at the feet of the mighty Alps. We think of her often, as do all who love her.

"So listen. I must leave you now, while the weather still allows me to cross the Piedmont. I must go to her. If she has died, and, truth be told, 'tis likely, then I need the peace of knowing. If not—and God be praised if it could be so!—then I must be at her side."

The pilgrims sat stunned. Most had not known Pieter before Genoa, but they had quickly learned to love him and to depend on him. One cried out anxiously, "Will *Herr* Heinrich stay with us?"

All eyes turned toward the baker. He and Pieter had formerly agreed to remain at San Fruttuoso until they all left together at Easter. The priest's sudden plan was unexpected and had surprised him as much as the others. With a cold stare he answered, "*Ja.* I shall stay with you all until we begin our journey north together."

The old man looked at the ground sheepishly. He knew he should have counseled Heinrich on the change, but the whole matter of Maria was awkward. "Heinrich, I am sorry for the surprise, but it is something I must do."

Heinrich had not resolved the confusion of feeling he had felt upon learning of the little girl. He knew he was not her father, and, according to his easy reckoning, he knew she must have been conceived while he was still in Weyer. It was a violation that haunted him—his feelings for his wife notwithstanding. He nodded.

"Then I go too!" cried Otto. "She is my friend."

Heinz echoed the same. The two had shared much suffering with the little girl and had loved her like a sister.

Pieter looked at the lads. Heinz was quick footed and keen. Otto was sturdy and dependable. The old priest fixed his eyes onto Otto's broad face and thought carefully. He scratched Solomon's ears and finally nodded. "Aye."

The group was unsettled at the whole notion of Pieter's leaving them, and more than a few grumbled. They had been happy to leave things as they were—they wished nothing would ever change.

"Now hear me, my precious children. *Herr* Heinrich and Wil shall bring you to Arona in the springtime, just past Easter. You shall all be in my prayers until then. Our reunion will be a glorious moment!

"Ah, but more. These good brothers may offer some of you this as your home. Lads, here you can learn the Scriptures, learn to garden and to fish, to make wine, to cure others. Perhaps you might choose to take the vows and take a new name.

"And, my dear maidens, they have told me of a kindly nunnery in sunny Tuscany that would gladly take you all. There you'd be safe enough. You might learn to read and to write, to embroider and prepare fine meals for travelers. You, too, may choose to take the vows. So, all of you, consider my words; think on these things in the months to come." His words brought them little comfort.

The next morning the sun shone brightly overhead, but the mood of the young pilgrims had not changed. They had become quite attached to the old man and were near tears as he prepared to leave them. With Solomon at his side, Pieter gathered his lambs close and led them to the edge of the water that lay flat and clean under a new day's light. "Little brothers and sisters, I shall not leave you until I show you something. Come. Each of you stand close to the water and look at your reflection."

The grumbling company obediently lined themselves along the shore and stared at the arc of long faces gazing glumly at them from below. Pieter chuckled. "Once before my flock faced themselves in such a way. 'Twas their time to see themselves as they were. Now look at yourselves; open your eyes wide, my beloved, and see what you've become."

"I'm clean again!" cried one.

"M'clothes are new; m'belly's full!"

"M'scabs are gone!"

Pieter laughed. "Aye! Rested, clean, filled with good food, and dressed in fresh garments; wiser, bolder, ever more free! Rejoice, my children. You've much to be thankful for."

Brothers Petroclus and Stefano stood at a respectful distance, nodding their approval of the priest's words. When he finished, they called to him and beckoned he follow them to the chapter house.

As the trio arrived, Petroclus turned to Pieter. "My friend, we did not expect you to be leaving quite so soon." He looked uneasily at Stefano. "We do have news you should know. We have kept it from you all this time so that you and your flock might have a season of rest."

Pieter leaned forward. "*Ja?* Go on."

"Within a week of your coming we learned of troubles in Genoa. One of the brothers spoke with a merchant at the dock in Camogli. It seems a group of crusaders, following a youth named Paul, I believe, did quite a thing in the city. They robbed rich and poor, set fire to a stable, and are accused of killing a carter and an old woman."

Pieter groaned. "*Ach, mein Gott!* I knew it!"

"The merchant's story is confirmed by our lemon trader. He tells us that a dozen children were captured and hanged. The rest fled into the countryside and are being hunted. The roads north have been scoured, as well as those to the south. I do not know any more than this, but you, Father, must have a care."

Pieter took a deep breath and nodded. He thought carefully, then concluded his Maria still needed him. "Thank you, brother. Can you tell me if we are safe here?"

The monks exchanged glances once more. Stefano spoke. "We have kept a guard at the path, and we have watched the waters each day. None of our brothers has spoken a word of you to any, and none of our traders has come. If a search is made, we'll need to hide everyone and quickly, but we've a plan for that as well."

Petroclus shook his head. "*Si,* but I believe the search will soon be over—if it is not already. The news we bring is a fortnight past. Our brothers have been to Camogli just days ago, and all was quiet. We tell you this so you are mindful of the road."

Pieter nodded.

"But," Petroclus said, "we've something for you that might mask your past appearance."

Stefano hurried away and returned with a fresh black robe draped over his forearms. With a respectful bow he presented Pieter with it. "You, too, Father, have survived a trying season. You should don this robe as a symbol of a new beginning."

Pieter took the garment and held it in front of him. It was made of finely loomed wool with an ample hooded cowl, a braided leather belt, and pockets sewn within. He looked at his own tattered robe and sighed. It had served him well, and he suddenly hated to part with it.

"I know, Father," smiled Stefano. "It has become a friend to you."

The priest nodded. "This tattered thing has kept me warm for longer than I know. It was a gift from poor peasants."

"My friend, I suggest you part with it before it parts with you inside it!" laughed Petroclus.

"Indeed! Then, so be it! Ha! A new robe—"

"And these," interrupted a monk, hurrying forward. He handed Pieter a pair of heavy leather shoes made from ox hide and stitched with strong cord.

The priest was astonished. "These are worth much!"

"You are worth more," added Petroclus. "These are our gifts to a brother who has suffered in the service of others. It is a calling that ought not to go unnoticed."

Embarrassed but delighted, old Pieter stripped away his old garments and stood for a moment adorned only by the wooden cross hanging around his neck. The monks abruptly turned away—they were more accustomed to the beauty of their inlet than the sight of wrinkled Pieter! "Ah, your pardon!" laughed the old man. "You should not be punished for your kindness!" He quickly dressed and danced about, only to be handed a new blanket as well. But when the cobbler offered him a new satchel, he declined politely. "Brother, this old bag has carried m'most precious things for much of m'life. It is not pretty, but neither am I. It is worn thin, like me, but not through. With sincere thanks, I choose to keep m'own."

The monks and the old priest embraced for the last time, each praying a blessing on the other. Pieter then returned to his children and summoned Otto and Heinz to his side. The two boys had been presented satchels as well as blankets and heavy shoes. They were delighted to feel so good again, and they stood by Pieter's side filled with enthusiasm.

Heinrich counseled with the old man for a brief time, reviewing the plan and the route to be taken. Pieter whispered the news of Genoa to the man and urged him not to tell the others. When finished, the baker embraced his wiry old friend, then bent to pet Solomon. "Until Arona, then," he said. "God go with all of you and ... and may little Maria be spared."

Pieter smiled. He knew how difficult it was for any man in Heinrich's place to see the child and not the sin. "Take good care of these, and I pray you find peace with your son." With that Pieter hurried to Wil's side and knelt by his litter. The young man was clear eyed and spoke with hopeful confidence. "Give Maria her cross, and tell her I am coming soon."

Pieter took the girl's wooden cross in his hand and remembered all it had endured. "*Ja*, my son. It shall be the herald of your coming."

The two stared at each other, then smiled in understanding. Their eyes assured them that hope had been restored. After a final prayer, the priest stood, bade Frieda an affectionate farewell, and walked to the others, whom he blessed. All things in proper order, Pieter, Solomon, Otto, and Heinz then boarded a small craft manned by two monks who would row them to Camogli and the perilous highways leading north.

෨

Fair Frieda had been born nearly sixteen years prior in the region of Westphalia that was once called the Lower Lorraine. She had kept her past a secret from her fellow travelers, though Gertrude had made comments from time to time that gave Pieter cause to wonder. Were the truth known, she'd have been relieved of a deep shame, one foisted upon her by circumstances for which she had no part.

The young woman had been born to a knight, Manfred of Chapelle, a landed vassal to Lord Rawdon of Bonn. Her father's modest manor consisted of some one thousand hectares that lay near the Rhine about three leagues from Adernach. Her mother, Clarimond, was the ravishing daughter of Lord Eginhard of Metz and boasted an ancient lineage of knightly sires. So by all counts, the young lady should have enjoyed a genteel life of privilege.

Unfortunately, Manfred was the firstborn of a marriage between first cousins—a union that had supported a necessary military alliance but violated the Church's standard. The man, like two of his seven siblings, had gone mad three years prior and had been taken to an undisclosed asylum somewhere in the marshes of Bohemia. His manor house and lands had been forfeited to his overlord and his family immediately deprived of its income.

Frieda loved her father, and she wept bitterly the day she watched him taken away. Her priest had told her it would be better for him to spend his days in some unknown cell than to be set loose in the world and that the family's overlord was owed a debt of gratitude. But when Clarimond and her children were presented to the haughty Lord Rawdon, Frieda slapped the man's outstretched hand and stormed away.

Were these not troubles enough, Clarimond, desperate to find some source of funds, then unwisely loaned her dowry to a well-intended uncle in Münster whose reputation for wagering was quickly proven to have little to do with his actual skill. After promising much, the downcast man could do no more than offer empty promises of better fortune and fill Clarimond's strongbox with scraps of payments due. Unable to pay her rents, she and her three children were eventually delivered penniless to the streets of Bonn.

Clarimond finally determined that God was demanding she yield her life to his service. She took her vows in a double monastery near Treves into which she placed her children as oblates. The experience proved immediately difficult for Frieda and her siblings. Frieda had caught the carnal eye of the bishop, who made every effort to override the protections of the abbess. The damsel was desperate to escape, and when rumors of a children's crusade found her ears, she conceived a daring plan to rescue her sister, her brother, and herself.

And so, Frieda, Gertrude, and brother Manfred escaped their plight to join the hapless crusade that had left Frieda as the sole survivor. Now the young woman was alone in the world, bearing the stigma of a mad father and a penniless mother. Reduced to the status of a peasant and with no place to call her home, she had maintained both her dignity and her belief that things would, even yet, be put to right.

It was Martinmas when Frieda wrapped herself warmly in an ample woolen blanket under the shelter of the monks' stone arcade. She stared peacefully at the bay now spattered by a cold rain. She had enjoyed a pleasant feast of roast pork and chicken stew. Flat fish had been provided, of course, as well as a large platter of shellfish and ample vegetables. But her thoughts were not of her plenty. Rather she was lost in memories of Gertrude and Manfred when a sound startled her.

The young woman spun about. Her eyes suddenly lit the dreary arcade, and she clapped excitedly. "Wil! Wil! You're walking without a crutch!"

The lad blushed and tossed his hair to one side. He wanted to cover his scar. "*Ja*, 'tis true. I swore to the infirmer on All Saints' that I'd surprise you before Martinmas!"

Frieda lightly brushed the hair away from his wound. She touched his cheek lightly, running her finger along the raised ridge. "I am proud of your scar, and you should be as well."

Wil looked down, shamefaced. "I ... I saw it in still water some time back, and it made me sick. It forever changes me."

The damsel shook her head. "'Tis not the scar that has changed you, Wil."

Wil turned away, embarrassed.

Frieda laid a hand tenderly on his shoulder. "You believed in the love of others. Then you fought for us like no knight I have ever seen. Those men ... oh, those men were fearsome, but you held them at bay ... you freed me from one's grip. I remember well."

The young man took a long breath, then spoke with a hushed voice, barely above a whisper. "It was like I was dead, Frieda. Truly, it was as though I were dead." He stared blankly at the mist now settling over the bay.

Frieda said nothing for a long moment. "So tell me, how are your wounds?"

The lad walked in a slow circle, lifting his shoulders from time to time and grimacing as his stitched skin stretched. "Truth be told, they hurt some. The one on m'belly is the worst. The brothers say by Christmas I should be able to stand upright and raise m'hands overhead. By Lent I ought to be able to carry baskets of lemons, and by Easter I should be fit as ever."

Frieda smiled. It was good news.

"But I can only think of Maria. I wonder if Pieter's found her ... or her grave." His eyes fell and he shook his head. "I loved her so. I can't believe I betrayed her as I did."

"She knew you loved her and she knew you to be sorry. Maria loved nothing more than forgiving."

"But she was near death when I asked her ... and she could not have heard my words. We ought not to have left her there alone."

"She was not alone. The monks were able to care for her, and Anna was there for her as well. Wil, listen to me. She *wanted* you to go. It would have been unkind to deny her that wish."

Wil shrugged. He wasn't so sure.

The two stood close to one another and stared at the gray sky. Even on the gloomiest day their refuge was not unpleasant. The air remained somehow fragrant, the sea still beautiful. Even the mists that curled about the mountains' feet were a wonder.

Frieda smiled and turned to Wil. "You ought to be glad you've been on that litter. The rest of us ache for the weight of lemons! The boys are tired of pressing grapes, and some are off to shake olives from the trees. The work is endless."

Wil smiled. "Helmut says his hands are like old canvas from pulling nets of fish, and Rudolf grumbles that he's spending more days threshing here than ever at his home!"

"He should never have told Petroclus that he knew the flail so well!" laughed Frieda. "But we girls are not spared! Besides the lemons, they've got us mending and washing, kneading dough and baking." The young woman looked at her callused fingers. "I've spent hours learning from your father. He's a good baker, you know."

Wil darkened and said nothing.

Frieda sighed. She understood his hurt. After all, according to Wil's reckoning, Heinrich had left the family nearly six years ago to the day that they had met again. The boy's mother had spent the years recounting a litany of the man's sins, and she had invented a few more for good measure. Abandoned to work the bakery and tend the fields, Wil had suffered the burdens of an entire household long before his time. "Will you not forgive him?"

The young man spat.

"Do you know the truth of his going?"

Wil shook his head. "Does it matter?"

Frieda was wise. "Well, perhaps it should not make a difference. Perhaps we should merely forgive another when asked … just as we want forgiveness when *we* ask."

The words stung the lad, and he clenched his jaw. "Sometimes there's too much to forgive!"

Now Frieda bristled. "*Ja?*" she snapped. "You must think your sins weren't *too much* then?"

Wil reddened, but he had no answer. Wounded by the maiden's rebuke, he turned away.

Frieda sighed. She wished that she could relieve the weight of bitterness that still bore so heavily upon Wil's broad shoulders. She kicked at the ground lightly, frustrated with herself. *I push too hard*, she thought. *I need to give him room.*

A damp breeze blew lightly, and Frieda turned her face to the gray clouds sagging heavily over the bay. Her thoughts turned to her sister, Gertrude, drowned in the sea, and to her brother, Manfred, drowned in the flood. "It is my fault they are gone," she muttered. "I brought them on this fools' crusade." A muffled peal of thunder rumbled in the mountains, and rain began to crash atop the tile roof of the arcade. The young woman shuddered. *Through what waters must I yet pass?*

୭

Pieter had calculated his journey to be about thirty-five leagues, maybe a little more. He and his companions were well rested and well fed, and he estimated they could travel five or six leagues a day on the easy roads of the Po River plain. They'd need to climb through the Appenines, but even so, he was confident they would arrive in Arona within ten days.

The morning he, Solomon, and their two young companions began was sunny and bright. The aquamarine bay sparkled, and the old man nearly fell asleep to the steady rhythm of the monks pulling steadily on their well-worn wooden oars. For their part, the brethren were content to hum happily or recite a psalm to the metered measure of their rowing.

The small boat splashed quietly forward, following the bending shoreline of the promontory about a bowshot from its rocky edge. Otto rested comfortably with Solomon dozing on his lap. The stout lad had been a faithful comrade from the first days of the crusade. He had left Weyer behind days before Wil, Karl, and Maria had taken their first steps.

As the miller's son, Otto had spent many hours unloading baskets of flour at Heinrich's bakery. For the six years the baker had been gone, the lad had watched Karl and Wil do the work. Otto understood Wil's anger. But Otto also understood Heinrich more than the man could know. The lad had heard rumors in the village for years—rumors kept very much alive by the man's bitter wife. But Otto had become friends with Brother Lukas in the few years before the crusade, so he had heard other things as well. "The man who speaks first seems right," the monk had once said, "until the other answers."

"I wish Wil would forgive his father," Otto mumbled.

Pieter stirred. "Eh?"

Otto shrugged. "I say I wish Wil would forgive his father."

"*Ja,* lad. Me, as well, but it is not something that can be forced."

Otto nodded thoughtfully, then blurted, "I miss Lukas."

"Eh?"

"I was thinking of a monk at home, in the abbey by Weyer. He was a clever man ... you would have liked him."

"Perhaps I'll meet him?"

"No. Wil found him dead just before he left."

"Ah. Well, you must tell me about him."

Otto beamed. His cheeks rounded like two red apples under a September sky. The boy had loved Lukas, just like Wil had—and just like Heinrich had in his own time. Otto proceeded to tell Pieter of Lukas's odd notions and of his wisdom. He spoke of his potions and his love for walks in the forests. "I helped him fill his satchel with mushrooms and berries and strange things. He loved to sneak away from the cloister whenever he could! He loved to play ball with us, and he showed me the place he called the home of the Magi!"

Pieter chuckled. He did wish he could have met the man.

"Wil carries Brother Lukas's satchel. Sometimes I like to touch it; it helps me remember him."

Pieter nodded and laid his hand on the lad's sandy hair. He looked into his broad face and realized that he had often taken the steady fellow for granted. "I am glad you've come with me, Otto. I pray we get you home safely."

The boy took a deep breath. "Sometimes methinks m'home's now with you ... and with Wil and Frieda ... and the others." Otto had been a good son to an unworthy man. His mother had died during a plague that had ravaged Weyer. Bitter and lonely, his father had become a drunken fool, oft beating the boy without cause and without mercy.

The old man sat thoughtfully and turned his face to the fortress of the Dragonara drawing close. He surveyed the muscled shoulders surrounding the sea and wondered where his own home really was. He looked into the sky and noticed it beginning to fill with gray clouds drifting from the southeast.

"Father," called one of the monks. He pointed to the sky. "Sirocco winds … they'll bring rain to this side of the mountains today."

The boys groaned. "No more sunshine."

"Ah, lads," chuckled Pieter. "The sun *always* shines … 'tis only hidden by the clouds!"

Within the half hour, the monks delivered their boat to the Camogli beach tucked tightly within a sandy cove surrounded by jutting rocks. The village fishermen had long since left for the day, and it was nearly empty. A few old women were picking mussels from tidal pools; others were mending nets. Pieter urged his two companions to keep a sharp eye at all times. "If challenged, you are novices on a pilgrimage with me. Our clothing is sound; we should look the part. I do the talking, and if you are asked about the crusade, you deny your part in it. Do you understand?"

The boys nodded. The boat was dragged ashore, and its occupants climbed out to stretch. They checked their gear and their clothing carefully. The cloister's cobbler had made sturdy rucksacks for the two boys, and the kitchener had filled them with many days' worth of meat and cheese.

The priest cast a wary eye toward the fortress perched nearby, then urged his lads to make ready. "We must begin. We'll follow the Genoa road until the first trail into the mountains. I've little interest in tempting the city guard."

The monks agreed. "*Si, si, Padre*, it would not be wise. Now, go with God." They recited two psalms, prayed over the travelers, and kissed each on their cheeks. With a final bow they turned away sadly and left Pieter and his companions quite alone.

Heinz waved to the monks and then turned his squinty eyes toward the roadway and grinned. He was suddenly itching to begin. The happy young man laughed and poked Otto in the belly. "Ready, fat fellow?" he teased.

Otto laid a thick hand on the scamp's shoulder and squeezed it hard. With feigned menace he growled, "Say it again and I'll bash yer nose … Elfman!"

Chapter Five

MARIA'S SONG

𝕻ieter and his companions hurried away from the fearsome Dragonara, through Camogli, and into the mountains. They hurried past the menacing fortresses dotting the ridges near Genoa, and within two days they felt confident that they had pressed their way to relative safety.

The November air was damp but not cold. Autumn rains fell, but the pilgrims continued steadily on, traveling along minor roadways and a few remote trails before descending onto a well-traveled highway that followed the stony shores of the Scrivia River. They continued without incident past numbers of clay-brick villages and soon entered Tortona, where all three paused to rest in a small piazza and to reminisce about their last visit to the city.

"If you could've seen yourself!" laughed Otto.

"*Ja!* I've ne'er seen the likes of it … and how the old gentlemen in the pool cried out!" Heinz howled.

Pieter chuckled. "Aye, lads. I couldn't see m'self, but I surely saw the fear in their eyes!"

The three were remembering the bath at Tortona, and they chortled about the cursing noblemen, the scowling bath matron, and the red-faced Frieda. "Ah, boys," said Pieter, "a good time, indeed." He sighed and smiled. "But we've a need to keep moving. I think it best we not follow our old route to Pavia but turn on the highway to Allesandria instead. The land stays flat all the way, so the walk should be easy."

"Methinks it ugly here," blurted Heinz.

Pieter nodded. "Aye, perhaps a bit. But most of the world is gray by Martinmas."

"Then white for Advent," added Otto.

"And green for Easter and yellow by All Hallows'!" chattered Heinz cheerfully.

"True enough, lads."

"But look, even the dirt is gray here, and 'tis all flat."

"Well, be thankful 'tis flat, lad!"

The three turned onto a wide roadway that led them through the plain west toward Allesandria. The air had grown colder, though not as damp as it had felt in Liguria. They marched on, north through the lands of the Savoy family and across the narrow Tanaro. They passed countless drab villages and a few walled fortresses until the landscape gradually began to change. They descended low hills lined with tidy vineyards and passed gardens tilled and fallow. Finally they stood at the banks of the Po River.

"We need to ford there," pointed Otto. A long line of rocks revealed an area of shallows.

Heinz stared at the water and grumbled. "Now we'll be wet all day!"

"Only your feet, lad," chuckled Pieter, "only your feet." The priest stepped boldly into the chilly waters of the Po and raised his staff triumphantly. "Now, lads, follow me!" He took three confident strides, then stumbled forward with a loud oath. To the wild acclaim of his comrades, the old man heroically regained his balance and took a deep breath. "Ha! Almost!" he cried. He ordered his fellows to follow, and he took another step—only to slip off an unseen rock and plunge headlong into a swirling pool!

Shouting every blasphemy the howling boys had ever heard, the old priest found his footing, then thrashed through the water toward the far shore.

"Only yer feet, Father!" roared Heinz. "Only yer feet!"

The Po was quickly left behind, and the trio spent the

fifth day of its journey marching past the brown soil of the northern Piedmont's fallowed fields. Soon they were within earshot of the graceful herons of the Sesia and then finally entered the town of Vercelli, where a church gave them shelter. Grateful, they stretched out comfortably before a generous hearth and accepted a meal of fresh wheat bread, olive oil, chicken stew, and a large platter of boiled vegetables.

The following night was spent farther north with some French pilgrims traveling from distant Lyons to the grand cathedral in Milan. At first glance, the Frenchmen thought Pieter and his boys to be a respectable trio of a priest and two novices. Believing them to be so, the pilgrims graciously shared their provisions under their canvas tent. Unfortunately, their fine red wine oiled Pieter's tongue, and he soon told them of the failed crusade. Upon learning of the children's past, the mood changed. In one voice they insisted the three be sent away. "We'll not share the night with the likes of these!" cried one.

Astonished, Pieter objected loudly.

"*Non*, old man. *Non! Mon Dieux!* We've heresies all over France! We've no need to suffer the spirits of these who have abandoned the faith as well!"

Pieter stood to his feet and shook his crook at them all. "A curse be upon you, *imbécile!* No faith in all Christendom has withstood such a test. You pitiful dogs are not fit to share your table with them." He spat, then snatched up his satchel. "We leave you to your crumbs! Come, lads; come Solomon. We've better places to be."

The two boys had not understood the Frenchmen's words, and Pieter chose to shield them. "Ah, you know those dandies! They think we Teutons to be barbarians and not fit to share their table. *Ach*, let them gag on their snails and their dainties."

It was late on the eighth day when the three made camp at the south shore of Lago Maggiore. The night was cold but clear, and the two boys scampered about gathering firewood under the cover of a starry sky. Pieter walked away from the fire and knelt alongside Solomon to pray atop the pebbly shore. From the moment he had left San Fruttuoso, he had thought of little else other than Maria. "Is she alive or with the angels, Solomon?" Now that he was within a half-day's journey of the answer, he secretly feared what they might find. *Oh, that I might see her smile again.* He remembered Maria's innocence, her unsullied charity, and her selflessness. *Such a sweet child,* he thought. *Cursed with deformity yet always giving.* His throat swelled, and he faced the dark, lapping waters of the lake sadly. "Another miracle, Karl?" he whispered. "Could there yet be one more?"

৯৯

"I confess I can barely take another step. My legs are trembling like a sinner at the Judgment." Pieter paused to stare some three bowshots ahead at the clay rooftops of Arona peeking above its sandstone walls. He swallowed hard against a mouth now dry with fear. His heart fluttered nervously, and he stooped to cup some clean water from Lago Maggiore. "I suppose I should feel comfort if she is with the angels now," he muttered. "But, by the saints, I pray she is yet here, with us still."

Otto and Heinz had said little that morning. They stared anxiously at the gray clouds above and at the silhouettes of the haze-shrouded mountains rising in the distance to the north. Heinz skipped a stone across the water. He counted three skips, and then grumbled and threw another. A light rain began to fall, dimpling the lake lightly until a blast of cold wind suddenly scratched the water's surface. To the boys it seemed like a dark omen.

"Pieter, we buried four by this lake."

The old man nodded as he lifted his hood over his head. "Aye, lad. One should have been me."

"And what of Anna?"

"I am chief of all cowards," moaned Pieter. "I fear for the both of them. Anna was such a quiet child. She asked for little and marched bravely. I can still see her little white head bobbing in the column." He filled his lungs with a deep breath and released it slowly. "Enough. 'Tis time to know." He drove his staff hard into the earth and set his face forward. "Follow, boys, and take heart. What is to be shall be."

The three said nothing more for a long while as brief gusts of wind rumpled their clothing. None wanted to go on, none wanted know, yet they knew they must. Anna, of course, was beloved to be sure. But Maria had given so much to all of them. It was she who had given them smiles when darkness had nearly overwhelmed them; it was she who would sing in the midst of misery. The little girl was uncommonly blessed with a quiet grace of which she was utterly unaware. She saw only others' needs and served them with an ineffable wealth of kindness. Maria's disfigured left arm had provided good sport to her many lessers—most of whom were pleased to believe that God's judgment had been foisted on the fair child and not themselves. Yet the long-suffering *Mädel* had returned charity for evil at every turn, saving her tears for secret places.

The three figures and their companion moved quietly along the lakeshore. In the distance they could see the rising foothills of the mighty Alps; behind them, the collapsing landscape leading to the plain from which they had just come.

Just ahead lay Arona, a prosperous town built directly on the edge of the clear lake where wide-hulled fishing boats and tangles of nets lined the stony beach. On Arona's northern edge was a sheer cliff nearly twenty rods high— "the first Alp," Pieter had said—and atop it sat the *Rocca di Arona*, the gray-stone castle of an aging lord.

"I remember the cliff, but not the keep," said Otto. "The cliff has two eye sockets ... it made me think it was the face of a giant!"

Heinz shuddered. "A fortress atop the head of a sleeping giant!"

Pieter said nothing. He was silently rehearsing the emotions he might expect to feel before the hour would pass. He withdrew Maria's cross from his belt and stared at it, suddenly lost in a swirl of memories. Little more than bumpy apple wood, the small icon seemed to have empowered the little girl with amazing faith. He could see it held high in her hand in the haunted forests of the Rhineland, in the horrors of Basel's dungeon, and high above the world in the mighty Alps. He then remembered it in Karl's belt, somehow remaining unbroken in the lad's awful death. The old man kissed it reverently.

Under a lessening rain, the three entered the town past the sleeping guard of the south gate and hurried uphill toward the Benedictine Abbey of Saints Gratian and Felinus. The cloister overlooked the town's market from a low ridge that paralleled the lake on its western side. It, and the attached church, the *Chiesa die S. Martiri*, had been founded nearly three centuries earlier by Count Ammizzone, a captain in the army of Otto I of Saxony. The church's reliquary boasted the remains of the martyrs Gratian and Felinus—soldiers in Rome's imperial army martyred in Perugia nearly one thousand years prior.

The abbey itself had become wealthy and powerful, owning lands all over the Piedmont and Lombardy. Its wealth, in turn, had created opportunities for the residents of Arona and the lord of its castle to enjoy the pleasures of good food, fine clothing, and trinkets of silver and gold.

"These folk do well," said Otto. "Methinks most to be rich."

Pieter didn't answer.

"What say you, Pieter?"

The priest said nothing. His face was hard, and he gripped his staff with whitened knuckles. So no more words were spoken as the three black-clothed pilgrims and their gray dog climbed the streets of Arona toward the walled cloister. It was a wet, gloomy noon, and the bells of *S. Martiri* pealed the hour of sext. Pieter paused for a moment and surveyed the folk milling past empty booths. "Not Saturday, I suppose, nor Wednesday. I've lost count."

In fact, it was neither Saturday nor Wednesday, but rather Monday, the sixteenth day of November when Pieter the Broken, Otto of Weyer, Heinz "Elfman" (as some were apt to call him), and their dripping dog stood before the portal of the abbey. The old man hesitated for a brief moment and lifted Maria's cross from his belt. Staring at it he mumbled, "*Ave crux spas unica.* Hail the Cross, our only hope." He then rapped firmly on the wooden door with the end of his staff.

A fresh-faced porter opened the small door. "Thanks be to God."

"Blessings, my son," answered Pieter. "We seek the two fair-haired girls left in the care of your infirmer two months ago."

The young monk hesitated for a moment. "I know little, for I am only just arrived from Milan. But come, follow me."

Anxiously, the three followed the quiet porter through the cloister grounds and past gardens now lying fallow in wait for the warm sun of spring. Pieter cast his eyes on the many thorny rosebushes and imagined Anna and Maria standing amidst them on a summer's day. Perhaps it was the girls' names, perhaps the Italian brick, but for whatever reason, the priest's mind suddenly flew to its place of secret comfort, the place no other living soul knew—the cherished memories of his long-departed wife, his beloved Anna Maria. She, too, had perished from fever, and all these years later the old man still grieved. A lump filled his throat.

The young porter walked quickly past the refectory, the chapel, and a building judged to be the herbarium by the musky scent escaping through its opened windows. They then rounded a corner where Otto spotted a small graveyard against a far wall beneath a grove of squat olive trees. He nudged Heinz. "There," he whispered with a groan. "A fresh grave with a pine wreath."

Heinz nodded and pursed his lips. Around another corner they passed the arcade that lined the dormitory, then walked along a series of small workshops until the porter finally delivered the trio to the prior's chamber. "The abbot is not in residence. He is presenting a matter to the curio in Rome." He lowered his voice. "I'm told he prefers the weather there between Martinmas and Holy Week."

Pieter grunted.

The young man knocked rather timidly on the door as Pieter tapped his foot impatiently. "I wonder if he's napping." The porter knocked again, still softly. Now no longer able to restrain himself, Pieter wrapped the oak loudly with his staff. "Someone open this cursed door!"

Within moments, a dark-eyed, elderly monk answered with a yawn. "*Prego*, come, enter in." He rubbed his eyes as he offered a quick prayer for the three and kissed them. He then turned to his porter. "Have the deans assembled to pray over these and wash their feet. Have the kitchener prepare a—"

"No!" interrupted Pieter impatiently. "Hear me. We come in search of two fair-haired maidens left in your care a fortnight or so before St. Michael's."

The prior nodded. "Ah, *si*. Brother Chiovo spent many an hour with them."

"And?" blurted Pieter.

The man lowered his head. "Ah, *mein Freund*, Brother Chiovo served them day and night by the reliquary of the church. He had hoped the relics might bring a miracle. For one, it seems they did, God be praised. But for the other blessed cherub, they did not. She died and was buried beneath the olives on the fourth day of October ... a bright Thursday. I remember it well. No sadder day has so darkened the sun in this place."

Tears began to course down the pilgrims' cheeks. They stood bravely and waited as the prior continued. "The two of them shall have a place in our hearts forever. They brought joy to all and served one another so very devotedly."

Pieter was now trembling and dismayed. He finally blurted. "Tell us!" he cried. "*Who* is buried here?"

The prior answered sadly, "The child called Anna."

No one said a word. The boys rocked awkwardly on their feet. Pieter was dumbstruck. Confused by opposing emotions, he squeezed his staff and groaned inwardly. He could not imagine that Maria had survived. It was beyond comprehension. Yet neither could he imagine the loss of Anna. She had been in improving health when he kissed her farewell. Her eyes had been bright and keen. Indeed, the man grieved for her loss, but grief had not been his first emotion—relief was, and he felt ashamed. "I ... I have no words," the old man muttered. He looked down and shook his head. *What manner of man am I?* he wondered.

"Did she suffer?" blurted Otto.

The prior answered gravely. "*Si* … I fear some, lad. On St. Michael's Eve a fever spread over her quickly. Brother Chiovo feared cerebritis, for the girl complained of severe pain in her head."

Heinz wiped tears off his face. "Was she happy here?"

"Yes, my son. Very. She cared for Maria with great joy and laughed often with the other oblates in our care. And Maria recovered in time for the two to play happily for a few days before the fever came. But come, let us walk to the grave."

The pilgrims followed the old monk slowly through the cloister grounds until they stood before the grave the boys had seen earlier. Solomon curled up alongside the sagging mound of earth and laid his chin atop the pine branches. "Maria comes each week with a fresh wreath."

Pieter and his boys stood respectfully silent by Anna's grave for a few moments. The old man then knelt and prayed over her remains. "Now may the Lord of peace Himself give you peace always in every way." Pieter stood and turned to the prior. "Thanks be to God for your care of them both. His ways are His alone. May the little one rest well.

"But I now needs ask of Maria. Is she here with the other children?"

"Nay, my friend. Before he left for Rome, our abbot instructed us to send Maria to the castle." He pointed to the fortress perched high above the shore. "It seems the girl accompanied Chiovo on his trips to serve the old lord, and the lord's lady fancied her. She paid a handsome sum to have the child released to her own household."

Pieter groaned and faced the imposing castle. "Well, we've come to take her home."

The prior shrugged. "A problem, perhaps. *Signore* Salito is very ill, and the girl brings him comfort. She and another sing to him."

Pieter darkened. "They have no right to hold her!"

The prior said nothing, and the boys felt suddenly nervous.

"Maria belongs with us!" stated Pieter flatly. "She'll be no servant to any! Brother, many thanks for your kindness and good care of our girls. May God's bounty fall upon all who served them, but if our little sister Maria has suffered in that castle, then I pray God's wrath consume your abbot!"

"But, sir, I vow to you—"

"Come, lads. We need be about our business!" With that command, Pieter planted his staff hard into the earth and spun around. He led his two boys and his trotting dog quickly through the courtyards of the cloister and out the portal.

"Should we not have made a thanks gift to them?" quizzed Otto.

"Humph! It would seem the lord has paid our debt for us." Pieter's anger did not fade. He had very much hoped that Maria would greet them within the safe boundaries of the monastery. Now he had no idea what kind of circumstance the girl was enduring. Grinding his gums, the old fellow marched through Arona. He focused all his anger on the castle looming over the town's walls and prayed for an army of angels to sweep from heaven's gate and stand by him. *What if they refuse us?* he wondered. *What if they will not release her?*

The three turned to wind their way up the western slope leading to the *Rocca di Arona*. They followed a steep, curving road and arrived at the gate panting. "A good place for a keep," muttered Pieter. He approached the sentry at the north gate.

"*Si?*"

"*Buon giorno.* I am come to see the fair child."

"*Si?*"

"The fair child, Maria."

"Ah!" The soldier smiled. "Maria. Yes, yes. Come in."

Pieter was surprised at the welcome. He had expected a grousing guard to bar the gate with the point of a lance. Somewhat relieved, he crossed under the raised portcullis and through the deep walls. Once inside he looked about quickly for any sign of Maria's golden hair. Disappointed, he surveyed the castle. The fortress had been built in three tiers that stepped up to the very top of the mountain. It was of gray stone, and Pieter thought it to be sturdy, though not well designed. *This lord has no love of warfare, else I'd see an inner curtain, turrets, and balconies.*

They climbed the stairs leading to the wall walk, and from there they paused to look about. To the south side the narrow list was filled with gardens, orchards, and a fishpond. At its edge was a sheer cliff that fell to Arona. To the east, another sheer cliff dropped to the shores of the lake. *Only two sides to defend,* thought Pieter. Having once been a warrior himself, he enjoyed considering such things. *Only two sides for escape, however, and methinks the future may hold a kidnapping.*

Pieter was further surprised to see few men-at-arms. Instead of milling knights and footmen, the bailey was busy with every manner of beast as well as peasants hauling carts about. Numbers of noisy workshops were at task with the hammering of iron or sawing of wood. Amidst the workers shuffled a few courtiers in their fine clothing, as well as many numbers of laughing children. Pieter strained to see a yellow head amongst the dark throng below.

"Here, *Pater,*" announced the soldier. "Here is the constable's chamber. He shall help you."

The old man nodded and stepped inside a small dark room where he met a coarse-looking fat fellow sitting at a squat table. "Peace to thee," offered Pieter. He lifted the cross from around his neck and held it out for the man to see. "*In nomine Patris, et Filii, et Spiritus Sancti, pax semper vobiscum.*"

"Eh?"

Pieter had hoped to impress the constable with his holy credentials. They were convenient tools from time to time. But the man seemed unmoved. "My son, we are here for the fair child of the northland, Maria."

The constable nodded and took a long drink of red wine from a glazed clay goblet. "Maria?"

"*Si.*"

The man belched. "I am Borgo. You needs speak to the *signora, Signora* Cosetta." Borgo gnawed on a piece of cheese and took another drink. He then tore a large piece of bread from a brown loaf and dipped it into a bowl of olive oil as Pieter and his companions waited with feigned respect. When Borgo belched and reached for more food, Pieter began to bounce his staff lightly on the floor, and the man stopped chewing. "*Si?* Yes, yes. No need to hurry. One moment."

The constable ate and drank a little more, and then stood and wiped his mouth on his sleeve. He wrapped his belly in a fine red sash, donned a dashing otter cap, and curled his finger. "Follow me."

Borgo led the three visitors and their dog in the direction of the castle's highest tier, where the lord's apartments were built alongside the great hall. In the village at the base of the cliff, the bells of the *Chiesa dei S. Martiri* rang the hour of nones.

Borgo's pace was slow, but the man had come very much alive. Passing through the central bailey, he paused to chat with friends and to bark playfully at others. Laughing robustly, he gestured crudely to a few passing maids. *"Bella donna!"* he cried. A young sergeant handed him an apple and a flask of wine. He stopped to drain the flask, and he tossed the apple to a beggar in the shadows. "Ha, the sun shines again!"

Pieter wanted to shout at the oaf. Instead he muttered to himself, *"Ach, mein Gott!* Could a grown man move any slower?"

Borgo stopped again, this time to pick from a peddler's cart three smoked fishes, which he tossed to the three behind him with a mischievous grin. He then swaggered toward the *acougue* and grabbed a fistful of meat scraps for Solomon. "Now," he belched loudly. "Now we go to the *signora's*."

They entered the lord's courtyard through a guarded gate and passed numbers of resting gardens placed neatly around a statue of the Holy Mother. A few well-dressed men-at-arms stood along the walls; others lounged atop the ramparts, keeping a casual watch. A tonsured head appeared beneath an arcade, and Pieter immediately recognized Brother Chiovo. "Ho, brother!" cried Pieter.

The large-bellied monk turned and faced the four, blank faced. Then a huge smile stretched across his face. "Father Pieter!" he answered as he came running. The two black-robed men embraced. "Father Pieter! God be praised!"

Pieter laughed, happy to see the good monk. "Oh, good Chiovo! Oh, my friend, I must find Maria."

"Of course! And wait until she sees you!"

"Is she here?"

"*Si!* And doing very well." Chiovo's face abruptly fell. "We lost your Anna."

Pieter nodded somberly. "We know. We were at the abbey."

"Ah, yes … God's will be done." He sighed, then laid his hand on Pieter's shoulder. "Come, follow me. All of you."

Chiovo hurried through Lord Salito's great hall and into a private courtyard, where he bade Pieter sit with his lads on a bench beneath a rose arbor. He winked and then disappeared into the shadows of the castle.

"Please hurry!" said Otto. "I can hardly wait another moment."

Pieter said nothing but stared at the doorway leading to the hall. The day was fast ending, and long shadows had begun to stretch from the statues of saints rimming the courtyard. The air now brought a touch of November chill, yet the man paid no heed. He had fixed his face to the doorway, and nothing else mattered. Pieter's heart pounded and his legs felt weak. His fingers tapped anxiously on his staff until, at last—at long last—he heard the voice of a child echoing faintly inside. It was a musical voice, high and cheery. It was *her* voice.

Pieter and his boys drew deep breaths. Then, like the bursting of the sun from behind a heavy cloud, flaxen-haired Maria emerged from the darkened hall. She obediently stepped into the daylight, ignorant of the surprise waiting for her. For a moment, she simply stood in her place and looked about innocently. She wondered why Chiovo had been so mysterious and why he was waiting in the hall behind her.

Pieter stared speechlessly. It was as though more joy had

filled his heart than he could contain, and he could do nothing but gawk in wonder. He stared through tear-blurred eyes at the beautiful maiden, and then suddenly dropped his staff and rushed toward her with arms outstretched. "Maria!" he cried.

The child's jaw dropped and she trembled. "Papa Pieter!" she squealed. She raced across the courtyard. "Papa Pieter!"

The two fell into one another's embrace, weeping and laughing. Solomon was leaping and barking happily, and the boys charged forward to wrap the pair with their arms, glad hearted and shouting. Oh, what a glorious reunion! It was hope realized, dreams come true; it was that rare moment when miracles are plainly seen and the goodness of God unquestioned.

Soon all four were chattering wildly, wiping tears and laughing. "Papa Pieter, I missed you so! And you, Otto and Heinz."

"We oft wondered if we'd see you again." Otto shook his head. "I am so—"

"Aye! Me, too!" Heinz's face was bright and cheery. "It was hard going away."

Maria nodded. "But you had to go. I wanted you to go."

Chiovo handed Pieter his staff. "The *signora* has agreed to speak with you in the morning. Until then, my friends, you are to stay in the guest quarters, where food and refreshment await you."

The old man thanked the monk. "In a moment, brother, just one moment." He retrieved the cross stuffed in his belt and slowly handed it to Maria. "Ah, my dear. This is your cross, the one Karl carried for you on his journey, the one sworn to be returned to your hand."

The girl took the cross lovingly. "Karl is gone from us," she suddenly choked.

Astonished, Pieter nodded. "But how did you know?"

She wiped her eyes. "I had dreams, Papa. I saw him lying in some flowers that were tended by angels."

The boys felt chills run down their spines.

"But all is well for him. He is at peace and happy. I know it."

Pieter's throat swelled, and he laid his hand atop her head. *A mystery to be sure*, he thought. "'Tis true, my dear. Karl is with the angels now. We lost him near Genoa."

Maria kissed the cross. "He was a dear brother and I loved him."

Pieter took her under his arm and held her tightly.

"And Wil lives," she then stated confidently.

"Aye, sister. So he does," answered Pieter incredulously. "He will join us here in the spring, with others."

Maria smiled and, with her good hand, touched both of her crosses. "Thank you, Papa. Thank you for coming back."

☙

Eventually, Pieter and the boys were led to a comfortable chamber adjacent to the lord's apartments. They were given a modest-sized room with one bed and a snapping hearth. Servants delivered trays of olives and fruits, some roasted duck and baked fish. Four silver goblets accompanied a tankard of red wine, and a basket of bread was set neatly in the middle of the table.

The *signora* had given permission for Maria to take her evening supper with her friends, and the little girl quickly joined them at the table. Wanting to know everything, the group shared tales of the lost crusade, memory to memory, from one tragedy to the next. In turns they spoke of the *San Marco*, the miracle of Wil's survival, of San Fruttuoso, and of hopes to return home. Maria talked of Anna and the abbey, of the lord and lady—and her special friend, a donkey named Paulus.

The conversation had continued for over an hour when Pieter noticed Maria beginning to glance frequently at the closed door. "Maria, are you expecting someone?" Pieter asked.

The girl's cheeks flushed pink, and she looked at her plate. "No."

Pieter thought her answer to be strained. "Are you sure?"

"*Ja.*"

"Hmm. Well then, please pass the wine!"

The old man had barely filled his goblet, however, when

the door was flung open. All heads turned with a start and Maria giggled. There, to the utter astonishment of all, stood a familiar face. "Benedetto?" cried Pieter.

"*Si!*" laughed the minstrel. "*Si*, 'tis me!" He ran to a very astonished Pieter and the boys and embraced them each. "You look well, all of you! And you've a dog?"

"Aye. Solomon is his name. 'Tis a long story! But tell me, my friend, how is it you are here?"

The small man flopped onto the bed and shook his head. "Well, it comes to this: my heart was so wounded by our sufferings that I thought I could endure no more. I wanted only my simple life again. I thought to return to my dock, where I was known and where I had sung so many songs." He pulled at his pointy black beard. "I hurried north, back to Fiesch before the snows. Soon after Michaelmas I was playing my lute along the Rhône, but it was not the same. I could think only of the two left here ... and of you all. The dock gave me no joy, no peace. It was as if I no longer belonged there. So I came running back ... nearly freezing in the Simplon, but I arrived in Arona to find Anna's grave and Maria here in this kindly place."

The room was quiet. The little minstrel sighed. "So that is my tale."

Pieter nodded, approving the man's decision. "You've done well, minstrel. You followed your heart along the path of love."

Benedetto shrugged. "I have failed in many ways. My heart is often weak."

"I am proud to be your friend."

The minstrel's spirit soared. He smiled happily. He had often remembered the old man's rebuke by the shores of this very lake. It had been a worthy gift at the proper time. Now he was glad to have the man's approval. Blushing, he reached for the lute ever hanging at his back. "So—" he winked at Maria "—shall we?"

Maria's face brightened. "*Ja!*" she exclaimed eagerly.

"Pieter, we've a song for you. Many times we talked of your return, and we pretended to sing it to you.

"You see, when Maria was near death, she had dreams ...

many dreams and visions. When I found her, we spoke often of them and, together, we wrote a song. She loved me to sing it as she fell to sleep. I call it 'Maria's Song.'"

The girl blushed. "*You* wrote it."

"*Si,* but *you* gave me the visions!" Benedetto smiled and plucked a few notes. Maria nodded and closed her eyes as the minstrel began to strum a pleasant, dreamy tune—one melodic for its time and enchanting.

Let me take you by the hand, and let us laugh beneath
    the sun.
Let us fly amongst the songbirds, in the springtime
    meadows run.

For with butterflies I've floated, toward the heavens I
    have raced;
In the valley of the flowers I have danced in God's
    embrace.

Like the moths and like the magpies, like the seabirds
    and the bees,
We are children of the Master borne by currents in the
    breeze.

We are butterflies emerging, we are buds about to burst.
We are spirits soaring freely far from hunger and from
    thirst.

Let us tiptoe on the sunbeams and swim across the sky;
Let us slide along the rainbows and sing from heaven
    high!

Chapter Six

GOD WITH US

Jn San Fruttuoso, Heinrich stood beneath an umbrella pine and stared unseeing at the blue bay. He had kept his suffering deep within—he thought it uncharitable to burden others with his private sorrows. But no day had passed without his heart rending over the loss of Karl. He had walked day and night along the quiet beach and he had sat alone in the citrus groves, but he had found no solace.

It would have helped the man if Wil had forgiven him, if his eldest could have shared in his grief. He had attempted to engage his son on a few occasions, but the lad would simply not respond. Heinrich finally had, perhaps wisely, chosen to offer distance in the hope that time might serve a healing course.

The man sighed and looked upward at the underside of the tall pine. Memories of Sister Anoush and the church of *Santa Maria in Domnica* filled his mind. The church had a garden shaded by just such a tree. He stared at the green needles and shuddered as he remembered his descent into misery. *Thanks be to God for the blessed sister and her kindness.*

"I've seen only sadness in your eyes since the day you came," said Stefano from behind.

Startled, Heinrich spun about. "Eh?"

The monk looked at the man kindly. "I said, you seem always sad."

Heinrich shrugged.

"Is it Karl that weighs so heavy on your heart?"

The baker nodded.

"I've no children of my own, so I dare not claim to know your grief. But I surely believe you suffer for it."

"I see his face and hear his voice everywhere," Heinrich murmured.

Stefano looked carefully at the man. "And why not? You loved him."

The two stood quietly for a few moments before the monk added, "And you suffer for the want of Wil's forgiveness as well."

"*Ja.*" Heinrich sat down and tossed a stone. "I've told him I am sorry, I've admitted all I know, and I've asked his forgiveness ..."

"Ah, my friend, the lad loves you, I am sure of it. He will forgive you in time. His love assures that."

Heinrich turned a hopeful eye to the monk. "It would be a good thing."

Stefano nodded. "Indeed." The monk's gaze drifted over the bay, and he soon lost himself in reflection. He and the baker sat quietly by the shore as the waves lapped lightly and gentle breezes blew. In time the monk spoke. "I fear we oft miss the mark when we think only of forgiveness."

Heinrich turned his face toward the man.

"It is wondrous, to be sure, but it is only part of something far greater. I used to walk about this very shore pleading for God's mercy. Day and night I groaned and beat upon my breast. Then, when I felt I had finally received His forgiveness, I would spend many days praising Him for it. It was all I knew of Him.

"One warm evening, I was rebuked for these things by a wise monk from Cypress. He taught me that God's mercy is not His *only* gift, it is just the beginning of gifts." Stefano leaned close to Heinrich. "My friend, He offers us so much more than forgiveness; He offers us the whole of His love."

The baker stared thoughtfully at the monk. He, too, had spent years seeking mercy. He had spent precious few moments considering the immeasurable vastness of God's love.

"Forgiveness, my brother, is something God *does* for us, but love is what He *is* for us."

Heinrich wondered, but suddenly enlivened by the monk's good news, his mind began to whirl. A voice from one side interrupted his thoughts.

"'Tis a good day."

The two men turned. "Ah, Frieda. Yes, of course," answered Stefano, slightly annoyed at the intrusion.

The girl stepped alongside the pair. "I wonder about Pieter and the others. Do you think they'll celebrate the Advent with Maria and Anna?"

Heinrich answered. "Well, we can only hope."

Frieda stared quietly at the water and wrapped a thin blanket over her shoulders. She had braided her hair and was dressed in her new black gown. Heinrich thought her to be beautiful, and he sensed Wil had noticed as well.

"How is my son?"

"He grows better every day," Frieda answered with a kindly smile. "His wounds are fast healing and—he is different than before the *San Marco.*"

"I wouldn't know about that," Heinrich mumbled with a sudden quality of self-pity.

Frieda looked at the man with compassion but answered firmly, "He's cause to be angry with you."

The man was surprised. He was also weary and frustrated. "How would you know about that?"

"By your words, sir, by your own words."

Heinrich fell silent. He had shared a great deal of his past with the girl while in camp in Genoa and here at San Fruttuoso as well. "I thought to protect them all from m'self by my penance."

"Who?"

"Wil and his brother ... m'wife as well."

Frieda thought for a moment. "True enough. But you also wanted to cleanse your own soul, and you failed to consider the cost to them."

Heinrich recoiled from her remarks and fell silent.

Always inward, always melancholy, the man retreated deep within himself. *She'd be right to say it; 'tis truth in her words*, he thought. *I did not consider the cost in full.* The weight of shame lay heavy on his spirit when he felt the touch of the damsel's hand on his arm.

"Good sir, I do not blame you, nor do I think Wil blames you. He only needs to know that *you* know. He needs to know that you understand how terrible the cost was to him and to Karl ... and to their mother."

Heinrich nodded and glanced at Stefano. "You are wise beyond your years, Frieda, and you humble me. I still have much to learn." He kissed her on the cheek and walked away.

෨

The season of Advent brought some sadness to the cloister. Old Brother Nectarious was found cold in his bed, but the smile locked upon his face gave the community a bit of peace as they prepared him for burial. Another was quite ill—a young monk who had arrived just two years prior from an abbey in Lombardy. His absence from the chapter was an immediate loss, for he was the only one blessed with a voice pleasing in song. The Rule of Benedict had expressly required readings at meals and singing be done by those so gifted. "Monastics will read and sing, not according to rank, but according to their ability to benefit their hearers." It was a simple enough rule, and the vacancy left by the young man's absence was making many a painful moment for the brethren and guests alike!

Though the monks were required to eat in silence (except for the readings), they were happy to invite their guests to a later meal offered for their pleasure. The children had followed the monks' schedule rather closely—from the fifteenth day of September until the beginning of Lent they ate in the midafternoon. From Lent to Easter they would be eating their main meal in the evening. So for the feast of Christmas, the monks invited their guests to a gracious meal beginning just before the bells of compline.

Seated on long benches along their trestle tables, the children stared open mouthed at the happy presentation the delighted brethren offered. Without a prior, the monks seemed happy to stretch the limits of moderation, if only a little. Heinrich had helped bake loaves of honey-laced rolls—his duties in the bakery had been assigned weeks earlier. To the hurrahs of the company, the man bowed deeply as baskets of his handiwork were passed about.

"And have them try my *focaccia!*" cried Patroclus. Focaccia was a flatbread topped according to the season. Patroclus had heaped anchovies and boiled mushrooms atop the many loaves, along with slices of fresh olives and chopped garlic. Eager hands reached for it!

The breads were followed by platters of roasted boar meat, still sizzling from the spit, and steaming shellfish. "Something green and something blue!" cried Stefano as he set them before the flying fingers of the children. A plate of bream seasoned with pine nuts was set beside a fricassee of ground almonds, juniper berries, olive oil, and rabbit on a bed of greens.

Frieda and Wil sat together and said little as they stuffed themselves. Wil had long since set the offense of the girl's rebuke aside, though he had not broached the subject again. They laughed and reached for mead and ale.

"Was it worth the work?" cried Wil to his company.

"Aye!" they shouted. Indeed, for every bite they took they had a memory. Whether threshing or netting fish, shaking olives or crushing them, hunting boar with Brother Risto, or filling the boats with lemons, the children had spent these past ten weeks hard at work. "And what 'ave *you* done?" shouted one playfully.

Wil nodded and stood. The room fell quiet. "My brothers and sisters, I am thankful to God for my life and thankful to each of you for helping Him to save it. Frieda has been my faithful nurse, and I owe her much." He turned an affectionate eye toward the blushing maiden and continued. "My strength is fast returning. None can know how much I wish to climb an olive tree or carry a load of lemons! Soon I will be working by your sides. Until then, I am banished to the monks' chamber, where I copy Scripture with them." He held up ink-stained hands and laughed. "Ink, not calluses!"

The room cheered and the lad sat down. He had regained much of his former weight, though he had always been lean. His skin had good color; his eyes were clear. Sharp featured and handsome—his scars notwithstanding—he inspired all who were near with a certain presence that defied words. His long blond hair and keen blue eyes conveyed a sense of regal disposition and authority. The son of a baker, he seemed more a prince.

Frieda, however, saw things more deeply. She had known the arrogance of his former self, the brooding selfishness that had so offended her. Through their short acquaintance, however, she had noticed the seeds of humility taking root in a heart softened by sorrows. The young man now seemed to be evidencing the presence of true strength and character. She had seen it in small ways: the way he helped the little ones, the way he worked with the monks, the way he touched her hand. She could see a change in his eyes; they had become softer, more apt to reflect the feeling of another's sadness. All that is, except his father's.

ൠ

It was the Epiphany, January 6 in the year of our Lord 1213—the feast that celebrated the wise men's visit with the Holy Child. The twelve days of Christmas were now ending, and quiet had settled over San Fruttuoso. After an ample midday meal and when the offices of the day were served, Brother Stefano summoned Wil to a quiet place in the arcade.

"My son, I've a gift for you."

Surprised, Wil waited.

Stefano reached behind a screen and retrieved a longbow and quiver filled with arrows. Wil's eyes widened and his mouth dropped. "For me?"

"Aye, lad. It seems our departed friend, Brother Nectarious, had a few surprises for us under his bed! He left us notes attached to a number of gifts." Stefano smiled. "Of course, we are all sworn to poverty, and the hoarding of possessions is a serious offense. His note began with his confession and a plea for the priest to pray loudly and often for his miserable soul … and he left him two gold coins 'in gratitude' for the father's faithful remembrance!

"I shall very much miss the old fellow. Ah, well, to you he left this." Stefano held the bow for a long moment, almost covetously, then handed it to Wil. "The note says it was given to him while on crusade by a mortally wounded Englishman."

Wil received the gift in astonishment. He stroked the smooth yew wood and studied the various designs etched on it. "Brother Nectarious was on crusade?"

"*Ja.* Nectarious was once a soldier named Morello. He served under three Christian kings of Jerusalem and fought against the armies of Saladin in the Holy City, in Tiberias, Tyre, Acre, and places I've since forgotten.

"This longbow is English yew, the best wood in all the world for archers; heartwood for the inside, sapwood for the front. And notice the etching, here, just above the handle. '*Vincit qui patior*'—'He who suffers, conquers.'

"He writes that the bow was given a name during a terrible, fearsome slaughter near Acre. The archer named it 'Emmanuel' … God with us."

Wil stared at the bow reverently. To imagine this had fired arrows at the infidels in defense of the Cross was staggering to the young man. To hold this instrument of judgment in his own hands, to carry a weapon that had once been in the holy places filled him with awe. "Emmanuel," he whispered.

"Nectarious believed the bow might serve in your recovery. By pulling its string, you'll strengthen your arms, your chest, your shoulders, and your back. You'll needs pull a short distance at a time, and over the weeks to come you'll find the string coming ever closer to your ear."

"I've ne'er shot one before."

"We'll be glad to teach you. None knew the old scoundrel had this hidden, else we'd have used it ourselves! We've a few poor bows lying about, but none such as this. You'll learn quick enough, then you can hunt game for us!"

"Ha!" cried Wil. "Indeed I shall!"

"And here, his quiver and arrows. Seems the heads need

sharpening, but the shafts are ash and seem strong enough. The fletching is sound; the feathers look like swan to me. You may want to steam them a bit. Cedar mist is best."

Wil took the leather quiver and lifted a few of the arrows from it. "Different heads."

Stefano nodded. "Most are barbed broadheads ... good for hunting man or beast. I see two for piercing armor."

Wil marveled at his gift. "But why for me?"

The monk shrugged. "He does not say."

Wil pulled on the bowstring and grimaced. "Perhaps by springtime."

࿊

Wil's company was soon invited to participate in the self-denial of Lent. The monks suggested they forego sweet rolls and mead, excess in any foods, and loud laughter. With so much to be thankful for, the young Christians agreed that taking time to consider the sufferings of Christ was a small thing to do, and so they quickly agreed. The season passed slowly, as one might expect, and the abundance of chores the monks seemed ever to require did not shorten it. Whether fishing or harvesting citrus, mending nets, repairing roofs, or plaiting baskets, many hands were kept very busy.

In this oft-drizzly season, Wil spent whatever time he could with Emmanuel. He gradually increased his draw by working each arm each day. By the Ides of March he was able to release his first arrow. His shot drew loud jeers from his laughing comrades as it careened away from his target and nearly pierced a wheel of cheese by the refectory! But the lad laughed as loud as the rest, thrilled to have the strength to feel the feathers by his cheek.

Heinrich had been kind to his son for these many weeks but had still not received the young man's forgiveness. It was a burden he was willing to bear, though it was heavy. He had hoped time might have prepared an opportunity to offer his heart, but it had not. He ventured a few comments, but his attempts were dismissed politely. So he spent his days helping the monks' baker.

The monk had been secretly taught the arts of confectionery by his teacher, a French monk, once a lord in Paris. The man loved testing his skills with jams and egg whites, and together with Heinrich, the two invented any number of crepes and memorable pastries that they tasted in private—the Lent notwithstanding!

But when he was not in the bakery, Heinrich spent long hours walking the shore with his Laubusbach stone rolling between his fingers. He was usually alone but sometimes was seen in the company of Stefano or even Frieda. Frieda loved hearing stories of Heinrich's life, especially of his times with Emma and Lukas. She oft sat spellbound as the man wandered through the years gone by, and for Heinrich the journey backward was comforting. For him, this season of denial was one of quiet reflection and rest.

Frieda spent her Sabbath days in the sunny arches of the arcade with quills in hand. The monks' priest, the oft-elusive Father Frederico, had presented her with a precious gift at the Epiphany—quills and ink. Her companions were astonished to then learn that she knew how to write—they had known nothing of her family's past station.

"I could read that if you'd let me," said Wil on Palm Sunday. He craned his neck, and the girl quickly turned her parchment away.

"I'd rather you not, for m'hand is poor."

"I would tell if it were so."

"I know," she answered. "Which is exactly why I do not want you watching!" She smiled flirtatiously.

Wil leaned close. The warm air of spring had begun to heat his blood, and the smell of the young woman's hair enchanted him. "Please?"

Frieda blushed and turned her head shyly.

Smiling, Wil reached his forefinger toward the girl's face and laid it lightly atop her dimpled chin. "I'd like very much to—"

Before the lad could say another word, the voice of Stefano rang loudly in his ear. "Wil, you're needed in the vineyard."

Both Wil and Frieda turned with a start.

"Come with me to the vineyard," Stefano ordered sternly.

"But 'tis the Sabbath!" protested Wil.

The monk growled. He was more concerned with pruning the young man's desires than nipping a twig! "*Ja*, Sabbath indeed. Come, follow me."

The monk and Wil walked quietly up the slope and paused at the first of many rows of muscat grapes. "I see buds," began Stefano.

Wil grumbled.

"Beware, my son. What say you to a wedding?"

Wil blushed. "A wedding? Me? Now? Ha, methinks not."

"Then as I said, beware."

The monk sat on a rock and bade Wil to follow. He set a weed between his teeth. "Now, on other matters. Seems we've but one week more together. According to your father, your journey begins the day past Easter."

"Aye, brother. I long to know of m'sister. I long to see her. It will be the middle of April before we leave and nearly the end when we arrive."

Stefano nodded sympathetically. "Are you so certain she is alive?" The question was intended to prepare the lad, but it stung.

"Aye!" snapped Wil as he stood. "I'll believe nothing else unless I see her grave!"

The monk changed course. "And what shall you say to her?"

The young man threw a stone and thought for a moment. His mind flew to the awful moment in the castle of Domodossola when he denied that Maria was his sister—when he was ashamed of her deformity and the pitiful condition of his other comrades. He could see the haughty smile of the lord's daughter he had hoped to impress, and he felt sickened by it. "I'll beg her forgiveness. I betrayed her ... and others ... and am still ashamed."

"*Should* she forgive you?"

The question confused the lad. "I ... I don't know if she *should* or not. I only know that I *hope* she does."

"Forgiveness, my son, is the fruit of humility, a gift of grace. It seems that some little children by nature still have that abiding touch of heaven in their spirits. They usually forgive with greater ease than a man. Men want justice, you see ... except for themselves, in which case they want mercy. But I say this: woe to him who seeks to be forgiven yet does not forgive. That man is a pathetic fool, one filled with arrogance and the disease of the self. A man like that gives no thought to the wonder of love."

Wil said nothing. He knew exactly what point the monk was making.

Stefano took a long breath. "Well, on other matters. We need to speak of your pilgrims. First, I must warn you of something. Before All Saints', a lemon merchant had told two of our brothers that some Genoese soldiers were asking the folk of Camogli if any had seen crusading children. Apparently a young man named Paul caused great mischief in Genoa, and many of his followers were caught."

Wil chilled. "Do you know their fate?"

"Some were hanged ... maybe most."

Wil shook his head. "And why did you not tell us before this?"

Stefano shrugged. "We wanted you to delight in a deep rest before your next trials. We've kept sentries deep in the mountain trail since then and have kept a sharp eye on the bay. We've seen or heard nothing since, so we are fairly certain the search is long since over. Nevertheless, you should be wary. The Genoese are spiteful, vengeful people.

"Now, a few more things. We have been approached by a number of boys and girls who would like to stay. Most tell us they were cast away from their homes or had severe lives in their villages. Others seem moved by pious devotion."

"How many?"

"Several. We've not taken a final count, but it seems nearly all the girls and about half the boys."

Wil stood and began to pace, deep in thought. "Can you take proper care of them?"

Stefano smiled to himself. *A true leader*, he thought. "*Ja*, young sir. We've need of more hands and can give them a good life until they know God's will for themselves. The boys would remain here; we've already received permission from our abbot in residence near Savona. We dispatched a messenger after Martinmas in anticipation of this question. Seems the abbot believes we'll soon have a prior to rule us. He's been granted some holdings from several benefactors in Milan and has visions of San Fruttuoso blossoming into much more than it is now."

Wil nodded. "I like it as it is. So what of the girls?"

Stefano brightened. "Ah, I have especially good news for the girls! It seems a new community is to be established near Assisi, one begun by a woman named Clare who's been given the blessing of the bishop. She was a wealthy lord's daughter, drawn to the message of Brother Francis— of whom we've heard much—and now given to the freedom of poverty. Her holiness has attracted many others who wish to shed the weight of their comforts for the liberty of service.

"We've learned of a group of seven ladies from Genoa who will be making their pilgrimage on the feast of the Assumption. A messenger has made secret communication with them, and they have willingly agreed to accept the girls who wish to join them."

"You know of this Assisi?" asked Wil.

"I once traveled there, about six years ago on my pilgrimage to Rome. It is a marvelous place—a wide valley of olives and rose gardens. Marvelous. However, we are told the community would probably begin in San Damiano, where Clare is at present. I've ne'er been there, but I would think your friends would have a good life wherever these women go."

Wil nodded. "I must trust you in this. Has the order a name?"

"It is no formal order yet, at least not that we've been told. Their desire has been approved by Brother Francis of Assisi, however, and some now call themselves the Poor Clares. I would expect the pope's blessing to be granted in due time."

"Did you speak to them about all this?"

Stefano shook his head. "Not without the permission of yourself and *Herr* Heinrich."

Wil sighed. The vineyard was terraced into the mountain's breast, and from that vantage one could see the cloister below. The young man turned his face toward the youthful, gangly bodies of his comrades, and he watched them frolic and play under the Sabbath sun.

"It is like paradise here," he said. "The air smells sweet, the water is clean and warm. The sky is usually blue, and at night it is filled with stars." He faced Stefano. "Are you at risk of pirates?"

"We've none for years. The Venetians swept most of them from the eastern sea and the Genoese from these parts. The times they did come, we spilled their blood ourselves."

"You'll teach the boys to fight?"

"Aye, but more to pray."

Wil nodded thoughtfully. "Well, I've no right to hold them. Seems a good thing for them to stay. Have you talked to my ... my father?"

"I have. He agrees with you."

Wil said nothing for a moment, then mumbled, "You think me wrong and stiff necked toward him."

"No man can force another to forgive. Your father has admitted his failings. I've heard you say that he has clearly confessed to you the great loss he caused your family. You said he was particular in his confession. He can do no more."

The young man looked away. "When I see him shuffling about, he seems old to me. Sometimes I feel pity for him, but ... but ..."

"He does not want your pity, my son."

Wil stared at the sky, then at the palms. It was early April, and all the world felt fresh. Easter was fast coming, and he thought of new beginnings. "I suppose I am no better than he, brother. I know this in my mind. And Pieter reminds me that *my* hard heart may be the greatest sin of all. These things I know, yet I cannot say the words to him."

ﾧ

Easter Sunday came on the fourteenth of April. It was a rainy day, but Father Frederico offered such a pleasant surprise that none gave it mind. He preached a brief homily to the monks, then turned to his guests and delivered a simple farewell message translated into German by Stefano. The pilgrims sat fixed on the man as he spoke of Christ as the Way of suffering, the Truth incarnate, and the Life to whom all belonged. They had traveled along their own journey of sorrows, and to imagine the Christ as having endured the same—and more—was oddly comforting. The God they worshiped was not without empathy; He had, indeed, touched His feet upon a world beset by hardship— upon the very world they themselves had been called to endure.

For Heinrich, the sudden realization that it was the Christ who had pursued him all along his own burdensome path was a moment of particular inspiration. The man nearly cried out. *This Christ, this Jesus, is the One to whom the others had been pointing! It is He who has given me sight; it is He who has set me free. The truth is alive and it is He!*

For all of them, the notion of new life as new persons— changed persons, redeemed ones—was one that abruptly began to create a change in their thinking. A vague excitement stirred in their bellies, an anticipation of a resurrection yet undefined. It was a message of mystery: They would soon become that which they already were; they would soon belong where they already did. For these former crusaders and their beloved baker, the priest's homily was one never to be forgotten.

The holy day was spent peacefully. The monks provided a generous feast, complete with many of the treats Heinrich and the Frenchman had concocted during Lent. But alas, the blessed day soon passed, and night fell upon a somber group of fellows preparing to bid one another a sad farewell on the morning to follow.

A misty dawn greeted the bells of prime. The church bell pealed slowly, most thought even sadly. Within the hour Wil and his company were fed and prayed over. Most fought tears as they assembled along the sandy beach they had learned to love so very much.

Heinrich stood erect and ready. He had gained weight,

and his spirit had healed some, though the distance between him and his son was becoming a great source of frustration. The gentle man had allowed the monks' barber to trim his hair and beard. His eye patch and old boots were oiled, his vest repaired. The Stedinger dagger was stuffed into his belt, and over his shoulder was slung his satchel, still bearing his Laubusbach stone and the pouch of Anoush's gold. He had offered the monks one gold coin for each child remaining, but they would not have it. Instead, they filled the remaining space in his satchel with food-stuffs enough for the journey to Arona.

"Heinrich," said Brother Petroclus as he approached with Stefano and the brethren. "Heinrich, we have prayed over all of you this morning."

"Thanks be to every one of you," answered the baker. He cleared his throat, stiffened, and then nervously offered, "And may God above always light your way with His truth and give you a life of belonging."

Stefano translated, and the amazed brethren stood dumfounded, astonished at the simple man's profound blessing. Brother Petroclus finally spoke. "Dear man, we receive your kindness with gratitude. Thanks be to God.

"Now this, my son." The monk turned to another and received a sheathed sword in the palms of his outstretched hands. He then returned to the baker. "Heinrich of Weyer, it was the desire of our late brother, Nectarious, to have this presented to you for the protection of your young pilgrims."

Heinrich's eye widened as he took the gift. A pang of fear ran through him suddenly. *I am a bound man, not permitted a weapon*, he thought.

"Draw the sword, Heinrich," said Petroclus. "Draw the sword."

The baker held the sheath between his knees and drew the gleaming sword into the morning's light. It was a heavy short-sword, about the length of his arm. It was perfect for one-handed use by a strong man.

"Look, there." Petroclus pointed to the inscription. "'*Veritas Regnare* ... Truth Reigns.' According to a note our old brother left, this was his own sword in Palestine. I saw it used here against Saracen pirates. It has drawn much blood in the cause of good.

"Now, we must tie it at your hip so you can draw it without using your knees!"

Heinrich let the sun glimmer on the sharp edge of the blade. "I've no words at all," he offered.

"None needed." Stefano laughed. "Old Nectarious can't hear you!"

The children laughed. Then Wil stepped forward. The lad was dressed in his new black garments, like the others. His leggings were of heavy cloth, his hooded tunic a bit thinner. A braided leather belt girded his waist. He had been given good shoes that laced at his ankles. A thick blanket was tied to his back alongside the quiver slung over his shoulder. The smith had sharpened his arrowheads and oiled his bow with resin and beeswax before wrapping it in canvas. The lad held Emmanuel proudly and adjusted his satchel. It had been repaired and oiled and filled with provisions. He raised his hands over the company and spoke. "Brothers and sisters, 'tis time. Those leaving with me need join me now."

Without a moment's hesitation, Frieda stepped forward. She moved through her companions gracefully, touching and kissing many until she emerged to walk boldly to Wil's side. The girl was dressed in a hooded black gown that fell to her feet. She walked in comfortable shoes not unlike Wil's. She had also been given a new satchel filled for the journey, and across her back was tied a blanket. In her belt she had placed a bouquet of springtime flowers, and her braids were tied with thin green vines.

Next came fifteen-year-old Helmut, the lad from the region of Bremen in the far north of the German empire. His hair had been trimmed, and his narrow face had filled a little. He had followed Wil for many miles and would follow him again. Rudolf of Liestal was the next to step forward. Broad shouldered and kindly, hardworking like his parents in the mountains so far away, he was ready to make his way home.

Thirty-four other pairs of feet began to rock. Eyes darted

about and a dull murmur spread. Wil was surprised. He thought at least four or five others were coming. "Do any others wish to join us?"

The group fell silent, many now looking downward.

"Do not be ashamed!" said Wil. "If you have chosen to stay, you have chosen wisely. I wish you the peace of God." He cast a quick look at Ava, the feisty little redhead. He thought she would surely have joined them.

The girl smiled and winked. "I like the sunshine," she quipped.

Wil laughed—they all laughed. Then, with no more ceremony but many tears, those few who were leaving embraced those many who had chosen to remain. Heartfelt thanks were offered to the good monks of San Fruttuoso, and their journey was begun.

☙

Brother Stefano helped row the boat carrying the five pilgrims away from their refuge. It was a quiet journey under a clearing sky that turned the waters of the bay deep blue. Light morning breezes nudged the curling mists away, and Wil's small company stared silently at the green mountains now emerging into full view. The heat of the sun, the rhythmic glide of the boat, and the melodic cries of seabirds left most drifting toward sleep. Wil imagined Pieter with Maria. *He'd have been there with her all this winter past,* he mused. *Soon she'll pick him springtime flowers by the bushel.* He took a deep breath, then groaned inwardly as the unbidden thought came. *Unless the monks buried her.*

As the craft moved from the bay and into the open sea, however, all began to stir. The breezes that had chased the mists had also nudged the water into easy swells. The small boat now dipped and rose lightly, occasionally plowing through a disappearing furrow that splashed the crew with a refreshing spray.

It was all too soon for Heinrich when the oarsmen pulled their final stroke and slid the craft against the pebbly shoreline of Camogli's cove. Most of the village's fishermen were far into the sea, having left a few old men behind to mend nets and pitch some leaky hulls. The baker noticed pairs of village women ambling along the brick streets. Each had one elbow wrapped round a friend's while the other cradled a basket filled with bread or cheese. He smiled and waved politely at an old woman who returned his gesture with a toothless grin.

"From here you know your way?" asked Stefano.

"*Ja,*" answered Heinrich. "The lad and I reviewed the route with Pieter before he left, and you agreed it to be a good one."

The monk nodded. "At least as far as Arona. From there, you need pray to God." He smiled.

Wil joined the pair. "After Arona we'll find no monasteries until the far side of the mountains."

"They are there for those who seek them," answered Stefano.

"Well, methinks I should have sought them on our journey south when I'd so many little souls to tend. Pieter suggested it at camp a few times, but he said he knew of very few close to our route, especially on our mountain trails. And I refused to stray from the quickest route ... we all thought we were too far behind the others."

"Perhaps you need to heed the words of the old man more. We brothers are here to serve others as a place of refuge in a dangerous world."

"Well, I'd reasons to not trust most monks in those times." He cast a quick glance at his father. "So I gave the idea little thought."

"Some brothers you should not trust. When I was a novice, I caught a monk in a grievous act. I could not understand. His piety and devotion were an inspiration to all of us. My dean told me this: he said, 'Where the light is brightest, the shadows are darkest.' Remember that, lad."

A weathered old woman suddenly appeared at Stefano's side and pointed to the castle. "*C' é un ragazzo nel prigione!*"

"*Si?*" answered Stefano.

The woman nodded, then pointed to the Germans. "*C' é un ragazzo nel prigione, ragazzo come quelli.*"

Brother Stefano thanked the woman and turned to

Heinrich. "She says a youth like these is in the prison."

"Probably a crusader," blurted Frieda.

"I fear for any held in Dragonara's dungeon," murmured Stefano. All heads turned toward the grim castle perched on the sea cliffs to their left. The fortress was dark and foreboding, even on a sunny spring day such as this. Heavy shadows filled hollow chambers, and it faced the sea as though it were daring the deep waters to rise against it. Workmen could be seen crawling from scaffold to plank with heavy ropes and mortar. Heaps of quarried stone lay piled at the fortress's feet, waiting to be added like so many new scales on the ribs of this Castle of the Dragonslayer.

Frieda shuddered and whispered to Helmut, "No good thing is in that place."

"What do we do about it?" asked Helmut.

"We cannot leave him," said Rudolf.

Heinrich had been thinking. He whispered to Wil and the two nodded. "Brother Stefano, could you stay here with the others? Wil and I have a plan."

Frieda stepped forward. "If you two are going to the castle, you'd best take us all."

"Nay!" snapped Wil. "One look at you and you'll be kept as their toy till the end of time. Helmut and Rudolf needs stay by you until we come back."

"And if you don't?"

"Then hurry on your way."

The words stung and the girl winced. His answer suggested no more interest in her welfare than for that of some stray cat. "Hurry on my way?" she retorted. "That's all? Just hurry along and have a life?"

Heinrich's lips twitched upward just a bit. *My son*, he thought, *has received little training in the curious ways of a woman!* "He only meant you ought to 'hurry' on your way," the baker quickly said. "He fears for your safety."

Wil stared blankly at the two. He could not imagine why the girl's cheeks were flushed and her eyes were flashing fire.

Helmut had paid little attention to the exchange. "What advantage is *two* of you?" he asked.

"What?" Wil's mind had been elsewhere.

"Why the two of you? It seems we ought to put only one at risk. Wil's going gains us nothing."

Heinrich quickly agreed. "Well said. Wil, I'll go m'self. I've some experience in these things." He removed his satchel and hung a small pouch on his belt.

Wil opened his mouth to protest, but the steely gaze of Frieda held his tongue. He nodded.

Stefano interrupted. "Surely, Heinrich, I should come. The robes of a monk oft have more power than a sword."

Heinrich hesitated, then Wil nodded, and in moments Heinrich and Brother Stefano were crossing the bridge leading to the half-built castle. The monk took a deep breath. "So, baker, *fortes fortuna adiuvat!*"

"What?"

"Fortune favors the brave."

Heinrich nodded. He surely hoped so.

Chapter Seven

A SON REMEMBERED, A SISTER FOUND

The baker and the monk approached the castle gate.

"Ho there," said Heinrich firmly.

"*Si?*"

The one-eyed man reached into the pouch and retrieved five silver pennies. "*Bambino,*" he said. "The boy in the prison."

The guard stared at the coins. "*Bambino?*"

"*Si,*" answered the baker. "*Bambino, prigione.*"

The guard nodded, now very much awake. He looked at Heinrich, then the pennies and then at the bulging coin pouch on the man's belt. He turned a sheepish face toward the silent monk and grunted. He ran down a corridor only to return with two others, one apparently the castellan.

The officer addressed Heinrich stiffly. When he finished, the baker simply held out his hand and said once more, "*Bambino, prigione.*"

The castellan sneered at the pittance being offered.

That, Heinrich understood. He nodded and reached slowly into the pouch to pinch a few more pennies. He held out seven.

The officer shook his head, and his comrade drew a dagger. Heinrich spat and quickly drew his sword, dropping the silver to the stone floor. To everyone's surprise, the monk then pulled a short-sword from within his robe. With unnerving confidence, the baker snarled, "*Bambino!*"

The castellan was fairly certain his men could dispatch the foreign barbarian, but at what cost? The man looked like a veteran of many battles. His patched eye and stump were no doubt losses for which others had paid dearly. But what would they do with the meddling monk? Perhaps the pouch for the prisoner was the easier way. He pointed at Heinrich's belt with the point of his sword. "*Bambino.*"

Heinrich nodded and backed up slowly. He replaced his sword in its sheath and unhooked the pouch. He bounced it in his hand, keeping it from the castellan's grasp. "*Bambino.*"

The deal was struck, and in moments a tall thin lad in tattered leggings was dragged into the light. The boy took one look and sneered. "Well, by the Holy Mother, it's *Herr* Heinrich himself."

The baker was confused. *How does he know m'name?* he wondered. He wisely said nothing as he traded his silver for the black-haired youth. With no more words, the boy's bonds were cut and the three hurried away.

❧

It had been more than an hour since Heinrich and Stefano had left, and Wil found himself surprisingly anxious. His stomach tightened, and an odd sense of remorse began to blend with his fears. Imagining his father imprisoned or worse troubled him more than he would have expected, and he prayed no harm had befallen the faithful monk.

Frieda suddenly cried out, "They're coming!"

The four burst from their cover and ran to meet the others. The rescued prisoner was hooded and walked on bare feet with his head down, but when Wil and the others arrived, he lifted his face and curled his lip with a snicker.

"Tomas!" cried Frieda.

Wil froze. Tomas had been his nemesis from the early weeks of the crusade. Before that he had been his helper in the family bakery. Wil clenched his jaw. "You again. The last we saw you, you were with that Dark Lord in the wood by Genoa."

"The last I saw you, you were hiding off the roadway south of here."

Heinrich took the young man by the arm. "You? You were the spy?"

Tomas smirked. "*Ja*. Me and two others." Suddenly, his face darkened and he threw back his hood. He turned his head for all to see the red scar on his right cheek and what was left of his ear. "You, y'swine, y'cut my ear in two."

"You ought thank the saints I didn't carve your throat!" snapped the baker with a growl.

Tomas looked at the others. When his eyes fell on Frieda, he smiled wickedly. "Ah, Frieda. I have surely missed your fine company."

The young woman looked away.

Wil pressed his face close to the lad's. "Tomas, I'll tell you this. You're free enough now," he growled. "We've paid the price for you. Now go away."

The black-haired boy's face changed abruptly, every trace of arrogance fleeing. He had assumed they would help him. "Go away? They'll kill me! The lord we followed sent us to scrump the city the same night your crusaders did. Nearly all of m'fellows were caught, most hanged." His voice became strained. "I was sent to follow you. But when I came back with m'wounds, I found the lord was imprisoned as well. Afore I could get away, I was caught on the road and dragged here. Some priest saved me from the gallows, but ... but if they find me again, they'll hang me for sure."

"When did you last eat?" asked Rudolf.

"Some days past," Tomas answered, now submissive.

Rudolf reached into his satchel as Wil kicked the ground and cursed.

Heinrich was still confused. "Wil, you know him?"

Wil grunted. "He apprenticed in our bakery."

Heinrich studied Tomas carefully. "You are from Weyer?"

"No, Villmar. The monks raised me there, then sent me to Weyer to help in your bakery when you left."

"I see."

"I've no parents that I know. I'm told I was dumped in a

shearing shed. None knew m'mother, but some say m'father was a shepherd near Arfurt."

Heinrich chilled. The only shepherds from Arfurt he knew were Gunnars, the family long hated by his own. "'Tis a sad tale."

"Humph," the lad snorted. "Sad enough."

The baker drew Wil aside and whispered, "Methinks we've little choice here. We cannot leave him to hang. He's one of us."

"One of us? Are you mad? He has been nothing but cause for trouble and abandoned the holy cause of crusade to consort with evil men. What makes him one of us?"

Heinrich paused. It was a better question than he had considered. "Well, son, he speaks our tongue, he lives in our village—"

"Wil, you've no choice in this," interrupted Frieda in a hushed tone. "We've enjoyed Christian charity all this winter past—you more than all. We cannot deny another, not even Tomas."

Reluctantly, Wil shrugged his assent. The band of pilgrims was now numbered at six.

Stefano had waited quietly at the edges of the conversation, but the hour was growing late. "I fear I am late for my duties," he announced, "so I must bid you farewell." He looked at Tomas. "My son, *Deus vobiscum*, may God go with you." He raised his hands over the others. "May the Lord direct your hearts unto the love of God and into the patience of Christ."

Wil reached for the monk's hand and grasped it firmly. "Our thanks, Brother Stefano, for your charity and your wisdom."

Stefano embraced Wil, then Heinrich, then each of the others. He prayed over the pilgrims and reluctantly returned to his boat, where his brothers were patiently waiting. Then, with a sad wave, the two groups parted company, never to see one another again.

⌘

By nightfall, Tomas proved himself to be of some value. He knew of an obscure trail that would lead the pilgrims safely around Genoa and deliver them to the main roadway north, in the foothills just beyond the city. All agreed that they ought not to risk the *podesta's* wrath. The city's guard was doubtlessly still fomenting over the night of grand theft. But Heinrich, Wil, and Frieda refused to leave Liguria without one final farewell to Karl, whose body was buried along the roadway just above Genoa.

The boy's grave had been dug in the "Angels' Garden" nearly seven months before. On the curving highway descending from the mountains to the city, the good lad had been lost to a reckless company of horsemen and their wagoner. Wil and Frieda could not blot the moment from their memories, and Heinrich's imagination lost nothing in conjuring the horrific event.

Indeed, while others slept, poor Heinrich walked about in the mountain's wood, lamenting the loss of his beloved child. Guilt heaped itself upon grief, and the weight of the burden was intolerable. He simply could not forgive himself for failing to reveal his true identity to Karl before it was too late. Would his cheerful, loving, and kindhearted son have forgiven and welcomed his father? Would Karl still be alive if he had been there to protect him? Heinrich could find no satisfying answers to these questions.

At dawn the man returned to the camp. He was drained, and his face looked sallow and drawn. He stood silently and waited bravely, and the sight of such a crushed soul caused more than one heart to clench in sympathy. Frieda ran to the man and held him tightly. "I loved him too, *Herr* Heinrich," she whispered. "I loved him too."

Wil stared at his father and wondered how a man so broken could have been as callous as others had once said. His mother had told him and Karl over and over again how uncaring, how utterly selfish, and how dangerous a man he was. Looking at him now, Wil wondered.

With few words the company gathered themselves and followed Wil upward along the crowded roadway. Most passersby thought them to be pilgrims from some holy order. Their black garments and somber faces even convinced a few to toss them pennies.

It was well before noon when Wil slowed his walk to study the shoulder of the highway in earnest. The grave had been dug on the east side in a clearing filled with wildflowers. It was mid-April, and he was sure some would be in fresh bloom. He wondered if Frieda's cross would still be there.

The pilgrims followed their leader quietly, respecting the loss that both he and his father so sorely suffered. Even Tomas admitted that he had liked Karl, though he had thought him a bit annoying from time to time. "His riddles could drive a monk to madness," the young man offered awkwardly.

No one answered. Finally Wil stopped. He beckoned Frieda close, and the two peered ahead at a distant clearing on the downside of a curve. From this vantage it looked peculiar, but something about it seemed familiar. The two ran forward with Heinrich close behind.

"Oh, by the saints," said Frieda in a hushed tone. "He is here."

Wil dashed ahead and fell to his knees. Frieda and Heinrich quickly joined him, and the three stared sadly at the sinking mound of stones half covered by winter debris. Wil leaned forward and began to pick away dead weeds and crumbling petals when he spotted the wooden cross lying on its side. The sight of it brought a flood of memories to his mind, and his vision swam into a blur. "See, Father ... Frieda's cross," he choked.

The man's gaze rested on the simple apple-wood cross as Wil and Frieda slowly set it upright. He could only imagine what sorrows that cross had witnessed, what sufferings it had borne along his sons' crusade of tears. He then laid his hand atop the grave and groaned woefully. It was a painful thing to be separated from his beloved boy by such a thin screen of dirt and rock. He only wished he could hug the happy lad one last time. Heinrich fell to the ground along-side the mound and cried out for heaven's mercy.

Wil drew short, shallow breaths and tried for all the world to hold back his tears. Unable to bear the raw agony of his father's grief, he retreated to the far side of the road and leaned against a tree, very much alone. Alas, there in his solitude he could not hold the flood tide of sorrow any longer. He covered his face with his hands and was soon weeping.

Large salty droplets also fell from Frieda's cheeks as she cleaned every bit of bramble off the grave. Humming softly as a mother would when tending one she loves, she smiled lovingly as she pictured the boy's red curls and ready smile. "Ah, Karl," she whispered, "you know the answer to the riddle now, don't you?" She reached for a few early blooms and sprinkled them atop the mound.

In time, Wil composed himself and started for the grave again. He stopped, however, and stared at his father, who was yet lying on the ground, still as death. The lad watched and considered this final evidence of the man's heart. *"Uncaring?" It hardly seems so. "Dangerous?" I remember how he was so easily tricked by the steward. "Selfish?" Perhaps. But I don't recall the times he was, other than his leaving us, and I've not seen a sign of it in all these months.*

Wil's thoughts took him to the Weyer of his childhood, and memories of his father began to take a more pleasant place alongside those of Karl. *He liked to laugh but was too easily shamed by others,* he remembered. *Ah, the Magi and the Laubusbach ... he and Karl loved them so. And old Emma and Lukas.... Odd they should be such friends to the man he was said to be.*

Frieda's touch returned him to the present. "Wil, perhaps 'tis time?"

The young man nodded. He walked to his father and nudged him with his boot. Heinrich lurched with a start. "What?"

"'Tis time."

The man's eye lingered on the well-groomed grave for another moment. It was hard for him to leave it, harder than he had imagined. He stared, emptied of all joy, drained of things happy. At last, he rolled to his knees and bowed his head. He prayed loudly and without reservation, pleading with the saints, the Holy Mother, and the Christ to share the bounty of heaven "with my good boy, Karl," to "show the boy mercy at the Judgment to come,"

and to "grant him all joy until the day I see him again."
Then, knowing he could do no more, he stood slowly to his
feet. With a heavy sigh, he turned to Wil and waited to
press his journey home.

≈

The April air was noticeably cooler in the Appenines than
it had been by the sea, but it was comfortable in the day-
time hours and surprisingly dry. Wil's company pressed
through the mountains under the watch of numerous
castle keeps perched on ledges high above their path. The
Ligurian lords who ruled them were in ever-changing tangles of alliances that kept their lives and fortunes in per-
petual jeopardy.

The six pilgrims camped at the eastern base of the mountains on a stony shore of the narrow Scrivia, and in the
morning they bathed in the river's rushing water. It was
cold and bracing—almost sacramental. Few words were
spoken, but somehow they believed they needed to be
refreshed in body and in spirit. It was as though the chilly
dip in running water might wash away the salty stains of
heavy tears.

Renewed and refreshed, they then journeyed northward
along the Scrivia toward the crossroads town of Tortona,
where they detoured westward in the direction of Allesandria. The days were mercifully dry, and the sky was blue.
The highways were not crowded, and the pilgrims made
good time.

They forded the shallow Po, then made their way to the
stone walls of Vercelli, where they set up camp alongside a
small caravan of merchants crossing the Piedmont from
Milan to Turin. The caravan was made up of some score of
merchants led by their elected doyen—a gruff, former Nor-
man crusader named Robert Fitzhugh. The band, or
"guild," included several spice purveyors delivering sea-
sonings from the eastern Mediterranean, a wine seller, an
oil merchant, a few potters, several cloth merchants, and
sundry others all riding in wagons groaning under the
weight of a bounty of goods purchased from the lands of
Islam.

That evening the band enjoyed a lively feast of good beer and tasty foods. By midnight, however, Tomas had indulged far beyond his limit and was sick in the alleys of Vercelli, leaving his fellows to settle into easy conversation with a silk merchant born in Oppenheim. "*Ja*, I've heard things of your crusade. Seems your leader's father was hanged in Cologne."

"Our leader?" quizzed Helmut.

"Nicholas of Cologne," answered Frieda.

"Devil's son," answered Helmut. "I hope he's dead!"

The merchant raised his brows. "*Ja*? Well, I have heard nothing of Nicholas, but well before Advent, methinks, an angry mob dragged his father into the streets of the city. They said the scoundrel had deceived them all. Then they hanged him and promised to do the same to Nicholas."

Wil grumbled. Nicholas was not *his* leader, but Nicholas's vision in the springtime past had certainly inspired the whole of the Christian world and affected the destinies of countless children, himself included. Thinking of being seduced by madness was troubling. *'Tis bad enough we failed*, he thought. *But now to know we were dolts as well!*

Somehow sensing his thoughts, Frieda leaned close and whispered, "The vision *could* have been true. How were we to know?"

Wil shrugged. He felt foolish no matter how it might be explained.

"Your hearts were good in the crusade, son. 'Tis the heart that matters," Heinrich offered.

"Well, a bounty of good hearts are not beating now," muttered Wil. "Next time methinks the heart and the head ought consider one another."

"Ha! Well said, lad," roared the merchant. "Well said, indeed! Would that *all* might see the world that way. Now, to other things. Where be y'travelin'?"

"North," answered Heinrich. "Home."

The man nodded. "Home is a worthy destination. I left my Oppenheim many years ago to fight the infidels. I served well, but my desires were fired by two things: a dark-haired beauty and the magic of silk—the both of them smooth and soft. *Ja!* Well, time came for me to make a choice. I found the woman to be quickly bothersome ... in truth, a vicious shrew! So I chose the silk!" He laughed and poured himself more wine.

"Now I spend my life traveling south of the mountains in wintertime and north in summer. I buy silk from the Venetians, sell it at the fairs, and then hide my money in the nearest Templar strongbox. They keep a fair accounting. We dare not carry much with us, of course. We've hired soldiers as you see, but sometimes the highwaymen come in whole armies. Here especially, what with the Visconti from Milan. They would seize all of Lombardy and the Piedmont if they could. Perhaps they shall in time."

At the sound of the word *Visconti*, Wil and Frieda chilled. The memories of their horrid days in the Verdi castle at Domodossola would never leave either of them. There, many had perished in awful ways, including three of their comrades. There, too, were other losses. For Wil, it was there where the Visconti had exposed his cowardice and the Verdi damsel his pride. It was there where Frieda had lost respect for him.

The two looked at each other until Wil turned away and stared at the ground. Frieda reached her hand forward and touched his. Refusing to look up, he mumbled, "Now I really am ashamed. First to be so easily fooled by a false vision, then to be reminded again of my deeds in that cursed castle."

"No more of that," answered the maiden. "We've all something to regret, but we must not let our regrets rule us, else they become who we are. Your father taught me that."

Wil said nothing. He was surprised by her remark and wondered what other things she had learned from his father. He cast a look at Heinrich, who was chatting with the merchant. "Well, 'tis time for sleep," he muttered.

The night passed quickly, and soon the pilgrims were enjoying a first meal of porridge and honey, fresh bread and red wine. "So now we part," the generous merchant said with a satisfied smile. He belched. "Was a pleasure to meet fellow survivors from crusade! I wish you all Godspeed."

With hails and grateful waves, the pilgrims then left Vercelli, soon to travel north across lands dotted with poor villages. Throughout the day Wil rolled the name "survivor" over and over in his mind. He liked the sound of it; it had redeemed his sense of failure in some small way. "Strange how a name can change a way of thinking," he blurted.

"What?" answered Frieda.

"A name. I say it's odd how calling someone something can change things. The merchant called us 'survivors.' Now I look at all of us differently."

Tomas sneered. He was often apt to sneer, for he took delight in casting shadows. "Ha! Wil, y'think to be honored by 'surviving'? Ha! Cowards are survivors, too!" He laughed and pointed his finger. "'Tis easy to see that you're desperate to claim something good from all this!"

"Shut yer mouth," snapped Wil.

"Aye, Tomas!" blurted Helmut. "Shut it, or I'll shut it with m'fist!"

The group stopped walking. Tomas leaned his face close to Helmut's and, daring the other to make good on his threat, he opened his mouth as wide as he could. With both forefingers he pointed to the gaping black cavern, goading the other with some indiscernible grunts.

To Tomas's great surprise, Helmut struck and struck hard, knocking the startled boy to the ground. He lay flat on his back, stunned and dizzy.

"Up, y'dung-breathed dolt!" challenged Helmut. "I've tired of yer whining, yer troublemaking talk. Stand up so I can beat you down again!"

"Enough, lads!" boomed Heinrich as he separated the pair. "Tomas, you'd be bleeding." He uncorked a flask. "Wash your face with this."

Tomas poured warm beer over his swelling lips. He glared at the lanky Helmut and then muttered a few oaths and wandered off the road.

Wil nodded his thanks to his ally but assured him that he

was perfectly capable of handling Tomas on his own. "Now, are we ready?"

A chorus of "ayes" answered, and the pilgrims were off again. They now marched quietly with Tomas some distance in the rear. They crossed the Piedmont under stormy skies, and it seemed that the weather grew more foul with each passing league.

Finally, at twilight on the twenty-fourth day of April, the six arrived at the southern shoreline of Lago Maggiore, where they made camp under a grove of trees. For the whole of the past ten days, Frieda and Wil had been restrained in their anxiety over the likely news of Maria. Neither wanted to mention the matter, each choosing to wrestle privately with their own expectations. Frieda retreated to her quill and parchment whenever she might steal the time. It was her way of escape. For his part, Wil found solace with Emmanuel, practicing with the bow at eventide and dawn.

As for Heinrich, the matter was more troubling than sad. *Who?* he had oft wondered. *Who sired this girl?* It was said that Maria was born in late May. According to Heinrich's rough counting, that would mean Marta would have conceived in late August—many weeks prior to his departure. Knowing that his wife had banned his touch long before then, the frustrated man was left to speculate. His mind struggled to recall the men of Weyer. *She hated all men*, he thought. *Who?* Such tortuous thoughts cost him his sleep, and he left the camp one night to roam under a clearing sky. *Who? Ach! All her boasts of right living, and all her charges against me and my "secret sins"!* The man pounded his fist against his thigh. "*Mein Gott!*" he cried.

Despite the dark, brooding cloud of dread hovering over the weary travelers, morning delivered sunshine and mist. The band arose quickly and followed a clench-jawed Wil as he led them on a hurried march along the western shore of the lake. Before noon, the town walls and clay roofs of Arona were in full view along with the silhouettes of the rising Alps beyond.

At long last, Wil and his five companions entered the town and hurried through its streets to the abbey. It was Thursday, and the market was closed, save for a few fish sellers and one badly crippled woman pleading with passersby to buy her plaited baskets. Brushing past a priest, a few carts, and two soldiers on patrol, the group made its way to the portal of the Abbey of Saints Gratian and Felinus. Pale faced and perspiring, Wil took a deep breath and rapped loudly on the door.

A young porter answered. "*Deo gratias.* Thanks be to God!"

"And to you. We come in search of two fair maids, an old priest, and two lads."

The porter twisted his face and shrugged. "*Momento.*" He dashed away to return with the prior.

"Thanks be to God. *Grüssen.* Come in, be fed." The prior bowed and kissed each on the cheek. He commanded two brothers to fetch trays of food and beverage as he led the others past gardens green with the fresh bloom of springtime and swollen with buds. The air was warm and humid, filled with the pungent odor of fresh manure.

Wil's company followed quietly, scanning the workshops and courtyards for any sign of their two fellows. At last they arrived at the prior's chamber, where they removed their shoes and submitted to prayers and a ritual foot washing. They nibbled impatiently on flatbread and cheese and then finally faced the prior.

"So, my children, how can we serve you?"

"We come seeking two fair maidens, an old priest, and two lads. Have you seen them?"

"Ah, *si!* And your name, young sir?"

"Wilhelm of Weyer."

The prior smiled and clapped his hands. "*Si! Si!* Pieter said you'd come. Ha! God be praised."

"So he is here?" Wil's brows were arched hopefully.

"No, no, my son. He is not here."

Wil's expression darkened. "No riddles."

"Your pardon. No riddles indeed. Pieter is with the others in *Signora* Cosetta's castle."

The group murmured. "The castle on the cliff?" barked Helmut.

"*Si, si.* The road leading to it is just beyond the north gate. You need only follow it up the back of the mountain and tell the gate guard that you have been sent by the abbey."

Frieda nudged Wil to ask that which all had been afraid to ask. He nodded and took a deep breath. "Prior, are our two girls with them?"

"Only one, my son. A sadder day there has never been for us."

Wil was staggered by the news, and Frieda sobbed. Bravely, the young man lifted his quivering chin. "*Ja,* brother. 'Tis as I had feared. Many thanks for your charity, but we must find Pieter."

Heinrich had remained quiet, but his heart was suddenly broken for the pain now evidenced on his son's face. He stretched his hand tentatively toward the lad's shoulder.

Wil paused to let the baker's palm rest lightly. The warmth and strength of his father's touch felt comforting for a moment. Then Wil pulled away and hurried ahead, wishing to run and weep where none might see him. *If only!* he groaned inwardly. *If only she knew of my love for her and my shame.*

Frieda hurried to his side. "Wil, she forgave you long before she was ever sick."

Wil pursed his lips.

"She was my friend. We spoke often. I've told you this before, yet you will not believe me. Please, Wil, trust me in this. She has forgiven you."

Wil would not yield. For him, grace needed to be earned— a paradox of residual pride. He could not imagine how he might be truly forgiven without evidencing the agony of a guilt-ridden confession. He wanted to rend his heart at Maria's feet, to pour out his shame in salted tears of blood. It was simply not enough to be granted pardon without penalty.

"She was a light-bearer, Wil. She was sent to show us the way."

The lad choked. "Then I am yet blind."

Frieda took his hand. "No more than I. Pieter says, 'We see through the glass darkly.' None travels the path without stumbling. Even Maria once stomped her little feet in anger at m'sister!"

"Aye?"

Frieda smiled. "It was a great relief to see she was not without her own faults!"

Wil dismissed the comment. "I pitied her so. Her arm gave cause for many to mock, yet she offered only kindness in return."

The company pressed its way through the crowded streets and alleyways of Arona, past carts laden with fish or barrels of olive oil. Shopkeepers hawked their wares, working hard to sell the disinterested pilgrims an assortment of colorful products such as blessed trinkets, straw hats, foodstuffs, and even kittens. On any other day the group would have enjoyed the scene, especially since Heinrich was carrying a pouch filled with gold and silver coins!

"There!" cried Rudolf. "There! Look between the roofs and you'll see the castle."

All heads bent backward, and soon the pilgrims' faces were fixed on the foreboding gray fortress perched high atop a sheer cliff rising from the shores of the lake. A few helmets glittered in the sun between the merlons, and Wil cursed. "I'm in no mood for this," he grumbled.

The six emerged from Arona through its north gate and soon stood at the foot of the massive cliff. "We need to follow that road like the monk said." Heinrich surveyed their location. He scanned the crowded roadway now clogged with ox-drawn carts and horses. He turned his face to the flat waters of the lake and suddenly wished they might all just sleep along the peaceful shore.

During the pause it was Rudolf who suddenly realized the obvious. "Wil, you didn't ask the prior *who* died!"

Wil's jaw loosed and he turned to Rudolf. "What?"

"Who died? Which girl?"

"What a fool I am!"

Frieda was reluctant to let hope rise in her chest. "But, but, Wil, methinks we know—"

"You can't be sure just yet," interrupted Heinrich. "You only know one thing ... that only one is lost."

"And that is sad enough," added Frieda. "I loved them both."

"*Ja*," said Wil. "And I as well. Yet I cannot hope but wish it is my sister who lives."

Tomas had said nothing all that morning. He had always liked Maria, though he often secretly wished misery for Wil. He grumbled, "Enough talk."

"Aye!" answered Wil with fresh life in his voice. "Aye. To the castle!"

~

"*Si*, you seek Father Pieter? *Si*." A guard led the anxious pilgrims through the *Rocca di Arona* slowly. He began to sing as he strolled, pausing to chat from time to time and stopping once for a tall clay goblet of red wine. Finally, the soldier pointed to the figure of an old man lying flat on his back in the middle of a rose garden. "Pieter."

In an instant, Wil and Frieda sprinted forward. "Pieter! Pieter!" they cried.

The napping old fellow didn't stir until the shadow of six encircling forms blocked his face from the warmth of the noontime sun. "Eh?" He lifted himself to one elbow and shielded his eyes with the other. "What—?"

"Pieter!" exclaimed Wil. "'Tis us! We've come!"

The old priest nearly leapt to his feet. He shouted his hosannas loudly as he took hold of his staff. "Ha!" He spread his arms wide. "God be praised!" Beaming his familiar gaping, one-toothed smile, he embraced them each. "Wil! My Frieda! Good Helmut and Rudolf! And m'friend for all time, Heinrich! *Laus Deo!*" Pieter was weeping for joy. He turned to the sixth figure and began to open his arms before he recognized the face. "Tomas?" He dropped his arms and stared.

"*Ja*. Tomas." The young man's face was hard.

Pieter was flabbergasted. "I ... I ... well, I—"

"We rescued him from the Dragonara," offered Heinrich.

"He wishes to go home with us."

Pieter smiled with reservation. "Well, God's will be done." He extended his hand.

Tomas stared at the old man for a long moment, then smiled wickedly. He placed his hand firmly in Pieter's and hissed, "God's will, then."

"Pieter," blurted Wil, "we must know of Maria's fate." His voice trembled at the sound of his sister's name. "Is she the one?"

"*Ja*," answered Pieter matter-of-factly.

Wil's heart sank and Frieda groaned. "I feared as much."

Suddenly realizing the confusion, Pieter cried, "Nay, lad. Maria lives!"

Shocked, Wil felt suddenly limp. "She lives? She truly lives?"

"Aye, lad! She lives! Come quickly. She is tending the *signora's* gardens."

Stunned and staring in disbelief, Wil and Frieda cried out for joy, then quickly turned to follow Pieter. They scrambled through the castle bailey, up the stone steps, past dozing soldiers on the battlements, and into the lord's private courtyard. Then they stopped, for there in the center of a rose garden, beneath an arbor of honeysuckle stooped Maria.

Wil smiled a smile such as none had ever seen. His skin tingled and his belly fluttered. Dropping his bow, he ran toward his sister with arms stretched outward. "Maria!" he cried jubilantly. "Maria!"

The little girl looked up, curious, then stood, her little lips pursed in uncertainty. Suddenly recognizing her brother racing toward her, she burst into tears. She had barely taken a few steps toward him when he swept her off her feet and into his embrace.

"Oh, dear Maria, my sister! Oh, I love you so!" Wil sobbed.

Maria held him tightly. She could not yet speak, but the joy she felt filled the whole of the castle with sunshine. A group of courtiers and workmen paused to line the garden and cheer. They knew her sad story and celebrated the fulfillment of her dream.

Hearing the joyous uproar, *Signora* Cosetta emerged from the shade of her arcade. She was a dark, plump *matrona* of some fifty years. She hurried toward the garden with her gown lifted high off her ankles and her gray braids tumbling off her head. "Maria! Maria!" She scooped the little girl from Wil's arms and held her close, crying loudly to the Holy Mother and praising the saints for the maid's good fortune.

Frieda would wait no longer, and she pulled the laughing little girl from Cosetta's grip and held her tightly. Then, finally, after hearts had quieted, Wil introduced his companions. "Maria, this is Rudolf. He is the son of the kindly yeoman near Liestal."

"I remember!" she exclaimed. "Your *Mutti* sent us with blankets and food!"

Rudolf smiled. "*Ja*, that is m'mother."

"And this is Helmut. He joined us in Genoa. He comes from the area of Bremen in the far north."

Maria nodded her head politely. "*Hallo*, Helmut. We shall be friends, I'm sure."

"And you must remember Tomas."

"I do. I am happy to see you again."

The black-haired youth shrugged. "Really? Methinks not."

Maria said nothing at first, then walked quickly to a nearby garden where she picked a swollen bud. "'Tis wanting to bloom methinks." She handed the surprised lad the bud with a sincere face. He took it, saying nothing.

Wil then turned awkwardly to Heinrich. The baker was standing stiff jointed and uncomfortable. He had wondered what he'd do. He studied the little girl carefully. *The sin is not with her,* he thought. *Mismade or not.*

Before Wil could speak, Maria brightened and ran to the man. "I remember you! You are Friend … from Basel! You saved us all, and you have one arm, too!"

The man's kind heart immediately melted. He knelt and squeezed her shoulder lightly. "*Ja*, little sister. I am he. I am very glad you are well."

Wil stared at the man incredulously. "He still denies her," he muttered.

Maria turned to Wil. "But Anna died."

"I know."

"I tried to care for her with Brother Chiovo, but her head hurt badly and her fever was so high. It was terrible."

Pieter stepped into the group. "Indeed, my dear, it was terrible indeed." He raised his face to heaven. "But God is good; His mercies endure forever, my children. We must grieve our losses and enjoy our blessings. And most of all, let us love one another."

Chapter Eight

HOMEWARD BOUND

The happy reunion of the former crusaders happened on the twenty-fifth day of April in the year of our Lord 1213. In the larger world, the blood of Christians and Muslims alike continued to soak the sands of Palestine. Reports of a few minor victories were doing little to encourage the waning spirits of Christendom's knights. After all, Jerusalem had not been recovered, Christian armies had been weakened over decades of discouraging losses, and now the savage Seljuk Turks were supplanting the Saracens as the lords of Islam. In response, Pope Innocent had recently rebuked his reluctant knights by referring them to the faith of the child crusaders. "While we slept, these children flew to the defense of the Holy Land. They put us to shame!"

In this regard, the pope did one more thing of which Wil's company had not yet learned. Considering all crusaders as having taken holy vows by either word or implication, he decided *not* to release the young survivors of the Children's Crusade from theirs. They would need to either honor their sacred duty again—perhaps at a more mature age—or pay their debt in alms.

The pope had also directed his attentions to another sort of crusade. Granting his warriors absolution if killed in combat, he commanded a gruesome campaign against the French heretics called the Cathars. Not yet concluded, it had become a horrid affair that gave many pause. Blood flowed freely through the streets and footpaths of French towns and villages as men, women, and children suffered the unmerciful steel of a wrathful Roman Church.

These distant circumstances had little present effect on the pilgrims resting in the *Rocca di Arona*. In time, the machinations of ruthless men would doubtless fall upon their heads as sure as soot falls from a chimney. However, it was fortunate for them that *Signora* Cosetta's late husband, *Signore* Salito, had negotiated peace with the emerging Visconti family of Milan the year before his death. Had he not, the tangle of the larger world might have been raining arrows and bolts upon them once more.

As it was, *Signora* Cosetta was content to enjoy her own final years with as little disturbance as possible. She ignored the appeals for alliances with either the Rusconi family or the Sforza. A cousin in the Dé Capitanei family had managed a small concession, but it was peace the widow craved and little more. To that end she had yielded quickly to the insistent pleas of Pieter and Wil during the May Day feast. She had agreed to release Maria to their custody on the provision that the girl would not be returned to a state of bondage in "that cold village you call Weyer."

"And," she had added, "you may not risk the passes just yet. You *shall* remain here as my guests until the feast of the Ascension!"

Wil presented the news to his cheering comrades gathered on the bailey. A few more weeks to linger under the Italian sun was good cause to be happy! Heinrich, however, was not as pleased. He was anxious about returning to the uncertainties of Weyer, yet he felt compelled to return. No matter the risk, he needed to learn of his bakery and of his wife, and further delays were frustrating. In addition, the man had spent many a sleepless night pondering his legal status as either bound or free. Walking across the bailey, he approached Pieter and Wil. "Pieter, the *signora* insists that we swear Maria's freedom. Yet how can Maria be free if we return to Weyer?"

"I am no lawyer, my friend, but it seems to me she is free already."

"How so?"

"No lord has claimed her for a year and a day."

Heinrich nodded. But it was his understanding that a man needed to be in an imperial city for that time, and he posed the point to Pieter.

The priest shook his head. "We can make the case otherwise. As I understand it, a man is free *de facto*, when not captured in due time."

The baker disagreed. "Without a passport no lord will honor such a claim. I fear for her ... I fear for us all." He looked at Maria. "But even if your point is true for Wil and m'self, perhaps even Tomas, the girl is still subject to the bound status of her mother."

Pieter grunted, then put his finger on his chin. "Hmm. Perhaps we've a problem." He looked carefully at Heinrich. "And you still swear you are not Maria's father?"

"Aye."

Wil growled. "My father and I will demand our freedom, and the daughter of a freeman is free." He turned a hard eye at the baker.

"Your father swears she is not his."

Wil stiffened. "He lies."

Heinrich took a deep breath. "No, son, I speak truly. Maria is not mine, so she is subject to the bound status of her mother."

Wil spat. "Let God be your judge!" He turned to Pieter. "Mother is surely dead. Pious saw to that."

"What do you mean?" blurted Heinrich.

Pieter answered for him. "It seems the priest gave Wil instructions to administer an herb to your wife ... that is poisonous."

Heinrich recoiled. "Cursed boar! Prowling devil! He had a coveting eye on our bakery and our land for years. May he suffer hellfire!" Heinrich was furious. Until that moment, he had imagined returning to his wife repentant and hopeful. To learn of her likely death was a shock, but to learn of Father Pious's scheme was infuriating. "May God forgive me, but I will carve that pig's throat and grind his head in the mill."

⮞

For the young pilgrims, the next three weeks passed in a most agreeable way. May had delivered a host of flowers and fresh vegetables that graced both garden and table. Heinrich, however, had become sullen and withdrawn. His rage had settled into a quiet, seething determination for vengeance.

Assigned by the castellan to work with the cellarer, the baker spent the days bartering his labors for his keep like his fellows. Frieda and Maria worked with the seamstresses who sewed garments for the poor of Arona and of Stresa farther north. The monastery of Sesta Callendo (a cliff-side cloister across the lake) had commissioned nearly a thousand ells of cloth to be sewn and distributed in the name of St. George.

Because of his age, Pieter had been given leave to lounge about as he wished. He offered an occasional prayer or blessing from time to time, usually in exchange for beer or wine—sometimes cheese or olives. And, while the grinning old fellow wandered the castle courtyards or the streets of Arona, Wil, Tomas, Helmut, and Rudolf worked long hours with the forester culling the woodlands for firewood. The work was hard but not demanding. Their wards were of a mind to grant one swallow of red wine for each swing of the axe! At the bells, they were all quick to settle into a dreamy nap while Benedetto sang for them.

Every evening Wil strolled across the lawns of the list with Maria or with Frieda, sometimes both, and always with Emmanuel. He talked of many things, some past, some yet to come. In every conversation, however, the lad's thoughts ran to his betrayal of his little sister on that awful night in the castle at Domodossola. He could still see her face fall, wounded by his words. He felt sick as he remembered denying her in order to curry the favor of the haughty princess, Lucia.

He had fumbled through a few general confessions over the previous weeks and had been assured of his forgiveness.

But he had avoided the specificity that his pride had guarded. This evening, he would open his heart. "Maria," he began slowly, "I've a need to speak of something once more."

The girl had been walking by his side. She stopped and turned her blue eyes toward Wil's face.

"I am so terribly sorry for what I did in the Verdi castle. I was a fool of fools, blind to the things I love most in this world."

Maria stood quietly, lightly slipping her hand into his.

At the touch, the boy's eyes swelled. "I have always loved you, Maria. I love you more than I can say. I denied you were my sister because, because …"

"Because of my arm?"

Wil swallowed hard and nodded. "I wanted the lord's daughter to think of me as a prince of high birth. I wanted her to think me special."

"I remember, Wil," answered Maria gently. "And we were all dirty and poor looking."

Wil shrugged. "And me, too. Only I was the dirtiest of all. I pretended you did not belong to me, that I was something I am not. And in that wicked moment I hurt you. It was a horrible thing to do. Then, later, even when I felt so sick about it, I could not say the words I wanted to say. Pieter says m'pride filled my throat so that the right words could not pass." The lad knelt and peered earnestly into the girl's kindly face. "Oh, dear Maria. Forgive me, I beg you. I was wrong. I am *proud* to call you my sister. I am proud that we belong to one another. I was a mad fool."

The girl smiled and fell into her brother's embrace. "I forgave you long ago … and I still forgive you!"

No herbal balm, no angel's song has ever cured an ailing heart like those three words. With them are painful wounds healed, warring realms put to peace, and the souls of men reconciled to Almighty God. Relieved beyond measure, the lad drew a deep breath, and when he released it, the weight of many sorrows blew away. "You are a wonder to me, dear sister," he said quietly.

Maria kissed her brother lightly on the cheek. "'Tis you

who are the wonder, Wil. It is no small thing to ask. But I saw a bit of heaven. That makes it easier for anyone to forgive. That makes it easier to do a lot of things! Now, no more word of it; 'tis all passed," she said with a grin. She then pointed to a large sycamore tree growing by the fishpond. "Follow me!" She led Wil to the tree and removed the ringlet of flowers resting atop her head. She hung her ringlet on a short limb and then stepped back to a safe distance. "Now, big brother, stand back fifty paces and shoot the center of m'flowers ... if you can!"

Wil laughed lightly. "*If* I can? Ha! Watch me!" The lad stepped off fifty paces and turned. He took a careful aim, pulling the bowstring steadily toward his face with three fingers. When he felt the fletching touch his ear, he released the string. The arrow sang through the air on a gentle arc as brother and sister held their breath.

"Yes!" cried Maria. "You did it!"

Wil beamed. His many hours of practice had made him an amazing marksman in a short time. "Ha!" he boasted. "Next time, sixty paces!"

Such was the way of that blessed May. It was a time of fresh colors, pleasant walks in balmy evening air, and early harvests of garden delights. Yet pleasure has its season, and the time to begin their journey was soon upon them. It was the feast of the Ascension, and on the morning to follow the pilgrims would turn their eyes northward. No thought was given to staying; all were ready to climb the mountains and face the destiny that lay ahead.

The feast day was bountiful, and *Signora* Cosetta was a gracious host. Tables were lined in long rows in the castle's great hall where trays of spring vegetables and steaming game delighted visitors from afar. It was an uproarious event, filled with loud singing and boastful claims. A papal legate nearly choked on fish bones, a drunken Visconti clerk disrobed, and the crooning Benedetto nearly fell to his death from his balcony far above the tiled floor! Otto and Heinz, Rudolf and Helmut exchanged flirtatious grins with a foursome of Italian maidens, only to be angrily chased away by jealous suitors. Solomon raced the *signora's* hounds in a wild scramble to gobble scraps tossed from greasy hands, and by night's end the shaggy beast lay panting on a swollen belly.

But alas, the night's merriment came to its inevitable end. The *signora* rose to bid her guests farewell. She gestured to Benedetto. "Leave them with a song, little fellow." The minstrel climbed wearily upon a table and sang of his Rose of Arona—a song about a beauty from this very town whom he had once seen for a fleeting moment. After spending years dreaming of her, he had been frustrated all this time that he could neither find her nor learn anything of her! The guests stood respectfully as their sleepy hostess slipped away from the table, then listened to Benedetto's heartfelt verse. The feast over, the hall emptied quickly.

Before retiring to her bed, however, *Signora* Cosetta summoned the eleven pilgrims to the door of her chamber. "I wish you all Godspeed." She smiled and laid a hand on Maria. "I am thankful you gave my husband joy in his final days. I could have asked no more for him." She smiled and winked at a servant.

All heads turned as a protesting donkey was led into the corridor. "This creature is more stubborn than any drunken fisherman I have ever met. Only Maria can move him without effort! We call him 'Paulus' because the priests say he is as stubborn and fixed of purpose as the apostle!" She took hold of the lead and handed it to Maria. "Now, my little dear, I present this old friend of mine to you. Treat him well and think of me often." She smiled as Maria's eyes widened.

"For me?" she squealed as she stroked the muzzle of the big-eared beast.

"*Sì.*" Cosetta motioned for the servant and turned to the others. "Now, Paulus shall wait for you all at the gate on the morrow. But as for me, I shall bid my farewell now." She handed Paulus's lead to the servant and summoned the pilgrims into her apartment. She sat on a chair and reached for Maria. Lifting the little girl up onto her ample lap, she began. "My husband was something of a poet. He was surely no warrior. I wish all of you might have known him. He learned to love Pieter almost as much as he loved the little one."

Cosetta pick a folded paper from within her gown and opened it slowly. Her eyes moistened. "As he was dying, he scribbled these words. I should like to share them with you, now, before you leave me to carry on with your lives. I think he would have wished me to do it."

She held the paper at arm's length as if to read, but she simply closed her eyes and recited the words from memory. "'Live life wisely, and have a care for the passage of time. For our world is a garden and we are like roses. Our blooms open and spread over others fading nearby. In time, new buds shall surely come, and they will bloom fresh and fragrant near our own withering petals. It is the cycle of life—the way it ought to be ... and it is good.'"

೩

It was Friday, the twenty-fourth of May in the year 1213 when the pilgrims rose to begin their journey home. The dawn was bright and warm; cocks and songbirds filled the air with the sounds of springtime. A light dew lay upon the green grass, and a gentle mist hung lightly over Lago Maggiore. The cliff-top fortress was beginning to bustle with the tasks of a new day, but few gave any notice to the travelers gathering at the gate. Only one servant was waiting for the group as they organized themselves. He was a disinterested young man who led them through the gate and to a braying Paulus tethered to a post just beyond.

Maria ran to her four-legged friend and hugged his long face. "I love you, dear Paulus! We shall go far away together." Solomon walked a tentative circle around the animal. He had been kicked twice and bit once over the past months.

Heinrich looked at the donkey with a satisfied smile. The beast was strong—he'd be a great asset for the journey. But more than that, he had been loaded with a generous stock of provisions that were tied in bundles hanging heavily across his back. "So many gifts!" the man exclaimed.

Eager hands quickly dug through sacks and bedrolls strewn about the ground as well. "Olives and fish!" cried Rudolf.

"Flatbread and spelt!" added Heinrich.

"*Ja*," laughed Wil. "And see here, arrows and string for me, blankets and cord, ells of wool and thread, flints, rope, salt—even fat scraps for Solomon."

"Salt?" exclaimed Pieter.

"*Ja!* A fortune in salt!"

Helmut foraged through a large bag. "Pots and a kettle, a ladle and tongs ... a dozen knives ..."

Maria laughed. "She said we were barbarians and ought not eat with our fingers!" The girl turned her face upward, and her smiling eyes accidentally met Heinrich's gaze. She held her smile shyly and hoped. For these weeks, the little maid had longed to hear the man call her "daughter," and she could not understand his apparent indifference. She had been told by Wil that he was her father, yet he had never said a word of it. She had heard the others prod him, and though he had not been unkind, his heart had not warmed to her. She longed for him to find her worthy of his love. Her gaze lingered and held the man's attention for a moment, and then he looked away. Maria's chin quivered and her heart sank.

Otto and Benedetto opened a small bag and showed it to Frieda. "Honeycomb and berry preserves. God's blessings upon that woman!"

Tomas had spent the previous weeks quietly. Though still somewhat distant from the others, he had taken the first steps toward reconciliation by sharing both work and respite. Now he tugged hard on the cork of a long clay bottle. With a loud "pop" it came out, and he held his nose to the opening. "Humph," he grumbled. "Olive oil."

"Good for most anything, lad," chuckled Pieter. "And see here, a set of wallets filled with herbs. We've horehound and dock for coughs, ground lemon rind for whitlow, garlic of course, and here's tansy, wormwood, thyme, lady's mantle for headaches, licorice for the belly, flaxwood, nettles ... God be praised!"

"And you stay away from those figs!" cried Otto.

Pieter grinned sheepishly. "Aye, lad, indeed."

Wil ordered his company to resecure Paulus's load before arranging the column. When all was in order, he faced his fellows quietly, then spoke in earnest. "We've a long journey ahead, and we know little about what faces us. I am in command, though Pieter and ..." he glanced briefly at Heinrich and forced himself to continue. "And my ... father ... are our counselors."

The sound of the word *father* comforted the baker.

"Otto," continued Wil, "you are my sergeant."

Frieda stifled a giggle. She leaned toward Maria and whispered, "The great general thinks he's in command of a mighty army!"

Hearing her, Wil quickly blushed. "Well ... now, Pieter and Maria follow behind me with Paulus. *Herr* Heinrich and Frieda are to be next, then Benedetto, Heinz, Otto, then Tomas, Rudolf, and Helmut. We need the rear well guarded."

Frieda was a little disappointed. Though she enjoyed Heinrich's stories, she would rather have walked alongside Wil. The baker leaned toward her and smiled. "Not to worry. After a day he'll miss you, too." He winked.

Wil continued. "We've agreed that we should follow our old route north to Weyer. A merchant in the castle told me that returning crusaders are being treated badly in the northland. Seems we failed in our faith and are now hated for it. So we must be clever and careful. As before, we'll not be near many monasteries, so we'll need to protect one another.

"Along the way we hope to find Friederich and Jon where we left them. Rudolf, we've hopes of returning you to your family." He turned to Helmut. "After we reach Weyer, you'll need find a way to your home."

The lad nodded.

"Frieda ..." Wil was in a bit of a predicament. "I ... we ... have you a plan for yourself?"

The girl paled slightly, but she set her face proudly and lifted her chin. "Well, master, I suppose my home is still in Westphalia. Perhaps Helmut can escort me there after we reach Weyer."

Wil threw a hard glance at the beaming Helmut. "I see." He squeezed his hands into fists. "And Benedetto, your wish?"

The little minstrel shrugged. "Once I thought I might find the village of my childhood, but I doubt it would feel like home to me now. The dock holds me no more. It seems I belong with all of you." He reached a tiny hand toward Maria and crooned,

Let each day bring
What each day will.
Just let me sing;
My cup, please fill.

Within the hour, the company of eleven souls had descended the castle road and were embracing the prior and a teary-eyed Brother Chiovo. The two monks hastily fed the group a meal of salted fish and red wine, then escorted them through the streets of Arona, chastising two peasants for eating mutton on a Friday—a fish day. Pieter chuckled to himself and gnawed on some salted pork. Breaking fish-day restrictions was one of his most delightful violations!

The company arrived at lakeside near midmorning, about an hour before the bells of terce. The road leading north ran along the water's edge and was bustling with horses and carts. The morning mists had lifted, and the sky was blue; the air smelled of fish and wet rocks. Above, the sun was warm and comforting. Heinrich lifted his face upward and looked at the few white clouds high overhead. He smiled.

Pieter gathered his flock into a tight huddle and raised his staff. "Brothers and sisters," he began, "our journey does not begin here; it merely continues. Let us honor those we have left behind, and let us walk in love with those yet by our sides." He held his staff to his breast and turned his face to heaven. "Come, Holy Spirit, fill the hearts of your faithful, and kindle in them the fire of your love. We adore you, O Christ, and we bless you. For by your holy cross You have redeemed the world." He proceeded to pray for their safety, for their health, and for the happy arrival of "hearts at the place you would have them call 'home.'"

The old priest then fell to his knees and implored the Almighty to shield them from all manner of wicked peril and pestilence of the world. Finishing his petitions, he rose and laid a hand on Maria's shoulder as he drew a breath deeply through his nostrils. "Wil, 'tis an astonishing journey we are on. Indeed, goodness and mercy have followed us, and the swords of heaven's legions go before us, each and every one."

Brother Chiovo stepped forward with a bowed head. "*Prego*, all of us. Together let us recite the Lord's Prayer."

When they finished, the group stood silently, each listening to the soft lapping of the lake against its stony shore. Then, with matters of both heaven and earth put to right order, Wil raised his bow and boomed, "Homeward!"

శ్రీ

The landscape rose rapidly from Arona, and the pilgrims followed the lake highway to Stresa where they took a rest at the edge of town. By nightfall they had said good-bye to Lago Maggiore and made their first night's camp by the roadway alongside the Toce River. Too weary for conversation, the group fell asleep quickly and rose at dawn, stiff and footsore.

"Too many weeks without suffering!" lamented Pieter. "We've become soft." His old bones were aching. "You see, Heinz? Look at m'feet!"

"Blisters *already*?" teased the imp.

"*Ja*, I fear so."

Heinrich distributed some cheese and fixed a quick mush for his fellows. He had been elected the camp cook, with Frieda and Maria as his helpers. He set a steaming bowl of boiled spelt in front the group and laughed. "Fingers in!" he cried.

The highway was oddly empty; only a few passersby hurried this way and that. It was a condition that did not escape the attention of either Heinrich or Pieter. "Saturday ought to be a busy day of market traffic," said Heinrich.

Pieter rubbed his feet and looked about. He nodded and scratched Solomon's ears. Paulus suddenly brayed, and all eyes turned toward a wide-wheeled carriage emerging from a bend ahead of them. Alongside the carriage rode a small escort of men-at-arms. Behind them appeared two squat carts laden with what appeared to be some furniture and personal effects. The travelers stood to their feet nervously.

"Scared, Elfman?" goaded Tomas.

Heinz growled.

"You'd be scared, too," whispered Otto angrily. "You left us afore the slaughter in the castle ahead."

Wil silenced the boys, but the reminder of what lay ahead left him feeling nauseous. The castle of Domodossola brought him only awful memories.

A lone rider trotted forward and hailed the group. Pieter stepped forward. The soldier was young and poorly armed. He approached the pilgrims warily but did not draw his sword. Pieter thought he looked somewhat familiar. "*Pater?*"

"*Si,*" answered Pieter with a smile. "How can I serve thee?"

Saying nothing, the young man looked past Pieter and studied the others, lingering for a moment on Heinrich's menacing form. Pieter laid a protective arm about Maria's shoulders. "Good fellow, you've naught to fear from us. Have we reason to fear you?"

The soldier shook his head. "No." He leaned forward in his saddle and studied Pieter carefully. "Smile again, *Pater.*"

Pieter grinned.

"Ah, *si,* I know you. You saved my lord's life." Relieved, he turned in his saddle and called to his superior.

Wil's company gathered close as Pieter announced, "They come from *Signor* Verdi!"

The veterans of the crusade were relieved but uncomfortable. Maria became quiet and leaned close into Frieda's side. It had been a horrible time for all of them, and the memory of the slaughter was unnerving.

An officer dismounted and approached Pieter. "God be praised."

Pieter bowed. "Blessings on you and your good lord."

"*Signor* Verdi is dead."

"Dead?" exclaimed Pieter. "How?"

"The Visconti attacked us on Easter Monday. When you were with us, we had not yet recovered from the battle months before. *Signor* died bravely; he fought to the end."

Pieter sighed sadly. "And Sebastiano?"

"Humph. Good old soldier. Tough as old leather. He perished early in the combat."

Pieter nearly wept.

The man recounted details of the surprise attack as more of his fellows gathered around. Benedetto sheepishly retreated as Wil listened intently, quite aware of his own failings in that horrid place. "Those that were spared are banished from the Piedmont and Liguria, so we are taking the lord's family to Rome in hopes of mercy."

Pieter sent Helmut to the donkey for flasks of wine, which the old man quickly offered to the thirsty soldiers. "Frieda, take some wine and cheese to the wagons. See if any are hungry."

"But ..."

The man's look left no room for argument.

The girl lifted two clay bottles of wine and a wheel of cheese from Paulus's packs and obediently delivered them to the first wagon. As she approached, the canvas was lifted and an aged, gray-haired woman reached a trembling hand forward. Frieda thought she looked like death itself. Her eyes were hollow, sunk deep in their shadowed sockets. Her skin was jaundiced, and the bones of her limbs protruded from beneath a peasant's gown. Next to her glared a young maiden. Frieda looked into the girl's dark eyes. They were blazing with wounded pride, but weary. Her hair was uncomely and her clothing of poor quality.

"Mother," said the maid in her own tongue, "take what you can from this wench. I'll not take charity from a peasant."

Not understanding, Frieda smiled kindly and offered the cheese to the girl. Suddenly, Frieda knew whom she was helping and she gasped. "Lucia!" Indeed, it was Lucia, the self-important daughter of the great Lord Gostanzo Verdi. For a moment, Frieda felt a wave of triumph. After all, the rich princess had been so very pleased to humiliate her just months before. Wanting for all the world to mock the maid's bankrupt condition, Frieda said no more. Graciously, she handed the *signora* her cheese and wine, then quietly walked away.

Wil had watched the exchange from a distance. He had already calculated who might be riding in the carriage. He was curious about Frieda's reaction, and when he saw his fair friend offer her prior tormentor mercy, his heart was touched. "Oh, Frieda!" he whispered. "Oh, good, kind Frieda."

&

After another quarter hour, the vanquished Verdi bade the pilgrims farewell, and most extended grasping hands of gratitude. Pieter offered them a blessing, then watched quietly as the broken men remounted and turned slowly away.

"Are we ready to move on?" boomed Wil.

"Aye, lad!" answered Heinrich.

"Then forward."

Each pilgrim took his or her assigned position, and the company began again. Within a few hours, they found themselves passing beneath the battered ramparts of the Verdi castle. The vanquished lord's soldiers had informed them that passage beyond the walls was probably safe enough, though surely a toll would be exacted. As predicted, a smug group of drunken Visconti soldiers barred the roadway and demanded a heavy fee. With a loud grouse and menacing look, Heinrich paid the exorbitant toll, and the pilgrims continued on their way.

The column advanced northward through the wide, rocky floor of the Toce Valley and under the watch of the high mountain peaks. Small villages dotted the narrow terraces, and from time to time, tall keeps jutted up proudly against the sky.

At last, the company began its climb into the southern slopes of the great Alps. The roadway was steep and stony, shaded by pine and softwoods. Winded and perspiring, the wayfarers passed the gray stone, dreary village of Gondo, where the ruling lord had erected an imposing watchtower. Pressing on, they hurried by a travelers' hospice and entered the stark, dramatic Simplon Pass.

Finally, Pieter begged for rest, and Wil was happy to accommodate the old fellow. The priest took a long draught of wine and sat atop a large boulder from which he faced south. He laid back and closed his eyes. He told no one, but he had been feeling more tired than usual. His feet ached, to be sure, and his joints were stiff and swollen. But he had also become short of breath and hoped he was not battling the onslaught of fever.

After a quarter hour of dozing, the old man gathered his strength and stood slowly to his feet. "Ah, my little Heinz," he said as he pointed southward, "we are leaving the people of passion behind. This mighty wall of mountains is the great divide between them and those who live in the north." He turned and pointed the lad northward. "Ahead is home to the people of purpose."

"So what?" groused Tomas.

"It may mean little, or it may mean much. These people of passion have given us art and beauty, song and philosophy. We, on the other hand, seem to be a people of determined ways. We are workers, and what has come to us through these passes has given us much to use." He looked about his group. "Learn from the wisdom of other peoples and places, discover what you can, then be who you are and make the world a better place."

Chapter Nine

THE WAGER

The pilgrims steadily made their way higher and deeper into the pass. Small pine groves stood in ever-thinning patches, and the air got colder with every step. Struggling upward, they followed the trail, still snow covered and packed hard by the many feet and carts of those gone before. To either side, the snow rose higher as they climbed, soon mounding far above a tall man's head and creating a white channel through which the travelers passed. Above, bearing the wind like the unflappable sentries of a beleaguered fortress, the green-stained rock face of the peaks stood, silently watching those below as they had for millennia.

The Simplon was difficult to cross, yet its grandeur was exhilarating. Pieter's heart, grown of late somewhat weary, now pumped vigorously, and his cheeks flushed with excitement. He surveyed the wonder about him and thanked the almighty Creator for such a gift as this. The old man drove his staff hard into the stony earth and considered, once more, his place in the cosmos. He laughed out loud. "What is man, that thou art mindful of him!"

The pilgrims wrapped themselves tightly in their cloaks and pressed on, finally cresting the pass and beginning the long descent. They stopped for one night under a rocky overhang where they made a hasty campfire with some scrub wood Rudolf had gathered.

At dawn, Heinrich breathed deeply. The man smiled, refreshed by the scent of pine and the tingle of crisp air. "Home!" he cried. "It is beginning to feel like home."

By the end of the next day, Wil's company emerged from the Simplon and began their sharp descent toward the sprawling village of Brig. Set along the rushing Rhône River, Brig was nestled neatly in a splendid valley cramped by jagged-edged mountains that seemed to reach into heaven. Stubborn winds dragged snow off the distant peaks and formed huge white pennants pointing southward. Wil's eyes turned from them and scanned the river northeastward along a narrowing green ribbon.

It was decided that Brig might be unsafe and that camp should be made beyond its borders. Benedetto had heard rumors over the years while perched on his dock in nearby Fiesch. "Too many Frenchmen," he warned. "They come from Burgundy to take the Simplon south. Many are thieves and rogues who fear the popular routes like St. Cenis's or St. Bernard's."

Just before compline, small clusters of quiet chatter ringed a snapping fire along the rapid river's edge. Wil had slipped away to practice with his bow, and Frieda sat alone with her quill and parchment. Otto, Rudolf, Helmut, and Heinz told tales of their crusade, and Tomas stared aimlessly into the rushing water. Singing rhymes and giggling, Maria sat with Benedetto and Solomon.

Heinrich relieved Paulus of his burdens and tethered the grateful beast to a nearby tree before sitting alongside Pieter. In the warmth of the campfire's heat, the two elders lounged comfortably and spoke of many things in low tones. The two had exchanged life stories over the past weeks, and both their mutual respect and mutual trust had deepened. Pieter leaned toward the baker. "So tell me, Heinrich, are you certain she is not your daughter? Wil says it could be no other, and he hates you for denying her."

The man sighed heavily. He looked through the flames at the firelit face of the happy little girl. With his eye lingering on her misshapen arm, he nodded sadly. "*Ja*, Pieter. I am *certain.* Would that she could be mine, for I could love her easily."

"And you do not now?"

Heinrich kept his face fixed on the maid. "I do try. But I know who her father is, and it is not easy to keep my hatred for him from falling upon her."

A small rustle in the brush turned both men's heads. Seeing nothing, Pieter faced the baker once more. "Are you certain of the father?"

Heinrich grunted.

"How so?"

"Once I owned a boar with a red ear. Each gilt of the litters he threw had a red ear as well. None others in the village herd had a single red ear, only the gilts of that boar."

Pieter waited.

"In the same way, Maria bears the mark of someone."

"Her arm?"

"Nay, not her arm. The village has its share of troubles like that. Most say 'tis punishment for sin. I say not. We've sheep with three legs, swine with half a leg ... a calf once with two tails. Nay, 'tis the way of the world as it is."

"Then what marks her?"

Heinrich nodded. "'Ave y'seen the little mole on the girl's left earlobe?"

Pieter nodded.

"The village has one pig with such a mole, and I've known him to be in my home when none else is about."

"And?"

"Aye. 'Tis our priest, Father Pious."

Pieter spat. "Humph. From what Wil says, I ought not be surprised."

Heinrich darkened. "A pig with the soul of a devil, playing the role of a churchman like some actor at a fair."

"So you are certain you are not the father?"

With a scowl the baker answered. "I've told you, I was banished from her bed long before I left Weyer."

The pair sat quietly for a few long moments. "You know, good friend, that the maiden is not to blame?" Pieter asked quietly.

"Of course." The man did not wish the girl to become a symbol of the offense, yet so many voices within him urged he see her as such. His mind turned toward those who had once so eagerly exposed his failings. *Hypocrites,* he thought. *They laid great millstones about my head ... they demanded so much suffering from me for my sins yet do not see their own.*

Sensing his anguish, Pieter laid a kindly hand on the baker's tight shoulder. "Seems you have been grievously wronged, my son."

Heinrich nodded.

Pieter sat thoughtfully. "And 'tis justice you ache for?"

"Aye!"

"Justice or vengeance?"

The baker hesitated. He wanted to be vindicated, to have the *whole* truth known. "I ... I suppose a bit of both."

Pieter smiled. "Good, an honest answer. Now, my caution is this: we oft want mercy for ourselves and justice for others."

Heinrich nodded.

"A very natural thing. Yet my heart tells me you would be truly content to simply have the truth known."

The baker nodded again. "*Ja.* Though I think Pious should be stripped of his robes and sent away."

"Agreed! And may it be so. But for now, consider this: the truth of these matters *is* known ... every bit of it. God sees all; He is perfectly aware of every stain on your heart, on the heart of Pious, and even on the heart of your wife."

The thought was mildly comforting to Heinrich. He shrugged.

Pieter looked deeply into the man's face. "Hmm. So, perhaps 'tis not so much that you want the truth known, as it is that you want it known in a *particular* way."

Heinrich shuffled in his place. He had not reasoned through his bitterness nearly so thoroughly. "I ... I suppose so."

"Good! To find a handle on trouble we must first name it. Your problem is particularity. You want someone in particular to know the whole truth. So *whom* do you wish to know?"

Without hesitation, Heinrich blurted, "Wil."

Pieter smiled. "Good! You love the boy, and you want him to love you. You think he hates you and judges you unfairly."

Heinrich was perspiring. He nodded. "Aye."

"Well, perhaps he does and perhaps he doesn't. But you can't *make* him see. You can't make him believe what you want him to believe."

The baker stared into the darkness. "I gave that up long ago, Pieter. I demand nothing from the lad. I wish he knew how much I loved him. I wish he knew that I did not abandon the family for wholly selfish things ... though I do confess some wrong desires in my leaving. I was truly in fear for them ... in fear of what horrible judgment the sins of my life might bring them. I believed with all my heart that the journey would cleanse me and free them."

"Perhaps it has," mused Pieter. "But hardly in the ways you thought!"

Heinrich shook his head. "I fear it has cost them far too much. Pieter, I am not a perfect man, and in that knowledge I have lived a life of fear that has wounded those I love most."

The old priest put his arm around the baker. "Sometimes we need to guard against our conscience. It is not always a proper master."

After several moments of silence, Heinrich finally whispered brokenly, "I have been given much mercy." Indeed, and so he had. It was a simple truth so oft ignored, but once grasped, a truth bound to bear fruit. The weary baker turned toward Maria and took a deep breath. Then, with a determined stride and a gracious smile, he joined the astonished girl and sat by the minstrel to hear a happy song.

≈

Morning broke brightly over Brig. Knowing the next days would require only a relatively easy march across the valley floor, the pilgrims roused themselves with ease. Wil, however, had not slept well. A great struggle of the heart had kept him tossing and turning through the night, for he had happened upon Pieter's conversation with his father and had heard everything. Hearing his father disavow all demands on the lad's affections had released Wil to forgive his father with greater ease. Hearing the man decry his own failings, acknowledge the suffering he had caused, and plainly state the truth of his motivations had moved Wil's heart greatly. He now understood the truth of Maria's parentage, and when he saw his father offering kindness to this daughter of Pious, his heart filled with respect.

Wil had secretly wondered if Pious was, indeed, the father of Maria. He had seen the man prowling about the hovel all the while his father had been gone. It did not shock him, therefore, to imagine that the priest had visited his mother even before his father had left. For as long as he could remember, he had hated Pious. Hearing his darkest suspicions confirmed only infuriated him all the more. The anger he had directed toward his father was promptly shifted against the village priest. Wil remained confused about his mother, however. *Perhaps she was lonely. Perhaps in great fear for all of us. The comfort of a priest was a temptation too great.* He wasn't sure what to think. Throwing a stone as far as he could, he took a deep breath. "Otto, is everyone ready?"

"*Ja.*"

Wil surveyed his company and let his gaze linger for a moment on Frieda. "And you, Frieda, are you ready?"

The damsel answered playfully, "I am, my lord."

"And me, too, sire!" Maria cried with a giggle.

So, in good spirits, the band of pilgrims began its nine-league march along the Rhône toward the majestic Grimsel Pass. It was a glorious day and the sun shone kindly overhead. Maria and Benedetto passed the time singing simple ballads, while the boys teased one another with jibes and taunts.

The company kept a brisk pace alongside the surging, chalky gray Rhône. The river was swollen and tumbling hard from the spring thaws. The group paused for a midday meal and reflected on their raft ride southward in the summer past. At Fiesch, however, Benedetto grew silent and urged Wil to hurry on. He cast one brief look at his former home and was shocked to discover his old dock was gone.

"It isn't there!" exclaimed Otto. "Benedetto, your dock is gone."

The minstrel nodded sadly, then looked away. He was surprised at the weight of melancholy that pressed his heart. The man had spent many years singing to travelers and those few brave enough to dare the rough glacier waters of the Rhône. It was a time that had surely passed. He was the minstrel of Fiesch no more.

The valley widened considerably as the pilgrims made their way northeastward. It was dotted with tiny hamlets whose poor residents pastured numbers of milk cows atop fields now carpeted with the most spectacular assortment of wildflowers. Maria dashed from the column from time to time to gather handfuls of them. She decorated Frieda's flaxen hair and her own, even setting a cluster behind laughing Pieter's ear. To either side of the splendid valley, the great mountains rose ominously, but not in an unfriendly way. They stood tall and proud, mighty sentinels of things glorious.

It was midday of the second day when the pilgrims stood at the base of the Grimsel Pass. There they gawked slack jawed and in wonder of the sheer magnificence before them. Huge spruce-covered mountains lay in wait, and behind them stood what seemed to be unending folds of snow-blown peaks.

"I can barely speak," mumbled Pieter. The old priest fell to his knees and gave thanks for the gift of God's handiwork spread before them all. When he finished, he turned to his little company. "God and nature do not work together in vain! See, whether we stand upon summits or walk in fertile valleys, the Lord is good. He gives us this earth as a glimpse of His greater glory. It is a gift. It is a reminder that He is present in all things, and from that we can draw hope. Look, there, at the mighty cliffs ... no, they are not divine in themselves, but He dwells in them. And there, among the tender flowers of the valley floor ... He dwells there, too. His Spirit abides in the heavens and in the forests, in the waters of the Rhône and the drizzle of the mist. He is with us, around us, above our heads, and below our feet. And there He shall be—always."

కళ

The pilgrims climbed through the difficult Grimsel with few complaints. The June sky remained bright and blue, and the air was pleasantly cool. About halfway to the top, the evergreens gave way to scrub brush that grew amongst lichen and moss. Streams and waterfalls abounded on every side, and eagles soared overhead. At the crest, the pass was surrounded by rock and swept with cold wind. Snow lay heavy on all sides. Yet, despite the harshness of the silent desolation, five-petaled purple flowers grew stubbornly in nearly every crevice and crack, boasting their beauty.

Delighted, Maria picked a handful of blooms and held them happily to her frost-reddened nose. Her companions, however, were far too cold and shivering to care and wanted only to simply hurry on. So, with a few barks, Wil pressed his followers into the descent—past rock walls striped with tints of green, past more waterfalls and lichen, scrub, and pines—and finally into the spruce, where the scented air was warm again.

The next day they pushed northward along the narrow Aare River and under the watch of three mountain peaks that Heinrich quickly named the "Magi of Mountains." Staring at them, the baker told stories of his beloved Magi of the Laubusbach. "Under their canopy we learned many things of heaven and of earth. You all would have loved my Butterfly *Frau*." The very sound of her name brought a lump to his throat. "Wil, do you remember the Magi?"

Wil nodded. "I do. And I remember Frau Emma very well. She made me feel free."

The road they followed took them toward the sprawling village of Meiringen and past a view of a castle keep set to the far end of the wide Aare Valley. There, numbers of pennants were flying over a large encampment of soldiers. Springtime was the most common season for warfare, and the company grew immediately anxious.

"We must hurry on," urged Wil.

The column entered Meiringen, where they decided to rest. Sprawling about the shoulder of the road, the group broke into its usual clusters and helped themselves to the remaining stores on Paulus's back. "Wil," said Pieter, "our supplies are getting low. Perhaps we ought to see what's about in the village."

"*Ja.* Methinks the same. Take my father and Otto … and Paulus."

"And me!" chirped Maria.

"And you," chuckled Wil. "But have a care. We don't know much about these parts." He watched the foursome meander toward the village, and he took the opportunity to call to Frieda. He picked up his bow and smiled at the girl. "Would you like to walk with me?" Frieda nodded, and the two disappeared into a small grove.

In the meantime, Heinrich, Pieter, Maria, and Otto led Paulus to the village edge, where they came upon two old men drinking beer. At the sight of them, Heinrich muttered an oath.

"Ho there, my brothers," began Pieter.

The two scowled.

"A miserable day for the two of you?"

"Humph," answered one as he released some gas.

"I see. Well, my name is Father Pieter, and these are m'friends."

The two looked away and did not respond.

Heinrich curled his lip. "I know you two! Y'sent me on the wrong path!"

One spat. He was a bald, wrinkle-faced farmer. "It would've been Edel what done that. He's daft and doesn't know it."

Edel cursed. "Axel is an old fool and dim as dung. Last night he tried pulling his leggings over his head … thought they were his shirt!"

The pilgrims chuckled.

"Did not, dolt. Y'd be dreamin' again!"

"Enough, good sirs!" laughed Pieter. "Enough! Can you tell us where we might find some cheese and bread?"

The two huddled, then began to argue again. Axel stood and pointed. "There, strangers. Go there, past the church, then past the smiths. The market is behind a row of barns."

"Nay! 'Tis the far way," griped Edel.

Pieter pursed his lips. "So who should I choose?"

"Axel," muttered Heinrich. "Edel cost me days of trouble."

Pieter hesitated. "Can you two not lead us there?"

The old men hesitated.

"I'll give you a blessing."

The men immediately stood. Pieter laid his hands on both their heads and prayed loudly. When Pieter finished, Axel and Edel bade the foursome follow them through a wandering labyrinth of narrow alleys and tight streets until somehow the old men delivered the foursome to the village market. Otto spotted a stack of cheeses piled in the shape of a pyramid. He ambled to the merchant who waited with his fists on his hips. "*Ja?* You've business with me?"

"We're looking for food."

"*Ja?*" The man stared at Otto for a few moments, then turned his face toward Maria and the two men. "Who be you?"

"Pilgrims," answered Heinrich.

The man shook his head and looked carefully at the children. "Their black clothes do not deceive me. Methinks the imps be failed crusaders."

"No," answered Pieter with a bite. "We are pilgrims, not crusaders."

The merchant sneered. "Nay? She carries a crusader's cross in her belt."

Pieter grimaced. "She's a pilgrim, and the crusade did not fail."

"Well, the caravans are full of talk of it! Yes, indeed it did fail. The little fools have caused good Christians great harm everywhere. They took pestilence with them wherever they went, they stole and murdered, then gave up the cause of Christ in their unbelief. Shame on them! Shame on all of them! They've failed the Holy Mother and the saints above. Now God is judging us all for their sins!" He turned a twisted face to Otto. "No, beggar boy, I'll not give you cheese. And if you try to steal it, we'll hang you quick. Begone from m'sight. You disgust me!" The man shoved the boy hard.

Voices from the crowd cried out, "Aye, Hartman! Strike him again!"

Pieter and Heinrich both reddened with fury, and Heinrich stepped forward with a menacing scowl. Two eavesdropping soldiers burst from a gathering crowd with swords drawn. "Hold, stranger! Hold or die."

Pieter whirled about and snarled, "Back away, fools. You've no business with us."

The soldiers' brows furrowed, and they stormed toward the pilgrims. Maria suddenly leapt in front of them. "Please, sirs! We mean no harm."

The men stopped and stared at the dirty-faced little girl. They began to laugh. "Well, now that's a comfort to us, *Mädchen*. For we were surely in terror of you!"

The growing crowd laughed loudly.

Maria smiled politely, but Pieter noticed a sudden defiance in the glint of her eye. The tyke set her jaw. "Sirs, we only want food for our journey."

A volley of hisses and taunts flew from the enclosing villagers. "Look at 'er arm!" shouted one. "A crusader," sneered another. "No wonder they failed. Look at 'er."

"Leave us, y'miserable waifs. Leave our sight! Hartman will not give even a nibble to the likes of you."

Pieter's mind was racing, and Heinrich was ready to draw his sword. A village boy threw a dirt clump at Otto when Maria stated firmly, "We've silver enough and gold to buy your cursed food!"

Heinrich paled.

"*Ja?*" blustered the merchant, suddenly surprised. "Well … well then, we ought take it from you and give it to the Church. That might pay a bit of the mighty penance you owe." He puffed his chest and held his bearded chin high. "But we're no thieves like the lot of you. Begone and take yer sin-stained coins elsewhere."

Maria was unaffected. To the dismay of Pieter and

Heinrich, she set her little jaw and walked directly to the man. The crowd hushed. "*Herr* Hartman, you are afraid of us. I see it in your eyes."

The man laughed. "Afraid? Afraid of the likes of you? Methinks not!"

"You fear to do business with us."

The merchant faltered.

Maria looked about the crowd. "Will any sell to us?"

Eyes shifted from one to the other, many tempted by silver and gold whether tainted or not. A few halfhearted "nays" were mumbled.

The six-year-old raised her brows. "Then, would any of you be willing to make a wager with us?"

The villagers leaned close, intrigued. "Wager?" asked the merchant incredulously.

"*Ja*, sir. Is our money good enough to be wagered for?"

A voice grumbled, "Aye! Gold is gold!"

Pieter was now as pale as Heinrich. The baker was nervous, for he had unwisely brought *all* their gold and silver with him. Inciting this growing mob might easily lead to a beating and a robbery. "Maria?" he said nervously.

The imp tugged lightly on the man's hand. Heinrich bent low and the girl whispered in his ear, "Trust me." She smiled.

Heinrich's heart raced, and Pieter's foot tapped nervously. The baker cleared his throat. "You heard her!" he boomed. "We've a wager to offer—unless you *all* fear this little maid."

The crowd murmured as Hartman pulled on his beard. Wagering was the one pastime few could resist.

Pieter lifted his chin. "Pathetic, cowardly women! You've not the manhood to make a wager with our little sister. Ha! Go to your beds ashamed."

"What's the wager?" shouted a voice.

"Aye! What's the wager, old man?"

Pieter had no idea. He turned a helpless face toward the girl and waited.

Maria's eyes twinkled. She whispered to Pieter and Heinrich, and when she was done, what little color had remained in their cheeks was drained away. The men took deep breaths and faced the crowd. Pieter raised his staff with feigned confidence. "Hear me, men of Meiringen. First, we've need of your priest as witness and guarantor. Second, we need your magistrate to pledge our fair treatment and safe escort away."

"What's the wager?" demanded several voices.

Heinrich looked anxiously at the little girl, then turned to the sea of encircling faces. "See the stack of cheeses? She is to be blindfolded whilst you make three new stacks of any size. She will then be allowed to touch only the bottom rows of each, and before the priest can say three *'Aves,'* she will tell you exactly how many cheeses are in each stack."

The crowd roared. "Not possible!" chortled one.

"How much to wager?" chimed another.

Pieter quickly took control. "Tell us, *Herr* Hartman, tell us the price of cheese enough to feed eleven for a fortnight. Add the price of six fresh loaves of spelt bread, a hogshead of dried pork, three gallons of beer, a quarter of vegetables, and a ring of ground grain. Oh, and four gills of honey."

Otto shifted uneasily as the man calculated his price. "A penny for the beer, three for the honey, hmm, then the bread ... the vegetables, grain ... and a shilling for the pork ... comes to two shillings, ten."

Pieter looked astonished. "Do not cheat us, man! I am a priest, and thou shalt have suffering aplenty!"

At that moment the village priest emerged from the crowd. "I am Father Mattias, and I say it is a fair price."

Pieter looked at the black-robed cleric and grunted. "You ask too much."

"Enough of this!" boomed Hartman. "Take my price or leave it be."

Pieter looked at Maria. "Are you sure, my dear?"

"Papa Pieter! What do you think?"

The old man grunted in wry amusement. He bent over and kissed the girl on the cheek. He turned to the priest. "Then we offer this: we wager seventeen pennies against the food."

A loud chorus of objections rang out.

"What? You ought wager twice my price, not half!" The merchant was ranting.

Pieter lifted his nose high in the air. "You fear this girl so?"

"Is she a witch?" cried a voice.

Pieter chilled. He hadn't counted on that. He suddenly realized they might have trapped themselves. *If she fails, we lose the wager; if she reckons rightly, she'll be taken as a witchling.* Masking his fear, he laughed loudly. "No, good sir. She is no witch. On that you've my word as a priest of the Holy Church.

"But now I fear you'll hide behind such a foolish accusation when you lose. So without a guarantee, we'll not wager a penny."

The village priest stepped forward and stared at Maria. The little girl was suddenly frightened. "Recite the '*Ave.*'"

Maria swallowed and began. "*Ave Maria, gratia plena, Dominus tecum. Benedicta tu ...*"

When she finished, Father Mattias nodded. "Now, the Lord's Prayer."

The little girl cleared her throat and spoke with confidence. "*Pater noster, qui es in caelis, sanctificetur nomen tuum ...*"

The priest laid his hands on her head and closed his eyes. Satisfied, he pronounced her clean of both demons and witchcraft, "though beset by the shame of unbelief and a disgrace to the name of Christ as are all these pitiful child crusaders."

Pieter snorted and spat. "You have offended us with your charge. We'll have no part in this."

The crowd protested loudly.

"Nay!" shouted Pieter. "I'll not let this precious child suffer the vile thoughts of wags like you."

"Two to one, then!" shouted a voice. "Take his offer, Hartman, two to one!"

"Eh?" Pieter looked at Heinrich with a mischievous smirk. He stroked his beard slowly. "Hmm. I think not. But perhaps three to one for Hartman's goods, and we'll take wagers for silver with the rest of you."

The men of Meiringen fell quiet for a few moments. They whispered among themselves until a number of "ayes" could be heard among the crowd. Soon, a long line of penny-bearing palms was passing by the magistrate and the priest who kept record of each wager. Within the half hour, the guarantor was holding a basket filled with ninety silver pennies—the equivalent of nearly four months' labor by a commoner. Heinrich handed the man one gold coin and six silver pennies. He then handed him eleven pennies against the foodstuffs wagered by Hartman. "A lot to lose," mumbled Heinrich to Pieter.

The old man's eyes twinkled. He loved the excitement of it all. "A lot to win! Have no fear, baker. No fear!"

"All is in order," announced the magistrate. "Blindfold the girl."

Maria's eyes were bound beneath a wide strip of black cloth, and she was led by the official to a long table where three stacks of varied numbers of cheeses had been piled. The crowd fell silent as she reached forward to the first stack. Her fingers were guided to the bottom row and she moved them slowly along the table, counting each out loud. "I count twelve," she announced. The crowd hushed as the little girl stood quietly. The priest began reciting his first "*Ave.*" He had barely finished when the girl blurted, "Seventy-eight!"

The merchant paled. The tyke was correct.

Maria was taken to the next pile, which had seventeen cheeses on the bottom row. The priest began reciting his "*Ave,*" this time more hastily. He finished the second recitation. Hushed and anxious, the crowd pressed forward. Father Mattias was standing with clenched fists, slurring the words as he began the final recitation of the race. "*Ave Maria gratia plena. Dominustecum ...*"

Maria was struggling. "Um ..."

"*Benedictatuinmulieribusetbenedictus ...*"

The pilgrims held their breath. Pieter gripped his staff with a white fist, and Otto stared open mouthed. The villagers ground their teeth.

"One hundred thirty-six!" shouted the girl.

Mattias groaned with the crowd, then finished. " ... *mortis nostrae, Amen.* "

Panicked hands now crawled over the stack to confirm the count. *"Ach!"* shouted Hartman. "One hundred thirty-six!" The blindfolded maid was led to the final pile. She took a deep breath, then counted nine on the bottom as Father Mattias began again.

This time, the poor priest had barely said his first Amen before the girl chirped, "Forty-five!"

Astonished, Heinrich removed the girl's blindfold as the villagers began to jeer and curse. The count was confirmed, and Hartman, Father Mattias, and Pieter quickly huddled with the magistrate, who then announced, "Hear me! Silence! The girl's right with her count ... on each. The wager is declared in favor of these ... these pilgrims."

Furious, the crowd grew louder and more surly. Heinrich hastily dumped all the coins into his satchel and ordered Otto and Maria to load Paulus with the food they had won as quickly as possible. Standing between two armed guards, Pieter climbed atop a barrel and pronounced a sarcastic blessing on the hapless men of Meiringen; then he smiled. With his yellow snaggletooth exposed by a cavernous grin as wide as the Aare Valley, the old fellow pointed to his dear little one and proclaimed, *"Ave Maria!"*

Chapter Ten

LOVE IN THE BRÜNIG PASS

Wil and his company rolled with laughter when they heard the story of the cheese told by Pieter that evening around a snapping campfire. "But how, Maria? How did you do it?"

The little girl was embarrassed by the attention but explained how *Signora* Cosetta had spent many hours teaching her mathematics. "Then a very old Persian man came to see the *signor*, and he taught me the secret of the triangle. I practiced a lot ... but never told Pieter!"

Heinrich finished his meal and stared at the torches of Meiringen. A feeling of uneasiness crept over him. "Methinks we need to leave at once. We should keep the fire ablaze to make them think we're here, but we ought to move on now. We left them angry and poor."

Wil agreed. So, well fed and in high spirits, the pilgrims hurried away from Meiringen under the silvery light of a half-moon. They traveled across the flat valley throughout the night and paused at daybreak for a brief rest at the first ascent into the Brünig Pass. Refreshed, they prepared to march again as the early morning sun cast brilliant color and shadow across the rock cliffs before them. The group marveled at the sight.

"It looks different coming this way," said Otto. "I don't remember those cliffs."

"The world always looks different when your vantage

point changes," mused Pieter.

"I think it's the most beautiful sight yet," sighed Frieda. She cast a sidelong glance at Wil and smiled.

Pieter nudged Heinrich with a knowing look. "Something seems afoot with those two," he whispered.

The baker chuckled. "Methinks you're right. 'Tis plain they have feelings for each other. I only wonder whether Wil sees what an uncommon lass Frieda is. Surely his head will soon follow where his heart is leading. He has long been a boy of good sense, though stubborn at times."

"Aye," agreed Pieter, laughing.

"Papa Pieter," interrupted Maria, "ahead is where Georg died for Karl? Otto said so."

Pieter nodded sadly. He remembered the lad's bravery as he hurtled off the cliff in a desperate, selfless attempt to save Karl. "Yes, my dear, somewhere in the Brünig ... but I doubt we'll find just where."

"But we'll surely know the tree that marks his grave," added Frieda. "We picked one we'd not easily forget."

The old man nodded. "It would be nice to visit him."

Wil interrupted. "We *must* find his grave, Pieter."

"Well, my son, you are our leader. Lead us there if you can."

The Brünig Pass was not as high as the Grimsel, nor as desolate as the Simplon, but was majestic and inspiring nonetheless. Sheer walls of rock marked its entrance from the south, and more cliffs abounded between tight channels of steep mountain slopes. It had its own "divine presence," as Pieter oft repeated. "God is here, my children! Can you not feel His breath on your face, smell the fragrance of His chamber in the scent of pine?"

Indeed, the Brünig had a special quality of enchantment, a welcoming way about it that drew the pilgrims in breathless wonder of the pleasant sights that awaited them at every turn of the roadway. Mountain wildflowers of purple or blue, orange and white peeked from crevices and filled sun-brightened glades. Birds chattered happily, and from time to time a proud stag emerged from the dark woodland to bare his chest for all the world to admire.

The wayfarers had not traveled more than a half day when Wil and Frieda sprinted ahead of the column and returned beaming. "We've found it!" cried Frieda. "We've found it!"

"Georg's grave?" cried Heinz.

"*Ja!*"

Surprised, Pieter leaned on his staff and patted Solomon on the head. "Oh, my shaggy friend! Have we e'er seen a truer act of love than what good Georg did on that awful day?" He turned to Heinrich. "You've heard the story?"

"Aye," he answered sadly. "I have."

The company hurried on and within a quarter hour was standing under the spreading arms of an ancient oak tree growing boldly in the center of a green glade. Beneath its wide-stretched boughs rested a mound of rocks marking the lad's grave. A crusader's cross was lying in the tall grass, and Maria picked it up. She then removed the cross she was carrying and fixed it at the head of Georg's grave. "Wil, I've given Georg back his cross. Karl carried it for him."

Wil's throat tightened and he nodded mutely.

The little girl then ran to Heinrich and handed him the cross from the grave. "*Herr … Herr* Heinrich, this was Karl's cross. He set it by Georg's head that day."

Heinrich's eye filled with tears as he received the cross reverently. Thoughts of his son were his constant companions. He touched the rough wood to his lips. "Oh, my dear Karl!" he moaned. He held it to his heart, then secured it in his belt. "Thank you, Maria. I shall take it home, home to Weyer."

Maria said nothing.

Heinrich wiped his nose, then looked carefully at the little girl. Her eyes were red and her cheeks stained with tears. Her braids were tangled and littered with wilted flowers. Heinrich dropped to his knees and smiled at her. "Come, Maria, let me hold you." Gently, the man reached out to the tiny maiden and embraced her, then kissed her on the forehead. He laid his thick, callused hand on her frail shoulder and looked at her tenderly. "Maria, you may call me 'Papa' or *'Vati.'* You are to be my daughter, and I will be your father."

The maid nearly fainted for the wonder of it. She collapsed onto the man's breast as a weary lamb welcomed to the shepherd's fold. There she sobbed great tears of joy. She had been accepted; she was loved and would be kept safe under the watch of a father who cared.

Maria did not rejoice alone. A short distance from the baker and the little girl stood a teary Pieter and a beaming Frieda. Wil had also witnessed the exchange, and tears streamed freely down his face.

"Well, he *should* claim her," griped Tomas with a hiss. He stood behind Otto with folded arms and sneered.

Otto wheeled about. "You'd take the joy from Christmas if you could!" he growled.

Tomas snickered. "Maybe I shall yet."

"Enough!" barked Pieter. "Tomas, you ... you—"

"Pieter," interrupted Heinrich, "leave him be."

The group settled, and Maria led Heinrich through the glade to gather flowers for Georg's grave. Wil and Frieda drifted to the shade of the nearby forest, while others rested. The air of the dark wood was cool and musty. A few squirrels rustled about, but the heavily needled floor muffled the sound. The needles made the earth soft beneath the pair's feet as they left the others behind.

With a light touch of his hand, Wil took Frieda's elbow and turned her to face him. The girl's brown eyes were wide with anticipation, yet she quickly lowered them. Wil laid his forefinger under her chin and lifted it upward. "Frieda," he said softly. "Oh, dear, beautiful Frieda ..." The young man's heart raced, and his limbs pulsed with vigor. He took her gently by the shoulders, and the feel of them, soft and firm in his grasp, made him want to pull her close.

At the gentle touch of Wil's strong hands, Frieda's body filled with warmth such as she had never known. The feeling was exhilarating, yet she wanted to melt away in his embrace. With a slight tremble she looked up into Wil's face, and as he leaned close to hers, she closed her eyes and parted her lips.

When their lips touched, the world stopped. For a seem-ing eternity, Wil and Frieda were aware of nothing and none save each other.

"Frieda," Wil finally breathed. "Frieda ... you are the one true good that has come out of this cursed journey. I've oft wondered if Karl would still be with us if I'd chosen differ-ently ... but even so, I do not regret leaving m'hearth and home if it meant I might find you."

Frieda was so overcome with emotion that she could not speak, but as she looked deeply into Wil's eyes, the warmth and depth of her love were plainly written on her face.

"Ah, Frieda, say you won't leave us when we reach Weyer."

Frieda lowered her eyes in despair. "But, Wil, what place is there for me? I can't wander about on my own for-ever. There is none left to me but my mother, and she is in Westphalia. I suppose I can return to the monastery ... perhaps they would welcome me if I were to take the vows."

"What!" Wil exploded. "You mustn't! What would become of you? You simply cannot think of it."

"What else can I do, Wil?"

For a long moment Wil was silent. As his thoughts tum-bled violently, he could not shake the inexplicable fear coursing through him. The idea of Frieda taking vows to the Church was simply unacceptable. He had not thought of finding love when he set out on crusade—but then neither had he anticipated suffering and death such as he and his comrades had endured on their journey.

The trials of the past year had matured Wil considerably. Young though he still was, he was no longer the same fool-ish lad who denied those closest to him at the castle of Domodossola. The true nature of love had become clearer to the young man, helped in part by the discoveries he was making about his father. In his newfound wisdom, Wil rec-ognized that denying his feelings now would cost him more than any man could afford.

How can I let her go? he asked himself. *There is only one way....*

"You must stay and become my wife!" declared Wil triumphantly.

Stunned, Frieda's head shot up, and joy filled her face. "You wish me to ... to marry you, Wil?"

"Aye, dearest, I would have no other. Will you marry me?"

"Yes!" cried Frieda. "Oh, most assuredly yes!"

The next hour passed all too quickly for the couple. Together they walked hand in hand through the forest, dreaming and planning as their two destinies became intertwined. Finally, they returned to the clearing. Seeing the others nearby, Wil cried, "All gather!"

"The boy's fidgeting like I've ne'er seen," whispered Heinrich.

"And look at Frieda. She's red as a beet!" Heinz giggled.

Wil waited impatiently until Pieter drew near. "Pieter, you once said this place is marked by love. Frieda has agreed to become my wife, and we do not wish to wait any longer than necessary. Would you ... would you marry us here, now?"

The pilgrims stood mute and dumbstruck. Heinrich's mouth dropped open, and Maria gasped.

"Did you hear me?" laughed Wil.

Pieter was suddenly weeping again. He raised his staff to heaven. "*Deo gratias!* Thanks be to God! *Ja, ja,* of course I will marry you ... here and now if you wish!" The old fellow leapt into the air and tried to click his heels. Apparently, he hadn't done that for quite some time, and he fell atop Solomon with a loud crash! Lying on the ground, he laughed heartily as the others congratulated the happy couple.

Heinrich beamed. He had secretly hoped for this very moment. *They are so good for one another,* he thought. *She makes him feel free ... I can see it in his eyes when she is near. And he makes her feel safe and treasured. Thanks be to God indeed.* He turned his face toward heaven. *Karl, lad, if you can see, be happy for them. And Emma, Lukas, Ingly, and Richard ... this is a good day under the sun!*

It was midafternoon when the joyous company gathered around the bride and groom. Frieda turned all heads with her radiant beauty. Maria had adorned the fair damsel in an array of wildflowers that the angels must surely have coveted. Atop her golden hair was set a ringlet of blue and white, and around her neck she wore a quick-woven wreath of green vines and yellow petals. The young woman stood pink faced and smiling, her beauty in full bloom despite the plain black dress she wore. Her happy eyes were moist with unshed tears, but her head was held high and her figure regal, bearing testimony to the proud lineage from which she came.

Wil had tied his long locks behind his neck and allowed Maria to fuss over him. The girl had picked all the brambles from his black leggings and brushed a journey's worth of debris off his tunic. She placed a single red poppy in his collar and insisted he borrow Karl's cross to place in his belt. The young man stood handsome and strong. His angular features were even and pleasing, now chiseled into a face matured by the harsh winds of struggle. Finally deemed ready by Maria, Wil turned his blazing blue eyes toward his bride.

Little Heinz spoke up. "We ought to hold hands round them!" With the exception of Tomas, the others agreed, and an effort was made to do just that. Of course, the idea had been offered without consideration of either Heinrich or Maria! It was an immediate source of friendly laughter.

The ring of fellows quieted, and Pieter joined the starstruck couple in the center, where he laid his hands on their shoulders. He closed his eyes, then lifted his face to the bright blue sky of June. "O God, King of heaven and earth, may it please You this day to order and to hallow, and to govern our hearts and our bodies, our thoughts, our words, and our works according to Your Law and in the doing of Your commandments...."

Pieter turned a kindly face to the pair and reached into his satchel. He retrieved his precious parchment and held it at arm's length to read. "Oh, blessed family of mine, 'twas in this very place these words were once read. I shall read them again with a heart now as happy as it once was sad. It is only God who can join such sorrow and joy together in the place of love." He swallowed hard against the lump filling his throat. He cast a glance in the direction of Georg's grave, then returned his attention to the bride and groom.

"'If I speak in the tongues of men and of angels, but have not love, I am only a resounding gong or a clanging cymbal.... If I have a faith that can move mountains, but have not love, I am nothing. If I give all I possess to the poor and surrender my body to the flames, but have not love, I gain nothing. Love is patient, love is kind. It does not envy, it does not boast, it is not proud. It is not rude, it is not self-seeking, it is not easily angered. It keeps no record of wrongs. Love does not delight in evil but rejoices with the truth. It always protects, always trusts, always hopes, always perseveres. Love never fails.'"

When finished, he folded the valuable parchment carefully and raised his hands in a prayer of mercy and of protection. "And may the womb of this woman be blessed richly with a bounty of God's children."

Trembling with joy, he then turned to Wil. "Wilhelm of Weyer, son of Heinrich of Weyer, do you take this woman to be your precious wife under God and before these witnesses? And do you promise to keep her and her only?"

Wil set his jaw hard and lifted his face proudly. "I do so swear."

Pieter turned to Frieda. "Frieda of Westphalia, daughter of ... of ..."

"Manfred of Chapelle," the bride whispered.

"Daughter of Manfred of Chapelle, do you take this man to be your blessed husband under God and before these witnesses? And do you promise to obey him and to give yourself to him only?"

Frieda's brown eyes filled with tears. She turned happily toward Wil and declared, "I so swear by heaven, by the saints and the Holy Mother, and by all things sacred."

Pieter turned to Heinrich. "Heinrich of Weyer, father of Wilhelm, do you honor and witness these vows?"

"With gladness, I do."

The old priest took the trembling hands of bride and groom and clasped them within his own. "Then with all the joy my heart can share and with all the wonder of the goodness around us, I do so declare you to be man and wife, *in nomine Patris, et Filii, et Spiritus Sancti!*"

A rousing cheer rose up from the jubilant ring, and the merrymakers began to dance round and round the smiling couple. Wil took his foot and set it lightly upon his bride's as the symbol of his taking her into his life. Then the two kissed.

Benedetto, nearly intoxicated with the happiness of the moment, leapt upon a boulder and strummed his lute. "Now, listen first, dear Wil and Frieda. Then sing to one another your wedding song!"

Take the roses from the gardens,
Take the fishes from the seas,
Take the starlight from the heavens,
But ne'er take her far from me.

Chase the snowflakes from the winter,
Drive the raindrops far and wide,
Move the sheep herds fro and hinter,
Only leave him by my side.

Though the world may fall asunder,
Though the grapes yield no more wine,
Though the storm clouds lose their thunder,
I'll be his ... and she'll be mine.

Fill thy goblets! Fill thy platters!
Sing with lute a kettle song!
What we claim here now doth matter:
With each other we belong.

The song over, a mad rush to kiss the bride ensued, and Heinrich cried, "Now we need to feast!"

Paulus had been standing quite peacefully by the tree to which he was tethered. His big eyes widened in fear as a rush of many hands flew toward him and the sacks tied fast to his back. Honey was quickly retrieved and poured atop loaves of Meiringen bread, while cheese was melted in the pot atop a hastily built campfire. Soon eager hands dipped bread into the bubbling mixture, while others passed flasks of beer. Strips of salted pork disappeared with speed, and even Tomas was prevailed upon to enjoy fingersful of berry preserves.

Benedetto strummed a ballad to which all danced the ring dance. Pieter brought tears of laughter to all as he frolicked about the circle in his rolling gait. He was as happy as a schoolboy released to the sunshine! The warm breeze tousled his thin white hair and beard, and his bony limbs creaked loudly with every step. Soon the old fellow was panting, and he staggered to the fire to rest.

From there, Pieter watched his beloved friends laughing and singing. The old man chuckled, and his heart swelled with love. "I am richly blessed, Solomon. Richly blessed indeed!"

As twilight descended on the merry camp, Heinrich knew the bride and groom would soon be off. "Pieter," he cried, "methinks we'll make camp here tonight?"

The old priest laughed loudly. "*Ja,* I am sure of it!"

The baker then called for his son and for Frieda. In moments, they and the whole of the company gathered together. Heinrich took Frieda's hand. "My dear, with my son's permission, I should find it a great joy to call you 'daughter.'"

Wil nodded. "Indeed, sir."

Heinrich embraced the girl. "We are family now. We belong to one another."

Frieda took the baker's hand. "I am honored to call you 'Father,' sir." She smiled.

Heinrich then turned to his son. He extended his hand tentatively toward the lad and laid it gently on his shoulder. "I am proud of you this day, Wil. I wish you and your bride every good thing under heaven." He closed his eye, then repeated what he had offered each of his sons at his birth. It was the blessing his own father had given him at his baptism.

For this circle of kin I vow
To stand by you (both) and humbly bow

To God above and blood below
To join our hands against all foes.

I pray you courage and arms as steel,
A mind of wisdom, a heart that feels.
Though battles may find you, may each one be won,
Your eyes turned toward heaven and lit by the sun.

Wil's throat tightened. He said nothing but nodded.

The baker then reached inside his tunic and retrieved something wrapped in a cloth. He looked at Frieda and at Wil. "I should like to give you both this thing as a token of a father's hope. Son, methinks you'll be the one to bear it, but it is to be borne for Frieda's well-being as well as your own. Take this and know that I love you both." He extended the gift to Wil's opened hands.

The groom received the present carefully, both eyes fixed on Heinrich. "Thank you, Father."

Frieda waited patiently as Wil turned his gaze to the thing lying in his palms. He removed the cloth, and the circle clapped. It was the Stedinger blade. "I ... we shall treasure it always! Many thanks." Wil leaned toward his father and embraced him shyly. Heinrich's heart soared.

Frieda smiled and touched the polished steel lightly. "What is the inscription, Father?"

"Father?" Heinrich smiled. "Ah, my dear girl. Yes. It says, *'vrijheid altijd,'* which means 'freedom always.' It is the language of the Stedingers of whom I have spoken. Freemen in a free land. Would that you both shall be free, like them."

The bride kissed the man on the cheek.

Pieter touched Wil on the shoulder. "And, good sir, I've a gift as well." He turned to Frieda. "Since Wil shall carry your gift from Heinrich, I should like you to bear this little gift I give to the two of you. Like the dagger, it is to be carried for the well-being of you both." The old priest opened his bony hand and offered Frieda his treasured Scripture.

The girl gasped. She took the parchment in her hand and held it lightly to her breast. "Oh, Father Pieter. *Danke sehr....* I've no words."

The priest laid his hands on each of their heads. "Love

one another always. It is your privilege as man and wife and as children of God."

The newlyweds thanked everyone for their good wishes and even cast a halfhearted wave to Tomas watching from some distance. Now blushing, they made their way nervously to the soft ferns of the shadowed woodland standing a respectful distance from the glade.

నా

In the next days, nine pilgrims, two lovers, one scruffy dog, and a donkey crossed through the Brünig Pass and marched within sight of a mountain-rimmed lake where the early morning light blurred the water like a distant green mirage. Through June mists they then entered the steep-sided, mixed forests of the Glaubenberg Pass, pausing only to watch screeching hawks soar overhead. At last, weary and footsore, they pressed beyond the hardships and the drama of the Alpine trails to enter the inviting charms of the Emmental Valley.

Fox and squirrel dashed about the rolling fields like happy children at Midsummer's. Deep green spruce plunged into inviting ravines, and streamside meadows abounded in deep blue cornflowers, pale blue meadow stork, orange moon poppies, and tiny white May bells. Thigh-high purple clover rubbed the legs of the laughing pilgrims as they descended to the gentler highways leading to Langnau and Burgdorf, and in every direction milk cows and oxen grazed on tender yellow-green grass.

"I like it here!" cried Otto. "It feels safe and warm."

The others quickly agreed. Indeed, it was a place of magic, a place of pleasant dreams and happy notions. Pieter hobbled along with a half-smile made larger each time that he cast a glance toward the light-footed couple floating at the head of the column. *A handsome pair*, he thought. *Long life to both of them.*

In truth, the old fellow was weary. Since the Simplon he had felt a growing weakness, and now he found himself short of breath despite the easier walk along the valley floor. *M'bones took a beating in those Alps*, he thought. *I'll not be seeing the other side again.*

As for the others, all were in good spirits. Heinrich was proud of his son and delighted in the lad's choice of bride. *He got to choose his own!* he thought. He was also glad hearted about the lad's sudden change of mood toward him. The man wasn't sure why, but it seemed that Wil's anger had subsided, that mercy had found a place in the boy's heart—and Heinrich was grateful.

Benedetto and Maria skipped along the trail, singing and laughing, the girl always picking flowers, of course. Helmut and Rudolf kept a quiet watch over all, each content to belong to a family of comrades, yet longing to return to their homes. Otto and Heinz spent most of the journey recounting events of the crusade. They spoke of the raft ride down the Rhône, of the pool of reflections, of Georg, and of Karl's near hanging, of the kindly *Frau* Miller, and of campsite spats. They laughed and mourned and fell into quiet melancholy, only to challenge Pieter with a riddle or to comment on his master riddle, "The Haven."

Tomas, however, kept mostly to himself. He lagged some fifty paces or so behind the column and at night made only a weak effort to join in the singing. He did his part in gathering wood, drawing water, or caring for Paulus, but beyond that, he had little to say and nothing to offer. Pieter and Heinrich oft watched him with wary eyes of pity, for none could know what troubled the boy. Tomas had spat at the baker thrice since joining the company. Each time he had pointed to his half-ear and scar. Heinrich had restrained his hand, however, and offered the boy peace in turn for each offense. It was those gestures of grace that some thought had begun to move the boy, if only a little.

For Wil and Frieda, the days had become little more than soft light and song. In sunshine they walked hand in hand, their conversation in lovers' whispers. At night they made their bed beyond the light of camp, where their love was joined with the gentle warmth of June starlight.

In all respects, it was a delightful and happy respite from the troubles that had dogged the steps of the weary pilgrims.

☙

Judging by the sun, Pieter guessed it was around Midsummer's Day when the walls of Burgdorf appeared in the distance. *"Ach!"* he grumbled. "We missed the Assumption last year, and I'd wager we'll miss Midsummer's this year!"

The company hurried forward, only to find the gates to the town barred and an angry, anxious troop of men-at-arms holding them at bay with leveled lances. "Begone, fools!" cried one.

Heinrich stepped forward. "And why, sir?"

A weathered old soldier cursed, then laid the point of his lance on the baker's throat. "We've trouble about and 'ave no need for the likes of ye!"

"Trouble?" mused Pieter. He shook his head. "Ah, it was bound to find us!" He walked slowly to the soldier. *"Mein Herr,* what sort of trouble?"

"What sort do y'think?"

Pieter shrugged in confusion.

"Well, we've warlords aplenty in this valley now that summer's come."

"And?"

"And we're at the ready. Seems the empire's war may never end. Otto has allies to the east, Emperor Friederich to the west. The pope's Templars are about. I'm told they've problems with some deserters they mean to hang."

"Who would desert the Templars?" quizzed Wil.

The soldier lowered his lance and turned his eyes on the donkey. "Have you any beer?"

Wil shook his head. "No."

"Then our little chat is done. Begone or swing." The soldier raised his lance again and set his jaw.

Wil scowled and wheeled about to his fellows. "We've no business here! We're off."

Otto's face fell. He marched past the soldiers and called to them. "When's the feast?"

"Eh?"

"Midsummer's. When is it?"

The soldiers roared. " 'Twas yesterday, ye fools!"

☙

Feeling discouraged for the first time in many days, the pilgrims marched sluggishly across the wide plain that stretched from Burgdorf to Olten. Behind them rose the great Alps, their rough peaks aligned like sentinels guarding their backs. Ahead, the distant horizon was softened by the gentler mountains that stood between them and Basel.

Murmuring and despondent, they had traveled less than a league when Pieter suddenly stopped, angrily raised his staff, and rebuked his fellows with a scalding reprimand. "Enough!" he cried. "You shuffle along like so many spoiled little lords and ladies. Minstrel, you've the look of an angry child. Otto and Helmut, stop your grumbling. By the saints, you turn your heads to the ground for missing a pitiful feast? How quickly you've forgotten what sufferings really are! Ahead we'll soon pass the graves of our friends who drowned; behind we passed the bones of others lost to fever and to violence. Look at yourselves. Well fed, well clothed, carrying gold and silver aplenty and yet wanting more!"

The pilgrims stared at their feet shamefaced. The old man had hit the mark squarely, and each knew it. Since San Fruttuoso they had been restored by mercy and refreshed by grace. How easily they had forgotten.

Pieter sighed, then withdrew from the line toward the shoulder of the highway. A mocking voice followed him from the rear. "Pieter, always rebuking, never rebuked." It was Tomas.

Ignoring the young man, Pieter bent low to the ground, then lay prostrate in the dust to pray for his beloved. "'Even when our wounds are scarcely healed, our ungrateful minds forget. If you hear us quickly, we become haughty from mercy. If you are slow, we complain in impatience.' O Lord, hear our cry. Forgive us our doubts; help our unbelief. Be merciful to all of us, Your ungrateful children."

Suddenly, the ground began to shake, and it was as the sound of thunder rolling across the landscape. All faces whirled about, wide eyed. "There!" cried Wil. "Soldiers!"

"Quick, everyone. To the cover of the wood!" Heinrich

snatched Maria under his arm and led the charge to a patch of woodland about a bowshot east of the highway. As they ran, more horsemen could be seen charging from the opposite direction. "Run!" cried Heinrich. "Run!"

Pieter struggled to his feet, then stumbled and fell. Wil abruptly reversed course to help. With a grunt, he picked up the spindly priest and carried him in his arms as he ran to rejoin the others. "Hurry, Wil!" shrieked Frieda.

Otto snatched Paulus's lead and pulled with all his might. The stubborn beast would not move! "Damn you, beast!" shouted the boy. "Move!" He pulled and yanked frantically, and with every straining tug the animal leaned farther back, planting his hooves deeply in the dust and nearly laying his rump atop the ground.

"Come on, Otto!" cried Rudolf. "Hurry!"

"I can't. He won't move!"

"Then leave him!"

Otto closed his eyes and grimaced as he pulled again. It was Solomon, however, who made the donkey move. With a snarl and a snap, he fixed his bared teeth hard into the beast's rump! Paulus leapt forward with a loud bray and threw a sideways kick at the nimble dog. With a victorious shout, Otto then dragged the donkey and a lifeline of provisions to the cover of the wood.

About a furlong ahead, a road that transversed the plain from east to west intersected the pilgrim's north-south highway. From opposing directions, two small armies now roared, and it seemed as though they would collide directly in front of Wil's company.

Panting and frightened, the pilgrims crouched low in the shadows of their leafy screen. "We ought to go deeper," counseled Heinrich. "They might join together and scour the whole plain for what they can find. We've two females, a high-piled donkey, and satchels heavy with coin."

Wil had strung Emmanuel and moved his quiver to his hip. He nervously fixed his grip on the handle of his new dagger. "Aye, but see. Both armies are pulling up. Look, their commanders are putting them to order. Methinks they'll fight one another."

"Then for the sake of heaven," cried Pieter, "keep out of sight."

The birds stopped chirping, and no living thing moved. Rudolf whispered to Helmut, "Listen to the wind ... it has stopped. 'Tis ne'er a good sign!"

Helmut nodded. Their ancient forbears had taught that the wind bore change into the world. Despite the relentless efforts of the Holy Church, it was these echoes of Odin—the ancient god of the Teutons—that yet moved lads as these. They feared both the stillness and the breeze, perpetually haunted by what might be.

"Look there!" cried Otto in dread. A distant field of winter rye began to bend beneath the insistent urging of a sun-heated gust. The shimmering green field now wended and welled toward the warriors. "The spirits are twisting in the grain!"

Chapter Eleven

TO ARMS!

The acrid smell of burning thatch wafted over the plain. "They've left villages afire in their wake," groaned Rudolf.

The group murmured and crouched lower as the armies prepared to fight. The knights to the east were gathering in close ranks, the flanks of each charger pressed up against the next. Wil strained to see the army gathering from the west. "Templars!" he gasped.

A line of Knights Templar stood waiting like a white curtain of steel. Wil noted how much smaller their horses were than those of their opponents. The Templars preferred their spirited Arabian mounts and rode them in deep-set saddles. The warrior-monks sat confidently upon their sweated steeds, souls safe for all eternity and ready to do battle against the disordered rabble of evildoers now facing them. Their white habits bore a red cross over the left breast, and beneath they wore chain mail coats. Atop their heads sat metal helms that capped their chain mail hoods. In one hand, each grasped a kite-shaped shield emblazoned with a red cross; in the other, long-swords or lances.

The standard-bearer raised the Templar banner proudly. Wil had seen it in Weyer years before and had never forgotten its chequered black and white panels with the Templars' red cross embroidered boldly in the center. "Methinks they've about two score horse in total and ... there! There comes some host of footmen and archers from behind." In fact, the Templars' small army consisted of eight Knights Templar, about two score mounted mercenaries, three score footmen, and a dozen crossbowmen.

To the east was a smaller army: heavy cavalry numbering some twenty knights and supported by an equal number of footmen and a tithing of archers. Garbed in the varied-colored robes of an assortment of lords, they, like their enemies, paused to receive blessings from their priests. In a few moments, the commander kissed a raised crucifix and inspected his men.

Heinrich whispered to Wil as he pointed to his right, "Methinks those to be men of Otto. There, to our left would be the army supporting Friederich. The Templars always follow the pope's choice."

Suddenly, the first glint of steel shined in the west as the Templar master raised his long-sword. With a loud cry he led his cavalry forward, first at a trot. At the sound, the commander of Otto's men answered. Undaunted by the white robes and the banner of the dreaded Templars, he abruptly ordered his own horsemen forward at a full gallop. His chargers thundered toward the dividing highway under shields glistening in the sunlight. In the dust behind, his leather-vested companies of footmen and archers sprinted forward with lances, pikes, and flails.

The pilgrims' heads turned from east to west as the close-ranked Templars answered with their battle cry, "*Vive Dieu, Saint Amour!*" They stormed toward Otto's line like a flashing fist of steel, lances leveled like a forest on end. Their ranks held tight and true as shoulder to shoulder they crashed into their foes. Otto's commander fell at once, his chest impaled by the hard point of an unbending lance. His line then collapsed in utter confusion.

The Templars and their allies seized upon their foes without mercy. They were skilled in butchery and fought savagely with long-swords and glaives. Some swung Turkish maces—thick-handled sticks bearing a heavy, spiked ball on the end. With them, they smashed through their opponents' helmets like rocks landing on eggs. In less than a quarter hour, many numbers of Otto's men were strewn about the roadway; others fled for their lives.

A loud cry was heard from a small pocket of trees just beyond the battlefield. Wil's spellbound company turned toward the sound and watched breathlessly as three of Otto's knights were chased from their cover by a half-dozen white-robed Templars. One of the pursued knights rode a small horse, like those of the Templars. This horse and rider were nimble and quick, dodging two shots from a crossbow and outrunning a mounted swordsman. His two comrades, however, were riding huge warhorses and proved to be no match for the speedier Templar mounts. In short order, they were slain as their lone comrade raced a wide circle around his foes and dashed for the cover of the very wood in which the pilgrims hid.

"We must run!" cried Heinrich. "They'll be upon us!"

The company panicked and began a desperate flight into the depths of the forest. Pieter stumbled and fell, only to be picked up by Otto and Helmut. Maria was snatched up into the arms of Heinrich again, but the two tumbled over a fallen log. Paulus reared, and his halter tangled in some brush as Benedetto scampered away in terror.

In mere moments, the fugitive's horse crashed into the wood behind them, and Wil cried for all to hold and hide. Like rabbits in the eyes of wolves, the pilgrims froze in place behind whatever cover was close by.

Heinrich held Maria close and peered through a green screen of weeds to watch. The fleeing soldier was spurring his horse through the brush directly toward the baker with a face set firm but not panicked. Suddenly, his white-foamed stallion turned a leg and toppled, dumping the hapless man forward with a crash. He groaned and hurried to his feet, only to trip backward as he drew his sword. Flinging his head from one side to the other, his eyes met the baker's. "Heinrich!" cried the knight.

"Blasius!"

It was all that could be said. The six Templars burst into the wood and, before Blasius could move, reined their mounts in a circle around him. Heinrich crouched low and held Maria tightly. The man's heart was pounding and his mouth was dry. *What to do ... what to do?* Blasius was the baker's friend. He had last seen him trotting away from Stedingerland those many years before. *O God above, what to do?*

Heinrich laid a trembling hand on his sword. His looked about the circle of six Templars, and he set his jaw. But before the baker could foolishly spring from his cover, Blasius was disarmed and bound. "They're not going to kill him?" The baker released his breath and watched intently as his old friend was thrown over his saddle and tied upon his own horse.

"You'll pay for your betrayal, Brother Blasius," grumbled a Templar.

"'Tis the Grand Master and the pope who've betrayed *us!*"

Fists pounded Blasius's face. "Blasphemer! Damn you to hell!"

With no more words, the soldiers mounted their steeds and charged out of the wood with their prisoner in tow. The pilgrims remained silent until, one by one, they popped out from their hiding places. Wil looked at his father now ghost-white and trembling. "Sir?"

"Yes?"

"Are you frightened?"

Heinrich wiped his brow. "Ah, lad. Do you remember our friend Blasius?"

"Of course. I'll ne'er forget him."

"That was he."

"Who?"

"The one taken and bound."

"*Ach, mein Gott!* Are you sure, Father?"

Heinrich nodded. Wil turned to his fellows and briefly recounted the history of Blasius. "And more than all that, he was devout to the true faith and a soldier of charity. He was all that I might ever wish to be. Father, he came twice to Weyer in search of you after you had gone. He was very worried."

The baker did not answer.

"I'll never forget when he tried to save the little boy from the hangman."

"Aye, lad. Now we needs save him."

Pieter asked gravely, "What's to be done?"

Wil looked about. "First, is everyone accounted for?" His eyes flew about the company. "Good. And I see Paulus and Solomon stood fast and quiet!"

"Methinks we need to first see where they take him," said Heinrich as he moved toward the margins of the wood.

"Aye," answered Wil. He led the others behind his father, and they watched helplessly as the Templar army finished its gruesome business. The soldiers moved midst their fallen foes, indifferently dispatching the wounded. No quarter had been given, and not a single conscience was pricked for it. Lord Otto, it was reasoned, had violated the sacred order of things, and the pope had ordained their swords as instruments of God's judgment. On that account, mercy had little role to play.

Blasius could be seen atop his horse, head drooping to one side. A circle of white-robed knights was gathered close by and seemed to be discussing the matter.

"We must know their plan," muttered Pieter. "I confess, I am grieved at what I see here. I have always admired the Templars. They are warrior-monks who have honored the cause of Christ in their piety and charity and have been the guardians of the innocent. But here, they seem no better than common rogues."

"Blasius is all that is good in a Christian warrior, Pieter. Trust me in this." Heinrich's attention was fixed on the captive.

"They're assembling to leave," added Frieda. "I see them pointing south."

"Toward Burgdorf, methinks," said Wil.

With no more business on the field, the Templar master commanded his small army south on the highway the pilgrims had just traveled. Crouching low in their cover, Wil's company watched carefully as the column of men-at-arms moved slowly away. Numbers of their own wounded were tied to litters carried by weary footmen, and their dead were shrouded in heavy blankets and hung over the rumps of horses. Blasius was still tied to his horse, his arms bound by thick cords that were wrapped around the whole of his body.

"To Burgdorf, then," stated Heinrich.

"*Ja*, Father. To Burgdorf."

෮

Wil, Pieter, and Heinrich left the others in the care of Otto and made their way carefully back to the timber-walled town of Burgdorf to spy. It had never been a place of hospitality, and entering its gates did little to make them feel welcome. The town was a disorganized clutter of low thatch-covered hovels and shops strung along deep-rutted alleys and crowded streets. Its folk were a typical assortment of poor peasants dressed in their short tunics and awkward-looking hats. Here and there merchantmen wandered about alongside two-wheeled carts filled with their treasures. These men were dressed in either knee-length tunics decorated with silk sashes or the more fashionable doublets beginning to make their way from the large cities. The mood of the town was surly and loud. On this corner and that, quarrelsome wenches were barking at one another, and the taverns were filled with brawling men.

"Not a place I'd like to stay long," noted Pieter. "'Tis good we missed the feast!"

The three made their way past booths of mutton slabs and pork. The meat was discolored and fly covered. Here and there tables were piled with wares from local parts and from afar. Cheese, of course, was everywhere, as were horn ware and items carved from wood. Hay was being harvested from the meadows, so the town's barns were quickly filling. "The hay is the only thing that smells good here," complained Wil.

"Aye," agreed Pieter. They rounded the corner and were greeted with a bakery's mouth-watering aroma. "Except for that!" Soon, the trio was crowding the baker's tables and breathing deeply of fresh bread.

"Buy or be gone!" snapped the baker.

Heinrich spat. "*Ja?* Well, the smell is free and so's the street." He looked at a few dark pretzels. "Your oven's too hot."

"Leave!" roared the man.

With a few oaths, the three moved on. "Pieter, even if we find the Templars, we'll not likely know their plan for Blasius," said Heinrich.

"True enough," answered the priest. "Methinks we ought to find an armorer or a smith. They oft hear things."

"There," interrupted Wil. "There, the armorer."

Down the street and to their right side was the workshop where chain mail was fashioned and repaired. It had been conveniently positioned next to the blacksmith, where several craftsmen were forging swords. "Good day, gentlemen," said Pieter smiling.

"Not so good," grunted the master smith.

"Good if you be a Templar man!" replied the priest.

The armorer shrugged. "What d'y'need?"

"We've heard of a battle nearby and wondered what y'might know of it."

The man turned away and hammered a small ring that encircled the round finger of a small anvil.

Heinrich lifted a penny to the air. "Does any know of the man captured?"

The workmen stopped and looked. A journeyman walked close, wiping his hands on his leather apron. He reached for the silver penny.

"And?"

The man took the penny with a snort. "*Ja.* 'Tis said he's a traitor and he's to be hanged by compline prayers. What of it?"

Heinrich reached into his satchel and retrieved another penny. "Where?"

"Why?" snapped the smith.

"And who needs to know our business?" growle Heinrich.

"I do." A soldier stepped forward from the shadows. was not a Templar, but he was a knight who had bee ing on his armor. He emerged into full light and fixed stare on the baker.

Heinrich's heart began to race. He turned to face the soldier. "This priest and his ... his novice were robbed in the mountains by a rogue knight. They wanted to see if it was he, and if so, they want their chalice and paten returned."

"Else we shan't bring the blood and body of Christ to our poor flock," whined Pieter sanctimoniously.

The knight turned toward a lady now entering the shop. Smiling, he reached to kiss her.

"And many thanks, m'lord. 'Tis time we were going," the lady said. She adjusted the jeweled chaplet ringing her head, then smiled flirtatiously.

The knight's eyes never left hers, and he walked after her until Pieter called after him. "Sir, the prisoner?"

Annoyed, the man answered over his shoulder, "He's to be hanged at compline on the Galgenberg."

Heinrich took a deep breath and turned to the smith. "So, for the penny you can now tell me where the Galgenberg is."

"Aye," the man snatched the silver coin. "'Tis about a furlong west of town. You'll see a widespread chestnut on a valley knoll. A good place for hangings!"

Soon Wil, Pieter, and Heinrich were hurrying away from Burgdorf and to their camp beyond the walls. It was approaching vespers when they arrived, and that left them only three hours to both calculate and execute a plan of rescue. "Look about us," whined Benedetto. "We've naught but smooth-faced lads, girls, a cripple, an old man, and a minstrel. We've a stubborn mule, no warhorse, and but one ˋlayful hound."

ˋmy like this
ˋt not to resist.
of knaves
ˋraves.

He
try-
hard

ˋ forefinger aimlessly in the dust and
ˋis brow. "Indeed. Sounds like the
ˋallad." He sighed and looked about
ˋk faces staring back. *Humph. This*

pathetic fellowship of castoffs and misfits against the Knights Templar? We must be mad!

Perspiring in the summer heat, Heinrich offered two poor ideas. Wil blurted some harebrained scheme, and Pieter struggled to find any solution. It was Tomas who stepped from the margins of the camp and offered a plan. The lad had been dark and brooding over the past weeks. He had taken what simple pleasure he could by sniping at the others from time to time, but his disappointment with the Dark Lord and his brief stay in Dragonara had plied his heart enough to let the occasional kindness of others bring a little light to him. "Blasius was kind to me," he muttered. "He was an oblate like me. Some say he was my cousin. Brother Lukas swore it, but I was never sure."

Heinrich leaned forward. "How a cousin, lad?"

"Seems we're both of Gunnar stock, shepherds by Arfurt. They had a feud with your family for generations. And I'm told you had some hand in the murder of some." The lad's expression suddenly darkened.

Heinrich felt sick. "I ... I murdered no one, boy."

"Killed, then?" Tomas sneered.

Surprised, Heinrich looked at Wil and struggled for words. "Well, we'd a fight on the Villmar road when I was young, a little younger than Wil."

Tomas cursed.

"It was long before you were born, lad. I had no hand in your father's death, and I know nothing of it."

"*Ja?* Well, perhaps you killed Blasius's father instead."

Heinrich's face hardened. "'Twas a Gunnar who killed my own father."

"Enough!" cried Pieter. "We've business to tend to."

※

Within the hour, Tomas's plan was begun. The black-haired youth led Wil, a trembling Benedetto, Helmut, Otto, Rudolf, and Heinz quietly through the alleyways of Burgdorf to the large corrals kept safe within the city walls.

Meanwhile, Heinrich and Pieter crept to their assigned hiding places in the brush rimming the Galgenberg—the hanging hill. The hill sprouted from the valley like a wart on a witch's face, and atop it stood a wide-limbed leafy chestnut tree dotted with green nuts. Here the pair waited breathlessly, hoping Frieda was obediently keeping herself and Maria out of view with Paulus and Solomon.

In Burgdorf, Tomas gave orders from behind a hay barn. "Heinz, go now."

The elfish scamp scurried away and sneaked past the marshal's guards to let his nimble fingers release the ropes that held the gates of the corral. Benedetto was then ordered to his duties. The little minstrel had determined to redeem his cowardice in Domodossola and now strutted bravely toward the doorway of a nearby hall where some soldiers were enjoying their supper. With a deep breath, he began singing loudly and playing his lute with all the bravado his timid spirit could muster.

Distracted, groups of drunken men-at-arms wandered into the street and stared at the tiny man. Laughing, they began to leap about the street like so many mad fools. The men drew others, and soon the pilgrims' troubadour was crooning over the din of an entire barracks.

With the corral unlocked and most of the soldiers distracted, Tomas and the others flew to their tasks. Wil and Otto ran into a nearby barn and set it on fire with torches taken from a vacant shop. At the first sign of smoke, the stable master's guards predictably ran from their posts, and the moment they were gone, Heinz, Helmut, and Rudolf dashed from their cover to chase the wide-eyed herd toward the far end of a street where the city gate was still open. The three lads heaved stones and sticks, shouted, and flailed their arms as the horses thundered past the grasping hands of surprised sentries.

With smoke pouring from the barn, the town erupted in confusion. Pieter and Heinrich spotted black smoke rising from behind the town's walls, and the priest began to pray loudly. "O Lord, tell me we are not truly mad!"

Before long, flames began to leap from the barn to another and then to another. In less than a half hour, the folk of Burgdorf were in a desperate battle to save their city.

With a third of the buildings now burning, the streets quickly filled with smoke. Benedetto threw his lute over his shoulder and crawled through a confused mob. Squeezing between the crush of bodies, the tiny man was soon trapped in the midst of a crowd beginning to stampede.

Wil and Otto rejoined a nearly panicked Tomas, who had moved to the street corner near the jailhouse. The smoke had become so thick, however, that none could see anything. Choking, the lads clung to one another and squinted painfully. "M'bow's no good to me," cried Wil. "I can see nothing!"

"We needs get out!" shrieked Otto.

"But Blasius?"

The three peered through the eye-burning smoke at the jailhouse door. Thankfully, it was not on fire. It had been Tomas's plan to have Wil shoot the guards during the distraction and then find a way to release the prisoner. With no horses to follow, they imagined that they might then find a way out of the town and across open fields to the safety of the wood. But it was not to be.

The smoke was suffocating. Coughing and tearing, they retreated inside a shop, where they gasped for air. "Tomas, we needs get out! We've no way to release him."

"To the other plan then," wheezed the lad. "Otto, can we find the gate?"

The stout boy was on his knees sucking air through the sleeve of his tunic. Overhead, a burst of wind dropped burning thatch alongside them. "Follow me!"

Otto and his two companions pulled their hoods over their heads and charged down a street they hoped would lead them to the walls. The town was a maze, however, and at each turn none could be sure of their whereabouts. A burning roof collapsed nearby. With hearts pounding, the three pressed on.

At long last, Wil, Otto, and Tomas ran into a chute of screaming townsfolk funneling toward a gate. Pushing and shoving their way through, the trio emerged, gasping. They fell to the ground, sucking for air. "We must hurry on," coughed Wil. "Now!"

The lads struggled to their feet and made way for their camp. Wil turned his face back and groaned. Black smoke and flames filled the sky. *O God, forgive us for what we've done.*

Hoping they had not been seen, the fleeing raiders returned to their camp. Frieda ran to Wil and hugged him tearfully. "I saw the smoke ... I was so worried."

The young man's face was black with soot, and his clothes smelled of burnt thatch. "We failed," he mumbled sadly as he wrung his hands. "We could not find the jail. The fire was to draw attention, no more. Now we've caused many a death."

Frieda nodded sympathetically. She looked at the other lads, whose heads were drooped in remorse. "The summer's been dry and hot. The thatch is tinder."

"*Ja*. So we should have known," moaned Otto. He wrung his hands and stared at the sky.

Frieda looked at the lad carefully, then at the others. "Confess the error but not evil intention. All of you, please listen. Your hearts were good in this—"

"But our minds were not!" groused Tomas. "'Twas my plan, 'tis my blame." The young man took a deep breath. "We've not time to think on it now. I have another plan if you'll let me."

Wil nodded. "Yes, Tomas. None shall ever blame you for the fire. We all had a part in it. Now, we've no time for this. We've need of your other plan."

Relieved, Tomas stared at Wil for a moment, then spoke. "My master told me to never have one plan alone. He said the world would always undo your first, but it wouldn't expect a second."

"Your master?" quizzed Otto.

"Aye, the prince of the forest you saw."

Otto gulped. "Aye."

Wil whirled about. "Pieter and Father?"

"In their places," Tomas answered. "They are part of our second plan. I'd hoped to not need them."

"And the others?"

Frieda pointed to a clearing in the wood. "I saw them back

there. They were able to catch six horses by their halters, and they're trying to keep them quiet in the wood. They took rope off Paulus's sacks and made some sort of reins. I've not seen Benedetto, though."

Wil looked back at the town. "If they catch any of us, we'll hang. We must not fail again. Frieda, you've the torches ready?"

"*Ja.*"

"Good," interrupted Tomas.

Maria finally spoke. "'Tis nearly compline. What do you think will happen?"

Tomas answered, "I'd think they'd be too busy to hang him tonight. We'll wait a bit longer, then plan for the morrow to—"

"Look!" Frieda blurted. "Look there!"

In the darkening twilight, four torches lit the white robes of four marching Templars who were dragging their prisoner toward the Galgenberg. Tomas cursed. "Make ready, then!" he barked.

The six lads prepared themselves. In about a quarter hour they emerged from their cover on horseback. None of them had ridden much—peasants rarely owned horses. They had ridden a few plow horses or nags, but these were neither. These animals were the great chargers, the mighty warhorses of Christendom with huge shoulders and broad backs.

Jerking on their short rope reins, the would-be knights circled and reared in every direction. Were it not so grievous a moment, it would have been a comical thing to watch! Young Heinz, looking no bigger than a large fly on the back of a black giant, fell three times.

"Saddles would've helped!" cried Otto.

Somehow, Wil and Tomas calmed their cavalry and turned to the girls. "We've need of the torches now." Wil adjusted his bow and quiver, nervously felt for his dagger, and then reached for his torch.

Frieda handed it to her husband, then helped Maria lift more to the others. Finally, all stood ready for the signal. "I hope this plan works better than the last!" sniped Helmut.

On Galgenberg, Pieter and Heinrich crouched low. Considering the confusion in Burgdorf, they were astonished to see the column of Templars marching toward them. "Why tonight? Why the devil are they so fixed on hanging him tonight?" grumbled Pieter.

"Do you think the boys are ready?" whispered Heinrich.

"Oh, by the saints above, I surely hope it. I tell you, baker, my old heart is pounding hard. This plan is far-fetched to my way of thinking."

The Templars soon were close enough for Pieter and Heinrich to see the torch-lit outline of their faces. And as they came closer yet, the pair could hear their conversation plainly. The knights spoke mostly of their fury with the stable master. "On the morrow, I'll have his head on a pike. I swear it. All the horses gone! Armor and robes ruined, two brothers burned badly, and the mercenaries killing each other in the looting. By the Virgin, someone shall pay!"

Blasius was praying quietly. As Blasius was dragged beneath the limb of his gallows, Pieter could hear him muttering the Lord's Prayer and quoting from the psalms. The priest and the baker prepared to act.

"Prisoner," began the master, "thou art charged with desertion in battle, with defending heretics against the crusade of the Holy Church, with blasphemy, and with treason against the empire. Thou hast been tried this very day by the brethren and declared to be an anathema in the name of the Holy Father. Thou hast disgraced thy order and despoiled thy name. Hence, thou shalt not enter hell as 'Blasius,' but rather as a nameless, corrupted soul, stricken from the Lamb's Book of Life. Thy once-good name is thus stripped from thee as are all benefits and merits of thy former brotherhood with the Order of Knights Templar.

"So, in accordance with the Rule of our Grand Master, Odo de St. Amand, and under the authority of Pope Innocent, I sentence thee to hang by this tree until dead. May thy spirit languish in the Pit for days and nights without end, amen."

Blasius lifted his head proudly. "Hang me if you must,

but I gladly go to God with the name of my baptism, Alwin of Gunnar." He said no more.

With that, the Templars tied a thick rope around his neck and threw the other end over the limb. It was the signal for Pieter. "Hold fast, fools!" cried the old man as he emerged from his cover.

Turning with a start, the Templars wheeled about. "What devil is this?"

"Release him!" shouted Pieter. He raised his staff in the air, hoping the others could see his signal in the firelight.

At the lifting of the staff, Wil and his fellows braced themselves.

"Who are you?" roared the Templar.

"I am a priest in the service of Almighty God. I say release this innocent man or bear the sting of the heavenly host upon thee, each and every one!"

"Hoist him up!" bellowed the master. Three sets of strong hands immediately pulled on the rope and lifted the flailing Alwin off the ground. They wound the rope around the gallows' tie.

Pieter raised his staff again, crying, "No! Come, legions of heaven, come!"

Instead of Gabriel, it was Heinrich who burst from cover with a drawn sword and filled with fury. And, two bowshots away, the second raising of the staff signaled Wil's little cavalry to charge, screaming like flame-bearing hellions atop thundering mounts.

Startled and confused, the Templars whirled about, and Heinrich caught the master completely by surprise. He plunged his sword into the man's unarmored belly with a bellow as the others drew their blades. The baker rushed toward Alwin's rope and swung wildly at it. The edge of his sword nicked the rope, but it was not enough. The Templars charged the man and would have slain him on the spot had not Pieter leapt between them. "You'd not dare slay a priest!"

"Move off!" one cried.

The air was suddenly filled with the sound of hooves and shrieking voices. The knights spun about to see torches surging toward them out of the darkness. "You two, charge them!" cried one. "I'll take these." As his fellows rushed past, the soldier turned his fiery eyes at Pieter. "Move, I say!"

"Burn in hell!" answered Pieter.

At that moment three riderless chargers burst by the tree, distracting the Templar for just an instant. It was time enough, however, for Heinrich to lunge forward and drive his sword into the man's neck.

Another horse ran by, and a moment later a Templar came running out of the darkness toward Heinrich. The baker stumbled backward to the ground, and Pieter jammed his staff in front of the knight's feet. The soldier fell forward, but before Heinrich could slay him, another riderless horse thundered through the camp, knocking both Heinrich and Pieter aside.

Meanwhile, in these few brief moments, Alwin had become limp. His limbs twitched slightly, save an occasional desperate lurch. Seeing his plight, Heinrich scrambled to his feet and stumbled toward the dangling man. There were still two other Templars, however, and one had retreated to the tree, where he dodged a passing horse. In that moment, he caught a glimpse of the baker rearing back to cut the rope. He flew at the man.

In the darkness, Wil hung on to the neck of his steed with two hands. He had thrown away his torch and pointed his horse toward the tree, where he could plainly see Alwin's body in the torchlight. Closer he came, and still closer. His mind carried him to a childhood dream very much like this. He reached into his belt and drew his dagger. *Not a dream, but a vision!* With a victorious cry, he roared past the hanging man and sliced the rope in two.

Alwin dropped to the ground with a thud and lay crumpled in the dark as Wil fell from his rearing mount. The lad hit the ground hard, and with a groan of pain, he pulled himself up and ran toward the gallows as he reached for Emmanuel still hanging on his back.

Under the tree, Pieter had collapsed unconscious, and Heinrich was scrambling for his life. Out of the corner of his eye, the baker saw that Alwin was saved, but both Templars were now upon him.

Into the clearing charged four shrieking lads. None were armed; they had hoped their bluff might have chased off the knights. Startled, the two knights turned from the helpless Heinrich, and one snarled, "Ha! You'll taste steel tonight!" The words had barely left his lips when a whiz and a thud caught all by surprise. The Templar stood as though stunned, then reached a limp hand toward the arrow now piercing his lung.

Astonished, the other knight whirled toward the darkness from which another arrow flew. The man gagged and gurgled, clutching the wooden shaft that had impaled his throat. Staring blankly, he coughed once and then collapsed.

Otto ran to Alwin and screeched for someone to cut the cord. Heinrich stumbled forward, but Wil charged from the darkness with his dagger drawn and laid its edge quickly under the thick hemp. He sawed carefully away from Alwin's throat and severed the rope. He took the man's face in his hands and prayed for God's mercy. "Breathe, breathe, I say!"

Tomas flew alongside and pounded Alwin on the chest once, then twice, then a third time. "Breathe, y'dolt, breathe!"

Alwin stirred slightly, and the circle stared down at him hopefully. His eyes popped open and he arched his back, sucking air into his lungs. Then, midst the cheers of all, the man rolled weakly to his knees and wheezed great gulps of air.

"God be praised!" cried Heinrich.

"Wil!" shouted Helmut. "Come quick. It's Pieter!"

Leaving Tomas to care for Alwin, the others ran to the old man's side. He was barely breathing and still unconscious. "He's alive," said Heinrich grimly. Before he could say more, Otto screeched, "Look! More's coming!" The boy pointed to a column of torches winding its way quickly toward them.

"Oh, by the saints!" shouted Heinrich. "The provost is

sending a company this way! Hurry, we must carry Pieter to safety!"

Wil and Otto lifted Pieter by his shoulders and legs and hurried into the darkness as Heinrich rushed to Alwin's side. "Men are coming. We must move you to cover at once."

Tomas laid hold of one shoulder and Heinrich the other as they helped the struggling Alwin to his feet. Heinrich quickly studied the Galgenberg. He checked to make sure he had his sword and that nothing was left behind. "Steady him," he said to Tomas. The baker then snatched another sword from one of the Templars. "*Ach,* if only I had two hands!" He looked about another moment, then stared uneasily into the darkness. "Something seems amiss."

Chapter Twelve

FRIENDS FOUND, FRIENDS LOST

here's Benedetto?" asked Maria. "And where is Heinz?"

Panting with exertion, the pilgrims cowered in the dark forest under cover of night. They had fled the Galgenberg and now stared fearfully at the group of torches gathered under the silhouetted boughs of the distant tree. "Benedetto!" whispered Wil loudly. "Are you here? Heinz? Where are you?"

All remained quiet. Squatting, Heinrich shifted his weight and peered into the inky darkness. A red glow radiated over the walls of Burgdorf, and the air smelled of smoke. Clouds hid the stars. "Wil?"

"Aye, Father."

"How is Pieter?"

"Awake, but weary."

The man took a deep breath. "Where are the minstrel and Heinz?"

Tomas answered, "I sent Benedetto to distract the soldiers at the tavern. It was near the jail. I heard him singing before the fire was set, but that's the last I saw him."

"And I saw Heinz on the horse when we first began to gallop," added Otto. "I said to him, 'Hold on, Elfman!' He never answered and I lost him in the charge."

"We all fell off, save Wil," said Helmut.

"I fell at the end."

Heinrich turned his face back to the darkness. "He must be out there, then. I fear the worst for him."

Maria began to whimper.

Frieda comforted the girl with an embrace as Wil stood. "Then he'd be between here and the hill."

The others stood, ready to begin a search for their comrade. "Rudolf," ordered Wil, "stay with Maria, Pieter, and Alwin. The rest follow me."

"And what of Benedetto?" asked Heinrich.

"He is either making his way toward us, else he is still in the town. For now, we need to find Heinz."

Solomon suddenly emerged from the darkness, whining. He ran over to Pieter and lay down alongside him. "Ah, good boy," sighed Pieter weakly. "Good old fellow. Help them find Heinz."

The dog's ears cocked.

"*Ja,* boy. Help them find Heinz."

Solomon twisted his head, then closed his jaw. Then, as though he truly understood, he spun about and trotted past the pilgrims and into the night.

For the next hour, Wil, Frieda, Tomas, and the others carefully picked their way across the open land between themselves and the hanging tree. To their great relief, the town's provost and his men had begun their slow walk back to town. The pilgrims would be safe until daybreak.

The bells of a church began to ring matins prayers when Solomon barked three times.

"Over there!" urged Frieda.

The searchers stumbled toward Solomon's whines. In what light the moon pushed through the night's fleeting clouds, the group soon found itself bending over the panting dog and the still body of Heinz. Frieda laid her head on the young lad's chest. The circle fell quiet. The young woman pressed her ear close and listened. All waited breathlessly. Finally, she moaned, "I ... I fear he's dead."

Wil quickly laid his open hand on Heinz's neck. He felt no pulse, but he did feel sticky blood. "Oh, Heinz," he muttered. "Good, brave Heinz." He lifted the boy's limp body into his arms. "We must go back," he choked.

Maria had waited obediently by Pieter's side until she heard muffled voices approaching. She sprinted toward the others. "Did you find him?" she cried.

"Aye," grumbled Tomas. "We found him."

The girl spotted Wil. "You ... you are carrying him." Her voice trailed at the end. She knew.

"We've lost him," said Wil sadly.

Hearing that, both Pieter and Alwin groaned loudly. The old priest hauled himself to his feet and staggered toward the group as it entered the camp. Without a fire, the man could barely see. He groped forward until his hands found the little chap lying in Wil's arms. Pieter whimpered at the touch. "By the Virgin," he wept, "I loved this little fellow."

"He must have fallen from his horse," moaned Otto. He turned to Tomas. "You! You put him back on three times afore we even left! How did you think he'd be able to hang on? You killed him!" Otto flew at Tomas, and the two crashed to the ground. Fists flew and curses filled the air until Wil and Helmut pulled them apart.

"I didn't kill him," Tomas sputtered. "He fell off his horse." The lad's tone belied a hint of guilt that few missed.

"Enough!" ordered Wil. "Otto, Tomas did not kill him. We all could have told Heinz to stay. And we all know he wouldn't have. Now listen. We must find Benedetto, and we need to put distance between us and this place as fast as we can!"

With no more to say, the pilgrims gathered themselves together. Helping hands steadied Pieter and Alwin, while Wil laid Heinz's body on the ground. "We'll bury him at first light," he murmured sadly.

Maria answered, "He should not be buried alone. You said we'll soon come to the graves of our friends who died in the flood. We should take him there."

"Perhaps we can," answered Pieter. "At daybreak we'll speak of it."

Otto knelt down alongside his friend's body and stared blankly into the boy's starlit face. Pieter leaned on his staff sadly. "'O Lord, how long?' How long must we endure this world of sorrows? How can we bear the mysteries of Your ways?" A weary anger rose in the man's belly and he could say no more. Looking about his band, his mind recalled countless memories of the boy. He could see Heinz's squinty eyes pinched shut in a good laugh, and he could hear him cheer his comrades when hope seemed lost. The man sighed. "I never knew where he joined us on crusade, Otto. He was as harmless a lad as ever was born into this miserable world."

"He was happy," offered Otto. "I've known none so happy as he and Karl."

"Not so happy now," murmured Tomas.

"Now happier than ever," answered Maria kindly.

The clouds fell off the moon, and wide shafts of silver light filtered softly through the leafy black canopy of silhouetted treetops. "Moonlight is mercy," whispered Heinrich.

Pieter gazed about the shadowed wood as the company gathered close. His beloved ones fully encircled him, and the old monk-priest touched them one by one. His hand was cold to the pilgrims, but reassuring. "Are you feeling ashamed?"

The group was silent.

The old man stood quietly in the middle of the group. He turned his eyes from face to face. "Do you weep for the innocents lost in Burgdorf?"

All heads nodded.

"As do I," answered Pieter.

Otto blurted, "We were fools. We ne'er gave a proper thought to the fire."

"Aye," came another voice.

The old man laid a finger on his chin. "Probably so, lads. But hear me. Confess to God your guilt, leave shame at the foot of the cross, and lift your chins. We are imperfect vessels in a broken world. Sadness is good to bear, but never shame."

"But people died for my foolish plan!" groaned Tomas.

Pieter reached a hand toward Tomas's hard shoulder. "Tomas, in this world I fear all things have a cost. Best to trust God for the price. Your plan saved Alwin."

The black-haired boy could not answer. Overcome by

the kind words, he stared at his feet.

Heinrich stepped from his place. "I speak for all when I say we are grateful for your help. None of us had a better way. Well done, lad. You belong with us." He offered his hand to the lad.

Tomas lifted his face. "I ... I ..." The young man faltered for words.

Wil hesitated, then stepped forward warily. "Tomas, we were once friends. I ... I forgive you for the past and hope you will forgive me as well. I'd like to call you 'friend' again."

The offer of reconciliation was sudden and unexpected. The hatred Tomas had once relished now felt oddly impotent, and an urge to weep came over him.

Pieter's heart soared. He was filled with hope. He knew that repentance follows forgiveness—it is the very essence of redemption—and he imagined the beginning of a new life for the lad. Sensing Tomas's discomfort, however, the wise old priest diverted the group's attention. He bent slowly to his knees and laid a hand on Heinz's head. "How easy to forget the good promises of God." He lifted his face in prayer. "O Giver of life and Companion in death, let the angels delight in the company of our little brother Heinz. Let him dance gladly in Thy presence; prepare his table for the feast we shall all share. And until that glorious day, forget not us, Thy suffering children."

ॐ

That same night, Frieda and Maria washed Heinz's body with rags dipped in water poured from the pilgrims' flasks. The others were gathered close together, grieving Heinz, fearing for the absent Benedetto, and still quietly preoccupied with their guilt over the fire. Pieter gave them comfort over Heinz, more counsel for their guilt, and finally confidence in the minstrel's sure return. Then, as if on cue, Solomon's ears suddenly cocked and he dashed ahead. For a long while no sound was heard as the pilgrims stared into the silvered woodland. Finally, the dog and a small shadow could be seen, and the group rose, hopeful. In moments, the soot-covered, shaken minstrel stumbled from darkness and fell into their arms. "*Laude a Dio!* Praises to God!" cried Benedetto.

Maria sprinted toward the little man with outstretched arms. "Oh, you are safe! You are safe!"

"*Si*, little maiden. Oh, I am very safe now." The happy man drank heartily from a flask of wine and recounted his adventure. But with the news of Heinz, the poor fellow choked and turned away.

With all now accounted for, Wil prepared his company to leave. Heinz was wrapped tightly in blankets and tied carefully atop Paulus's back. "In the morning the roadways will be searched carefully. Alwin is in great danger, as are we all. We must leave at once," instructed Wil.

The quiet company hurried away. They traveled through the night quietly, most lamenting the loss of life and property they had inflicted on Burgdorf. The air was cool and the highway was empty, save two patrols that the pilgrims avoided by dodging for cover along the shoulder.

"As I recall," said a weary Pieter at daybreak, "Olten is about six leagues northeast of Burgdorf. Methinks we've traveled about two leagues by now."

Tired, Wil ordered everyone to the cover of a ridge just beyond the road. "We need to rest."

The fugitives collapsed in a grassy field and nibbled wearily on salted pork and cheese. They filled their flasks from a nearby spring but set no fire. Forlorn, they murmured among themselves until Otto finally asked, "And what of Heinz?"

Wil looked about at the wide green valley surrounding them. Maria stood. "No, Wil," she stated firmly. "The others are by the river. We must take him there."

"The day may get hot," grumbled Helmut.

Pieter took a long draught of beer. He looked to the sky and shook his head. "Clouds coming from the east. We'll have some rain for sure." He turned to Wil. "He would have wanted to be buried with the others. I am certain of it. We've about three leagues to go ... at this rate, perhaps a day's journey. Shall we try?"

Wil looked at the imploring eyes of his sister and at Pieter, then up at the clouding sky. "I'd rather you be riding Paulus than he, and we needs walk off the road. It'll slow us."

"First, I'd rather put the boy to proper rest than ride. Next, I know these parts. We can parallel the highway with ease." The priest was firm.

"Fine, as you wish. But we needs hurry. If we don't find the graves by nightfall, we'll bury him where we must."

It was a gray twilight when the pilgrims finally came upon the quiet shoreline of the Aare River. Maria quickly spotted the mill near the broken dam and the large rock that marked the place where the crusaders had been buried the summer past. The company hurried to the spot and found the earth still mounded beneath the river stones used to cover the shallow graves. Their wooden crosses had disappeared, and weeds had overgrown the site, but to these former crusaders, the place was yet hallowed.

Large tears fell from Frieda's eyes as she stood at the head of her brother's grave. "Oh, dear Manfred," she sighed, "I've missed you so." She pulled the weeds from the stones and cleaned away the bramble. "In the morning I shall bring you fresh flowers," she whispered. Humming lightly, she sat down alongside the mound. "You know, Manfred, I'm married now. I married Wil! I think you would have liked that." A large lump filled her throat, and she could say no more. She closed her eyes and groaned midst visions of the horrid flood that had taken so many.

In the meanwhile, the graves of the others were cleaned, including those of Albert, Jost, and Otto's old friend, Lukas. The broad-faced lad let the tears fall as he remembered the fateful storm. "I'll not ever forget the sound of the water," he muttered.

Tomas and Wil worked with Rudolf to dig Heinz's grave as Helmut gathered large smooth river stones. When the hole was ready, Wil summoned the others.

"I shall miss you, Elfman," choked Otto.

"We shall all miss you," added Pieter. "You tried to save a man you never knew. Would the earth be filled with the likes of you in times to come." The priest then prayed a quiet prayer and blessed the company. He held the weeping Maria in his arms and kissed her lightly on the cheek as Wil and Otto lowered the shrouded body into the ground.

"Papa Pieter, will you leave us, too?" asked Maria.

The old man looked deeply into the little girl's frightened face. "Ah, my dear. *Ja*, I shall someday leave this earth, per-haps one day soon. But I'll ne'er leave you alone. Fear for naught, my angel, for you are loved by many."

Each traveler set about the task of covering Heinz's remains, first with soft earth and then with stones. Once finished, the company stared quietly at the rock-mounded grave as Maria and Frieda fixed a neatly fashioned wooden cross at its head. Then, each one bade the brave little fellow farewell in his or her own way and drifted off to sleep under a starless sky.

ঔ

Considering the next day's rain and the need to stay hidden from the dangers of highway patrols, it was a wonder that the forlorn pilgrims arrived at Olten as quickly as they did. But it was that evening just outside the gates that Alwin bade the brave pilgrims farewell.

"No, Father Pieter. I am a danger to you all. You have saved me and I am fast healed. The Templars will never stop hunting me, and as long as I am with you, you will be hunted as well."

Heinrich stepped forward. "You must not travel alone. You'll have no hope at all. And you're not yet well. I've seen your steps fail a few times."

Alwin set his jaw firmly. "I'll not have your deaths on my conscience."

Pieter spat. "So, monk, 'tis all for you, then."

The knight looked surprised.

"Aye, you heard me. You'd deny us the defense of your sword and the skill of your eye so that your conscience might not be pricked! Go then! The self-serving have no place with us."

Astonished, Alwin gaped at the old man and then at the pilgrims gathered about. "I ... I ..."

"We hoped you'd protect us, *Herr* Alwin," said Maria gently.

"But ... but, my dear sister, I bring you danger, and—"

"You bring us no more danger than what we've been hardened to," barked Pieter. "Look at these faces. They have been guided through hardships that would make your own heart tremble. Then God sends them a seasoned knight who now wants to run off to protect his own conscience. I, sir knight, am fairly disappointed."

Alwin looked at Heinrich. The baker nodded. "We need you, friend." He walked to Paulus and retrieved the Templar sword he had taken. He handed it to Alwin. "We need your honor."

The knight took the sword and cast his eyes about the circle of faces imploring him to stay. He took a deep breath. "Well, for now, then."

The pilgrims cheered, and Pieter winked at the smiling Maria. Their knight would stay!

The group made its way through the darkness to the gates of Olten, where Wil hesitated. He cocked his head toward Pieter and shrugged. "What do you think?" The young man was nervous about the reception they might receive at the hand of Lord Bernard. After all, Pieter's earlier efforts at dentistry may or may not have provided the promised cure!

Pieter climbed down from his seat with determination. "Methinks we've a duty to Friederich and Jon. We left them behind in hopes of seeing them again. Knock and let us take what's coming."

Wil rapped loudly on the gate.

"'Tis past curfew. Begone!" grumbled a guard through the oak.

"Open the cursed door, y'fool!" answered Pieter.

The door flew open, and a long-nosed soldier stormed toward the company with his lance leveled and his torch raised. "Who dares call me 'fool'?"

Pieter ground his staff into the ground. "I do."

The soldier wheeled about. "You!" He tilted his smoky torch close to Pieter's face. "You, the old priest from the north! Ha! I remember you." He cast an eye at Heinrich, then stepped closer, raising his lance. "And I've seen you here before as well."

"*Ja.* Some months past. I was looking for the child crusaders."

"Seems y've enough light to know us by. Now let us in," growled Pieter. "We've business with Lord Bernard."

Wil shifted uneasily. He leaned toward Frieda. "Pray the lord's tooth is fixed."

"What business 'ave you?" quizzed the soldier. "Lord Bernard is in Bern."

Wil released his breath, relieved. "And how's his tooth?"

"The old man here took the pain away. 'Tis how I know his face. Our priest thinks it was witchcraft."

Pieter was in no mood for this. "Witchcraft! By the saints, I ought—"

"And what of the two we left here? They belong with us," interrupted Wil.

"The little crusaders? They came back hurt after you left. We helped them."

"Aye!" answered Wil impatiently. "And?"

The man's face hardened. "We had plague in October past. I lost m'wife and my two *kinder.* Most say you crusaders brought it. One of yer boys perished in it. The other is doing penance."

"Which?" Wil blurted.

"Which what?"

"Which of them died!"

"The older one. He had a broken leg."

"Jon!" groaned Frieda.

Heinrich was bristling. "And what of the lad doing penance?"

"What of him?"

"Why the penance?"

"The priest says the waif's to purge the sins of you all. Lord Bernard and his daughter objected, but they dared not oppose the Holy Church in this." The soldier shifted on his feet uncomfortably. "Some say you disgraced good Christians, what with yer losing faith and thieving. Some say y'cast spells and ate infants. You went to crusade in Christ's name but defiled our Lord and the Holy Virgin Mother with yer weak ways. Now we all suffer for it."

Despite his rising anger, Pieter had been oddly quiet. He stepped forward with his staff gripped by fingers whitening with rage. Barely controlling himself, he said, "I see. And what say you?"

The man shrugged. "I am unsure in this. I've a nephew who left on crusade last summer. He's a good boy but has not yet returned. Methinks him not one to eat someone's baby. And m'sister swears these stories are lies."

Pieter relaxed his grip. "And what of Dorothea?"

"What of her?"

"What says she of the crusaders?"

The guard nodded. "She makes sure yer little penitent is well fed and clothed. She finds ways to lighten his penance. I've heard her reprimand the priest on more than one occasion."

Relieved, Pieter released a deep breath. "I should like to speak with her."

"*Ja.* Perhaps you may. She's dining on a late supper, no doubt, or ..." he leaned close to Pieter and whispered something the rest could not hear.

Pieter's brows raised and he cast a glance at Alwin. "*Ja?*"

The guard nodded. "But tell no one. Now, seems all is in order here. If you've money, you can follow me to the lord's inn."

Worried that the knights at Burgdorf would be hunting the killers of the Templars, Heinrich had been anxious. It would be good for them to get off the roadway. He looked nervously at the sword riding on Alwin's hip. *Should ne'er have kept it!* he thought. *What a fool I am.*

The pilgrims quietly walked through Olten's dark streets and alleys until they were introduced to Lord Bernard's innkeeper at the doorway of a comfortable two-story building. The house was dimly lit within by oil lanterns and a few thick candles. The innkeeper bade them enter as he greeted the weary pilgrims. "Good evening," he murmured with a bow.

Wil stepped forward. "We've need of shelter. We served your master well some months prior, and we hoped to meet him again."

"He's in Bern."

"Aye, sir."

"We've a few drunken guests, but I've room for some of you. For the lot it would cost you four pennies, and it buys you fresh bread and beer in the morning. The beast needs go to the stable along with four others."

Heinrich laughed and pointed to Otto. "He's a good one for the stable!" He then whispered in the innkeeper's ear, and the man nodded. "You, boy," he said as he pointed to Wil. "You and your woman follow me. I've a room in the attic. 'Tis a bit warm on summer nights, but it has a good straw mattress."

Blushing, Frieda lowered her head and hurried past the others to join Wil and the innkeeper climbing a flight of curling stairs.

"Sleep well!" roared Otto. The pilgrims howled.

In a few moments, the innkeeper returned to escort some others to a small closet whose floor was covered with a thick mound of fresh hay. "We've no mattress but soft hay. But he who sleeps here sleeps well."

Pieter was relieved. His bones ached from walking through the rain. He was thankful it was summer, to be sure, but he was nearly ecstatic to sleep under a good roof and atop a soft floor.

"Now, who shall sleep with the beast?" chuckled the innkeeper.

The children looked at one another warily.

"Heinrich, you must guard the provisions," Pieter finally blurted with a wide grin.

"*Ja*, seems right enough," he grumbled. He shuffled toward the door midst the guffaws of Otto.

Alwin followed. "I'm well again, well enough to sleep with a beast, a miserable baker, and a stable full of *Scheisse*!"

The pilgrims roared.

"Well, who joins us?" sighed Heinrich. The words had barely left his lips when the man's eye fell on Tomas. "You're one of us, lad. You ought to come too."

Surprised at the dubious invitation, Tomas brightened.

Being denied the inn was less important than belonging. "*Ja*. I'll come."

Heinrich smiled. "Good. Then if it's Weyer men for the stable, Otto, you're the other!"

Muttering under his breath, Otto followed the others to the stable that stood to one side of the inn. Unfortunately, the stable was crowded with two heavy-wheeled wagons and many horses. Grumbling, the guests clutched hands full of what clean straw they could find and piled it along one wall. "The straw is wet and packs hard! A pox on the others," groused Otto.

A shrill voice startled the four. "*Mon Dieux!*"

"Eh?" Heinrich spun about.

Alwin grabbed his sword. "*Qui venir!*"

A trembling old man stared wide eyed at the four pilgrims now standing in a row before him. "*Non, non! Je m'appelle Michel! Je ...*"

"We do not speak your tongue!" snapped Heinrich. He stepped forward with his sword drawn.

"*Non, non!* I ... I am *voyageur*. I mean no ... no evil."

Alwin stepped close to the man and held a lantern by his face. The Frenchman looked down at the Templar sword now pointed at his belly and nearly swooned. Something about the man's sudden and inexplicable terror caught Alwin's attention. "Cathar?" he asked.

The old man closed his eyes and trembled. Alwin lowered his sword and laid a hand on the man's shoulder. "*Non* Templar," he said kindly as he pointed to himself.

Michel's eyes opened in relief, and the pilgrims thought he might burst into tears. "*Ah, mon Dieux!*"

"Sheath your sword, Heinrich," said Alwin as he set his own aside. "He's a Cathar."

"Cathar?" Heinrich was confused. "I thought he was French."

"The Cathari are heretics from the region of Provence and Languedoc. He would not think himself a Frenchman at all, and his language is not quite the same. I don't know it very well."

Alwin turned to Michel and studied his clothing, then

smiled at the egg clutched within one closed hand. *"Credente?"*

The man hung his head and nodded.

Alwin smiled. *"Depuis Toulouse?"*

"Non, Avignonet."

The knight walked into the dark corners of the stable and chased away a clucking hen. He retrieved two eggs and handed them to the old fellow with a smile. At first, the man looked ashamed, but when he saw the twinkle in Alwin's eyes, he grinned. Placing the eggs into his pockets, the Cathar cast a fleeting look at his horses and wagons, then hurried away.

Chuckling, Alwin set the sword aside and then sat with his confused friends. "Gather close."

The four huddled atop the straw in the yellow light of a smoky lantern. Alwin stroked his beard and stared into the flame as he collected his thoughts. Heinrich thought the knight to have aged considerably since he had last seen him ride away from Stedingerland. That was six years prior, in the time when the monk had worn white robes and was known by another name. The baker remembered him as a sinewy young blond with the heart of a lion and the spirit of a saint. Still handsome and ever disposed toward compassion, Alwin had changed nonetheless. His hair and beard were now longer than the Templars allowed, and his dark eyes belied a deep sorrow. The man had become seasoned by a world of troubles, and the baker easily recognized the telltale marks of suffering. Heinrich waited quietly.

"I should tell you my story," began Alwin. He settled comfortably against a stout post. "I was proud to serve the order," he said slowly. "I tried to serve my Lord with both sword and alms to the very limits of my strength. I was obedient to my masters in the preceptories, kept to my prayers, my reading of the Holy Scriptures, my endless fasts, and to the service of the Church. I honored my vow of chastity and only sought to offer kindness to the helpless and sharp steel to evil.

"Yet, as God is my witness, I sit before you as a man confused."

A voice distracted the group. It was Pieter. "Ah, I've come with news. Dorothea ... the lord's daughter ... has been told of our presence and bids us come to first meal before prime. She thinks it best we gather *before* the bells."

Slightly annoyed at the interruption, the four grumbled a bit. "Why before the bells?"

Pieter shrugged. "I've no idea."

"Sir Alwin is telling us his story," said Otto.

"His story?" Pieter set himself atop a mound of hay and called Solomon to his side. "Your pardon, Alwin. Please, continue."

The knight began again. "I kept the rules of my order and the rules of the Church, but I fear I violated the law of love."

"Order and love are not always friends," muttered Pieter.

The others stared at him.

"Ah, pardon, Alwin. Please, go on."

"As I was saying, I served the order well and our Lord poorly."

Pieter spat.

"Heinrich, when I left you in Stedingerland, I delivered the taxes to the preceptory in Cologne, where I remained until our Grand Master, William de Chartres, ordered a contingent of knights to England. I was sent as an escort along with the seneschal and three grand preceptors to the London Temple, where we met the horrid King John.

"I remained in London for a year or so. It was a terrible time. The king is surrounded by fools, save one ... a man named Sir William Marshal—a Christian knight of courtesy and honor for whom I have only respect. But I found the realm odd. It is filled with a great sense of liberty amongst the nobles, and even the middling freemen speak incessantly of their ancient rights. It seems they've come upon another way, yet their king is as ruthless a tyrant and as greedy a thief as I've e'er seen ... save, perhaps, the pope."

"Well said! He—"

Once again all eyes turned toward the priest, who sighed. "Pardon, again, Alwin. Please, say more."

"*Ja.* It was near Pentecost when I was ordered to France

along with a small company of Templar knights and lesser brethren. We numbered about twenty-eight when we gathered in Paris. Our orders were to protect a papal legate soon to be sent to counsel an army arrayed against a growing heresy in the south of France.

"We were told that the heretics teach that two powers control all things: Jehovah, the benevolent Lord of light, rules the realm of the spirit; while the equally empowered lord of the material world, Lucifer, rules things temporal, including the flesh in which men's spirits are imprisoned. They preach that Christ was spirit only; He had no physical, earthly body, so our Holy Mother had no pain in childbirth. He was sent by Jehovah so that men might be liberated from all things temporal.

"They deny the sacraments, the Holy Trinity, the resurrection, prayer, and the Holy Church. They are forbidden to eat eggs or meat of any kind. To them sexual union is the greatest sin, for it perpetuates the world of the flesh by causing birth. They have their own bishops and deacons, and they lay hands on one another to pass on spiritual power. Their elite live plain lives, utterly committed to the laws of their creed. They are called the *perfecti*. The followers are called the *credentes*. I suppose they do their best, but they are weaker men who hope to enter a higher state on their deathbeds."

Pieter rose angrily. "Bondage mongers! They abuse the fools that follow them. They are no better than the Church they oppose!"

"Are you finished?" Heinrich groused.

Pieter grumbled, then sat down once more. "Aye. Pardon, Alwin. Please, go on."

Alwin walked toward the provisions piled near Paulus and withdrew the Templar sword. "Father Pieter, it is teaching such as yours that defeats the snares of heretics, not this." He drove the sword into the earth at the center of the circle. Sitting, he continued. "The pope insisted that King Philip of France destroy the Cathari and eliminate their creed by violence. The king, however, was more concerned with the English. Unfortunately, a papal legate, one

Pierre de Castelnau, was murdered in Provence. We were then ordered to prepare a holy war against the heretics, that 'sinister race of Languedoc,' and soon the pope issued his bull that granted all knights crusader status. This meant that in death our souls would fly to heaven and that in life we'd be offered the lands of the slain heretics. So you might imagine how quickly the army filled with landless knights feigning piety!

"I was told we numbered nearly fifty thousand men-at-arms. We followed the Rhône toward Provence, where we joined a papal legate named Arnaud-Amaury. He was to act as the spiritual adviser to the crusade and was later elected archbishop of the conquered territory.

"We learned that even the local Catholic lords were preparing to resist us. Our army ransacked countless villages on our way to Béziers, then destroyed a pathetic sortie sent from that woeful town. It was there that my faith was crushed. We seized the town with ease, of course, but then I hid in a dark corner as our army slew nearly twenty thousand men, women, and children—Cathar and Catholic alike. In the middle of the slaughter, my preceptor challenged the papal legate. 'We ought spare the Catholics!' he cried. To which Arnaud-Amaury replied, 'Kill them all; God will find His own!'" Alwin shuddered and fell silent.

The listeners shifted uneasily, looking at one another with troubled faces. Alwin proceeded to tell more of the unspeakable cruelties inflicted upon the terrified citizens of Béziers in such descriptive language as might give nightmares to the most hardened of hearts. He went on to speak of other battles: the siege of Carcassonne and the death of thousands to disease, hunger, and thirst; the mutilation of prisoners in Bram; and of stake burnings in Minerve and Lavour.

"Then Montfort ordered us to attack small fortresses and towns all around Toulouse. I'd had enough. It made me vomit to think of what we were doing in the name of God. I wanted to slay the pope! I could barely pray, I ate during fasts, and I refused to read the psalms at chapter. No, the confusion of it was more than I could bear.

"Then, about four months ago, I was sent with two brethren and a company of German knights to a small village near Albi. We were to demand the lord release all known Cathari to our custody for burning. When we arrived—and we numbered about two score—we were met with a pitiful group of armed Catholic farmers wishing to defend their neighbors and their own homes. I was astonished. In their midst was a brave priest. I remember his final words. 'The conscience is reached by love!' he cried. I suppose he would have said more, but an arrow was shot through his head, and we charged the brave defenders.

"As for me, I lowered my sword in tears and could not swing it at any of the poor wretches. Instead, when I saw a brother Templar dismount and run toward a fleeing old farmer, I filled with rage and charged at him on my stallion. I can still see the astonishment on his face as I cried out and trampled him to death. I then turned and slew a French knight, then a German. Confused, others reined their horses and stared at me. My preceptor stood in his stirrups in utter disbelief. It was in that moment that I tore my robe away and cast it down.

"'Brother Blasius!' he cried. I said nothing but wheeled my mount hard around and fled. With no money and nothing to eat, I begged my way slowly east over the weeks that followed. Finally, I came upon a band of knights in Sion who were recently hired by a lord in the service of Otto. With no other choices, I fought with them until the day you found me."

Alwin's eyes were swollen, and he looked away from his companions in shame. He walked over to the provisions to draw a long drink of ale. Heinrich stood and followed him, then laid a kindly hand on his shoulder. "My friend, we are never too far gone for grace to find us, nor too close for us to need it. Do not be so proud as to carry shame. There is another way."

Alwin turned. "Then you must teach me, old friend, for I am lost."

Chapter Thirteen

TROUBLE IN OLTEN

rieda and Wil descended from their room before the bells of prime rang over Olten. Smiling, the pair leaned into one another as lovers do, and despite the catcalls of their teasing fellows, they kissed one last time before the day's beginning.

"We're to meet with Lady Dorothea!" exclaimed Maria. Her cheeks were flushed with excitement. "She was so pretty."

"And I am sure she'll remember you," said Frieda.

"Hurry, then," called Heinrich from the door. "We're to be there before the bells."

The company walked briskly through Olten's waking streets. They were narrow and cramped by tight rows of one- and two-story shops and dwellings. Shutters were opened over window boxes of early summer flowers. The dirt streets were heavier with manure than what was common, but the ruts that Pieter remembered had been filled.

The eleven pilgrims followed the winding streets according to instructions offered by the innkeeper. They turned at the cutler's guild and hurried on, passing the town fishpond and the lush common gardens surrounding it. Finally, they rounded one last corner and approached the three-storied timber-and-mortar home of Lord Bernard.

Two guards gave them entrance, and they were quickly ushered by a servant to the lord's firelit hall, where

Dorothea rose to meet them. "Ah, *wunderbar!* It is so wonderful to see you again!" The graceful fair-haired woman brushed past her attendant and took each by the hand in turn. "Maria! Yes, I remember you. Your friend Friederich talks of you all the time ... he talks of all of you!"

Pieter stepped forward with a wide one-tooth grin.

"And Father Pieter! You rascal! The priest says you are a sorcerer, you know. He says no mere man could fix a tooth as you did." She kissed him lightly on the cheek.

Embarrassed, Pieter blushed like a schoolboy, then introduced Alwin as a landless knight and old friend of Heinrich.

The woman looked at him and admired his handsome form. Her eyes fell to his vacant hip. "A knight with no sword?"

Alwin's hand flew to his side. "Well ... I left it in the stable, m'lady. I ... I thought it not proper to bring it to your house."

Dorothea smiled. "I see. Well, now, all of you, welcome. Please, be seated at my table. The ushers shall take you to your seats. I am sorry for the early rising, but I'm to begin a journey to St. Gall before terce."

Pieter and Wil stepped past several hounds and were positioned on either side of the lady, who sat at the end of her trestle table. From there, the pilgrims were placed in order of acquaintance, leaving Alwin and the minstrel on opposite sides at the far end. With all things proper, Pieter was asked to say a blessing and Benedetto to sing a song. Then, at long last, the lord's baker delivered a silver tray heavy with wheat loaves and pretzels. To this, the cook added two trays of cheese and a clay bowl of cherry preserves. A wooden goblet was set by each guest and filled with red wine.

Summer air wafted through the damp hall, and the first hint of the day's light peeked through the shutters. "My regards to your baker, my lady," offered Heinrich. "The bake is nearly perfect."

"Nearly?" quizzed Dorothea.

"Well ..."

"A poor choice of words from a simple man!" quipped Wil

with a laugh. "I think the whole table is quite perfect indeed!"

The guests clapped. Dorothea then motioned for another servant to come to her side, and when he did, she whispered in his ear. The man scurried away, and the diners continued their meal with little more conversation until Pieter could wait no longer. "My dear sister," he said, "might we see our Friederich this morning?"

Dorothea nodded and swallowed a portion of bread. She slowly took a draught of wine, then answered. "Yes, of course. The priest was told that the archbishop's emissary demanded the boy for a penance in Mainz." Her eyes twinkled. "He should be here soon."

Pieter raised his brows.

Dorothea laughed softly. "I've learned from you! First, though, I have gifts." She clapped her hands, and to everyone's wonder, a group of servants bearing armloads of clothing scurried toward the children. Dorothea rose with a smile as big as an autumn sunset. "The innkeeper told me you were all dressed in black! He said you look like novices and nuns. So my chamberlain demanded the clothier open his shop at matins, and we've fresh, well-loomed garments for you." She turned toward Heinrich, Pieter, Benedetto, and Alwin. "It is our thought to serve the young ones as I have little to offer the three of you." Her glance lingered playfully on Alwin. "But I do have something for you, sir knight."

A servant hurried over to Alwin and presented him with boots, heavy-spun leggings, a long brown tunic, a padded leather vest, and a sleeveless green robe. The man was speechless. "These were my husband's. I am a widow," Dorothea said calmly.

Alwin received the gifts with a humble bow. "With thanks, m'lady. God's blessings."

Happy hands reached for new leggings and tunics, overgowns, and scarves. Dorothea motioned for her seamstresses to descend upon the group with needles and thread to adjust gown lengths and such, and before long, the pilgrims looked less like pilgrims and more like free wayfarers.

Maria twirled about in her new hooded overgown. It was a deep and rich forest green, linen weave—perfect for summertime. It was belted with a heavy braided cord and fit her wonderfully well. Frieda was simply stunning in a gown similar to Maria's, only paneled in cherry red and mustard gold.

Wil proudly displayed his own clothing for his new bride. He and his fellows had been given tightly woven brown linen leggings, and their tunics were knee length like those of freemen of means. They were hooded and made of finespun English wool—and dyed the color of baked rye. Each was given a different belt: Wil's was braided leather, Tomas's a rather dashing red sash, Otto's a wide leather belt with a brass buckle, Helmut's a black cord, and Rudolf's a green sash.

The travelers looked at one another in the early day's light and clapped. Looking like free persons, they suddenly felt like free persons. Tomas lifted his head proudly and thanked Dorothea with an eloquence that raised the brows of all. Each, in turn, bent a knee before the kind lady and kissed her hand.

"Now, my dear guests, would I be permitted to give your former garments to the poor?"

"Ja!" answered a chorus of happy voices.

At that moment, as if on cue, the door to the hall burst open, and young Friederich rushed toward his fellows with a happy cry. "Oh, Pieter! Wil! Frieda! All of you!"

Immediately overcome with tears, Pieter rose on wobbly legs and stumbled toward his lost lamb. The two embraced with halting sobs as the others crowded close. The reunion was joyous. Benedetto leapt upon the table and sang loudly as the boy greeted one old friend and then another.

At last, Wil asked that which all needed to know. "Tell us, Friederich. Tell us more of Jon."

The hall fell quiet. "It was some sort of pox, methinks. After St. Michael's, many in the town were sick. Most blamed us. We were both beaten, though Lord Bernard sent his guards to stop it. The priest said we ought to be ashamed for our failure, that God would punish the town for helping 'faithless fools' like us. He told the lord that we'd need to work a great penance for all the town, else everyone would die. He made us walk naked in the streets each day at terce to show our shame. And Jon's leg was not healed well, so it hurt him. I tied a splint as best I could, but it was growing crooked.

"Then he made us clean the latrines day and night. My wrist was weak, and I had trouble with the shovel, so I was beaten for it. We were given little to eat and were not allowed to speak. There were other things, too, but I cannot mention them." The bony eight-year-old hung his head.

Heinrich and Pieter were nearly bursting with rage. They turned hard eyes on Dorothea, who shifted in her seat with her eyes downcast in anguish. "It … it was the Church's business. I did what I could to help them both."

"*Ja*, she did," said Friederich. "She was scolded often, but she hid bread about the town and sent her servants to tell us where. I heard her arguing with the priest, and she once threw over the chalice!"

"And Jon?"

"His face broke into red marks, and he was sweating day and night. Then he began a terrible cough. Blood came out his nose."

"And the doctor?" queried Wil.

"The priest said it wasn't allowed. He said Jon was paying his debt to God."

The table shook with the pounding fists of the outraged pilgrims.

"Where is this priest?" roared Heinrich with a drawn sword.

"No!" exclaimed Dorothea. "I'll not have this at my table!"

An usher suddenly rushed into the hall and flew to Dorothea's side. He was visibly frightened and whispered awkwardly into the lady's ear. Dorothea paled, then looked about the hall.

"Quickly!" ordered Dorothea. "All of you to the cellars."

"What is it, m'lady?" asked Pieter.

"Soldiers are at our gates. They're demanding the right to search." Dorothea's face was drawn and her body stiff.

"What do they want?" asked Heinrich.

The messenger answered. "Two Templar knights are with them along with some brown shirts. They claim four of their own were murdered, and a refugee is about. They've some thought for youths dressed in black, but they suspect Cathari as well." The man looked sideways at Dorothea and licked his dry lips. "M'lady?"

"Father Pieter, you must all do as I say at once. We will hide you in the cellars until—"

"Bar their entrance!" cried Wil. He picked up his bow and set a hand on the hilt of his new dagger. "We'll fight with you!"

"Fool boy!" growled the servant. "They've two score horsemen and footmen, archers as well. Our garrison is a score at best. The rest of our soldiers are with Lord Bernard."

Heinrich's mind was racing. "Lady Dorothea, the innkeep has seen us, and you've servants as well. They'll be sure to search your house."

A guard ran into the room and whispered into Dorothea's ear. Pale, the woman answered, "*Ja.* So it may be. You all have been seen together, but my servants and the innkeep are loyal to the death." She turned to her servant. "Tell the gatekeepers to hold fast until I come. Tell the Templars they must ask my permission directly."

"Hold fast?"

"Yes!" cried Dorothea. "Do as I say. Then send me my captain."

The servant raced away as Dorothea pointed to a dark corridor. "There, all of you. Follow my man down to the deep cellar. Leave the dog here with my hounds."

"Our donkey?" squealed Maria.

"Give it no thought, *Mädel.* He'll be safe enough in the stable." She set a kind hand on the girl's head. "You shall be safe, my dear. Now all of you must go quickly."

Wil and his company followed a terrified clerk down a slippery flight of narrow stairs and across a candlelit cellar crowded with wine barrels, sundry baskets of root-foods and cheese, a few racks of fruit preserves, and a collection of broken furniture and pottery. Reaching a far wall, the clerk pushed away a large trunk and reached down to lift a dusty wooden hatch. "God go with you," he muttered as he pointed to a short ladder leading into utter blackness. "And, by the saints, keep silent!"

Above, Dorothea summoned her handservants, who fussed about her clothing and her hair. "My circlet," she ordered anxiously. A young girl ran to a drawer and returned with a silver ring, which she placed neatly over the woman's silk wimple. Now dressed in a flowing green overgown and her shoulders covered by a lace mantle, Lord Bernard's lovely daughter drew a deep breath and bravely stepped from the burgher-house.

Feigning confidence as she entered the town's abandoned streets, the young widow smiled at her father's townsfolk peering fearfully from behind half-shuttered windows. The radiance of her fair beauty and the bold gait of the soldiers at her side quieted many a racing heart. Dorothea made her way calmly to a set of wide steps at the base of the town wall. She lifted her gown and began her climb to the wall walk that rimmed the top edge of the stockade. She then made her way to a position just above the main gate, where she raised her face to survey the army arrayed before her. *Never show fear to an enemy,* she thought. They were wise words from both her father and her late husband. So when Dorothea's eyes scanned the angry faces staring at her from impatient chargers, she did not flinch. Instead, she let her mind fly to the young soldier she had married three years ago. *Oh, dear Jurgen, I wish you were with me now.*

"Who commands this town?" roared a knight. The man was the surly, unkempt commander of several companies.

"I do," answered Dorothea firmly.

The soldiers below laughed. "As tender a wisp I've ne'er seen, m'fair lady," the knight said as he bent forward in his saddle. "I am Sir Roland von Esselbach. My men are tired and hungry. Would that we might dine in thy halls this very morn."

"I doubt your manners are equal to the task," declared the lady.

Insulted, Sir Roland growled. "Open the gates, wench, and we'll soon see of what stuff you're made!"

Dorothea's eyes shifted from Roland to the Templar a few mounts to one side. The monk seemed agitated. The woman placed her hands on her hips. "Who of you is in command?"

Sir Roland pounded his chest. "I am."

"You command the Templars?"

"Aye."

The goad showed immediate promise. The Templar barked at Roland, "We serve the pope, y'fool, not the likes of you!"

For a few moments, it appeared that a sudden rift had divided the army. The Templar knights and a few of their lesser, brown-habited brethren formed a knot in defiance of Sir Roland. "You've no authority over us in this or any other matter."

"I am ordered by the emperor against all foes of the empire. This is my army and—"

"I declare this army now to be an army of the Holy Church!"

Dorothea held her breath.

Sir Roland spat. He would not raise his sword against the Templars and risk the vendetta of their brethren from all over Christendom. "*Ach*, blood is blood for me. I am in command of m'men—"

"And I am in command of you!" The Templar nudged his stallion close to the knight's and faced him squarely. "Enough of this, then. We've fugitives inside to find. Take from the town what you will, but the Church seeks justice for our slain and an end to heresy. Do not interfere again."

Defeated, Roland said nothing more as the Templar turned his face toward the disappointed Dorothea staring at him from above. "Woman, I am Brother Cyrill, commander of this army. Four of our brethren have been murdered, and a prisoner has escaped. We must search this town for him and for the heretics that are said to be harbored here."

"By whose authority do you come?"

A loud chorus of jeers rose from the ranks. "We owe no woman an answer! Open the gates or we shall burn them down!"

Sir Roland pointed his sword at the lady. "Did y'not hear us? We'll burn yer cursed town to the ground."

Brother Cyrill shouted for silence. "Woman, we come in the name of the Holy Church, and I command you to open this gate."

"My father, Lord Bernard, is lord of this town and lands surrounding. He is en route with men-at-arms even as we speak. In his name I grant none entrance."

Olten's guardsmen shifted in their places. They looked nervously at their lord's daughter. "M'lady," whispered the town's captain, "we are at half strength, and some are sick with fever. With what we've left, we cannot resist them."

Looking at the man with sudden contempt, Dorothea stiffened. "This town is not yet chartered. It is the property of my father, and you are his subject. Your duty, sir, is to do as I say, even unto death!"

Chastened, the soldier backed away. Dorothea looked across the thatched rooftops and leaning buildings of her town. Not a soul was in sight. *It is hopeless*, she thought. *Would that our whole army were here; we'd have enough men to make a fight of it!*

Unwilling to yield easily, she took a sword from a nearby guardsman and pointed it directly at Brother Cyrill. "Hear me, warrior-monk. 'Let all things be done in decency and in order.' Lord Bernard is a vassal to the abbot of St. Gall. When you deliver the seal of the abbot, you may search this town. Until then, Brother Templar, be content that you have not bled on Olten's soil."

Dorothea's captain of the guard went wobbly. Pale and shaking, he whispered, "My lady? What are you—" They were his final words on earth, for a crossbowman shot an oak dart squarely into the man's chest, and he toppled into the courtyard below.

Shocked, Dorothea whirled about and cursed the Templar and his army. "Murderous army of hell! Serpents and demons, may you all be cursed to the Pit!" The brave young woman threw her sword from the wall with a loud cry.

"Open the gate!" came the angry reply.

Defeated, Dorothea nodded to her gatekeepers. In moments the lock beam was lifted away, and the heavy timber gates were pulled apart. Horsemen and infantry roared through the opening and descended on Olten in a wild rage. Like angry hellions, the soldiers surged across the courtyard knocking over carts and merchants' tables, spilling racks of wares, and trampling cages of fowl. Homes and shops were immediately looted as terrified townsfolk crouched ever deeper in the shadowed corners of their homes.

On the wall, Dorothea waited for the enemy. She ordered her guards to drop all weapons as footmen scrambled up the stairways to the wall walk. At last, with her face lifted proudly, she yielded to the grasping hands of two large knights, who dragged her down to the courtyard. Thrown to the ground at Cyrill's feet, she fought back tears of outrage. She climbed to her feet and brushed the dirt off her silk gown. Her chin now trembled slightly, and her fair face had lost its prior flush of anger. Nevertheless, she stood erect and proud. "Whom do you seek?" she asked flatly.

The Templar stroked his short beard and shook his head. He muttered a few words to the other white-robed knight at his side, who galloped away. Then he shook his head at the disgusting display around him. Laughing footmen were carrying screaming women into vacant sheds, and knights were filling sacks with silver goblets and sundry treasures. The inns were crowded with men happy to slake their thirsts with fresh ale and red wine.

At last, he turned to Dorothea. "Brave woman, look about you. I am ashamed of the wanton vice and excess I see. These are Roland's men. Unlike mine, they are under no vows. Do you see there, those horsemen in brown robes behind their commander in white? They are our lesser brethren, Templars nonetheless. They'll not touch the women nor steal for themselves. No, my lady, be thankful we are here."

"Thankful? I think not! If you were truly in command, you'd spare this carnage."

"I see. Well, perhaps it is carnage or perhaps it is justice. Like the locusts of Egypt, they may be the mighty hands of God's wrath." His mood darkened and his voice now rose. "You are harboring heretics, doubtlessly the murderers of four of my brothers—four Christian soldiers with whom I served our Lord in Palestine."

"We harbor no one."

The man took a deep, restraining breath. He wrapped his fingers around the handle of his sword and watched a footman slay an old man in the doorway of a shop. "Before this day ends, we shall have our justice. Either you surrender those you are hiding, or I shall order the entire town slaughtered and burned."

Cyrill's tone was matter-of-fact, and his ultimatum was delivered with such seeming familiarity that the woman's spine tingled with terror. "Now, hear me well. We are told of youths dressed in black. They were seen freeing our horses in Burgdorf and setting fire to that town."

"And?" Dorothea's mind whirled.

The Templar set his jaw. "And we are certain that they are those who later murdered my four friends and set our captive free."

"Children bettered the swords of four mighty Templars? Methinks not."

The knight reddened. "Silence, wench!" He slapped Dorothea hard across her face, knocking her to the ground. "We've also been told of Cathari venturing to and from this town on their flight eastward. The man who was rescued is a traitorous Templar who served their cause! Does it not seem odd that he is rescued near the very place the Cathari are known to hide? By God and the Holy Mother, I can almost smell them! We shall find them and slay them under thine own eyes! Now where are they?" he roared.

Dorothea fell silent. Her heart raced, for she knew that if either Pieter's company or the Cathari were discovered, she'd suffer death as well. *Oh, Pieter, stay deep in the cellar!* she thought. Before she could answer, the town's priest came scurrying toward the two of them. "Brother Templar!" he cried.

Dorothea chilled. Aside from her innkeeper and a few servants, this meddlesome churchman was the only one to know of Wil's company. One of her guards had spotted him prowling the gardens by the hall's windows during breakfast. *If he speaks,* she thought, *all is lost.*

~

In the dim light of a single yellow candle, the travelers stared at the heavy shadows of the cellar. Each sat deep in private thought, wrestling with conflicting urges of both fear and duty. Wil leaned against his bride with one hand clutched firmly around Emmanuel. At last, the young man broke the silence. He kissed fair Frieda and stood determinedly. "Dorothea needs me on the wall!" he blurted. "This town has treated us well. I'll not let it fall without raising my hand for it."

"Aye, lad! I am with you!" cried Heinrich. The baker turned to the others. "Pieter, Maria, Frieda ... remain here with any other who wishes to stay."

Frieda rose. "I'll not stay—"

Wil put his hand on his wife's arm. "*Ja!* You will stay. I demand it. You must keep Maria safe."

Frieda stiffened. She would not give in easily and pulled away. "I go where you go!"

"No! Obey me in this, wife! I need you to stay by Maria."

"What shall we do?" asked Otto.

Wil and Heinrich looked at each other as Alwin joined them. "No, this will not do. Listen well. The Templars demand justice at all cost. They will burn the whole of Christendom to find me and those who rescued me. I must surrender myself and quickly. I'll confess all deeds and swear by the Holy Virgin that it was Otto's men who saved me and left me here to heal." With that, the man abruptly shuffled through the damp cellar toward the squat ladder amidst shocked protests from his comrades.

"No!" cried Heinrich. "They'll hang you on the square afore terce!"

"*Ja,* and then spare the town. You'll not dissuade me

again." Alwin reached for a rung. "I am not the warrior I once was. I even forgot my sword this morning!"

Pieter stood and leaned heavily on his staff as he called after the man. "Good Alwin, one moment. Please, my son. Hanging you shall not stay their swords against those who have given you shelter."

"It will save some."

Pieter nodded. "Perhaps. But I should also say that your story shan't hold under scrutiny. What of Burgdorf?"

Alwin hesitated. "I'll … I'll be ready for that. No, you cannot change my mind in this. It is the only way."

Pieter sighed. "Then I ask you this: would you pause just a brief moment so that I might share the holy doctrines, hear thy confession, and pray over thy soul? It would give me peace."

Alwin hesitated.

"Please," urged Heinrich. "My friend, I beg you. At least do this."

Alwin released the rung and turned toward Pieter. The old man's craggy face looked sad yet consoling; Heinrich's, familiar and assuring. It would be comforting to be alone under his hanging hood with these images as his final companions. He nodded. "Very well, but be brief, Father Pieter."

"Good, my son." Pieter reached for the candle and lifted it to cast a soft yellow light about the dusty room. He eyed a clear spot on the floor at its very center, away from the stacks of sundry wares piled about. "There, brother. We shall kneel together there."

The priest handed Heinrich the candle and hobbled behind Alwin to the place where he bade his penitent bend to both knees. Still holding his staff, he laid one hand atop Alwin's head. "Alwin of Gunnar, prepare thy soul to be received in thy Savior's embrace."

Alwin bowed and folded his hands.

"First, do you confess belief in the truths of the Apostles' Creed?

"I do."

"Does thine heart lean upon our Savior by faith alone for the forgiveness of sin?"

"*Ja*, Father Pieter. It does so lean." Confused by priest's unusual liturgy, he opened his mouth to add, "But I—"

"Might I ask if you have been perfect as he is perfect: in thought, word, and deed?"

Confused, Alwin answered obediently, "No, but—"

Pieter smiled. "Ah, good, my son, the truth lives within you. Do you then lean upon the perfection of our Savior and receive it as His gift for thine own perfection?"

"I ... I ... suppose I do, but—"

"*Gratia Dei tibi!* Now, recite the *confiteor* if you must."

Baffled, Alwin shrugged, then bowed his head low to the ground. With a groaning, heartfelt voice, the penitent began. "I confess to Almighty God, to blessed Mary ever Virgin, to blessed Michael the Archangel, to blessed John the Baptist, to the holy apostles Peter—"

He never finished. To the astonishment of all, Pieter slowly raised his staff over the praying man, and with both hands he swung the sturdy stick against his head! Alwin slumped to his side, unconscious. "Quick! Tie him up!" Pieter cried.

At first, none moved. Speechless and utterly stunned by the old fellow's surprise, they simply stared at one another slack jawed.

"Quickly!" barked Pieter.

With that, many hands scrambled through the darkness to run fingers over dusty crates and jars, broken shelves and baskets. "Here!" shouted Helmut. "Here's rope!"

"Good! Tie him up and find a rag to bind his mouth." Pieter whirled about and faced the dumbstruck face of Wil. "Now what?"

"Huh?"

"I said, now what?"

The sounds of heavy horses suddenly shook the earth above them all. "They've broken through the gate!" exclaimed Otto.

Tomas spoke. "We've new clothes. If they'd be searching for the arsons of Burgdorf, they'd be looking for youths dressed in black."

Heinrich answered, "True enough. But if they find us all together here—"

"And they'll likely remember me," interrupted Benedetto. "They'll know I played to distract them."

The group was quiet. "So how do we disguise you?" grumbled Rudolf.

The cellar fell utterly silent until Maria chimed, "All lords have minstrels! Would be common for one to be here, too! They won't remember your face."

"She's right, Benedetto. You should be safe if you claim to sing for the lord's court."

"And the rest of us?" chimed Helmut. "Ought we not hide here as well?"

"No, methinks Dorothea was wrong," Heinrich said. "The army will search the burgher-house from top to bottom. If they find us here, they'll know. We ought spread into the town and hide amongst the folk."

"We've the servants to fear," said Helmut. "Others may know we've come, but only the servants know we've new clothes."

"The servants are few and loyal to the house. None would confess, I swear it," said Friederich. "I've lived here, I know. But the priest surely knows. He didn't trust Dorothea's message ... I heard him tell a novice that something was amiss, and he's oft seen spyin' about the gardens."

"Then it's the priest," muttered Heinrich.

Maria asked nervously, "But are you sure?"

"*Ja*. I know he does," Friederich continued angrily. "I can *feel* when he's about, and I felt his prying eyes at first meal. Perhaps he was listening under the windows."

Frieda had been hovering over the unconscious Alwin. "Thank God, he's breathing evenly, Pieter. You might have killed him!"

Pieter shrugged. "There are some advantages to knowing one's weakness, my dear girl. But I confirmed the condition of his soul to give me peace if I was wrong." The priest smiled. "Either way, be assured Alwin would have been in a good way."

Frieda shook her head in disbelief as Wil and Heinrich

summoned Pieter to come close. After a few moments of consultation, Wil turned to the group now gathered around the candle. Above, muffled screams could be heard, and more horses thundered through the streets. "My father is right. We cannot all stay here. So, we've a plan. We'll hide Alwin behind those sacks, and we'll leave Benedetto here to watch over him. The rest of us will spread into the town and hide with other townsfolk as if we are one of them. Pieter will linger near the gate; none should bother with an old priest. When he thinks you can pass safely, he'll make himself easy to see. So when you see him plainly, get through the gate and beyond the walls. Pieter will keep an accounting."

"And if they close the gate?" asked Helmut.

The cellar was quiet.

Pieter stroked his beard. "Then we hide until the day it opens."

Heinrich nodded. "Now listen. If you are challenged by anyone, do not act like a fugitive, else you'll be taken as one." His voice became firm. "You know who you are: free travelers ... so act like it."

"Just use your wits and get out as you can," said Wil. "Pieter says the road north takes a hard turn at the base of a mountain about a half league away. He says he thinks there is a water pool to the east side of the highway. We'll meet there. Now, I'll keep m'wife with me. M'father's to take Maria. Would be good for you others to stay apart." Wil peered through the heavy shadows and took a deep breath. "When the time is right, I'll come back for Alwin and the minstrel. So is it clear?"

The company nodded soberly. "Godspeed, everyone," murmured Rudolf.

Wil took Frieda's hand and looked tenderly at his sister. "Fear not. All will be well."

Chapter Fourteen

RELIEF

orothea's heart pounded as the town's priest drew near. "He's ... he's a mad fool," she stammered to the Templar. "He has visions of virgins attending him at his bed, and he thinks snakes slide out his nose at Hallowmas. Whatever he has to say is a lie or some fantastic deceit. If you want justice, Brother Knight, do not listen to his words."

Brother Cyrill said nothing. He was distracted by the vile behavior of Sir Roland's men, who were continuing their savage rampage of bloodletting and rape. As the priest called out, he paid him little notice.

"Brother," panted the priest, "we've Cathari by the inn's stable and the black—"

The man did not finish. An arrow, seemingly from nowhere, flew and struck the priest in the center of his back. He gasped and fell forward to the ground, where he flopped about with one arm reaching futilely for the shaft. The Templar whirled about, scanning every shadow until another arrow hissed through the air and penetrated his thigh. Screaming, the knight fell backward. Dorothea turned and ran as a company of brown-robed sergeants stormed toward their fallen captain.

"The stable!" he cried. "Cathari in the stable by the inn!" The Templar grabbed hold of two fellows and lifted himself to his feet. He pointed to the priest. "See if he is alive. He had more to tell."

The priest was lifted and found still breathing, though weakly. "He's alive!"

"Bring him to me!" barked Cyrill. "Let him talk afore he dies."

The sergeants pulled the priest to a standing position and dragged him limp legged to their commander. The Templar lifted the man's head by his hair. "Tell me! Tell me more!"

The priest's eyes fluttered as he struggled to whisper. "Cathari ... stable ... black ..."

"And what of the murderer? We're in search of a murderer!"

An arrow sang again, this time piercing the priest's neck. The man went limp, and his holders dropped him to the ground. Into the vacancy immediately flew another shaft, hitting the Templar captain squarely in the eye. Falling backward with a sickening cry, the man landed dead upon the ground.

"Find him!" cried a voice. As men went running in the supposed direction of the archer, others mounted their horses in search of the other Templar knight. Once found, he was informed of his comrade's death and of the priest's words. Messengers were sent in all directions, and within the hour, much of the army had descended upon the inn and its adjoining stable.

"Innkeeper!" cried the Templar.

The door opened slowly, and a trembling man came out. "He is not here, my lord knight."

"Where is he?"

"He's gone to Bern, m'lord."

"Bern?"

"Aye, sir. With Lord Bernard."

At the Templar's signal, several footmen appeared with torches and tossed them into the inn and into every building nearby, including the stable. The army tightened its noose around this corner of the town as white smoke poured through thatched roofs. Soon flames licked the morning sky, and within moments, a stream of terrified folk poured into the streets from their burning cover.

A large company of horsemen trotted dispassionately among the coughing wretches and looked with only mild interest at a one-armed man and a little girl dragging a stubborn donkey into a smoky alley. Something else caught their attention, however. A comrade spotted a particularly closely huddled group just beyond the heat of a large warehouse that was belching flame and smoke. The lay commander summoned the Templar. "There." He pointed. "Something's odd about them. See, the others are running hither and yon, thinking only of themselves or their children. These are different. They seem unwilling to leave each other."

"Good eye, soldier," mumbled the Templar. He nudged his horse closer as he motioned for more soldiers to join him. "Circle them and move them from the smoke!"

In short order, the terrified group of men, women, and children was herded down the street and into the square by the fishpond near Dorothea's burgher-house. The Templar ordered the prisoners to spread apart.

Suddenly, one of Roland's knights shouted. "Over there, sir. A group in black!"

The Templar plowed past the crowd with a drawn sword and came upon a handful of gaunt youths dressed in black tunics and leggings. From another part of the street, a footman appeared, dragging by the hair a young woman dressed in a black gown. The Templar commanded silence. He ordered all those dressed in black to be brought before him. "Where is my prisoner?" he roared.

Confused, all were silent.

Another of Roland's knights dismounted and knelt by a little girl who was clutching her mother's legs nearby. He took her by the hand. "My dear, can you help us?"

"*Non. Ju n'parli ...*" The tyke's mother quickly clapped her hand over the girl's mouth, but it was too late.

The soldier abruptly stiffened. "*Langue d'oc!* She speaks with dialect. Cathari to be sure."

At the word, a great cheer resounded in the ranks. The Templar nodded and dismounted his horse. "Can you speak their language?"

"*Oui*, a little. But I am Catholic."

The Templar smiled. "As you say. Ask them to swear by whatever God they worship that every one of them is here in our little net."

The man posed the question, and an apparent leader stepped forward. He spoke in fluent German. "*Mein Brüder*, we may not lie. One of ours is missing." The man pointed to the stable that had been reduced to ash and charcoaled timber. "I last saw him enter there, and he never came out."

The Templar grabbed the man by the throat. "Tell me, demon, if he is the one who killed my brethren, if he is the betrayer you protect."

"Oh, not that poor man—"

"Liar!" The knight threw the fellow to the ground. "Another sound and I shall cut your tongue from your blasphemous head m'self." He ordered men to search the ruins of the stable. "We shall see what we find, Cathar, and if you lied to us, you and yours will perish this day."

"Kill him now," roared Roland as his horse trotted to the scene. "Kill them all now. What's the wait?"

"First we see what's in the stable. Then proper justice shall be served."

Within a quarter hour, a sooty soldier ran out of the stable and to the commanders. Whispering to both men, he led them to the place where the charred remains of a faceless body lay near a blackened Templar sword. "As I thought!" growled the Templar as he covered his nose. "Search him."

A footman delicately picked his fingers within the burned remains of the victim's clothing looking for any sign or symbol of identity. He found nothing in the man's shirt or sleeves or around his neck. But when he came to a pouch sewn on the side of the man's leggings, he paused.

"Well, what is it?"

The soldier reached carefully inside the yet-intact pouch and retrieved two blackened eggs.

"Ha! It must be he!" shouted the Templar. "He is not a Cathar, for they are forbidden eggs. The sword, the eggs, the black clothing on those youths ... 'tis quite enough. Slaughter them all!"

~

Once word of slaughter had echoed throughout Olten, drunken soldiers carousing the taverns abandoned their tankards to join in the holy dispatch. It was during that horrid distraction that Wil's company realized its opportunity.

Heinrich and Maria had rescued Paulus just moments before the disaster and had led the beast warily to the gardens behind Dorothea's hall. "Maria," whispered Heinrich, "no doubt Wil shall come soon. When he does, you'll flee with Frieda. Your brother and I will get Alwin and Benedetto. Do you understand?" He had barely finished speaking when Wil and Frieda came crashing through the bushes, flushed and wide eyed. "The gate is still open ... the town's guards are helping many escape. Seems the army is busy elsewhere. We must go—now!"

"Aye, lad."

Solomon leapt through an open window and pounced happily on Maria. "Oh, we almost forgot him!" she gasped.

"Frieda, take Maria ... and Solomon ... and go now. Pieter is at the right side of the gate by a barrel. Hurry and keep an eye for him. When you see him, move quickly through the gate. Do not come back ... not for anything!"

As the two girls and the two animals hurried away, Heinrich followed Wil in a wild race to the subcellar, where Benedetto was trembling behind a barrel. "Here!" he cried.

"Good. You've been spared. And Alwin?"

"He's awake and not very happy."

"Alwin?"

From behind his screen of sacks, the man grunted angrily through the cloth binding his mouth.

Heinrich informed the man of matters at hand as he and Wil released him from his bonds. The four men then climbed up the short ladder to the main cellar, then up the tight stairway leading to the main floor.

"Hurry, Father. Listen to the screams. The soldiers are drawing near."

The pilgrims joined a stream of others fleeing the hapless town. Smoke now billowed from all sides, and the sounds of clanging steel suggested the town's guard was attempting to defend its own. "We should help!" cried Wil.

"Our first duty is to our fellows," answered Heinrich. "Frieda and Maria need us."

Pieter was pacing near the gatehouse, the air filled with a blinding, choking black smoke. Less than a bowshot away, a furious battle raged between a large company of the army and a brave band of the town guard. Pieter knew the army had intended to close the gate and trap everyone within its grasp. He had accounted for all his company except for the four he now spotted pressing desperately through the panicked crowd mobbing the gate. "Oh, hurry, lads! Hurry!"

A mounted troop suddenly appeared to the other side, and in the lead was the Templar and Sir Roland. Shouting, the pair demanded the gate be closed. "Kill the guard!" bellowed Roland. "Kill them all!"

Wil saw them and heard the order. The young man's eyes swept the scene, and he quickly deduced that without the Templar and Roland, the army would be headless for a time and that, left to its own devices, chaos would surely follow. "Keep going," he shouted to his father. "I'll see you on the other side!"

Wil raced to a corner and drew his bow. Without hesitation, he released his first arrow toward its target, and the shaft hit its mark. The Templar fell from his horse, mortally wounded in the neck. But before the young man could reset, Sir Roland reined his horse hard toward Wil and dug his spurs into the stallion's flanks with a loud cry. Trampling his way through the shrieking, scattering crowd, he charged directly toward the lad.

As Wil saw the oncoming rider, his fingers fumbled. He notched his arrow hastily and drew his string too tight. The arrow spun away from the bow and fell harmlessly to the ground. Fortunately, Heinrich and Alwin had not left the lad. With a shout, Heinrich drew his sword and led Alwin on a mad rush to intercept the charging knight.

Quaking with fear, Wil set his arrow and drew his bow

taut once more. This time the string at his ear danced, and he released his shot to fly impotently away from the looming knight. The lad had no time to draw again; the knight was mere rods away. He snapped the dagger from his belt and crouched.

Then, to his left came the roaring sound of a charging bear. Heinrich lunged from the crowd and swung his sword hard across the fore shoulder of the man's steed, tumbling horse and rider upon the hard earth with a crash. Wil, no longer the frightened boy of Domodossola, raced forward with his dagger, and father and son fell upon their victim together. Roland was dispatched to his eternal end with the sharp edges of freemen's steel.

Realizing that Wil and Heinrich had the situation under control, Alwin quickly turned about in search of more trouble. Sucking air hard into his lungs, he slew an onrushing footman, then cast a wild eye at the terror all about. "There!" he shouted. "Benedetto!"

Joining Alwin, Heinrich and Wil fought their way toward the minstrel. Wil clutched the man's sleeve. "Come!" he shouted. As Wil had hoped, the army was suddenly confused, but the men knew that they must escape now—in that brief moment of uncertainty.

Pieter watched the four men struggle toward him within the crushing mob. "Hurry!" he cried over the din. "Hurry!" He waved his staff and urged them on, and when he thought them close enough, he ventured into the flood tide to join them.

Fearing for the old fellow's safety, Wil wrapped his arms around Pieter's waist and hoisted him over his shoulder. "Hang on, Pieter!" he cried. "Hang on!"

"Keep moving, son!" shouted Heinrich. "Hurry!" The band struggled forward, hard pressed on all sides by the crushing torrent of screaming folk. They finally burst through the narrow, choked gate and sprinted awkwardly forward within the widening stampede into the free air beyond. It was then that the baker looked over his shoulder. "Oh, dear God above!" he exclaimed. "Archers!"

The group ran frantically as a volley of arrows flew

toward it. To either side tumbled men, women, and children writhing in pain. Another volley then flew and yet another. Pieter, bouncing along over Wil's shoulder, lifted his head and groaned. He could see the terror in the faces behind and the agony and pain of those struck. "Have mercy on us, Lord. Have mercy on us!"

The comrades ran on, beyond the reach of the arrows, and did not stop until they were unable to take another step. Gasping for air, they collapsed in a shadowed wood a safe distance from the burning town.

All eyes scanned the carnage and the death strewn about Olten. Thankful to be alive, the five retreated deeper into the wood, where they rested before moving on to join their fellows.

"By God, what happened to me?" Alwin finally croaked. "Methinks my skull is broken!"

"Thy life was spared," answered Pieter sarcastically.

"You! 'Twas you who struck me on the head!"

"Aye, and what of it?" The old priest was in no mood for a lecture.

Alwin rubbed his head and grumbled, "Thank you."

Pieter nodded and grinned.

"Seems a second town now burns in your wake, Pieter!" Alwin said with a painful chuckle.

"Nay." Wil sighed. "This makes three."

≈

By midafternoon, the weary pilgrims were reunited by the spring-fed pool Pieter had described. Wil took an immediate accounting of his tired, dirty, and still trembling band and was relieved to confirm that all had survived. A few of their provisions had fallen from Paulus's back, but all their coins were still safe.

All were accounted for, but all were not well. Pieter collapsed into Otto's sure hands, and the old fellow was laid gently down upon the green grass. "Pieter?" asked the lad.

"*Ja*, boy. I am weary beyond words." His voice trailed away and he fainted.

Maria ran to the old man's side and wiped his face with a rag dipped in the cool water of the pool. "I love you, Papa," she whispered. Frieda joined her, and soon Pieter stirred, only to smile and drift into a peaceful sleep.

With their beloved shepherd resting, the other travelers circled the pool and quietly rinsed their soot-blackened skin with clean water. Saying little, they each watched the grime swirl slowly away, and they stared into their reflections with wonder. Some had done a similar thing so many months before in a different place and at a time when they had no knowledge of things that were to come. The innocence of their former likeness was now clouded with the residue of a world beset by sorrows. Yet for most, the visions of themselves were not fouled by the stains falling from their bodies, but rather bettered. For the curling shadows drifting by their rippled faces were certain evidence of wisdom gained.

Lowering his fingers from his scar, Wil pulled himself away from the water's edge and took his bride by the hand. She, still anxious from the day's horrors, embraced her young husband and began to weep softly. "Oh, Wil, thanks be to God."

The lad nodded and kissed her before turning to call his company to order. He glanced about the nearby roadway with some concern and then surveyed the faces gathered about him. "We must give Pieter some rest. There, in that forest we should make our camp. 'Tis out of sight, near this good water, and cool with heavy shade."

"And what of Dorothea?" challenged Otto.

"*Ja*, Wil. She's likely in need of help," added young Friederich. "She was always there for me. We cannot leave her to those devils."

Wil nodded. He had been thinking the very same thing.

Pieter awoke with a start and opened his eyes to the blue July sky above. "Pray, lad."

"Eh?"

"Always pray first."

Wil grunted. "I'm no priest. You pray."

Pieter took Heinrich's hand and sat up slowly. With a moan and a heave, he then stood on wobbly legs and sighed wearily. "You need to learn, boy."

Wil grumbled, then beckoned all to follow him away from the pool and to the cover of a hardwood forest rising steeply against the breast of the round-topped mountain they'd soon cross. The forest floor was free from brush and soft with a thick blanket of rotting leaves. Mighty oaks and beech spread their arms wide and rustled happily in a light, cool breeze. It was a good place to rest.

Friederich smiled and cocked his ears. "The trees say we're welcome here!"

His remark was met with a few snickers until Otto scolded them all. "He has a special gift, believe me. He hears the whispers of the trees when the breeze blows."

The boy planted his fists on his hips. "'Tis true!"

Maria led Paulus to a young tree and tied him loosely to its trunk. She rubbed his soft muzzle and kissed his long face. "I love you, Paulus!" she whispered. The beast shook his head, as if delighted, then brayed happily.

"A good friend is worth much!" Heinrich chuckled.

The six-year-old giggled. "*Herr* Heinrich—"

"Nay, child. Remember you are to call me 'Papa' or '*Vati.*'" The baker knelt and, with his only hand, took Maria's only good hand.

The man's kindness illumined the girl's pink face with a happy joy that could have softened the blackest heart of Christendom. "*Vati,*" she said. She recited it to herself almost reverently until she pecked Heinrich on the cheek and danced away.

The baker's eye followed her as she pranced happily midst the sturdy timbers of the forest. Her flaxen hair had been plaited into braids that bounced by each ear. Her new gown was a bit too short and revealed her skinny ankles that rose out of her slightly oversized shoes. Heinrich chuckled. The man was happy for her. He had noticed Frieda's kindness to her over these past months. Unlike Maria's mother, Frieda was concerned to shelter the girl from the ridicule that her deformed arm so often prompted. The young bride had charitably offered to sew one of Maria's sleeves closed. *Two angels among us,* he said to himself.

Within the half hour, Wil's company had built a small fire and had shared a much-needed meal of cheese and salted pork. With the loss of some provisions from Paulus's back, it was hoped they'd have enough food for the three-day journey to Basel. However, they were not yet ready to march on. The question still nagging them all was immediately raised once more. "Now, what of Dorothea?" blurted Friederich.

"I've not forgotten," answered Wil.

"And?" Otto's brows were furrowed and his fists were clenched. Loyal to things right, the stout lad would not rest as long as the beloved lady was at risk.

Heinrich was cautious. "Boys, we cannot venture to Olten now. The highway is filled with those fleeing; the soldiers are likely having their way with whom they will. We cannot save her."

Friederich's bony face hardened. The eight-year-old was brave to be sure—and loyal, like Otto. His intuition was more respected than his reasoning, however, so when he insisted they storm the town, the whole of the company rolled their eyes! "But they'll not be expecting us!" he insisted.

Tomas and Helmut had been whispering together, and Helmut spoke. "First, we needs find a way to see what's about in the town." He ran his hands through his long hair. The fifteen-year-old was generally quiet and unassuming—odd traits for the son of a merchant. He was intelligent, however, and well reasoned. "Tomas and I think we ought to go as spies near the walls. We'll come back before matins to report what we've seen."

Wil listened. He looked to his father for an opinion, and the baker reluctantly nodded his approval. "Right. No plan without knowledge."

"Then we have it. Tomas and Helmut will scout the town first, and when they return with news, we'll make a plan."

Pieter grumbled a bit and cast a glance at Wil. "And a prayer, lad?"

Wil shrugged. "*Ja*, Father Pieter, please do." Despite the lessons of their journey, the lad could still be stiff necked and self-reliant—traits apt to yield slowly.

The old man nodded and raised a quiet prayer to heaven for Dorothea's safekeeping and for the protection of their two scouts. When he was finished, Tomas and Helmut scampered away.

తి

The two did not return to camp by matins as was planned but did arrive sometime past noon of the day following. The night before, they had found themselves close enough to Olten's gate to hear the drunken slurs of some soldiers draped over a few hitching rails. They had learned that Dorothea was being held in the town's jail, that Lord Bernard's house was pillaged and burned, and that his servants had been slaughtered. Dorothea, it seemed, was destined to be tried for harboring "murderous heretics and fugitives of the Church," namely the Cathari, who had, themselves, been killed by either sword or stake.

The pair had positioned themselves dangerously close to the wall, and when a fresh company of sentries took a position nearby, they feared to move. At dawn, however, all heads had turned toward the sounds of thunder rolling toward the town from the west. To the dismay of the occupiers, Lord Bernard's soldiers, along with a host of hastily hired mercenaries, stormed the town. The lads seized the opportunity to dash from their cover and watched from a safe distance as Bernard and his men reclaimed their town. Dorothea was surely safe.

Hearing the story, Frieda and Maria both pointed to Pieter. "His prayer!" they cried together.

"God be praised," said Pieter. He turned to Wil with a look of reprimand. "Pride still shadows you."

Wil ignored the man's comment and turned to the others. "We should return to offer our thanks to the lady and to her father."

The company murmured among themselves until Alwin answered. "Wil, I fear the risk of ill will from either Bernard or his men. I have seen the sort of things that happen when even good men are heated with bloodletting. I think it not safe. Perhaps at a later time we might send a message?"

The others voiced their assent, including Heinrich and Pieter. "My son, we ought not to go back. Some may blame us."

Wil looked about the nodding group, then agreed. "A message someday then." The matter was settled.

The pilgrims quietly gathered in a circle around their midday fire and let their thoughts return to Olten. They spoke of those who had helped them: the innkeeper; Lord Bernard's servants; Dorothea, of course; and even the old Cathar with eggs in his leggings.

"I hope someone killed the priest," grumbled Friederich.

Heinrich glanced at Wil, then stared at the young boy with a heavy heart. *What turns a happy child to such a thought?*

Finally, Wil spoke to his company. "On the morrow we begin the journey to take Rudolf home." A small cheer rose up, and many hands patted the blushing Rudolf on his back. The gentle lad was buoyant and grinning as thoughts of his parents' mountain home rushed through his mind. What a joy it would be to see his mother's round face again. Rudolf laughed out loud. "Oh, *Mutti!* I'm almost home!"

The next morning the pilgrims rose to a pleasant summer's day. The sky was clear and streaked with color as the sun peeked over the horizon in the east. A fresh morning breeze felt clean and cool, and soon the happy band was washing once more in the refreshing pool.

Alwin was well rested and laughing. The bruises across his throat were still red, but his voice was no longer hoarse. "Can y'not keep that crusty old priest out of the water until we fill our flasks!"

Heinrich laughed and came to the knight's side. "Good friend, we really do need you with us. Will you vow to stay with us to Weyer?"

"To Weyer?"

"Aye."

Alwin hesitated. Heinrich entreated him earnestly until the man finally agreed. "I pray this is not foolishness. I am still a target; I can feel it."

"Let God shield us all then," answered Heinrich.

The knight nodded, then clasped the baker's hand. "To Weyer then."

Revitalized, the group gathered and cheered Heinrich's good news. Clean and ready to press on, they had assembled in their column when Wil whispered to his father. Smiling, Heinrich nodded in agreement.

Pieter was summoned to Paulus's side and ordered to climb atop the beast. The red-faced priest laced his furious indignation with nearly every known expletive and even threatened Alwin with his staff! It was Maria's gentle insistence that finally quieted the old fellow as Alwin and Heinrich lifted him atop the unhappy donkey's back.

Despite the tragedy lying in their wake, the wayfarers began their journey northward in high spirits. They traveled several hours along the rapidly rising highway ascending from the wide green valley of the Aare River. Looking back only once, they paused to bid a final farewell to the distant, craggy, snow-capped mountains appearing behind a rising curtain of morning haze. The ragged horizon seemed so very, very far away. It was hard for them to imagine that they had come from even farther places.

"Somewhere beyond is my home," lamented Benedetto. The minstrel had said little since Burgdorf, and the trauma of Olten had nearly finished him.

"Your home is with us now," said Frieda. She set her hand lightly on the man's shoulder. "You are one of us."

"*Si*," he answered. "*Grazie, signora.* It is true, but sometimes I do yearn for the past."

"The past, good minstrel, is just that," Heinrich offered with a hint of introspection. "Methinks it is oft a good place to remember, but not a good place to dwell."

"I sometimes pretend I'm sucking lemons with Brother Stefano and the monks at San Fruttuoso," said Helmut. "Now *that* is a good place to remember *and* to dwell!"

"Aye!" answered a chorus of others.

The pilgrims stared for a while longer at the distant view, then turned to look forward. During the brief respite, a cloud of heavy melancholy moved in to hover over them. Quiet conversations carried them to faraway homes and distant places, to the way of life before the crusade. Heinrich now felt especially despondent. For all his bravado just moments before, fear of the past had abruptly ensnared him, and he began to perspire. *What of Weyer?* he wondered as dread filled his belly.

Conversations fell to whispers, then ended altogether as blank stares were fixed at the horizon. The way of the past had cast its spell.

"Enough!" cried Pieter suddenly. "Enough of this. You have left the old order behind. Do not go back to it. You must live life freely and without fear, bound only by the laws of grace." His voice was firm but not harsh. He leaned on his staff and reached for Maria. "Believe in what you have become."

Sudden chills of inspiration tingled along his listeners' spines, and in that moment the power of evil oppression was broken. Heaven had sprinkled the old man's mouth with admonitions of hope, and the brave pilgrims were now ready to press on.

Heinrich and Alwin shifted Paulus's sacks to make room for Pieter. "He'll not be refusing us again," insisted the baker. "He will do as we say!"

Alwin looked at Pieter and shook his head. "How old is he?"

"Nearly seventy-eight," Frieda replied. "But my heart tells me he still has much to teach us. He'll not be taken from us yet."

The sun was directly overhead when Pieter was finally hoisted upon Paulus. He did not complain nearly as much as the beast below him, though he admitted a certain wounded pride. "Ah, it is what it is," he finally muttered. "Lead on, Wil. Lead us on."

Chapter Fifteen

A FAREWELL, A MONKEY, AND A CARAVAN

he region of Liestal lay southeast of Basel. It was a land of lumpy-shouldered mountains and easy valleys. Small fields of spelt and rye checkered clearings here and there, and hardwood forests covered what was not green with pasture. It was a quiet place, save for the bountiful numbers of songbirds fluttering happily amongst the heavy boughs. Tucked out of sight were the timber farmsteads of the mountain peasants. From their hidden chimneys, thin columns of smoke streamed slowly upward like white ribbons, rising from the unseen hearths hidden deep within the mountains' many nooks.

Rudolf was flushed with excitement. It had been just over a year since he had left his family to join with a different band of crusaders that had passed nearby. He began to point to familiar landmarks—first a few, then many more as they grew closer. "There! *Herr* Ernst's well! And see, down there, old Emil's mill."

He began to trot ahead, down a long descent toward a waiting valley. Laughing, the others followed close behind, with poor Pieter grumbling atop his bouncing perch. At last, Rudolf stopped. He held his breath and licked his lips nervously as he and his friends faced the homestead.

The house was a long rectangular structure, "built of mostly hardwood logs, judging by the bark still hanging on some," reckoned Heinrich. The baker stared at the rock chimney standing proudly at one end. "Better than a smoke-hole!"

The scene was made all the more inviting by the low mooing of milk cows grazing in a nearby meadow. To their deep song was added the grunts of contented swine rooting mast from the woodland floor and the clucking of hens bobbing and scratching along the footpath. The pilgrims looked about, enchanted by the healing green of the forest, the farmyard's comforting sounds, the sprinkling of colorful wildflowers, and the warm rays of golden sunshine piercing between leafy boughs. And were that not blissful enough, the air was soon sweetened with a singsong melody of the *Hausfrau.*

Backe, backe Kuchen, der Bäcker hat gerufen!
Wer will guten Kuchen backen, der muss haben sieben
 Sachen:
Eier und Schmalz, Butter und Salz, Milch und Mehl,
Safran macht den Kuchen gehl. Schieb in den ofen rein!

(Bake, bake the cakes, the baker has cried!
Who wants good cakes baked, he must have seven
 things:
Eggs and lard, butter and salt, milk and flour,
Saffron makes the cakes yellow. Shove them in the oven
 pure!)

Rudolf's eyes watered and a lump filled his throat. He had heard that rhyme for the whole of his life. Pieter dismounted and wrapped an arm about the lad. "You are home, boy. Go and greet them."

The lad embraced Pieter. "God bless you, Father. God bless you always." He turned, then sprinted toward his timber home, where he flung open the door and disappeared into the darkness behind. The singing stopped abruptly. Silence seized the woodland, and nothing stirred until cries of joy rose to heaven as Gerda ran to her son.

Maria and Frieda had been holding hands anxiously. At the sound of Gerda's happy cries, they burst into tears. It was a precious moment, indeed, one filled with shining eyes and broad smiles.

Then, to the pilgrims' right, the earth suddenly shook with the sound of feet crashing through the woodland brush. Storming toward the opened door of his home charged the barrel-chested, bearded man of the house, Dieder. Hearing the shrieks of his wife in the trees beyond the fences, the bear of a man roared past the amused travelers and burst through his doorway, axe in hand and readied for battle. Again, utter silence seized the moment until, unashamed, Dieder bawled loudly, like a small boy swept away by utter joy.

"Ha, ha!" laughed Pieter. "Wonderful!" He skipped about on his bowed legs with his face flushed by his glad heart. "I love it!" he cried. "Sing, O ye angels! Sing!"

The group waited in their place until the household settled. In a few moments Dieder and his plump wife emerged from their doorway with arms stretched as wide as their smiles. They called to the pilgrims with shouts of thanksgiving. As Gerda hurried toward Pieter eagerly, the teetering old fellow suddenly had cause to fear! He braced himself as the happy woman fell upon him and lifted him off his feet with both arms wrapped tightly round his bony waist. "Father! You found him ... you found my boy!"

Gasping for air, Pieter wheezed, "*Ja*, God be praised! Please ... I can't breathe!"

"Ha!" roared Dieder. He pried Pieter from his wife's embrace and squeezed the old man's aged hand with one of his huge paws.

"Aahh!" cried Pieter. "Aye, aye, you are surely welcome!"

Dieder pulled the limp-limbed priest to his chest and hugged him crying, "Ah! Old fellow! God be praised indeed!"

From the sheep pen, a young girl came running. "Rudi!" she cried. It was Beatrix, his younger sister. The lad ran to meet her, and the two greeted each other with joy.

Sore and breathless, Pieter grinned, and at the sight of his snaggletooth, the farmer roared with laughter. "Come! Come in and eat with us, all of you!"

The rest of that day was spent in tale-telling and feasting.

Gerda scurried about her kitchen delivering baskets of freshly baked cakes and loaves of spelt bread to her guests. She raced to her larder for sundry berry preserves as Heinrich studied her bread. "Ah, good woman," he exclaimed as she returned, "a finer bread I've not tasted."

Gerda blushed.

"'Tis true. I am a baker by trade, and I've an eye for these things."

"Only *one* eye!" laughed Otto.

"*Ach!* So be it." Heinrich feigned anger. He turned to Gerda. "Long ago I was reminded that the baker is the priest of the kitchen table. Like the Eucharist at the altar, bread gives us life. It may seem a simple thing, but it is *bread* that our Lord chose as His body for us."

"And it is feasts like this one that is our Lord's vision for his true kingdom!" Alwin stood, his dark eyes swollen red with emotion. "Look about, all of you. What do you see? I see love and charity. I see kindness and grace. See the table, about to be filled with the bounty of God's goodness." The knight's voice thickened with the lump filling his throat. "Oh, dear Heinrich, dear Gerda ... bake your bread always with thanksgiving ... it is a taste of the feast to come."

Dieder stood and toasted the knight with a fresh tankard of ale. "To the kingdom, then!"

"Hurrah!" cheered the diners.

Then, with the frothy tankard fixed securely in his grip, Dieder lifted his eyes upward. "O Lord of field and forest, rivers and seas, I thank You for our Rudi, and I thank You for our brothers and sisters round m'table who've brought him home. Forgive us our failings. Heal our weaknesses. Strengthen our charity. Amen."

"Amen."

Wil had listened to many prayers, mostly in Latin. But here he heard a humble, grateful man lift his voice directly to the Almighty in the common tongue. There was such simple honesty in the man's tone and such directness in his words that Wil thought all heaven was surely moved. Perhaps it was.

With an unwavering smile stretched as far across her face as it might go, Gerda then filled the table with platters of salted pork, entrails, mutton, cheeses, and numbers of summer vegetables. She poured mead generously amongst the young ones, while Dieder reached for some ale and a bottle of good red wine for Pieter, Heinrich, Alwin, and himself.

Later, three chickens and a duck were boiled in beer, and a slab of venison was set to sizzling on a spit above a snapping fire. Before long, the stuffed pilgrims lounged about the summer evening like spoiled little lords and ladies. They spoke of the crusade, of adventures, and of friends lost. Wil informed a saddened Dieder of Karl's death. Then others spoke of the terror of the *San Marco*, the wonders of San Fruttuoso, and of the journey north.

At long last, night fell. The sounds of a woodland's summer evening calmed all hearts with as soothing a lullaby as ever was sung, and, one by one, the pilgrims fell to a peaceful sleep in the embrace of the kindly mountains near Liestal.

∾

It was a sad farewell when Rudolf was left behind. He, too, had changed. But his world was unusually suited to both what the boy had been and to what he had become. For the travelers, though, thoughts turned to things ahead, particularly Weyer and the troubles that might be waiting. Until then, many more leagues needed to be traveled.

It was early in the second week of July when Wil's company looked down on the walls of Basel. The city brought them nothing but dread, and none wanted to enter. "But, Wil, we are now in need of foodstuffs," insisted Otto.

"Dieder gave us a good supply."

"*Ja*, but it is not enough."

"We can cross on the ferries and find food in the Rhine Valley."

Otto spat. "In a place like Dunkeldorf?"

The group fell quiet. Pieter hung his head sheepishly, remembering his own failings in that horrible town, but it was Frieda who gasped at the name. "No! I'll not go near that awful place."

Wil laid his arm around her and whispered words of comfort. It was in Dunkeldorf where she had been rescued by Wil's company, along with her now-departed brother and sister. She shuddered.

"Then we need to travel west of the Rhine and cross at Mainz," stated Alwin flatly.

The group discussed the plan until there was general agreement. Heinrich added rather insistently, "Aye, but we still need to send someone into Basel for provisions."

Alwin agreed. "I think it best as well. The prices ought to be better here than from some thieving merchant along the way. The free villages along the borders by France are the worst."

Wil nodded. "Then you, Father, along with Helmut, Tomas, and m'self will go. You others make a camp off the roadway."

Otto and Friederich grumbled some, but Benedetto was greatly relieved. He made his way to Solomon's side and sat beside the dog, nearly out of view.

"And how long before we send someone to find you?" Friederich cast a sideways glance at Pieter.

The priest smiled weakly. "They'll be back in proper time, lad. Not like some fool priest."

A conversation quickly ensued in which a list of necessary items was made. Frieda wanted more thread and a needle; Maria asked for honey for Pieter's sake; the others added various items such as salt, fishing nets for the Rhine, fresh flint, replacement arrows for Wil, and a whetstone for the blades. "Several baskets of flour would be good," added Frieda. "We lost most of ours in Olten."

"And what about some vegetables ... late peas and the like?"

Helmut added more. "What of some fresh-baked bread? What we have is hard as stones. And I'd like a few turnips, some garlic and onions, some—"

"My, how times have changed!" mused Pieter. "Might I add some butter, a bottle of French wine ... perhaps from Bordeaux ... no, Provence ... no, make that the region of Lyons—"

"It'll be red," grumbled Heinrich. "Is that all?"

Alwin stepped forward hesitantly. "It would cost much, very much, but what of a sword for me? I fear we might need one."

The group hesitated. Swords were very expensive. Heinrich thought it a wise purchase however. "How much is one of our lives worth? We need Alwin's arm."

"Why not give him your sword?" challenged Otto.

Wil stepped forward. "What money we'll spend is mostly m'father's! His sword is his to use, and he uses it well. We'll buy Alwin what we can."

The matter settled, Frieda asked for one more thing. "If you could find a bowl of ink, sir, it would make me glad."

"Ink?"

"*Ja.*"

"What are you writing, anyway?"

Frieda flushed with embarrassment. "Oh, I'll show you another time."

The group was intrigued by the secret. "Eh?" quizzed Tomas. "Why another time?"

"I'm not yet finished."

"Finished with what?" challenged Friederich.

Frieda turned to Wil with imploring eyes. He came to her defense. "Enough. She'll reveal it when she's ready."

The matter settled for the time being, Heinrich shrugged. "Aye, girl. Ink it is."

The four made their way toward the city on a roadway filled with travelers. Every manner of cart and wagon groaned between men-at-arms, pious pilgrims, merchants with heavy-laden horses, and clerics bearing crosses. It was a noisy, uncomfortable press of people dressed in woolens on a hot summer day.

"Everyone stinks," groused Tomas.

As they neared the city gate, Heinrich handed each shopper some coins and assigned a list of wares to purchase. When they entered the marketplace, the four divided with a plan to meet by the gate again at the bells of nones.

Bidding the other two good fortune, Heinrich and Wil walked together into the market and scanned the tables of produce that were brought into the city each day from the farms dotting the countryside. Cheese was abundant, along with various assortments of green vegetables. Fish was plentiful, particularly codfish from the Rhine. Game was scarce, of course, considering that the local lords refused to allow hunting by anyone other than their own huntsmen. But joints of pork and heavy slabs of ox-meat were plentiful and hung on iron hooks alongside droop-legged fowl and mutton.

Heinrich was pleased to walk alone with his son, and the two spoke earnestly of things past and things to come. Heinrich was informed—in rather great detail—of the events in Weyer since his leaving, and Heinrich, in turn, told more of his own story. Sitting under a linden and sharing a jar of beer, the two nearly lost track of time. For each, the other's accounting was a fascinating glimpse into the soul. It quickly became a time of mutual repentance and the beginning of healing. A loud voice interrupted their conversation.

"Do you like m'monkey?"

"What?"

A strange old man with a monkey on his shoulder leaned forward. He was fat and bald, and the reek of his foul breath was overpowering. Father and son winced. "I say, do you like m'monkey?"

Heinrich looked at the wide-eyed creature. "I suppose I do."

"Good, then have him." The man set the four-legged little beast on Heinrich's shoulder.

Objecting loudly, Heinrich stood, and the monkey bit him on the ear. "Ahhh!" cried the baker. He swatted the dodging animal as it scooted back and forth across the man's broad shoulders.

Wil roared with laughter—as did the gathering crowd—while the old rogue watched through squinting eyes. At last, however, the trickster began to shout. "Thief! Thief! He stole my monkey! Call the guard!"

"What!" roared Wil. His father was too busy to respond. He was dancing about the marketplace trying to shed himself of the mean-spirited creature. "He's no thief!" the young man cried furiously.

A troop of soldiers came trotting around the corner. "Thief!" cried the old man, pointing at Heinrich. "Thief!" The commander immediately rushed toward the hapless baker and knocked him to the ground. The chattering monkey dashed away, running wildly in a wide circle around the laughing crowd until bounding upon his master's shoulder and kissing the old man on the cheek. "Oh, thank you, officer," cried the man, bowing. "This fellow tried to steal my little friend here. You were a witness. Arrest him at once."

Wil bounded to the soldiers. "The man's a liar! Arrest *him*."

By now, Heinrich had gathered his wits and climbed to his feet under the points of two lances.

"Hold fast, stranger. He says you tried to steal his monkey."

"He's a liar."

The soldier looked about the crowd. "Have we any witnesses?"

"*Oui*," came a voice. It belonged to a lovely young damsel dressed in a flowing silk gown. She peered from beneath a gauze wimple that covered her hair piled neatly atop her head. She pointed to Heinrich. "He is a thief."

It was enough. The guards grabbed both father and son and began to drag them away when the old man cried out again, "Hold, sirs. Hold a moment."

"What?"

"Well, truth be told, this fellow caused me no harm. Perhaps he might just pay me for m'trouble, and we can let the matter rest."

"He'll pay nothing!" shouted Wil. A soldier slapped him.

The officer nodded to the old man. "And how much would be fair?"

"Well, he gave m'little friend quite a scare and me as well. And he ought be taught a lesson for the sake of other helpless folk such as m'self. I should say ... hmm ... methinks a shilling should do."

"Burn in hell, old man," cried Wil. A fist knocked him to the ground.

"Two shillings, now," grumbled the guard. "Else we'll invite you to our little feast in the dungeon."

The very word sent chills through both father and son. Heinrich clenched his teeth. "Sirs, methinks a shilling and a beg of pardon from my son should do. I've no more than a shilling on m'person anyway. 'Tis all I've left after a long journey."

Wil was impressed. His father had learned a few things since his days in Weyer!

Annoyed, the officer agreed, and Heinrich picked carefully through his satchel. His fingers found the silver, and he carefully counted twelve pennies. He lifted them from his bag in a closed fist and presented them to the officer.

Releasing their prisoners with a shove, the soldiers grunted. They took four pennies for themselves, then handed the old scoundrel his eight as Heinrich and Wil walked slowly away. "Old bag of gas," grumbled Wil. The pair turned to see the man who now beckoned his apparent accomplice to his side. He handed the damsel some coins, and the two waved at the hapless pilgrims.

"I hate this place," said Wil as he rubbed his jaw. "Let's be off."

The pair hurried to buy the items on their lists, then paused briefly in the square by the fish market. Their eyes scanned the brownstone buildings, the towers of the churches, and the passersby. A few men sitting nearby were talking of the dangers in the Rhine Valley, both along the east and west banks. "Outlaws and mercenaries, errant knights and rebels are everywhere. The war never ends and the innocent pay the bills. It's best to board a riverboat or travel with a caravan if you can find one. The boats are costly, but there ought to be numbers of caravans headed toward the Champagne fairs this time of year. And the road north is flat and easy walking."

Heinrich listened carefully. He'd had his fill of troubles and wanted no more. "These caravans—they'll let us travel with them?"

"For a lesser fee than a boat. They hire men-at-arms to guard them, so they charge others to sleep under their watch."

Heinrich nodded. "Seems fair enough. I'd not travel with infidels, though."

The others agreed. "Times go bad for them ... as they should. Landless crusaders fill the ranks of the highway-men, and they want nothing but vengeance on the cursed devils."

⌒

The following morning, the company agreed they'd forego the expense of sailing the river and would venture north along the west bank of the Rhine in hopes of finding a cara-van. With Pieter riding Paulus, they followed the highway as it bent northward across a landscape that had become flat and easy to walk. They were quickly unsettled, how-ever, when they realized they were among a very few travel-ers on what should have been a crowded thoroughfare. After all, it was this road that led the way to the fairs at Champagne, to Paris and Strasbourg, and even to dreary Bruges and the Low Countries.

"Keep a sharp eye about," said Alwin. "'Tis all we can do."

The group marched north quickly but cautiously. Few words were spoken as all eyes were kept fixed on distant points. At the end of the second day, they made camp in a light wood about three bowshots beyond the red-block walls of a free, growing village called Neuf-Brisach. It was on the morning of the next day when it seemed good fortune found them.

"Look," cried Helmut. "A caravan!" The lad pointed to the north gate of the town from which a column of wag-ons and horsemen was emerging. The company hurried forward to have a better look, and as they drew near, they smiled.

Led by an armored knight in gaily colored robes and accompanied by a cacophony of sounds, a long line of per-sons, beasts, and sundry vehicles streamed forward. Heavy-laden packhorses followed yawning servants, and strong-backed Frisians yielded to the cries of the carters as they hauled many numbers of canvas-covered wagons and two-wheeled carts

A host of walkers were intermixed, including freemen of middling means dressed in knee-length tunics and well-loomed leggings. Pilgrims in broad hats, servants under heavy packs, and knots of monks moved along as well; the shavelings were working hard to keep their eyes from lingering on the sampling of "erring sisters" strutting about. Here and there were a few jugglers, and two balladeers were singing a farewell song to the captain of Neuf-Breisach's guard. Benedetto wrinkled his nose. "German music ... always about bloodshed and honor!"

Ambling along either side of the column were two lines of disinterested and rather unseemly men-at-arms mounted on a collection of palfreys and a few chargers. These were mercenaries, mostly landless knights with swords for hire. Dressed in flowing gowns of silk or linen, numbers of ladies were traveling as well. These rode sidesaddle on elegant Spanish-Normans or on small coursers.

But Wil's company took the greatest delight in the assortment of animals accompanying the parade. Besides carts of swine and fowl, hounds and cats scampered about as pets of the lords and ladies. Hooded falcons rode tethered to perches affixed to numerous wagons.

"And see!" exclaimed Otto. "In those cages. A black bear, and there ... a strange bird ..."

"'Tis an ostrich," added Pieter.

"Oh."

"They make huge eggs." Pieter licked his lips.

"And see there." Tomas pointed. "Giant cats with spots."

"Leopards from the Dark Continent," replied Pieter. "And over there, carrying that fat lord on his litter, are men from that very same place." The company stared at the oil-black skin of the giant men who had been brought from the mysterious land of spirits and odd tales.

It was a passing cart carrying a group of chattering monkeys, however, that seized Heinrich's attention. The baker growled. "Wil, see that one!" He pointed to one particular little creature who was pointing back and chortling. "'Tis that blasted devil from Basel!" he shouted.

Frieda laughed. "How do you know it's the same one?"

Heinrich rubbed his bitten ear lightly and swept his eye across the scene in search of the old swindler and his young accomplice. He shrugged.

"Well, should we join them?" asked Alwin.

Wil looked about his group. His companions were nodding hopefully. After all, they had just spent two days walking in tremulous fear, and the caravan seemed safe enough. "Well?"

"*Ja!*" was the unanimous response. Wil turned to Heinrich. "Help me find the master, then, and we'll pay the fee."

ૐ

Wil's company joined the caravan at the rear, behind the lord's servants but still within the protective reach of the soldiers. They walked happily along the highway northward, past numerous villages recently liberated from the diocese and from their local lords. It seemed that concessions were being successfully wrangled from the feudal order. With cities rapidly expanding and towns emerging across the countryside, serfs had been fleeing their lords' lands and successfully finding both refuge and employment elsewhere. Inspired by news of the Stedingers and others, peasant rebellions were strengthening in frequency and in effect. The brave village folk were slowly reclaiming some semblance of their divine birthright that had been long since suffocated: liberty.

The landscape was still flat and easy to walk, so the caravan made good time as it passed by Colmar and drew close to Strasbourg. It passed meadows of orange-red poppies and sparkling ponds of turquoise blue. "Each land has its own beauty," said Pieter as the column was halted for a wagon repair. He looked upward and pointed to a skyscape of fluffy white clouds. "Do you see, baker?"

Heinrich lifted his eye to the sky boldly. It was a simple act for most but a demonstration of much more for him. "Aye, Pieter. I look up often now."

Alwin smiled and nodded. "God be praised, good fellow. A curse on those fools who bound you otherwise. They had no right."

Pieter's gaze drifted across the land until his eyes rested peacefully on a barley field moving softly in the breeze. He followed the wending of its green grasses as they yielded to the skipping currents of air. "The angels are playing again," he mused.

The others watched as a stronger breeze etched the green field with dashing paths of silver made bright by the sun's reflection on the bending blades. A couple of merchantmen walked by, completely unaware of the sky above but pausing briefly to look at the healthy field of grain. Their conversation turned to prices of springtime plantings and the likely harvests in the month to come.

Pieter sighed. "It is my observation that all men are either poets or merchants. Poets see beauty for what it is; merchants see it for what it does!"

Alwin agreed. "I daresay we are in a long line of merchants who'd squeeze deniers from the stones at our feet if they could! Look there." He pointed at three squabbling peddlers. "One sells cloth; the other, metals; the third, feathers. They've naught in common but greed."

Heinrich grunted. "They'd quarrel over a comfit."

Pieter nodded and studied the column. "Seems we'll be spending the day with the song of hammers. That wagon's leaning badly, and it looks like an axle broke on the other."

Wil joined the three and heard the news that the caravan would need to make an early camp. "Will we ever come to Weyer!" he groused.

"I shouldn't be so much in a hurry about it, lad," answered Alwin. "Much can happen in a year's time."

"I swear, if that old hag Anka stole our land or if Pious stole the bakery, I'll lay them both in new graves!"

Heinrich darkened. "We own both for all time. It is the law."

Pieter sighed. "Nothing is owned for all time, baker. *Omnia mutantur.* All things are changing."

"No!" retorted Wil and his father simultaneously.

Heinrich's face tightened. "The land was m'father's father's. It is only a half hide, but it is *my* half hide! The bakery is mine by law as well. The abbot bartered it to me in fair exchange for land I inherited from a dear friend. No other shall have it!"

Wil felt suddenly anxious, and he turned sheepishly to his father. "I ... I did swear to Father Albert that I'd give a quarter of our land to *Frau* Anka if mother is alive when we return."

Heinrich stared blankly at his son. "A quarter of our land? By the saints, boy! That would be seven hectares!"

"Enough to feed a family for six months," added Otto as he joined them.

"Aye!" The baker's face was flushed.

"But she gets it only if mother is alive when we return," blurted Wil.

Heinrich's conscience was suddenly snagged. He would prefer to keep his seven hectares, to find them plowed and planted and still recorded in his name. Yet choosing a plot of earth over the life of his insufferable wife was shaming. "I ... I ... well, what's right is right, boy. Pray you've yet a mother."

Otto interrupted. "My mother died soon after Lothar was born."

"I know, lad," answered Heinrich. "Your mother was a good woman."

"She hated my father."

Heinrich was not sure how to answer. "I wouldn't know much about that. Your mother seemed content enough when she came for bread. Your father kept a distance from me, and I ne'er knew him very well ... even though he was baptized the same year as m'self. He has a strong way about him, and it was good when he got the mill. Better him than that fool Dietrich, I thought. He'll be happy to see you."

Otto shook his head. "He swore he'd beat me and throw me out of the village if I didn't bring Lothar back unscathed." The lad's voice became thick, and he wrung his hands. "He loved m'brother like no other. After the wild *Schwein* killed my sister, he was never the same. Then Lothar was born and *Mutti* died."

"I remember when your sister was killed," said Wil. "It was horrible."

"My father found her lying with two dead lambs. He said she had been torn in pieces. He keeps a lock of her hair tied round his neck on a cord."

The group fell quiet while they made camp for the coming night. Wil ordered a few to tasks, and then built a small fire and sat by Otto and Tomas as they spoke of home. Frieda and Maria had spotted mushrooms on some trees in a woodland they had passed, and the pair imagined adding these to the afternoon meal along with a sprinkling of poppy petals.

"Wil, we'd like to gather some mushrooms from the wood," Frieda said. She pointed to a dark stand of forest not far from the roadway.

Wil was lost in his conversation. With a distracted wave of his hand, he sent the two smiling girls away, and within a short time, Frieda and Maria were skipping across a narrow field with baskets on their elbows.

The day was warm, almost hot. An hour or so before, distant bells had rung the hour of nones. But, as this was near the middle of July, the day would be long. The young woman and her little sister sang happily as they dashed through waist-high barley. Their flaxen braids shimmered golden under the bright sun, and their pink skin flushed with joy as they raced toward the cool of the woodland shade. In moments, the pair disappeared from sight, swallowed into the shadows of the silent forest.

Chapter Sixteen

FOREST HAUNTS AND A MERRY INN

As though drawn by an invisible spirit of some ancient myth, the two hurried deeper and deeper into a magical realm of heavy timbers and soft ferns. The air smelled musty, and the earth beneath them was padded with the crumbled black residue of centuries. Now quiet, the girls slowed their pace and looked about carefully. A slow, creeping sense of dread had just begun to crawl over Frieda when Maria's happy voice cried out, "There!"

The tyke sprinted toward a damp, shallow dish in the forest floor that was covered with mushrooms. She stopped at the edge of the heavily shaded clearing. "Frieda! Look how many!"

Indeed, before the two girls stood a veritable world of mushrooms on their stout, singular pillars like a field of multicolored umbrellas. Frieda smiled. "There, steinpilz, the fat brown ones. And there, see the pretty blue caps? They're blewits, and those huge gold ones! Those are pfifferling and they're delicious! I remember them from m'*Mutti*'s kitchen."

The two girls stared wide eyed at the enchanting glade. Covering the moist earth was a host of varieties. Some flat, some rounded, many brown, others red or blue. A large arc of fairy-ring mushrooms encircled a splattering of dark-capped ones standing tall on their cream-colored pillars.

Ledge like flattops grew from the sides of rotting logs, and white-toothed semmelstoppelpilz mingled with many others to boast nearly every color of the rainbow.

Frieda led Maria carefully into their newfound mushroom kingdom. The two tiptoed gingerly among the host of fungi at their feet, staring incredulously at their treasure. "These are too soon ready," whispered Frieda. "It is summer; most are not ready until St. Michael's!"

Maria nodded, suddenly a little fearful. "Are they witched?"

Frieda paused. The word had always frightened her. She looked about for any sign of spell-casting or charms. "I ... I ... methinks not."

Maria waited as Frieda thought hard to provide some other explanation. "It is cool here. Perhaps they grow differently in this wood."

The answer seemed right enough, and, relieved, the girls were soon bobbing amongst the little pedestals, snatching this one and that with grasping hands. It took very little time to fill the baskets, and with broad smiles the pair stood and faced one another proudly. "Well, methinks we've too many!" boasted Frieda. She set down her overflowing basket and Maria giggled.

"We've enough to feed the whole of the caravan!"

"Aye. But we wanted poppies as well," answered Frieda.

They looked about. "We should find a more sunny place," said Maria.

Frieda turned in circles. "I saw lots of them along the highway. Shall we go that way?"

Maria stared vacantly at what suddenly seemed to be endless forest. She shrugged. "I'll follow you."

So the two wanderers began a brisk walk with their baskets in hand. They spoke of things touching both their hearts, and Frieda probed Maria on the secret particulars of Wil's past. "He was always kind, but he liked to be alone mostly," Maria said as she thought carefully. "He seemed to be unhappy a lot."

Frieda nodded.

"*Mutti* was usually angry with him."

"For cause?"

The little girl shrugged. "Methinks not. *Mutti* was angry with everyone. Karl worked hard to please her, though, more than Wil did."

"And you?"

Maria stopped and her face fell. "I tried to be good, but she thought this"—she lifted her deformed arm—"was a punishment. I think she was ashamed of me."

Frieda set her basket down and hugged the girl. "No one is ashamed of you, Maria."

The maiden smiled.

Scanning the forest, the two spotted a distant dip in which a pool was likely lying. They hurried forward and, to their delight, they did, indeed, come upon a clear spring filled with crystal water and laced with watercress. "Ah, Maria, we should have brought another basket!"

They removed some of their mushrooms and topped their baskets with the green water plant. They took long, refreshing draughts of water and sat to speak of times past once more. It was a restful conversation that wandered between Frieda's life as the daughter of a lord to Maria's and the particulars of Weyer. Frieda spoke in somber tones of her lost siblings and her father's shame and lovingly of her mother. Maria giggled over May Day tales and cried a little when she remembered Karl playing bladder ball with his friends.

Frieda turned the talk toward Wil again but suddenly stopped. An uncomfortable breeze had chilled her, and she sat erect, looking about with wide eyes. The woodland had become ghostly quiet, and the shadows had slowly thickened around the two like creeping villains enclosing their prey. Frieda took short, anxious breaths. She stood and whirled about, first this way, then that.

Sensing her sudden fear, Maria stood and clutched Frieda's gown, scanning the view for whatever had given Frieda such unease.

"Maria, I think … I think we're lost," murmured Frieda.

The word struck terror like few others. "Lost!" exclaimed the little girl. Her eyes arced upward and widened. "But it will be dark! And what of trolls? What of wild boar or bear? What of spirits? What of—"

"Enough, Maria," interrupted Frieda with a faint voice. She squeezed her fists tightly, as if to press courage quickly into her own body, then knelt before the frightened tyke. "My dear, we can't have wandered so very far. We'll try to find our way, but Wil and the others will come looking soon."

"But ..."

"No. We've both faced far worse than this. Look about. We've water, food aplenty, shelter under these old trees." Frieda swallowed hard.

"Which way do we go?"

Frieda did not know.

⌒

"Where is my wife?" asked Wil. He searched the faces of his comrades now ringing the campfire.

"And where is Maria?" added Heinrich.

"You said they could go for mushrooms," retorted Otto.

"What? When?" answered Wil as he stared into the distant wood.

"When we were talking. Must have been some hours ago."

Wil stood and looked up at the dimming sky. "I don't remember that. 'Tis past vespers, to be sure. Compline is but two hours away!"

The whole company now stood. Alwin cast a worried glance at Heinrich, who was turning pale.

"They may be lost," said Tomas anxiously. "Lost in that wood."

"Lost!" gasped all. "Lost at night, lost with what devils lay about that place?" cried Friederich. He stared at the trees standing nearly motionless. "Something is amiss," he muttered. "I can feel it."

Licking his dry lips and wringing his hands, Wil paced back and forth. "What to do? What to do?" he mumbled. The lad looked at the sky, then at the wood, at the sky, and at the wood again. Highwaymen and rogues ... the forest is filled with them! He turned to his father when his eyes fell on Pieter kneeling quietly nearby. Wil hesitated, then took a step toward the old man. He paused, looked at his companions, then at the forest one more time. Finally, with a deep breath and a slow release, the worried husband—the worried brother—walked slowly to the old priest and knelt awkwardly at his side.

Pieter's heart soared. He continued petitioning the Almighty for mercy, to "shield the fair maidens from what evil might be lurking near and comfort them in this moment of terror. Guide them, O great Shepherd of Israel, like your people of old, and return these two lost lambs to the fold. Hide them in the comfort of your mighty hand, and be a sword of might to any who would wish them harm!"

Wil's spirit echoed the priest's words, shyly joining the yearnings of his heart to the old man's. And when Pieter pronounced his "amen" loudly and with confidence, the lad did as well.

But such noble submission was not limited to the priest and the young man at his side. It had also touched the whole of the company, which had fallen quietly to its knees. So, when Pieter stood and faced the silent ring of his rising brethren, the man cried aloud for joy; his flock had learned and learned well after all.

"Now," exclaimed Wil. "Now we need a plan."

Alwin stepped forward. He wiped his hands through his hair and turned his dark eyes toward the flames. "Darkness can be a friend in the forest ... it is when light is most easily seen. We once hunted for a wounded comrade in a heavy wood near Grenoble. We took torches and formed a line within sight of one another. We moved forward slowly, calling for him as we went. Every bowshot we held fast and listened until we found him."

Wil nodded his approval. "That we can do. Pieter, you remain behind with Paulus and our provisions. Leave us have Solomon."

The old man yielded. He had become increasingly aware of his failing strength, though it was a painful admission. He looked forlornly at the donkey. "Paulus, I have now aged beyond aging ... I shall soon be the man that used to be," he mumbled.

"Pieter?"

"Eh?"

"You'll stay with Paulus?"

"*Ja*, lad. I will stay behind."

Heinrich was sent in search of oil with which to soak long-burning torches. He returned promptly with a reminder from the master that the column would leave at daybreak with or without them. "Here, I've oil enough, and I've found two horns. Soak the torches well and let's be off!"

∂

"Frieda, I am scared," whispered Maria.

"Me, too," answered Frieda slowly. "But fear gives us our wits. Now, we needs put the breeze to our backs. It was in our face when we entered the wood."

"Are you sure?"

"Yes, quite." The young woman feigned confidence. "Now, let's have a good drink from the spring and be off."

The pair drew ample draughts of water from the spring fast losing its sparkle in the fading light of day. Ready, they peered into the darkening canopy overhead for some sign of rustling leaves. The trees were still. Frieda licked her finger and held it in the air, feeling for the cool side. "There." She pointed. "The air is coming from there."

Hurrying across the soft floor of the forest, Frieda and Maria made their way into an ever-deepening thicket of unfamiliar saplings and tangled bushes. Both soon realized that they had not come that way before. They stopped. The sun had now set below the unseen horizon, and cool breezes swirled from each direction. Frieda was perspiring and pale. She dared not display her growing terror to the little girl at her side, but she wanted for all the world to burst into tears.

Maria took her hand. "Listen!" she whispered.

The two became perfectly still.

"There!" answered Frieda. "I think I heard a voice." The two stared blankly into the thickening blackness of the wood. The muffled trumpeting of a horn faded away.

"Here!" shouted Frieda suddenly. "Here! We are here!" The young woman ran toward the sounds, stumbling and tripping in the increasing darkness. Maria raced behind her, shouting frantically. The two crashed through brush and bramble until finally pausing to listen again.

"Do you hear anything?" whispered Maria.

Unable to hold back her tears, Frieda shook her head.

Maria looked up with imploring, trusting eyes. She took the young woman's hand in hers and waited.

Frieda stared fearfully at the dark images of trees now rising about her like so many silent creatures of the night. She shivered and spun about. *We are lost!* she thought. *Lost!*

"In the morning, then?" asked Maria. "Shall we wait until the morning?"

"I ... I ... yes, of course. In the morning they'll surely find us."

The two said nothing more but felt their way to a clearing they could barely see. All had become shadows and shades, mere hints of blacks and grays with eerie slivers of silver sent from an unfriendly moon. They crouched nervously against a wide trunk and held each other tightly as the sounds of the night stirred about them.

Neither dared to sleep. They had spent many hours at the knees of elders who had told them of the woodland spirits, of the secret kingdoms of wicked gnomes, and of dragon's lairs. "On the half-moon, sprites go to war with fairies," Maria whispered.

"'Tis a crescent moon tonight, methinks."

"On crescent moons the spell-casters meet in the hall of the toad queen. They seek the tongues of little girls," Maria whispered in a tightening voice.

Frieda opened her mouth to answer but suddenly remembered the daughter of her father's bailiff who was born mute under a crescent moon. "We mustn't think of these things."

At that moment, an owl burst from its unseen perch and swooped overhead, flapping its wings violently. The startled girls cried out, then held each other all the more tightly. The curtain of night now hung fully over the wood. The air was heavy, and a silent mist began to gather along the forest floor. Staring into nothingness, the pair trembled. New shadows seemed to appear, then disappear, only to give rise to another here and yet more there. It was as though the woodland was silently taunting them, daring them to move from their place and wander amidst the hauntings.

Maria and Frieda held each and leaned into the smooth bark of a night-blackened beech. The older maiden closed her eyes and sang to the little one her "Maria's Song."

Let me take you by the hand, and let us laugh beneath the sun....

The words comforted them both, and Frieda's confident tone soon filled them with courage to endure the blackness of the forest. When the song was over, the two settled under their black canopy to imagine sunbeams and springtime meadows, rainbows and butterflies—and a splendid valley of wildflowers.

And so they waited until the morning songbirds coaxed the darkness to yield. And yield it did, for despite its stubborn, stiff-necked pride, the forest did not rule the sun; it could command nothing and finally submitted to the insistent sky above.

"Maria! The morning is finally come!"

The little girl nodded wearily, greatly relieved to have survived the ghostly terrors of the night.

"Now we need move."

"Where?"

Frieda looked about. She licked her dry lips, then ran her fingers through the dew at her feet. She turned her face to the treetops and closed her eyes. She finally took a deep breath and spoke to her little companion with a commanding voice. "There." She stared at a wide sunbeam pointing to a bright patch some distance ahead.

"Why there?"

"I don't know. But it beckons me somehow."

The two walked hopefully toward the clearing and finally emerged into a small glade filled with soft ferns and the sweet smell of a nearby grove of pines. "Look up!" cried Maria.

Three seabirds swooped toward the pair and cried loudly. They dove deeply and then sped to the sky, only to fly in rapid circles and dive again. "They're calling us," marveled Maria.

Frieda stared at the three birds as they glided toward her. Their white underbellies were clean looking, their gray wings preened and healthy. "What are they doing here? I've only seen them by the sea."

Maria stared at them for a long while, laughing at their chatter. "They are waterbirds. Maybe they'll lead us to the Rhine!"

Frieda smiled. "Ah! Of course. So we should follow them!"

And follow them they did. Doing their best to keep one eye on the birds and the other on the path ahead, the two sisters ran. The three gulls cried happily overhead, sweeping eastward as they soared away, only to reappear above the heads of the racing girls. On and on they ran, pausing for nothing, now certain of their faithful escort. They dashed through stands of hardwoods, through bloom-spotted clearings, beneath the boughs of heavy spruce, and over fallen timber. At last, they paused, panting. Maria claimed she had heard a voice. They listened carefully.

"Frieda!" came a faint cry. "Maria!" A horn sounded.

"Here!" the two screeched. "Here!"

Running toward the sounds, they soon heard more. Now laughing and waving to the three birds above, the two emerged from the forest and charged across the grain fields by the Rhine. Downstream about a half league, they could see several figures now running toward them. The two sprinted until their legs burned. Closer and closer they came until, at last—at long last—Frieda's eyes fell on her desperate husband's face.

The young bride dashed forward. Closer and closer she came until, to the loud cheers of her comrades, Frieda fell into the happy embrace of her exhausted groom.

❧

"No more adventures," said Wil wearily. He was still holding Frieda's hand in his as the relieved pilgrims returned to Pieter and Paulus. "I just want to sit in my poor hovel and bake bread with m'father. I want to enjoy feast days with the village and hear Father Albert do his Mass. I want no more of this."

"And what of Pious?" grumbled Otto.

"What of him?" growled Wil.

"You said you wanted to hear Father Albert do the Mass, but it is usually Pious."

Wil spat and his father grumbled, "Pious needs to burn in the Pit."

Pieter sighed. "I've heard much about the man. Seems he is in need of redemption."

Tomas stood. He cast a faraway look at the empty roadway leading toward home. "Pious is a wicked fool." He touched his half-ear and looked at Heinrich. "You took m'ear, but he nearly took m'soul. He had me lie and cheat others. He's more wicked than your uncle, Arnold."

Heinrich agreed. "*Ja*, lad. 'Tis true. Uncle Arnold with his penny sins is vile and cruel, but Pious ... I have no words for him."

Pieter laid a hand gently on Tomas's shoulder. The two had spoken often of late, and Pieter had helped soften the lad with grace and wisdom. "We all become the ugliest face of our idols. If we worship wealth, we become greedy. If we worship power, we become tyrants. From what I have heard, it seems this Father Pious worships stature and has become utterly vain. He has hated others and become a murderer."

"Vanity? Murder? More than these, Pieter," growled Heinrich. "He is all things wicked! The lusts of his fat-pressed heart are boundless."

Wil nodded. "As evil a man as I've ever known, Pieter. And he wears the robes and the tonsure."

Pieter nodded sadly. "It is the mask of false faith that is, perhaps, the worst face of all." He took a deep breath. "I confess my fear for you in Weyer. He shall not happily welcome any of you, save Tomas, perhaps."

The lad grunted. "He'll not have me doing his bidding again."

Otto threw a stick onto the morning fire. "So what awaits us in Weyer?"

The circle was quiet. Frieda looked at her husband's darkening face and took his hand. Maria cuddled against Heinrich's broad chest, and Otto faced Tomas blankly. Who could know?

~

Now beyond the protection of the caravan, the travelers made their way warily along the left bank of the Rhine, pausing briefly in the city of Strasbourg for provisions. Their purchases made, the group then returned to the highway and moved toward Mainz, which lay some forty leagues beyond. Paulus slowed them slightly, but traveling the flat highway under a blue sky afforded the company a pace of some five leagues per day.

During the eight days since leaving the caravan, the group had been accosted only twice. A pair of drunken rogues had emerged from some rocky cover and made a bumbling effort to drag Frieda away while she was drawing water from a well. It was Helmut who heard the girl's cries, but it was Wil who hastily launched two arrows from his bow, each missing its distant target but landing close enough to frighten the brigands away. Suffering only a torn gown and a bruised cheek, Frieda found herself sobbing in her husband's arms once more.

The following day, two ruffians armed with weighted staffs accosted the weary band. They believed it was God's will that they should punish any returning child crusaders. But judging the quality of their clothing and the unbroken spirit in their lifted chins, the men determined them to be pilgrims and "not that unfaithful rabble daring to return home." Fortunately, Wil and his company managed to restrain their tongues and avoid a bruising brawl.

Finally, on the evening of Friday, the nineteenth of July, the weary travelers arrived in the busy city of Mainz, where they sought lodging at an inn near the scaffolded cathedral. Mainz was an ancient city lying directly on the river of myth and legend. Its narrow streets were crowded with all manner of peddlers, clerics, and fools. It reeked of manure and human waste, of garbage and standing water. It was filled with sundry buildings made of plankboards, clay, or wattle. Thatch covered most of the pitiful hovels that crowded the poor neighborhoods, as well as the countless assortments of sheds, barns, and workhouses set haphazardly about. It was place where a single torch might destroy everything in sight within moments.

Everything in sight, that is, except for the cathedral climbing high above the lesser sights scattered at its feet. From here the Archbishop Siegfried ruled his expansive diocese. His miter commanded souls as far south as the Italian Alps and nearly to the city of Bremen in the north—from the vineyards of the Rhine's west banks to the markets of Augsburg in the east. His diocese was rich and prospering. His feudal territories had grown to such proportions as might corrupt even the most honorable men, and so Alwin reminded his companions that "the wearer of the pallium and buskins in Mainz is another cleric to fear."

"Siegfried is an arse. I don't like him," Pieter crowed from his perch atop Paulus. "I've crisscrossed his little churchdom most of my life. I've found little true piety. The dolt is a count of the empire, like that fool Conrad before him. His tastes are high. Look, the alms boxes are emptied on this cathedral, while the poor under his very nose suffer! Maybe God shall burn this one down like he did the old one."

Wil hurried his company through the city, past the wharves where wool was piled high in great bales and countless ells of linen were rolled and stacked. The marketplace was nearly empty except for a few Jews in rich robes and pointed hats chattering by their booth. "Moneylending Jews do well here," said Alwin. "They do in England as well. The Christians in London are quick to borrow from them, but few have paid them back! 'Tis little wonder they charge such outrageous fees."

The group looked confused.

"Like us, Jews do not permit themselves to loan money to

one another at interest," Alwin added. "But a Christian may charge usury to a Jew and a Jew to a Christian!"

"Aye," said Helmut. "My father says the bishop makes good business from that somehow. I don't understand it, though."

The children stared blankly at the Jews until Pieter added, "Some of the lords make them wear special clothing. I've seen some required to wear the Star of David on their breasts so that Christians know to keep a guard."

Alwin nodded. "The pope's talked of requiring all Christendom to do the same ... to make them dress in special ways and to make them live in their own neighborhoods of the cities."

"Some call them 'Christ-killers.' Does he want them killed for their crime?" asked Tomas.

"Nay. The pope granted them a constitution of sorts a few years ago. He ordered that no Christian may cause them harm since they are the sons and daughters of Abraham. But they may not dwell with us nor keep Christian servants and the like."

The darkening sky had clouded and was now heavy and gray. A brief shower dampened the wayfarers, and their thoughts turned to other things.

"More rain is coming, Wil," said Heinrich. "We're all tired and your wife is coughing. It's time we found an inn."

The young man nodded and looked about the busy streets. From atop his braying friend, Pieter pointed to a corner with his staff. "I remember a good roof over there," he said. "And they have good beer."

The group followed the old man's directions and was soon facing a busy tavern. Curiously, three seabirds were perched on the crooked ridge of the building's roof, crying lightly and shaking themselves loose of the rain. Frieda stared at them for a moment, then smiled to herself.

Finally, with Paulus stabled and their provisions locked away, Wil and his fellows gathered around a wide planked table within the warm confines of the inn. Here they reached hungrily for salted Rhine codfish and hearty ales. The hearth fire choked under a poor draught, but fresh rye bread and a few roasted joints of pork kept any from complaining.

That night in Mainz was like few others. Good food, uproarious tales, and an engaging mix of patrons made for hours of well-deserved pleasure. Maria spent most of the long evening half-hidden in the safety of Heinrich's broad shadow. Frieda positioned herself strategically near her less-than-happy husband and away from the grasping hands of harmless but coarse and unseemly men. Laughing, she managed to hold her own against the leering taunts of the uncouth diners as well as the barbs of their jealous companions. Wil, however, found himself spending much of the evening trading blows with the bumbling fools who pressed his young bride beyond the rules of tavern fun.

It was late when Wil's exhausted company found their way to their beds. They had rented one room, it being covered in a thick layer of straw upon which all fell fast asleep. Morning came quickly and the company roused slowly. Stretching and yawning, most complained loudly of Pieter's persistent and unfortunate digestive failures. Quickly leaving the room, the group gathered for a first meal of red wine and bread. Then, well before the midmorning bells of terce, the pilgrims, their donkey, and their dog stood alongside the docks, waiting for a ferry to take them across the Rhine.

"Soon, lad," muttered Heinrich. "Soon we'll be home."

Wil looked wistfully across the river. He often thought of his brother, Karl, but seeing the crossing and knowing they were a mere two days or so from Weyer filled his mind with memories. He turned to his father. "Do you think of him too?"

"Karl?"

"*Ja.*"

"I do. Every day. I was just remembering him now."

"And me."

Both men fell quiet. They stared blankly at the green treetops of the eastern shore lying beyond the busy docks. "He was a good lad." Heinrich choked. "No bad bone in him."

Wil nodded.

"I ..." Heinrich sighed and wiped his eye. "My sorrow keeps him close to me. I pray I shall feel it always."

Wil looked at his father sadly. "Can you not feel joy in his memory as well?"

The baker drew a deep breath. "Sadness seems easier to carry than joy. It is not what I would wish for you or any other, but it is my way, methinks. Perhaps in time, lad. Perhaps in time."

Wil nodded. "And what of Mother?"

Thoughts of Marta filled his heart with darkness and shame. Heinrich felt suddenly sick. "I ... I only ever wished her well. I could hardly bear her, lad, but I hold no hate for her. I am both sickened and saddened for her, I fear, and that makes me ashamed."

"She is a hard woman."

"She is your mother. She loved you."

Wil kicked a stone from under his foot. His face tightened with a confusion of feeling few besides his father could understand. "No doubt she is dead. She was dying with fever even before I poisoned her."

"You did not poison her. It was Pious. And if she is dead, he needs to pay for that crime."

"We've no witness."

Heinrich thought for a long moment. "What of Anka? She knew of Pious's instructions to you."

Wil shrugged.

"But she had a motive to keep your mother alive. You promised her land."

"Aye, 'tis true enough." Wil paused. "But she'd never swear an oath against Pious, never. She fears him like Mother did."

"Would Pious even accuse you?"

Wil shook his head. "No. I've given him cause to fear me some; I know of things. I think he'd rather let the matter lie."

Heinrich wasn't so sure. "Well, we needs first see your mother ... or her grave."

Chapter Seventeen

HOME?

A lwin was, no doubt, a hunted fugitive. On numerous occasions he had offered to spare his fellows all risk by leaving them, but his pleas were soundly rejected. Heinrich had sternly reminded him of his prior vow. Now that they were nearing the lands of his home, he was secretly happy that he had made such a vow. He wanted to stand once more on the "Golden Ground" where he had been raised. He wanted to see, once more, the manorland of Villmar's abbey, and he was overjoyed to imagine seeing it with his beloved friends at his side.

So, walking warily behind the hedges and hurrying cross-country along the banks of the Emsbach, Alwin and the rest of Wil's company detoured Limburg, then arrived in Oberbrechen, where they followed the southeastern bank of the beloved Laubusbach until they arrived atop the slope overlooking Weyer. It was Sunday, the twenty-first day of July in the Year of Grace 1213.

At long last, the weary pilgrims now stared into the smoky green hollow of home. For those who had lived there, it was a moment of true homecoming, a time of returning to that singular place of belonging. They were suddenly awash with unnamed images of times past, of long-lost family and dear friends, a blur of memories bathed in colors, sounds, and scents. It was home—that inimitable place to which roots yearned to cling and the place from which all the world is measured.

Heinrich's eye filled with tears, and he could see little more than a blur of thatch beneath a wide landscape of green as he peered into Weyer. The village, still ruled by the monks of Villmar, was tucked tightly in its nestling hollow like it had been for more than four centuries. Beyond it lay the wide horizon dipped with gentle valleys and striped with forests and fields. The summer sky was grand—bright blue and blotched with puffy white clouds. Heinrich wiped his eye and looked up, smiling. He fixed his gaze on a chubby cloud overhead. *Emma*, he chuckled. *Emma, you're welcoming me home!* The man's mind swept him quickly to his Butterfly *Frau* and her wonderful hovel. He could see her illuminated pages, her gardens, her smiles.

The baker sighed, then turned his face to the haphazard assortment of hovels and sheds that was so very familiar. His mind flew from his boyhood along the babbling Laubusbach to the anxious day he had left his family behind. He closed his eye and drew deeply of the fresh, grass-scented air. He lifted Karl's cross from his belt and held it to his heart. His mind carried him to memories of the cheerful lad laughing and dashing about the footpaths below.

Heinrich sniffled, then kissed the wooden cross. He stared blankly into the waters of the silver Laubusbach below and pictured his father and his poor mother, the angry face of Baldric, and the imploring eyes of Ingelbert. A vision of Katharina and the Christmas star raised bumps on his skin, and the terror of that horrid night of feud turned his belly sour. Memories of feast days and harvests, of bitter winters and warm Sabbaths, of people beloved and others hated, all quickly melded into a single impression of what had been—in a word—his life.

And so it was for the others. Each crooked rooftop made for a memory either good or bad, but all surely familiar. And in the comfort of habituation, in the security of habit, an oppressive temptation began to climb from this "Golden Ground" through the soles of weary feet and toward the hearts of each melancholy pilgrim.

"Will be good to be home again, methinks," muttered Heinrich. "I miss what I know."

"Ja," added Otto. "Enough of this crusade or pilgrimage ... or whatever it has been! I want to be back in m'own bed under m'own roof."

Maria smiled politely, but she looked at the village with some reservation. For a girl of a mere six years, she was wise and insightful. She had wanted to share in her father's hopes, but a sense of dread had kept her still. She walked away from the others to search the field for some flowers to pick but saw none, and then turned her face to Friederich, who was solemn and troubled. "Friederich?"

The boy wrinkled his smudged face and shifted uncomfortably on his feet. "Something is amiss," he whispered.

Wil had been standing quietly with one hand in his wife's and the other wrapped around the hilt of his dagger. He withdrew the blade from his belt and stared at its inscription. "*'Vrijheid altijd,'* 'freedom always,' Frieda," he said. He stared down on his village and wondered.

Tomas shifted uneasily on his feet. He, too, had learned to treasure his freedom, and he was no more certain than Wil of the conditions that now faced them all. "So are we free or bound?"

The company turned away from the view and faced one another. "Eh?" asked Pieter.

"I say, are we free or bound? We've all wondered about it since we began the journey home, but none would e'er speak of it." Tomas turned his face to Heinrich. "What say you?"

The baker shook his head. "I ... I cannot surely say. The law says if we live for a year and a day unclaimed by our lord we are free."

"That's what *Pieter* says the law is," added Alwin. "I am not so sure of this."

"But we've served on crusade!" blurted Otto. His green eyes were now blazing, and a tone of insistence laced his words. "By the saints, I'll not be bound again! We paid our price. The lives of the others should have been manumission enough."

Wil nodded. "*Ja*, Otto. It should be so. Weyer's paid the debt for us all with the lives of many. You, Otto, have given your brother, Lothar, and I m'brother, Karl. Ingrid and Beatrix are gone, and m'cousins Wolfhard and Richarda are probably dead as well. Weyer sent more than a score to the cause, and I doubt any are come home."

"It will not matter," said Pieter slowly. He sighed and knelt by Solomon. "Perhaps I've put my hopes for you ahead of the facts. I fear the order is what it is. It cannot abide its folk declaring themselves free. The lords and the churchmen see you as bound to them. They conspire to keep you in your place under the ruse of it being for common good. But what they *say* we are and who we *really* are is oft not the same at all." The priest turned to the baker. "Heinrich, do you really believe that the abbot shall deem you free?"

The man looked at his feet and shrugged.

Pieter drew close. "But do you *want* your freedom?"

Heinrich raised his face angrily. "Of course!"

"Are you so sure?" The old priest peered deeply into Heinrich's soul. He knew the baker had been badly bitten by sentiment and nostalgia. The siren call of security in things familiar had already begun to tempt the exhausted man away from his calling. "Are you?"

The company stared at the man quietly. His answer would guide them all. Heinrich turned his face toward the village once again and toward the clearing where Emma's cottage once stood. *Oh, Emma, would that you were here.* A breeze brushed the field of grasses at his feet, and as it whispered by his ear, it was as if he could hear the beloved illuminator's voice.

... Come flutter 'tween flowers and sail o'er the trees
Or light on m'finger and dance in the breeze.

Since change is your birthright, fly free and be bold
And fear not the tempest, the darkness, or cold.
Press on to new places, seek color and light,
Find smiles and laughter and joy on your flight....

Filled with fresh vision, Heinrich answered boldly, "*Ja!* I will not yield that which God has granted me: liberty!"

A loud cheer rose up around him. "Aye! And neither shall I!" cried Otto.

"Nor I!" cried the others.

Pieter was leaning on his staff and smiling broadly. "Men may call us bound or free, foolish or wise, brave or cowardly, even saintly or wicked, but it is *heaven* that has already declared who we truly are.

"Hear this, my precious ones: we will live as we have learned to want. Freedom comes from the wanting." He stretched his arms over his beloved and pronounced, "It is for freedom that Christ has set us free! Behold, old things are passed away; all things are become new. Forgetting those things that lie behind, let us reach forth unto those things that lie ahead!" He then lifted his face to heaven. "God is good; His mercies endure forever! O Lord, protect us from our enemies. May God have mercy on us all. Amen."

The circle echoed, "Amen."

The company faced one another with hearts lifted, then turned to look at Weyer once again. "So will you enter to make your claims, or do we go elsewhere?" Helmut asked.

Wil shuffled uneasily. "I think—"

"I needs first find my wife," blurted Heinrich flatly. "It is a matter above all else. Then I must know about my bakery and my land, else I shall never rest." He laid a hand on his son's shoulder and looked at him squarely. "I do sincerely pray for your mother's good health, lad. I'll not pretend a heart of great affection, but I do wish for her well-being."

Wil nodded, then added, "And I pray for the law to fall upon Pious."

ॐ

It was noon, and the bells of sext pealed gently over Weyer when the homecoming crusaders descended the eastern slope that rimmed the village. They soon stood in the shade of gray-barked beech trees and old oaks, of pungent pine and ash. At their feet bubbled the happy Laubusbach as it had since time was not recorded. Heinrich reached into his satchel and retrieved the stone he had carried for all these years. He held it in his palm and stared at it quietly until Frieda joined him.

"Your baker's mark," she said.

The baker nodded. "*Ja.* I etched it on this streambed stone before I left as a keepsake from home. Your husband and his brother made the shape. It was long ago along some dusty footpath."

"Ha!" laughed Wil. "I remember the day. Karl was so happy. He saw the cross in the *E*.... He saw the cross in everything."

Heinrich smiled. "No artisan in all the empire could have done as well as you two. I stamped it into a thousand loaves, methinks, and each one with pride."

Alwin laughed. "Only *you* would stamp oat bread!"

The company chuckled. "'Tis true enough. I thought the poor should be granted a bit of art as well as all the others," answered Heinrich.

The baker knelt by the stream and let its waters rush over the little stone. "I baked bread for the table, but Emma gave us the bread of life. I shall miss her always."

Wil squatted by his father's side. "I remember playing in her gardens, and I remember how she'd hug me and I'd disappear in her bosoms!" The group laughed. "I used to run from her so I'd not smother!"

"Ha! Ha!" roared Heinrich. "I remember well."

"And what of the Magi?" quizzed Frieda. "I've heard so much about the Magi."

Wil pointed upstream. "There, a quarter hour's walk or so. They were like three giants protecting us from all danger."

Maria giggled. "I was lost once, but I saw them and then I could find my way home."

"Lost?"

The girl blushed.

"*Ja?*" scolded Frieda playfully. "That's two times now!"

Heinrich stood and faced Alwin. "You, me, and Brother Lukas had some adventures here of our own."

The knight nodded. "Indeed. You saved my life once. Not

far over that ridge." He turned toward the village and drew a deep breath. "My beard is long now and my hair as well. I've not been here since you left. I doubt any will remember me."

Pieter was concerned. "If they do, you'll be arrested by the reeve. No doubt word of your troubles has found this place. Heinrich, how many bear arms in the village?"

The baker turned to his son. "Wil?"

"We'd about a dozen freemen last year, counting old Oskar and that dimwit Rolf of Metz. So I'd venture about ten worth fearing. Only Ludwig has a crossbow; the others have swords, and methinks Yeoman Franz has a halberd. Only he and Yeoman Rudi serve in combat; the others pay the scutage. But everyone hides slaughter blades, and many have pig mallets, which are as good as a warrior's hammer."

At the mention of Ludwig, Heinrich scowled. The man was Katharina's cruel husband.

Pieter frowned. "So you've a full tithing to face if the reeve sounds the horn. And you'd have the others with their hoes and mallets and such." He faced Heinrich and Wil. "You two would not easily raise arms against your own, and you, Alwin, knight or no, would be badly outnumbered. All of us would soon be bound, gagged, and hauled away." He set his finger by his nose and thought carefully. "We needs have a care. Weyer was once home to some of you, but it may no longer be. Can y'not check on your wife and bakery without the whole place knowing?"

Heinrich thought carefully. "This is Sunday, and most are either drunk or sleeping...."

"We can wait until dark and find Herwin," blurted Tomas.

"Herwin!" cried Heinrich. "Is he still alive?"

"Aye!"

"He must be old by now." Heinrich was smiling. "He's as good a man as ever walked the earth. He loves the soil *almost* as much as he loves his wife."

"*Loved* his wife, Father. Varina died on Martinmas Eve the year you left."

Heinrich groaned. Varina was a good woman, and she had brought great joy to Herwin. "And what of their children?" "Wulf lives with Herwin along with a wife and one son. Irma died in childbirth about two years ago. The other girls married men from Oberbrechen and Selters."

"Enough reminiscing, Heinrich. What's our plan?" Alwin said with an impatient bite. "I see a group assembling for a Sabbath forest walk over there, and more are starting to mill about. I'd not want us seen until we're ready."

Heinrich nodded and stared across the stream into the village. "My bakery is just beyond those sheds. Since we're here, let me have a quick look."

Pieter frowned. "If you must, but hurry and, by heaven, don't be seen!"

Stooping low behind the cover of brush, the baker and his son left the others and made their way across the ford toward the bakery standing just beyond a shed. They crept slowly and cautiously forward, then stretched their heads to have a look.

"There." Heinrich choked. "My bakery." His thoughts ran to the day he baked his first loaf of bread in the building built by Katharina's father. Then he remembered that glorious day when it was sold to him by the abbot. *A good day, indeed!* he thought. The man looked at the sturdy building and remembered so many days within its walls. He closed his eye and imagined he could smell the bake. He wondered who was stoking the ovens and kneading the dough. Then he wondered how he could ever come back. He turned to his son. "What would a baker be without a bakery?"

"A baker still," answered Wil quietly. "And a good one. He'd still be a father, a husband, and a friend as well. But it is still yours by right of law."

The man took a hopeful breath but shook his head. "I'm not so certain." He turned his face toward the village. From a distance, the place had felt warm and inviting. Up close, however, it seemed oddly unfamiliar. It was as if he had become a stranger. He said nothing to Wil, but he was suddenly anxious, like prey precariously positioned at the edge of a snare. He motioned for his son to follow him back to the others waiting nervously across the stream.

"Now what?" asked Otto as the pair returned. "I'd like to see m'papa."

Heinrich looked at Wil, then at the sandy-haired lad.

"And what about *Mutti?*" asked Maria.

Wil nodded and set a kindly hand on his sister's shoulder. "Otto, we'll get you home soon enough. We need to think a bit more on this."

Friederich, Benedetto, and Helmut said nothing. They had all been anxious about the others' homecoming. In the first place, they feared being arrested as fugitives along with the others. They also were terrified of being charged as accomplices of Alwin. But they also wondered about their own fate if their fellows were able to make Weyer their home again. Friederich finally spoke. "You ought to go in at night. We all feel danger here."

Wil looked at his friend. He thought the eight-year-old's face seemed tight and haggard. Friederich's hands were trembling, and Frieda put her arm around him. As if she knew what troubled the little boy's heart, she kissed him on the cheek. "You'll be safe with us, and whatever happens, you've a home with us."

"He's right, Wil," said Helmut. "It'd be safer at night."

The pilgrims murmured amongst themselves and finally agreed. "Just past compline bells then," said Wil.

࿊

The company retreated to the fern-softened environs of the Magi, which stood within a brief walk of the boundary pole of Villmar's manorlands. Here, in this place of fond memories and cool air, the pilgrims lounged, albeit warily. Pieter patiently listened to Heinrich and Wil chatter about Brother Lukas and the Butterfly *Frau*, of Richard and Ingly, of things magical and things tragic. But when talk finally turned toward things more imminent, the priest became ever more insistent that those from Weyer give heed to the likelihood of their abandoning home for a new life of freedom elsewhere. To this, angry objections were offered. Wil paced about the wood, confused and struggling to answer the challenges his old friend posed.

Heinrich was equally distressed. He was no longer living in his dreams but rather standing at the very edge of his former master's manor. A gnawing realization crawled over him. *Perhaps the old man is right. Maybe I cannot be home and be free.*

The group finally settled quietly midst the lengthening shadows as summer sunbeams slanted their way between great timbers, splashing golden patches throughout the brushy woodland floor. Soon, twilight would fall, and the long-awaited bells of compline would echo from the stout tower of Weyer's brownstone church. Frieda and Maria had built a small fire upon which they had boiled water for a stew of vegetables, mushrooms, and pork. Heinrich stared into the steaming pot and thought wistfully of Katharina once more. He sighed.

The company whispered amongst themselves, and the light began to fade. A flask of ale was passed around the circle, and soon Benedetto strummed softly on his lute. He smiled at Maria with dark eyes now twinkling in the firelight.

Not far away, Weyer's church bell rang. Its deep, soulful peals rolled through darkening woodlands in slow, rhythmic waves, and each pilgrim's heart began to race. "'Tis time," said Wil as he stood. The young man secured his dagger in his belt and gripped his bow tightly. *Emmanuel,* he said to himself, *I needs leave you here.* He handed the bow to Helmut while staring at its inscription. "'*Vincit qui patior,*'" he whispered. "'He who suffers, conquers.' Indeed."

Heinrich and Alwin, Otto and Tomas joined Wil. "We're ready," the baker said.

Wil looked at his fellows and nodded. He reached for his wife and embraced her, then kissed her tenderly. "Frieda, I shall return with news. Then we'll make a plan. Take care of Maria and the others."

The young woman nodded. She lingered in Wil's embrace until he lifted her arms gently from his sides. "Have no fear, wife. I shall be back."

Pieter stepped forward. "I should like to come with you.

I've little strength in my arms, but I've yet m'wits."

Wil laid a hand on the old man's bony shoulder. "Ah, indeed you do. Use them to help the others." The lad leaned low and whispered into the stoop-shouldered priest's ear. "If we do not return by dawn, come looking, but come alone."

Pieter nodded. "*Ja*, me and the hosts of heaven!"

Helmut was made second in command, just below Pieter, and was told to keep those remaining safe in the woodland near the Magi. "If you must," Wil further instructed, "take them east into the heavier forests by the Matins Stone. Maria, can you find it?"

Maria twisted her face and rolled a finger through her braids. "I was there twice," she said. "Both times with Karl. I think I remember."

Heinrich looked at the little girl with a furrowed brow. "That rock is off the manor! You and your brother could have been beaten ... or worse! I thought you were an obedient child!"

Maria giggled. "Sometimes!"

"No matter now, Father. If they need to hide, she'll take them there. Otherwise, we meet here, at the Magi by dawn. Helmut and Pieter, keep a sharp eye on our satchels, and keep the two beasts quiet! If Paulus brays, he'll bring you trouble for sure."

The young man turned to look carefully at Alwin. The knight was staring into the dark canopy of leaves above and muttering a prayer. "I still say you should wait behind."

Alwin said nothing for a moment, then adjusted his sword. "Nay. You may need me yet. I'll surely not be known under cover of darkness, and we'll be out of the village by light."

Wil nodded. "Otto, are you ready?"

Otto was nervous and wringing his hands lightly. "*Ja*."

"Then we go."

With no more to be said, Wil led Heinrich, Alwin, Otto, and Tomas toward the small bridge that arched over the Laubusbach. Once they crossed the bridge, the path would lead them past the ruins of Emma's cottage and into the sleepy village. It was a warm summer night, almost sultry. Few hearths were burning, though a thin, eye-burning haze hung lightly along the footpaths and alleyways.

Otto's hovel was positioned as the farthest hut from the village center—a place believed fitting for all millers, tradesmen cursed for their thieving ways. The group arrived at its door quietly. Inside, an unattended candle burned, and through the one window, the lad could see his snoring father stretched atop a straw mattress. The young crusader swallowed hard and looked to Wil for courage. His fists were clenched and he did not speak.

"He will be glad to see you," whispered Wil.

"Do you think so?" choked Otto.

Heinrich laid a hand on the lad's broad shoulder. "I'd be proud of you, boy. And I'd have a feast to welcome you!"

Otto smiled. "If there's trouble, I'll be at the Magi by dawn."

"There'll be no trouble, friend," answered Wil confidently. "You're home."

With that, all clasped hands, and the lad was left to rally his courage alone. The four others faded into the shadows, their silhouettes gliding silently past a half-dozen darkened buildings. They crouched and turned to watch Otto walk through his door.

It was a long pause before a voice suddenly boomed from within the boy's hut. "Otto! By the saints, you little fool! Where's yer brother?" Within moments Otto's father began to curse and shout. A few sleepy villagers in nearby huts groused a bit, and then a few staggered to their doorways. "Shut yer mouth, miller!"

"Burn in hell!" the angry man answered.

"A curse on yer children!" roared a drunken man.

The miller burst from his door and dragged Otto by the hair into the path. "A curse you say? A curse? I've been cursed with this coward!" To the dismay of Wil's group, he punched the poor lad in the belly and threw him to the ground. "He let his brother die on that fool's crusade! He broke his vow to me and to the Holy Church! Come, all of you! See this worthless scrap of dung who calls himself m'son!"

Wil's band watched in disbelief as bleary-eyed villagers emerged from their huts and gathered on the narrow street. A menacing group moved toward Otto, shouting curses. "You, boy, tell me where's m'Ingrid?" growled one.

A mother suddenly shrieked, "And where's my little Oskar?" More names flew from angry, grief-stricken lips as more and more villagers funneled their way toward the miller and his terrified son.

"My Bruno is gone!"

"And m'Etta and m'baby Pepin!"

Names of lost children rose from the gathering mob as the forlorn folk of Weyer finally released their sorrow. Shaking their fists at their unseen God, bitter fathers shouted blasphemies at the stars. It was the mothers, however, who shook the heavens with great shrieks of sorrow as these broken women finally faced the tragic truth of their heart-wrenching loss. Seeing poor Otto stand before them alone and with no news of the others was their final proof that their own sons and daughters would not return the way they had left; they'd not be marching home together; they'd not be coming home at all.

For Otto's comrades hiding in the nearby shadows, the sudden turn of events was startling. They stared wide eyed as the clamor drew yet others. It seemed barely a quarter hour had passed when much of Weyer was aroused, its streets now aglow in torchlight. "What of Otto?" blurted Wil. "What will they do to him?"

Heinrich licked his dry lips. "I ... I don't know. He's no runaway; he's committed no crime."

"But listen. They're calling him 'devil' and 'murderer.' There, that one called him 'son of Lucifer!'"

Indeed, the grief of the village folk was turning toward vengeance. "Why him?" cried one. "Why did he live and not the others?"

Otto's voice cracked above the din, "But others may come even yet!"

"Liar! You're the only one shameless enough to come back. You betrayed the faith, and now you come back? You need a flogging! You ought be hanged!"

"He'll not be harmed," growled Alwin. The knight had already drawn his sword.

"Hold fast," urged Heinrich. "Listen."

The reeve had summoned two armed deputies, and the three now shouldered their way through the crowd. The man turned his voice against the folk. "Nay! The boy is not to be harmed!"

The mob grumbled and fell quiet. "Now hear me! Any who lays a hard hand on the lad, save his father, is to be punished by the law. He's but a boy come home. 'Tis you fools who sent yer waifs on crusade."

"No!" answered many. "We told them not to go. We barred our doors and tied them fast."

Reeve Edwin laughed. "Ha! A pitiful lie to ease the conscience. You'd best have the priests say a prayer for that." He turned to Otto's father. "He's yours. Do as y'please, but if another interferes, I'll bring justice on your heads."

The miller spat, then grabbed Otto by the scruff of the neck, and dragged him inside his hovel. Then, to the sound of Otto's pitiful cries, the folk of Weyer drifted slowly to their own homes.

Heinrich cursed in the shadows. "We'll not leave the lad with the likes of him."

Tomas had said nothing. Like Otto, he, too, had felt the whip, only it had been wielded by monks. "Leave Otto to me," he whispered. "I'll set him loose, and we'll meet at the Magi."

Wil looked carefully at the stone-faced lad. He had learned to trust Tomas, even respect him. He and others had marveled at what change a little patience and some grace had wrought in the young man's heart. "We all will go."

Otto cried out again.

"No," said Alwin firmly. "I'll go with Tomas. You two have other business, and we must all be away afore dawn."

Wil nodded reluctantly. Alwin was right; the two of them should be enough. "Then we'll meet at the Magi."

The four separated, and soon father and son were

padding softly along Weyer's footpaths. Behind closing doors, mothers could be heard sobbing softly. These folk did love their children, sometimes more, it seemed, than the lords who'd beat their little ones for dropping a comfit. They loved them and missed them, and their hearts were torn by the knowledge that they had released them to die on a fool's errand.

"There." Wil pointed. "Home!"

Heinrich and his son stood in the shadow of an ox-shed and faced their two-room hovel quietly. For Heinrich, it was a moment like few others. There, before him, was the simple wattle-and-daub cottage that had sheltered him since the day of his birth. It was here that his mother had died. It was here that all his children had been conceived and born—and where two had died. Under this very thatch he had laughed and wept for so many of his thirty-nine years. Built by the sweat of his father, it was still his along with the adjacent garden plot and fowl coop. The baker took a deep breath and stepped forward boldly.

Arriving at the door, Heinrich paused. "Just open it, Father," insisted Wil. "It is *our* house!"

Heinrich hesitated, then knocked. A booming voice thundered from within. "Can a man not sleep this night! Who goes?"

Heinrich set his jaw. It was not Marta's voice. "Heinrich of Weyer, owner of this place!"

The door flew open, and a large man held a candle angrily toward Heinrich's hardened face. Seeing the patched eye, the wrapped stump, and the handle of a sword, the man stepped back. "So what's yer business?"

Heinrich pushed his way past the man and into his former home. Wil followed with his dagger drawn. Putting his hand on the hilt of his sword, the baker turned a stiff eye toward the startled family within. "Hear me, thieves, and hear me once. I am Heinrich of Weyer, son of Kurt of Jost. This house is mine and mine alone. It was given me by my father, and I shall pass it to my son."

The hovel had become home to six: a yeoman, his wife, two grown sons, and two young daughters. The yeoman was a burly, brown-haired fellow from a village near Wetzlar. He was about Heinrich's age, and his sons were broad-shouldered lads who now reached for their swords. The yeoman grabbed Heinrich by the cloth of his tunic. "I am Horst, a freeman and owner of this cottage. I bought it from the priest for a high price that is paid in full. Any who tries to take it shall need to take it by force!" The women faded into the sleeping chamber as the man's sons stepped forward.

Heinrich shoved the yeoman, then jerked his sword from its scabbard as he answered, "We've two to your three. If you think that makes you the rightful owner to this place, you're wrong."

Horst growled and took hold of a sword of his own. "We can strike you dead where y'stand, fool."

"Or you can prove your claim in the morning in the abbey."

"The law says it is mine. I've no need to prove anything to anyone."

Heinrich snarled, "The law be damned! This is *my* home! This is my chattel. The land is mine and the bakery, too!"

"None is yours!" roared the yeoman. "This miserable house, the garden, and the coop are all mine. And the bakery is owned by the church, along with your land."

Wil had remained oddly quiet. "What of the woman who once lived here?"

"Dead." The answer was hard and unsympathetic. Horst's eyes now fixed on Wil's.

"She was my mother," hissed Wil through clenched teeth.

The family murmured. Horst nodded and turned to Heinrich. "And she was yer wife?"

"*Ja.*"

"She was murdered, we're told."

"Murdered! By who?"

All eyes turned to Wil. "By her son," Horst answered.

Chapter Eighteen

TROUBLE IN WEYER

Wil paled. He looked blankly at his father, then at the family staring at him. "I ... I did not!"

"Father Pious says you poisoned yer own mother, then ran away on that crusade of idiots. He said you killed a monk and an abbey guard."

"He's a liar!" roared Wil.

Horst smirked and turned to Heinrich. "And you are the father?"

"Aye."

"The priest says you were killed in the northland."

"Well, I wasn't."

Horst shrugged. "Might as well have been. You were declared dead, and yer wife gave the Holy Church all you owned. As she was dying, Father Pious told her the boy had poisoned her. He says she died cursing the two of you."

"No!" cried Wil. "No!"

"Hold, boy! Hold fast," commanded Heinrich. The baker curled his lip. "I've come back to life to claim what's mine. The boy's no killer. You own what you have by fraud and thievery. You'll not keep it, not for long."

No one spoke. Wil and Heinrich stood shoulder to shoulder, and Heinrich raised his sword to Horst's throat. The baker looked down on his blade, and its inscription seared confidence into his heart. "*Veritas Regnare* ... Truth Reigns." He lifted his eye to lock on to his foe's, and there he stood, stiff as stone, unflinching.

A dreadful quiet hung over the room. There was no rustle of garments, no squeak of leather boots or creak of wood. Horst's nostrils flared, and it was he who finally broke the silence. "Enough of this!" he groused. "Leave my home."

Heinrich's mind was whirling. *Outnumbered and me with one arm, Wil with only a dagger.* "Yeoman, I've a rightful claim. I'll take the matter to the abbey in the morning. Prepare to live elsewhere."

Now Horst's mind began to whirl.

As though he could read the man's mind, Heinrich interrupted. "You could try to kill us, and the matter might be settled. But this I do vow," he leaned close. "You'll lose a lad and most likely your own life."

The menacing baker had a firm confidence about his way, one seasoned by hard times. Horst hesitated, then quickly reckoned that the court would be delighted to have the murdering Wil walk directly into its grasp. The yeoman relaxed. He lowered his sword. "Take yer lies to the abbot then, but if you come to m'door again, we will cross steel!"

With a grunt, the baker slowly lowered his sword and bade Wil to sheath his dagger. Father and son slowly backed out the door as Wil snorted a thick phlegm into his mouth and spat it on to the floor at the yeoman's feet. "I leave that until we return."

☙

Cursing in frustration, Heinrich walked away from his own threshold and stumbled into the village. "That devil Pious! He's stolen what's mine." The man stopped. He closed his eye in shame. "Your mother ... is dead, you are accused of murder, and I think of nothing else but my property."

The pair said nothing more and walked toward the Laubusbach slowly. They passed the village well when Wil paused. "We should find Herwin. He can tell us what more we need to know."

Wil led his father through the footpaths of the village now fast returning to sleep. He found his way easily to Herwin's door, and when he knocked, a blurry-eyed Wulf answered. "Eh?"

"Wulf, 'tis me—Will!"

Herwin's son of thirty years squinted and studied the two men who were lit only by starlight and a setting moon. "Wil?"

"*Ja!*"

"Wil? We thought you were surely dead!"

"No, I've come home!"

An old woman in the neighboring hut poked her head out of her door. "Wil? The baker's son?"

Before Heinrich could hush him, Wil snapped, "Aye. What of it, hag?"

The woman's head disappeared.

Wulf bade the two to come inside. His wife hurried to light a candle as he called to his sleeping father. Herwin climbed to his feet slowly, then stared incredulously at his old friends. "Can it be true?" he asked.

The one-armed man and the aging thatcher embraced. Herwin had been a part of Heinrich's life since the baker was a boy. He had once been a faithful tenant of Heinrich's father, then suffered under the rule of Baldric until Heinrich owned the hovel. Now in his early fifties, Herwin was gray and frail. His teeth were missing and he limped. "A fall, Heinrich. Actually, two falls and now I'm lame. I still do some thatch on the low sheds. But, now, oh, I've much to ask you! First, what of Karl and Maria?"

Heinrich lowered his face. "Karl is dead. He died on crusade near Genoa. Maria is safe."

"Ah, poor friend." Herwin laid a trembling hand on Heinrich's shoulder. "And where have you been all these years?"

"I've a long tale," answered Heinrich. "I shall tell you more when I can, but now we must know of some things. We are told that Marta is dead and our house is sold to another ... to a yeoman."

The thatcher hung his head. "I did what I could to challenge the matter, but within days of your leaving, your wife swore all her earthly possessions to the parish. She was near death when Pious had her words witnessed quite properly by himself, Reeve Edwin, Father Albert, and a clerk of the prior. You had already been declared dead on account of your being missing, so your property was rightfully your wife's to give away. She could do with it as she pleased, my friend."

Heinrich cursed.

Herwin sighed. "Pious quickly sold the house to the yeoman, but he kept your land and the bakery for the parish. He's raised the prices over the objections of the abbot. He sends quite a profit to the diocese, and he's been rewarded handsomely by the archbishop's secretary.

"But I fear I've other news." Herwin turned his face toward Wil. "*Frau* Anka has given testimony against you, lad ... at the urging of Pious, no doubt. She told the bailiff that you told her to give your mother an infusion of an herb. Pious proved it was poison...."

"I did! But I didn't know it was poison! Pious told me to give it her. It was he who knew what it was!"

Herwin gasped. "Pious? Pious did this? We thought you were simply mistaken about the herb!"

"Aye, it was Pious!" exclaimed Heinrich.

Herwin was dumfounded. "Wil, he ... he wanted you arrested on sight if you ever returned, and he'll have Anka swear against you in court. And there's more. Pious has argued that you murdered Lukas and an abbey guard."

"Miserable, fat bast—"

"Enough, lad!" cried Heinrich. "Pious is a liar! Lukas died in his bed, and the lad had nothing to do with the guard."

Wil sat down hard on a stool. "I ... I might have killed the guard that night. Ansel was his name."

"But—"

"He was chasing me, and I tripped him with a heavy stick. He fell and must have broke his head on a rock. I thought he was only knocked out."

Heinrich groaned and looked at his son, astonished. "Did any see?"

"No, none at all." Wil was now pale and perspiring, and he stared into the looping candle, blankly.

No one spoke for a long moment. Herwin motioned for his daughter-in-law to give the two a drink of mead. "Old friend, I fear your son is in a frightful tangle. If he is caught, he will be hanged."

Heinrich began to pace. "Pious'd have no chance to prove any of it. Priest or not, he has no good ground to stand on."

"Wil, the abbot would not see me, but I complained to the bailiff that the charges against you were madness. I fear it mattered little," said Herwin sorrowfully. "Pious told him that you are a hateful, wicked devil who hated your mother and bore a grudge against Lukas. He claims that God opened his eyes and that he saw you do the deeds in a dream. He said he knew of a spell cast on you by the witch. Words like these from a priest might sway the court ... even without another witness ... but Anka's testimony will be make it certain."

"No! It cannot be so!" roared Heinrich. "We'll accuse *him*! *He's* the murderer!"

"On whose word?"

Heinrich was silent, and he stared at Wil thoughtfully. "The abbot and his prior have always hated Pious. Now with the bakery prices and his life of gluttony, the monks must surely despise him. Someone might help in a charge against him."

"With no more than Wil's word you'll not be proving a thing," added Herwin. "Your uncle Arnold told the prior that the boy is innocent. He told him that Pious is up to some mischief. But he knows no one could ever prove it. No, I fear you need to run far, far away and quickly."

"Arnold? Why would he care?" grumbled Heinrich.

"He's some different than you remember. Methinks he wants to cleanse his soul before he dies."

"When did you say m'mother died?" muttered Wil.

"Less than a week after you left."

The lad fell silent.

"Heinrich, believe me, I took an oath for your son. I swore that the lad had no malice toward his mother nor knowledge of herbs. I swore the witch had cast no spell. I swore on my eternal soul that he had only love for Brother Lukas."

"You swore true enough," groaned Wil.

Wulf had been listening quietly. "So the poison was Pious's then?"

"Nay. I ... I took it from Brother Lukas's chamber."

The cottage fell silent until Herwin murmured, "Perhaps we've heard enough."

Wil ground his fist into his palm. "Pious and I had an agreement. He agreed to keep silent about that night if I did not accuse him of ... of having his way with m'mother." He darted a glance at his father.

Herwin stood, shaken. It was all too much for the weary man. "Boy, I love you and your father like no others, but you cannot stay here. Pious will destroy you. He is more powerful now than then. Your threat against him would matter little. Get out of his web whilst you can, lad, else you'll surely swing from Runkel's gallows."

❧

"You lay another hand on that boy, and I'll cleave you in two!" Alwin stood in the door of Otto's hovel and pointed his sword at the miller.

The miller pushed his son to the floor and took a step toward the knight. "Who be you to tell me how to raise m'brat?"

Alwin's dark eyes burned red with rage. His blond hair hung over his shoulders, and his beard was long. For most men, the sight of this strapping warrior would have been reason enough to yield. But Herold, the miller, was unlike his fellows; he was a fool of fools. The man lunged for the truncheon he kept near his bed and whirled about at the charging knight, swinging wildly at Alwin's head.

Dodging the stout stick, Alwin kicked the man in the belly and sent him sprawling on the floor. "Otto, get out!" the knight cried.

The lad hesitated.

"Go!" added Tomas. "Go now!"

Bruised and bleeding from his beating, Otto backed slowly toward the door with his eyes fixed on his father now climbing angrily to his feet.

"Boy!" the miller shouted. "You'd run from yer own father? You'd betray yer own for some stranger?"

Otto's eyes flew from his father to Alwin, then to his father again. "Just ... just let me come home in peace," the lad pleaded. Tears streamed down his face. "Can y'not forgive me? Can y'not have me back?"

Herold spat and cursed, then lunged once more at the knight. Alwin deftly blocked the man's blow with his sword and countered with a carefully placed slice along the man's shoulder.

"Aahh!" Herold cried. He fell back and grasped his wound, then turned hateful eyes on his son. "You! 'Tis your fault, you little *Scheisse!*" He looked at the blood seeping down his arm. "Pathetic fool. You are no son of mine, and I'll not have you stink up my home. Get out! The sight of you sickens me. Get out, else I'll kill you in yer sleep!"

The words pierced Otto's heart like no mere lance might ever do. The hard man who had once fed and sheltered him was now discarding him like so much refuse. Yet the boy longed to remain in his most familiar refuge with one whom he did somehow love. The brave lad's chin quivered slightly, and then he held out his arms as if to beg his father's mercy one last time. "I ... I ..."

"Shut yer fool mouth. I curse the day you were born. You've never been the son I wanted, and you killed the one I loved. Would that Lothar had come home and never you!"

Alwin's chest heaved. He had no son; he had denied himself that joy by taking his Templar vows. To see this fool now curse and spit upon a lad as worthy as Otto filled him with rage. "By heaven and by hell, I ought take your head and put it on a pike! You miserable old fool, take a step toward me so I can send your soul to the Pit."

Herold stared at Alwin, tight faced, then spat at Tomas, who was scowling to one side. What courage he had, he had already expended on his first go at the knight, and he had no interest in trying again. "You two, take this worthless scrap of dung out of m'house. He's no son of mine no more." With that, he turned his back on Otto forever.

Alwin lowered his sword and cursed, then looked at the trembling boy. "Lad?"

Tomas laid a hand on Otto. "It's all changed now. Come with us."

Otto nodded sadly. He turned to his father and opened his mouth to speak, then held his tongue. Hesitating for another moment, he let his eyes linger on the little hut that had been home to him for his fourteen years. He ran his fingers lightly along the bruises rising on his cheeks, and then, saying nothing, he followed Tomas out the door and returned to his comrades by the Magi.

෨

"Open the door!" boomed a voice.

Herwin's color drained away. "The reeve!"

"Open!"

Herwin's eyes flew about the dim-lit hut. It was a one-room hovel with no good place to hide Heinrich or Wil. "To the corner!" he whispered urgently. Wulf blew out the candle, and Herwin answered. "*Ja?* Who's there?"

"Reeve Edwin and five deputies. Open, else we'll break it down!"

Herwin lifted the bar, and the men burst into the dark room. "Where are they?" shouted the reeve. "Make us some light!"

Heinrich and Wil were crouched low in a dark corner, but they knew it was hopeless. There'd be no hiding. With a shout, they rushed toward the open door. At their cry, Wulf threw two of the reeve's deputies away from the threshold. Midst grunts and heaves, a tangle of struggling men then tumbled out of the hovel and onto the moonlit footpath.

There, Wulf, Heinrich, and Wil engaged six shadows in a wild brawl. The large Wulf dropped one deputy with a solid fist to the face, but he was quickly felled by the strike of the reeve's flail. He collapsed sideways, falling like a great timber. Bouncing against the hovel's wattled wall, he rolled to his side, unconscious.

Wil traded blows with two others, then yanked his dagger from his belt, which was immediately sent to the shadows by the strike of a mallet. The two grunting forms then wrestled the howling lad hard to the ground. "Hold fast, y'devil," cried one. "Y've a hangman to greet!"

Heinrich kept the three others at bay with his sword, while old Herwin begged for calm. The baker backed slowly toward his son now being tied at the wrists and ankles. "Wil!" he cried.

"Aye, Father, they've bound me!"

"He's to hang, baker. He's a murderer." The voice was familiar but the face unseen. Suddenly, the figure lunged toward Heinrich with a long-sword of his own. The baker dodged and parried, missing his mark. Another rushed him and he swiped at the man, cutting him lightly across the belly and sending him rolling away. Reeve Edwin roared forward with his flail. Heinrich leapt to one side and tripped the aging reeve, only to quickly dodge the jab of the other's sword once more. Instinctively, the baker returned a ferocious thrust of his own, driving the point of his sword squarely into the ribs of his foe.

The man cried out and fell forward with Heinrich's sword jammed into his chest. While struggling to jerk his blade free, the one-armed baker was quickly pounced upon by the reeve and another and knocked hard to the ground.

"I'll kill you, y'fool!" cried a deputy.

"Hold!" begged Herwin. "Hold easy!"

With a loud cry, the reeve struck Heinrich on the head with his flail, knocking the man unconscious. He then spun around to Herwin. "I should arrest you as well, you and your son. You've harbored a fugitive."

"We didn't know."

"Aye, y'did know! You know Wil and his father well, and you know the boy's been charged with murder. You'd a duty to summon me! That makes you guilty." Reeve Edwin was panting. He was a man of middling years and had served as Weyer's reeve for a decade. He had always liked Herwin, however, and as his breath returned to him, so did his reason. "Why didn't you send for me?"

"I ... I had barely spoken with them when you came to the door. Who sent you?"

"I did!" It was Horst, the yeoman occupying Heinrich's hovel. The man cursed and rubbed his jaw. "Boys?"

One son answered. "Fitz is cut in the belly!"

Horst stumbled to his son's side. "That one-eyed fool!" he cried. "I'll kill him where he lies!"

Reeve Edwin spun about and stuck the end of his flail against Horst's chest. "Nay. He'll be taken to Runkel. You'll not have at him nor his lad."

Horst spat and cursed. "My son lies with a belly wound."

"Then load him in yer cart and get him to the abbey! But leave me with these."

The two glared at one another in the darkness until Horst yielded. Edwin then ordered Herwin to tie Heinrich's ankles together and to wrap the man's arm to his side. The reeve then hurried over to his fallen deputy and groaned. "*Ach, mein Gott!* Ludwig's been killed."

Another deputy hurried to Edwin's side on wobbly legs, still rubbing his jaw where Wulf had pummeled him. The two bent over the dead yeoman and cursed. The reeve yanked Heinrich's sword from the man's chest and threw it on the ground. "Baker, you'll surely swing as well," he muttered.

Several peasants with torches had emerged from their hovels and now stood gawking in a curious circle around the reeve, his deputies, and their two prisoners. Behind them, crouching deep in the shadows, were Alwin and Tomas, recently arrived from delivering Otto to the Magi. They had hurried back to the village and had been drawn to the sounds of struggle. Now they found themselves utterly unable to help their captured friends.

Edwin ordered four onlookers to carry the body of Ludwig to his wife. "And give her the killer's sword. She can sell it for her keep." Heinrich's sword was laid across Ludwig's corpse, and the grunting men carried the body away.

"Now, you others. Hear me. We've captured Wilhelm, son of Heinrich, and he'll be hanged for murdering his mother … and maybe for others as well." The folk murmured.

"And it seems our missing baker's come home. He's murdered Yeoman Ludwig, and he'll dangle with his son."

That news drew loud gasps of disbelief. "Heinrich's come home?" cried one.

"Where has he been?"

Numbers of them hurried to stand over Heinrich and Wil, where they stared at the two in the dim torchlight. Wil scowled and countered a few mocking words with answers of his own. But those looking at Heinrich were stunned. "Are you sure 'tis him, Reeve?"

"Aye. 'Tis him, sure enough. Ask Herwin."

The frail fellow nodded. "*Ja*, it is he. 'Tis m'old friend come home."

The folk stared at the one-eyed, one-armed, bearded man in disbelief. "He's different. He's old and ... and ..."

"And he looks like a freeman," grumbled one.

The others nodded. "Aye. Look at his clothes. And they say he had a sword."

"Well, he's come home now!" mocked one.

"Aye. He's come home to hang."

෴

Alwin and Tomas stayed hidden until the reeve had carted his prisoners away and the curious peasants had returned to their hovels, shaking their heads in disbelief over the night's events. Stealthily, the knight approached Herwin's door and knocked quietly. The trembling thatcher opened it slowly, and then, astonished, he bade the knight and Tomas inside. "Come quickly!" he whispered.

Once inside the hovel, Alwin listened carefully as Herwin offered what details he could of the matters at hand. He and Tomas gave a sketchy review of the past year's events and assured the man that the baker and his son would not be abandoned to their troubles.

"We shall help you as we can," said Herwin. "But Alwin, have a care. The Templars search the lands for you often. They want you hanged, sir. They say you turned your sword against your own."

The knight nodded. "I know what they say. Herwin, you've known me many years. I tell you this: I turned my sword against evil. That, my friend, is my duty under God."

Saying no more, the two turned toward the door and slipped away. They hurried through the night to the Magi, where they told all of the night's worsening events. The pilgrims groaned with the news. Otto's story had been tragedy enough, but this was far worse. "Wil's charges are grievous, and I fear Heinrich's fate is sealed," moaned Alwin. "Our baker struck a man dead in full view of many."

Frieda started to sob loudly. "This cannot be! I knew we should not have come here!" She stood and paced about the campfire. "Oh, what do we do? What do we do?"

Maria sniffled as she leaned into Pieter's side. The old man patted her head and stared into the low flames. His mind was spinning, and he sat with his gaze fixed on the fire for an hour or so. No one disturbed him; no one spoke. With Maria at his one side, Frieda had come to his other. Across his legs sprawled Solomon. Around the fire the other troubled pilgrims sat silently.

Pieter did not speak. It was as if he were in a trance, as if his spirit had left his body and were floating somewhere far beyond sight. Finally, his mouth moved and he whispered, "*In nomine Patris, et Filii, et Spiritus Sancti.*" He took a deep breath and turned his face solemnly toward his fellows. "Yes?"

The group looked at one another. Maria looked at him. "Papa Pieter, what shall we do?"

"I've no idea."

The circle murmured. Friederich wrinkled his nose. "Then what were you thinking about?"

"I wasn't."

Alwin tossed a stone into the fire and groused under his breath, "We need a plan, Pieter. And we need to be quick about it."

The old man rose and leaned heavily on his staff. "The dog's been uneasy since we've come here. I don't know why. And I have as well." He stared into the small red-coal fire. Frieda thought he looked suddenly beaten. *His face is so thin,* she thought, *and the light has left his eyes.* Dark shadows etched his cheeks, and he looked almost ghostly. The girl shuddered.

"The day soon comes, my beloved, when you'll not have me to guide you. I am weary, and my mind is beginning to fail. So I was not thinking, but praying." He smiled a little. "It is good to be free of my mind sometimes. We are not called to know all things, but to trust in the One who does." Pieter's voice became gentle, and he looked into each distressed face. "When I am gone, you still have Him. You'd best learn now to run there first. I will not talk of things to do until each of you has begged heaven for counsel on this grievous matter. I cannot do this alone; we need each other." With that, he walked away.

Alwin, the former monk, nodded. He hung his head in shame, for he knew that when he had abandoned his vow, he had nearly abandoned his faith. The Church had failed him, yet God had not. The troubled but devout Christian knight fell to his knees and began a prayer of such heart-wrenching despair that the others soon knelt close by his side. Then each in turn—some in whispers, some unheard—lifted his or her supplications to the One who held all things in His grasp, to the One who might grant these harmless lambs minds as clever as serpents.

From deep in the wood, Pieter watched with joy as his beloved prayed. And when their heads were lifted, he walked boldly toward them, refreshed anew by hope, inspired by this remnant that would surely pass truth to generations not yet born. "Now, to work," he said. "First, we needs move our camp to the Matins Stone I've heard of. We are not safe here. Douse the flames now, bury the embers, and scatter brush about."

The company's spirits were lifted by Pieter's newfound vigor, and they hurried to task obediently. Tomas led them eastward for about an hour through the heavy wood until they arrived at an odd-shaped boulder known in legend as the Matins Stone. According to local lore, the stone would rotate at the ringing of matins bells, as long as no eyes were upon it. It was also said to be a favored haven for the witches of the region.

Pieter ordered Paulus to be unloaded and tethered to a tree. He wanted their provisions hidden about the forest, and he insisted that Heinrich's and Wil's satchels be buried under brush for safekeeping. "Just someone remember where all this is, for I shall surely forget!"

A fire was built and some food distributed. Pieter then

summoned all to his side. "The sun should rise in about two hours, methinks. When it does, we must act and act quickly." He turned to Alwin. "You must remain as our reserve. You cannot be discovered. If you are, we'll lose the sword we may need." He whirled around to Otto and Helmut. "You two must stay with Alwin and protect Frieda and Maria, here, at our camp. Helmut, you've been practicing with Wil's bow. Maybe you can hunt us a stag or a boar?"

Otto protested loudly.

"Nay! Otto, you must now stay away from the village. Tomas can guide me."

Frieda jutted her jaw forward. "I will not stay behind!"

Pieter narrowed his eyes. "You are a fair damsel in a place I do not know."

"I will not stay behind. He is my husband."

Alwin objected. "This is not a woman's business!"

Frieda spun about and lashed the man with a fiery tongue. "Woman's business? Is not a husband's life a woman's business?" The young woman's nostrils flared like an angry mare's, and she stomped her foot defiantly. Before any could speak, she snatched a burning faggot from the fire and reached toward Alwin's beard. "Say again I may not go, monk, and I'll set your face afire!"

Alwin did not move. He fixed his eyes on Frieda's, then tilted them toward Pieter. The old priest shrugged, and Alwin yielded. "Go, then, sister," he mumbled. "Go with God."

Frieda flung the faggot back to the fire and stormed away. Pieter raised his brows and smiled at the others. "Well then, here it is. We can do nothing until we know more. We do not know where the two are being held or when they might face their trial.

"So, I shall take Tomas, Friederich, Benedetto, *and* Frieda with me to the abbey and shall do my best to learn what we may."

Benedetto nearly swooned when he heard his name. He had done his best to keep from view. "But, *Padre*, what can I do?" If the sun were up, the others could have seen how very pale the little man had become!

Pieter shrugged. "I don't know yet."

"But—"

"But I shall know when I need to know. Trust that."

"But why are we *all* going?" the minstrel pleaded.

Now the others began to scowl. "You don't want to help?" barked Helmut.

Benedetto licked his lips and answered carefully. "I ... *si,* of course I want to help, but I wonder if I can."

"You can," snapped Friederich. "Your lute is oft as good a weapon as Pieter's wit or Alwin's sword."

"Enough of this," interrupted Pieter. "First, we learn what we can. Knowledge is power."

Suddenly, an unfamiliar voice came from the darkness. "I can help you."

Startled, the group spun around and faced the silhouette of a shape drifting toward them. Maria gasped. To her it was as though a woodland spirit was approaching. "Do not be afraid," the voice added serenely. "I am here to help you."

It was then that the figure emerged into the firelight of the camp, and all mouths dropped open.

Chapter Nineteen

A JEW, A WITCH, AND A MONK

$\mathfrak{I}$ am sorry, son," lamented Heinrich as he awoke.
The two had been tossed into the small jail at the
abbey's garrison. The baker's head was covered
with dried blood, and he was dizzy.

"No, it was me. It was me they were after." Wil took a deep
breath. "I was a fool to ever trust that devil Pious. I did not
murder Mother, but it was at my hand she died."

Heinrich sat quietly, listening to the snoring guard
sleeping outside the door. Wil changed the subject. "I saw
the reeve strike you."

"Well, I didn't!" grumbled the baker. "Never saw it coming."

"No, I suppose not. You know, the townsfolk could
hardly believe it was you lying there. One said you looked
like a freeman."

The word sounded good to Heinrich. "And so I am ... so
we are." He squirmed in his place. The guards had not
released either from their bonds. Straining to see Wil in the
darkness, he said, "And so we shall ever be! I want the land
of m'fathers to be yours someday. But I'd rather leave you
with your freedom than a plot of dirt!"

"Greetings," said another voice.

Startled, father and son looked blankly into the black.
"Who's there?"

"I am Beniamino." The man's voice sounded old but still
vigorous.

"Beniamino?" answered Wil. "What kind of name is that?"

"I am from the kingdom of the two Sicilies."

"You speak our tongue."

"*Ja, si, oui, sim!* I speak many tongues. I am a money-lender and so I must."

"A Jew?" snapped Wil.

"*Ja.* A Jew. But I do not eat babies or steal money from the dead."

Wil spat. He had oft been told of these strange people and their dangerous ways. A village elder had once said they spread evil in their path. He had said they were tricksters of a high order. "Keep away."

The man laughed. "I'd prefer to. You stink."

Wil grumbled. "If I wasn't bound, I'd smash that big nose of yours."

"And how do you know I've a big nose?"

"You all do. I've heard it from the priests."

"Ah ... but I thought you said you ought not have trusted your priest."

Wil grunted. He could hear the grin in the man's tone.

Heinrich was wary. He wished he knew where the Jew was standing. Being bound and lying on the floor made him feel vulnerable. "Why are you here? Who did you steal from?"

"Ha! Ha!" laughed Beniamino quietly. "Do you think I could be caught? No, I'm here for quite another reason."

"And what is that?"

"That is why I am here."

"*What* is why you are here?"

The old Jew was, indeed, smiling in the dark. "I am here so that I do not say why I am here."

"Go to Jerusalem and die," grumbled Wil.

"Ah, my dear boy. And why are you here?"

"None of your concern."

"He is falsely accused of murdering his mother," Heinrich answered.

Beniamino said nothing for a long moment. When he answered, his tone had changed. "So I heard you say. A more horrid crime I do not know. When you hang, know that I shall be dancing."

If Heinrich could have, he would have torn the man's throat out of his neck. He cursed and flailed about the floor until, panting and exasperated, he simply groaned. "He did not murder his mother!"

Beniamino was an old man and wise. Traveling Christendom he had become wily and intuitive. The anguish in Heinrich's voice was genuine. "Then who, good sir, did?"

"The priest."

In the darkness, Beniamino's lips twitched. "The priest?"

"Aye. Father Pious, the priest of our village, Weyer."

"I passed through your charming hamlet early this morning. But why would the priest kill the lad's mother?"

"He wanted my land, and he's always coveted my bakery. He thought it could further his ambitions."

Beniamino was quiet. "So, you are the lad's father, and the woman was your wife."

"Aye."

"So why are *you* here?"

"What does it matter?" Heinrich groused.

"Oh, it doesn't really. But since you wondered about me, I thought I'd return the kindness."

Wil grumbled at the man's sarcasm, but the baker had no ear for such. He answered plainly. "Well, I killed a man defending my son from false arrest. Now, sir, why are *you* here?"

The Jew thought for a moment. He felt sudden pity for the two. "It cannot hurt to tell a little of it to dead men," he answered in a whisper. "It seems the clever prior thought it was better that I spend the night far away from his brethren. As I recall, he said, 'Temptation and good wine might pry loose thy lips.' So, I was sent here to sleep ... with a kind apology, I should add."

Heinrich did not understand. "Seems like an odd way of business."

Beniamino chuckled. "Dear man, not so much odd as careful. You see, I am a man with a secret, and secrets, my friend, have value! So I willingly suffer the unpleasantness of one night to secure the profit of this particular secret I bear."

"Sounds like Uncle Arnold," muttered Wil.

"Uncle Arnold?"

"Aye," answered Heinrich. "My old uncle peddles secrets in the village. You would like him."

"Ha! Perhaps."

Heinrich's curiosity was stirred. "Can y'not tell us something of this?" he asked.

The Jew hesitated, then laughed quietly. "It is true; secrets are very hard to keep. It is so tasty to let them roll over one's tongue and out one's lips!"

"Then tell us, Jew!" growled Wil. "What could it hurt?"

Beniamino chuckled. "Such spirit from one who will soon hang for a crime he did not do."

"So you believe us?" asked Heinrich.

"I do."

"Why?"

"I know the sound of a father's pain." The jail was quiet. At last, Beniamino sighed. "Ah, well. I've no bread to share with you, so why not share a secret?" He felt his way toward Heinrich and cut him loose with a sharp knife, then stood over Wil. "I should let you lie there for your lack of courtesy."

"Then let me," Wil growled.

"As you wish then." Beniamino took a seat between the two and proceeded to speak in a low voice. "So you want to know my business. Fine. I am to remain here in utter silence until I leave in the morning. I've assured the prior, on risk of future dealings, that I will travel far away with no single word to another." He smiled. "Ah, the web of Christian politics.

"I am a moneylender and am welcome in the company of your churchmen. You see, my business is to loan money to desperate Christian warlords at a high interest."

"Usury," grunted Wil. "'Tis a sin."

Beniamino grinned. "Well, only between either Christians and Christians or Jews and Jews. It is not so much a problem between a Christian and a Jew."

"The tricks of lawyers," muttered Heinrich.

"Indeed." Beniamino went on. "At first the lords pay a little back so they can borrow more. I happily loan them more, and soon they refuse to pay. This, you see, delights me beyond words, for I then sell the note of debt to your bishops or abbots for my profit. They, in turn, add their own profit to the value of the debt, then demand payment from the lords under threat of excommunication ... a power a poor Jew simply does not have."

"A shrewd business, to be sure," interrupted Wil.

"Indeed. What is the best, however, is when a note is bought by an ambitious man like your prior. He was willing to pay more than my normal price to keep the abbot from knowing. You should have seen him smile when he set my little parchment in his box!"

"Prior Mattias?" asked Heinrich.

"*Ja*, it is he."

"But why would he be so anxious to buy a debt from you?"

"Here's the wonder of it: the debt was between myself and the abbey's protector, Lord Heribert of Runkel!"

"Heribert!" exclaimed Wil.

"Shh, lad!"

Wil's mind was racing. "What would Prior Mattias do with a debt owed by Heribert? And why would he not tell the abbot?"

"I am rather certain that the man intends to wrest something of great value from either the lord or the abbot. If the abbot needs to press the lord, he might reward Mattias for providing a way. Or it may be that your prior will conduct a private business for profits of his own."

Heinrich was dumbstruck. He had known Mattias to be a shrewd man, particularly when in league with the steward. "And Lord Heribert's steward?"

"Ah, yes, Hagan. He is a cursed thief to be sure, a man of avarice. He sent Lord Heribert to me in the first place. I suppose it shall be he who will act as judge in your trials. It is my belief that he and Mattias are conspiring together in this."

Heinrich grumbled. "I know him. He's a wicked demon if ever one lived."

"Indeed. And he is in a good position to plot with Mattias either for or against either the abbot or the lord."

"And you could spoil the secret," blurted Wil.

"Yes, I surely could. But it would not profit me to do so. I've a handsome sum already set in my strongbox. I'd not want to lose that!"

"So you're leaving on the morrow?" asked Heinrich.

"*Ja.* At first light." The man finally cut Wil's cords, while Heinrich lost himself in thought.

After a long silence, Heinrich spoke. "Beniamino, might I ask a kindness of you?"

"You might ask."

"When you leave, would you be traveling through Weyer again?"

"No. I'm going to Limburg."

Heinrich's mind was racing. "The uncle I mentioned— Arnold, the peddler of secrets—methinks he might be willing to pay you for what you know. You would be long gone, and he has never once betrayed a seller. This I know."

"Hmm. Would he pay a Jew?"

"I don't know. But tell him his nephew says to give you a pound of silver. Tell him Heinrich will pay him back when he is free."

Beniamino was quiet, then answered with a smile. "*When* you are free? Ha! I like that. *Ja*, my friend. Heinrich, I am an old man. I'll be spending the rest of my days under the sun in Brindisi with my cousins far to the south. I'll not be back in these cold forests again! So why not? For you and your stiff-necked boy, I shall gladly tell this uncle. And if he doesn't believe me?"

Heinrich thought for a moment. "Tell him I have news of his son, Richard."

Beniamino looked carefully at the shadowed figures of the baker and his son. "Done." He laid a hand on the pair. "You inspire me with your hope. You have not yielded to the moment. May the God of Abraham, Isaac, and Jacob grant you favor."

༅

A tall slim woman slipped into the campsite. "Wilda!" cried
Tomas and Otto in unison. "Wilda the witch!"

The company froze. The woman smiled and took a place
near Tomas. She was tall and graceful and quite beautiful
despite her years. She touched Tomas kindly on the arm
and turned to the others. "I am Wilda, daughter of Sieghild
known as the witch of Münster. I *was* a witch, like
m'mother, though I was baptized on this Easter past by the
priest in Münster."

Pieter stepped forward bravely. He extended his hand.
"Welcome, Wilda of Münster."

The woman smiled and turned her shining blue eyes on
Alwin. The knight blushed in the firelight, and his heart
fluttered within him. He guessed the woman to be about his
own age, perhaps a bit older. Her hair was white, but it was
white like a little child's, not like an aging woman's. Her
skin was smooth, and her eyes twinkled like Pieter's in the
flames. Her smile was warm and tender, conveying an
inner joy.

"I am Alwin, Alwin of Villmar." He bowed.

"I know," she answered.

Each in turn then made introductions until the circle
was completed.

Wilda spoke again. "I've spent most of m'life here, near to
this stone. Mother and I lived in these woods. We were not
welcome in the villages—at least by most of the priests—
and when mother was killed, I was still not welcome, save
for the monks at Villmar who fed me sometimes." She
looked at Tomas. "I saw you there last summer."

The young man nodded.

"In the winter past, the new priest in Münster found me
by the springs that feed the Laubusbach. I was cold and
hungry, and he was kind and fed me. He taught me stories
from the Scriptures and showed me to the way of life. I was
baptized and then offered a home with a tinker and his wife,
where I now live. But I still like to wander this mountain on
summer nights.

"I've been listening from the wood, and I know your

troubles," she continued. "Mother said the baker, Heinrich, was kindly and was kin to us. She oft wished she had not cast spells on the village on his account, but she was bitter about her past."

Alwin leaned forward. "Kin?"

Wilda answered, "*Ja.* She was the baker's aunt."

"His aunt? His aunt? I … I don't think I ever knew of an aunt … Wait! He once said he had an aunt who was raped and disappeared—"

"It was she."

The circle hushed, and Alwin shifted uncomfortably in his seat. It had long been rumored that some of his own Gunnar kin had raped a woman from Weyer a few years before his birth. He had heard the monks speak of the blood feud between his own family and Heinrich's. It was said that it was vengeance for this rape that had cost him his father and several uncles, though they had never been proven to be the woman's attackers.

Pieter invited Wilda to share in some food. He handed her some salted pork and a small wedge of cheese and then sent Maria for a flask of ale. "So, cousin of Heinrich, how can you help us?"

Wilda proceeded to tell all she knew about the charges against Wil; about both Anka's and Pious's parts in the accusations; of the last testament of Heinrich's wife, Marta; and of the taking of the baker's property.

"You are certain that the bakery is rightly owned by the archbishop now?"

"Yes. Heinrich was declared dead. He had been missing for so long. His widow granted Pious all the family property. When she died, Pious nearly ran to Mainz with his little success, and he came back with new robes and some silver. And, I'm told, he was allowed to add a portion of the bakery revenues to the treasury of the parish."

Otto cursed. "You know it was Pious who told Wil to give his mother the poison herb?"

Wilda was stunned. "I … I never thought it was Wil, but … but Pious?"

All heads nodded.

"In Münster we thought it was the hag Anka. The dung-hauler said she'd been a false friend to the widow always and had an eye for their land."

"That is true," Maria answered. "She was *Mutti's* friend, but she always talked about the land."

"And where was Heinrich all this time? We thought him to be dead."

"He was first sent to the north to serve the Church against rebels," Alwin answered. "Then he was caught up in troubles and went to Rome to do penance. He was returning when he found his son ... and daughter, as well as these others on crusade. He had hoped to come home to what is his as a freeman."

Wilda sighed. "It cannot be. He should have known that."

The knight nodded. "Aye, indeed. None could tell him. It seems he thought he might win the favor of his masters. A fool's mission, I fear."

Pieter looked at the sky. "We needs be on our way. Heinrich and Wil are in grave peril, to be sure. We must learn still more, and we need a plan quickly. Would you come with us, Wilda?"

The woman shook her head. "The monks in Villmar have been kindly. They've learned of my baptism and rejoice in it. But I am not welcome amongst the parish priests in their manor. They still believe me to be a witch, and they all fear me. If I am seen with you, you will be cast aside as well.

"If you seek help in Weyer, though, I should tell you this. Heinrich's uncle Arnold lives alone in a comfortable cottage by the sheepfold. You'd know his because it has good thatch and straight walls. He has an old green barrel by his door where he keeps his walking sticks.

"As these children can tell you, Arnold's been known all his days as one to fear. Since his son went away with Heinrich, he's been sullen and broody. But I hear of late he's in fear of his soul, and he even vouched for Wilhelm. He may be the friend you need."

Tomas agreed. "There's none more shrewd in all these parts than Arnold. If he could be a friend to us, we'd have a friend indeed."

Pieter nodded and took a deep breath. He fixed his hand tightly around his staff and called his group together. "Good, we shall see about this Arnold. But first, we *must* learn more." With that, the company divided, and Pieter's group hurried downslope toward the Laubusbach. They crossed the stream and entered Weyer while the sun edged over the horizon to their right. They had decided they would simply march through the village and directly to the road leading to the abbey, where they'd beg for food as pilgrims oft did. Once inside the abbey walls, Pieter believed he might wrest some information from the monks. It was a skill he had not lost. He wanted first to learn of the prisoners' whereabouts, and then of the time and place of their trial.

It was Monday, and a parade of peasants was already winding its way through Weyer like it had on every other summer workday for four centuries. Two-wheeled oxcarts lurched along rutted byways, heavy-laden with manure or filled with men being delivered to the fields of winter oats nearly ready for harvesting. Chickens and geese cackled and honked as Pieter planted his staff firmly along Weyer's footpaths. With his face set hard toward his destination, he ignored the curious housewives pausing to gawk at the strangers passing through.

At Pieter's urging, Tomas had lifted his hood over his head. It would serve no purpose to be recognized, but his eyes were needed to guide the others. The group marched past the village well, past the widespread linden tree standing in the center of the commons, and they were soon past the smoke and thatch and hurrying around the base of the knoll upon which the brownstone church was perched. All eyes lingered on the squat building above. "Karl the Great built it," said Pieter. "'Charlemagne' as the French call him. Heinrich told me so. He had hoped to visit the graves of his family. He said he'd a daughter and two sons resting there, as well as his parents and the like."

The company pressed up the steep slope leading north from the village. Gasping for breath, Pieter paused for a brief respite, then dragged himself behind his comrades a little farther up the hill. Panting, he once more begged the others' pardon as he collapsed along the shoulder. Eventually, the pilgrims reached the crest of the ridge and stopped again. They were all breathing hard, so they were glad to rest and marvel at the wide landscape before them. It was as Heinrich and Wil had always described: gentle, rolling fields as far as one could see, and in the center of the view was a dark ribbon of deep green marking the banks of the distant Lahn River.

Tomas pointed. "There, straight north of us along the river lies the village of Villmar and the abbey. If you follow the river to the left, you might see the towers of Runkel Castle. That's where they'll be taken for trial."

Frieda strained to see. "There, I think I see a square tower."

The others nodded.

"*Ja,*" added Friederich. "I see it too. It gives me a fright deep inside."

Benedetto trembled. "We'll not be going there, will we?"

Ignoring the little man, Tomas continued. "The castle is about two leagues from the abbey and about four leagues from Weyer. It would take less than two hours to get to the dungeon by cart."

"Not much time to free them by force," stated Friederich.

"By force?" cried Benedetto. "By force? Are you mad?"

"No, minstrel," interrupted Pieter. "Have no fear. We'll not be taking them by force." He took a deep breath and continued glumly, "Actually, I've no idea how we'll help them or *if* we'll be able to do anything more than offer them comfort as they're hanged. I tell you, friends, they are in terrible danger."

࿐

Visions of Heinrich and Wil dangling from the gallows in Runkel Castle silenced Pieter's company for the rest of its descent toward the abbey. The journey would normally have been a pleasant walk under a large sky and through fields glistening with morning dew. Ox-teams dotted the landscape along distant roads beyond the Lahn, and clusters of wool-clad peasants could be seen plodding through thigh-high grain.

The group soon entered the village of Villmar, a village not unlike Weyer but more directly affected by the business of the abbey set at its edge. Hence, the arrival of strangers prompted little interest from the folk so familiar with such things. Pieter's company walked through the village curiously, nearly colliding with an old Jew riding atop a sway-backed palfrey. Arriving at the walls of the monastery, Pieter turned to Tomas and to Frieda. "As we agreed, you two will wait over there." He pointed to a small inn. "Take these pennies, and have a beer and some bread. Tomas, keep away from the door. The abbey's porter is likely to know you. Frieda, I am sorry, but a female in the cloister makes the monks nervous. You understand?"

The young woman nodded.

"Good. We shan't be more than an hour or so." Pieter looked at Benedetto and Friederich. "I shall speak; you two must listen and look about. See what you can; hear what you can. Are we ready?"

The pair nodded. Pieter approached the portal and knocked on the wide oak door with his staff. Immediately, the door opened and the porter greeted his guests with a bow. "Thanks be to God."

"Indeed. We come in search of charity. We are weary pilgrims in need of a little rest and a merciful morsel or two."

The porter looked compassionately at the trio and bade them enter. The young man was dressed in his summer habit: a lightweight, cowled robe with a white scapular and thin sandals. He kissed them each, prayed over them, cupped water over their dusty feet, and begged them to follow him to the guestmaster.

The pilgrims hurried behind the man through the courtyard of the gray-stone abbey, where brothers were hard at work tending their many gardens or at task in their workshops. Friederich's eye fell upon a rotund old monk sleeping soundly at the base of a large tree. In his hands he gripped a large ring of keys.

"That's Brother Perpetua, our beloved friend who is

always either eating or sleeping!" commented the porter. "Though, in fairness, he is the keeper of keys and must be awake most of the night to bid travelers in and out. I am told, however, that the old fellow is usually snoring by the wine cellar door!"

"Keeper of keys?" mused Pieter. "A new title?"

"Well, 'tis not part of the Rule, but Father Abbot says it is his way of reminding us of the authority of the Holy Church. Do you understand?"

"Of course, my son. The apostles were granted the keys of heaven to bind and loose what they wished on earth."

The porter stopped and looked at Pieter with some surprise. "Ah, a priest who knows his Scripture! I thought there were no more."

Pieter chuckled. "Well, 'tis true that there are few left. Seems most of us know our liturgies, but few know the truth!"

The porter threw back his head and laughed. "Good brother, well said! You make me think of a dear friend who died but a year ago. Brother Lukas was his name." The young man leaned close to Pieter and spoke softly. "I believe the Holy Bible was written on his heart. He taught me much."

Pieter wisely held his tongue. He smiled and laid a kindly hand on the young man. "Then write Scripture on the hearts of others, my son. It is the only way of hope."

The porter delivered his guests to another earnest young monk, who welcomed them into a small room. This one ordered some novices to bring him bowls of water. He kissed each guest and prayed over them. "I shall wash thy feet in a moment."

"I already have," answered the porter.

"Why?"

"It is my duty when the abbot and prior are not about."

"No, it is mine, brother."

"No, look to the Rule."

"I have."

The porter grunted. "Well, 'tis done."

The guestmaster muttered, then fed the amused pilgrims

porridge, wheat bread, berry preserves, and one egg each. During the meal, Pieter made an effort to have a conversation with his host, but it was not in the character of the man nor in the order of things for the monk to reciprocate with idle chatter. It was their good fortune, therefore, that the porter returned.

"I am relieved of the gate to take my duties at chapter. I failed to pray a blessing over you."

The guestmaster growled. "Thou ought to be keeping away from our guests. Thou art not to mingle with visitors. *That* is plain enough in the Rule!"

Pieter quickly interrupted. "As thy guest, brother, I do ask some gift of charity from you. I should be most blessed if the young brother could sit by us for a few moments more."

The guestmaster grimaced. It was a request that put two rules of his order in opposition. The bells of terce rang, and he needed to go to his prayers. He had arrived late at prime that same morning and had missed the first of the three psalms. He knew he shouldn't press the patience of the abbot. "Well, uh, yes. We are to be hospitable to strangers." He bowed, prayed quickly over the group, and then scurried to the church.

The happy porter took a seat by his guests. "I am Brother Egidius, named for a beloved porter of this same gate some years past."

"I am Pieter, once warrior, once student, once monk, once clerk, and now a priest serving the poor of Christendom. These are my fellow journeymen, pilgrims to the holy places."

After more friendly conversation with the porter, Pieter finally turned the conversation to the matters at hand. "A peasant told us of some terrible things in one of your villages on the night of Sabbath past."

Egidius nodded. He looked out into the courtyard anxiously. "Well, Father, I am not to speak of these things, but you are a man of the cloth so ... well, hear this. The reeve of that village delivered two peasants to our garrison late in the night. One is under suspicion of killing his mother, a beloved monk of ours, and perhaps an abbey guard as well. He foolishly returned from that wretched crusade of children."

"Why do you call it a 'wretched crusade'?" challenged Friederich, unable to hold his tongue.

"They should never have gone. If only they could have known that God would not ever send them to such certain misfortune."

"But the Church wanted it!"

Egidius looked closely at the lad and shook his head. "Were you a crusader?"

Pieter answered for him. "Yes, he was a brave soldier for God."

The monk bowed his head. "I fear the Holy Church did not do enough to dissuade you. Perhaps the fault should be laid at our feet, for we say you ought seek truth from us. I am told that few of your priests ever tried to stop you."

"And I am told that, here, in this very abbey, a papal legate sounded the call!" Pieter's face was tight and anger laced his words.

Surprised, the porter faltered. "I ... I have heard the same, brother, but I was not here then. I was on a pilgrimage to the tomb at Aachen. It is said the abbot was not pleased. The pope has such an earnest fervor for crusading that it seems his legate may have been overzealous in this matter. I beg thy forgiveness for the error of my brothers."

Pieter took a deep breath. "Good monk, it is not you who should beg anything. Now, let us let the matter lie. We've other business. The young man falsely charged with murdering his mother is being held in your garrison's jail?"

Egidius looked up with a start. "You know him?"

"We do."

"I ... I surely must not speak of these things, then. You ... you deceived me."

"Brother," said Pieter in a fatherly tone, "we ask only this of you: do you know what is to happen to the lad and his father?"

"His father?"

"Aye."

The monk groaned. Looking nervously into the court-yard, he leaned forward and spoke quietly. "I am told they are to be taken to the castle for trial."

"When?"

"Today."

"The trial is today?" blurted Friederich.

"No, little brother. They'll be taken to the dungeon today, but we think the trial is not for several days ... maybe at week's end. Steward Hagan acts as judge in these matters, and he is en route from business elsewhere. Lord Heribert has no interest in things of the court and has just recently left on a pilgrimage to a shrine in the east. 'Tis all I know."

Pieter clasped the man's hand and prayed over him. "With our thanks, brother. Forgive us our deceit."

Egidius bowed his head. "I do. And what will you do?"

Pieter looked at his companions, then back to the sym-pathetic monk. "Surely, I shall pray."

Chapter Twenty

A COLLABORATION OF LOVE

By the bells of sext, most of Weyer's men had enjoyed a midday meal and were returning to their fields. The day had grown very warm, and the air had become humid. Perspiring and thirsty, Pieter and his worried companions returned to the ridge overlooking the village and scanned the endless green of the landscape beyond. The priest drew a long breath and rested his eyes on a flock of sheep grazing peacefully on a distant slope that was sprinkled with tiny flowers. He smiled. "Oh, if we might only have a day to sleep in the sun in a place like that!"

With a sigh, he turned his eyes toward the smoky nook in which Weyer was nestled. The village was crowded and busy. "We need to find Arnold's cottage."

The group hurried down the steep descent past chatting peasants, a team of oxen, and a peddler's cart until they faced a short row of hovels set against a fence. Tomas immediately pointed to a sturdy cottage with a moss-green barrel by its door. "There! That'd be Arnold's!"

Nearly running to the open door, Frieda arrived first. "Sir? *Herr* Arnold?"

A narrow-faced, thin old man rose from a stool upon which he had been dozing deep within the shade of his thatch. "Eh? Who calls m'name?" He rubbed his eyes and stepped to the doorway to gawk at the company standing before him. "Tomas?"

"*Ja.* I've come home."

Pieter stepped forward. "I, sir, am Pieter, wandering priest and servant of these friends."

Arnold spat and waved them off with a mumbled blasphemy.

"*Herr* Arnold!" cried Frieda. "You are my husband's great-uncle!"

The man stared at the young woman, then stepped slowly out of his house. Frieda trembled, waiting nervously. The man's taut face was hard as iron, and his skin clung to his bones like wet leather wrapped around an old oak. He was lean and gray, and his face was etched with the bitterness of broken dreams. Approaching sixty, the man had bettered nearly all his foes by ruthless cunning, but he had been soured by the vanity lately discovered in such vacant conquest. "Who are you?"

"I am Frieda, wife of Wilhelm ... son of Heinrich the baker."

Arnold said nothing for a long moment. He studied each face before him. He looked at the minstrel. "And who are you, little mouse?"

"I am Benedetto, troubadour and friend to these."

"And you?"

"I am Friederich of ... of ... well, I don't know where I am from."

Arnold laughed. "I like that," he said. "A plain-speaking lad. And you, old man, you say you're a priest. I tell you this: I don't like priests or shavelings of any sort. They are all deceivers, liars, and pretenders."

Pieter smiled. He had already judged Arnold to be a cantankerous old devil, but he sensed the man had a keen understanding of the world as it oft was. "Not all, sir, but some, to be sure."

Arnold grunted. "They walk with bowed heads as if they be humble, yet they do not walk at all—they strut!"

Pieter laughed out loud. "Aye, I've seen it m'self! Some only pretend to be forgiven, for they pretend they are sinners!"

"Ha! Good one, old man. I like that one. I shall remember it. Now, why are you here?"

Pieter proceeded to tell Arnold much the man already knew. Arnold listened carefully, feigning ignorance while attempting to discern the hearts of the group now gathered around his table. He asked them of their journey and of their trials, of their present wishes and their fears. At last, he poured them each a generous tankard of warm beer and tore apart a large loaf of wheat bread. "What do you know of my son, Richard?"

Pieter thought for a long moment. "Is he the cousin who traveled with Heinrich to the north?"

"He is."

The man leaned forward. Pieter took a long draught and set his tankard down. "Heinrich told me that his cousin was killed in combat with the knight who crippled him as a youth. I am sorry."

Arnold's eyes misted and he turned away. He rose from his table and went to a small window facing the sheepfold to the rear. The room was quiet as the old man absorbed the news. At last, he returned to the table and sat down again. He poured himself another tankard of beer. "Was his death avenged?"

Pieter nodded. "It was, sir. Your nephew buried your son's killer in a heap of dung."

The answer satisfied Arnold. "Good man, that Heinrich, though sometimes I thought him to be too soft, like his mother. My boy, Richard, was spirited like his grandfather and me. 'Tis fitting he fell fighting." He took a drink. "I fear his children are perished as well. Have you news of them?"

"No," said Frieda quietly. "Some of us are still finding our way home."

Arnold nodded sadly. "A brave thing, that crusade of yours. Foolish, methinks, but brave enough. My son Roland said he had talked to his children—but they said the visions of others was proof enough. They left and have not come back. So now it is only me, Roland, and his terrible wife, Elsbeth. 'Tis all the kin I've left except for Heinrich. Once our family was strong and growing. We kept the code of our forefathers and their cause as well. It was a different time then, and I think I was a different man."

"You've Wil and Maria," blurted Frieda. "They'd be kin of yours and mine."

Arnold looked thoughtfully at the young woman. With a nod he answered. "You've a kind heart, fair damsel. Have a care with it." He took another drink. "Wil's a good lad. He's spirit like my Richard had."

No one answered.

"No matter. This life is naught but dark shadows and wicked things. Mine is ending far from what I had expected. There was a time m'brother Baldric and me ruled Weyer! He as woodward of all the abbey lands, and me as forester of the manor. Ha! I learned to fill bags of silver with the secrets of others—secrets they paid to keep hidden. I've coins from monks, prelates, peasants, housewives, and even a gold coin from old Pious himself. The Templars keep my money safe, but ... but I fear it is not enough to keep me from burning for my sins in the ages to come." The man shuddered. "I met a demon once, outside the hut of a witch. He made me pay alms to save m'soul then. I suppose I'll need do the same again."

Pieter shook his head. "I hear the voice of a man humbled into honesty. As you know, my friend, *'multi timor, conscientiam pauci verentur* ... many fear their reputation, but few their conscience.' Some take their pride to their grave with a sneer at things to come. It seems your heart is touched by grace."

Arnold grunted and swallowed another draught.

"Yet, my friend, the conscience can be a tyrant as well. It is not always a wise or proper master."

Arnold looked at him blank faced. "What kind of priest are you?"

"Oft a bad one, I fear. But one who's been given small bits of truth along the way. Your nephew is one who has taught me much from his own amazing journey. You ought to spend time with him."

Arnold grinned a wide, toothless grin. "You are a clever one!"

Pieter laughed. "I love your nephew and his son, so please forgive my feeble attempts to sway you to our cause." The old priest looked deeply into Arnold's eyes, and his tone became earnest, even pleading. He leaned forward. "Listen to me, sir. I do not ask your help so that you might purge your soul ... forgiveness is not to be earned. I do beg your help simply because it is right.

"You, *Herr* Arnold, have seen men and women at their worst. You know their secrets—secrets of betrayal and lust, wicked, horrid deeds and hypocrisy. You've made it your trade. But methinks you have discovered the truth of life's rotted underbelly. It is an ugly serpent that crawls about us all. Can you not help us spare two of your kin from the stench of such evil?"

Arnold stared evenly into the old man's face. None spoke as they waited breathlessly for the man to answer. At last, Arnold turned his eyes to Tomas, Friederich, then Benedetto, and, at last, to the imploring face of Frieda. He nodded. "Aye. That I can."

అ

Elsewhere in Weyer, Herwin and Wulf were desperate to find a way to help the baker and his son. "They've no chance, Father," moaned Wulf. The large man was nursing a deep cut in his scalp from the reeve's flail.

"We must help them!" cried Herwin. He looked at his table and picked up the dagger that had been knocked from Wil's hand in the melee. He had found it at sunrise. "This must have a story. It has an inscription."

"You'd best hide it," answered Wulf.

"Aye, lad," Herwin sighed. "I confess that I've no idea how to help. Perhaps I'll just beg mercy from the court."

"I fear we've already been given what mercy is to be had," grumbled Wulf. "The reeve was good to not arrest us."

A woman's voice sounded at the door. "Herwin? Might I speak with you?"

"Frau Katharina! Aye, come in, come in."

The graceful woman slipped into the cool shade of Herwin's hut. She sat down sadly on a stool and shuddered. Herwin went to her side and rested his arm kindly over her shoulders.

"I am very sorry for your loss," Herwin began.

The woman nodded. "He's to be buried this evening. I've washed the body, and others helped me shroud it. Father Albert will pray over him."

"Oh, my dear, with no husband and no children to care for you, what shall you do?"

"Dear Herwin, I did not come for your sympathy. I shall be well. I am now the free widow of a yeoman with chattels enough. I've a dowry with the Templars and two hides of land that I now own." She stiffened her back and fumbled awkwardly for words. "Old friend, I am told it was Heinrich of Weyer who killed my husband. Is it so?"

Herwin nodded.

Katharina's heart raced. Her spirit soared, yet she lowered her eyes. "I did not believe it to be true. I thought Heinrich to have been long since dead."

"So did we all. I still do not know his story."

Katharina stood motionless, fighting tears and swallowing hard against the knot in her throat. Then, no longer able to dam the flood, she burst into tears and buried her face in her hands. Father and son looked at one another in alarm. "Katharina?"

"I miss him so, Herwin. I have missed him for so very long!"

Herwin was confused. "Who?"

Katharina looked sadly into the aging man's face. Then with a voice tainted by shame, she whispered, "Heinrich."

Herwin did not answer. He held her kindly as his mind whirled. He had always respected Katharina, and he had been a good friend to her over the many years she had lived in Weyer. The woman had endured much under the heavy hand of her husband. She was known for her charity— sometimes despised for it. He knew she had spent many an hour in old Emma's gardens, and he knew that Heinrich had a soft place in his heart for her.

"No, Herwin, it is not as you may have heard. Heinrich was a faithful husband to Marta," said Katharina. "It was *I* who longed for *him*."

Herwin nodded sadly. *Methinks he longed for you as well,* he thought. He lifted her chin and smiled. "Good woman, I know Heinrich's heart, and I know it was held fast by his duty. And you were a faithful wife to a monster. I oft wished I was a younger, stronger man when I'd hear him beat you." He brushed her cheek lightly. "I see the purple of a bruise lingers even after he is gone."

Katharina nodded and pulled away. She sat at the table and dried her eyes. "I must deal with my shame and bury my husband. But tell me this: did Heinrich murder him as I am told?"

"Nay, child! He only sought to defend his son. None could know what the reeve and his deputies were about. I believe Heinrich thought they were going to kill them both. My son, here, was knocked to the ground and young Wil wrestled down. See here. The lad lost his dagger in the fray.

"But Heinrich fought against shadows, not faces. He thrust his sword only when he thought his son's life was in peril. Your husband tried to kill him, but Heinrich struck hard and fast. No, sister, he did not know, and methinks he still does not know whom he slayed."

Relieved, Katharina closed her eyes. "Thanks to you, Herwin. Oh, dear God, I prayed that if it were truly Heinrich, he did not know whose life he was taking." She looked at the man again. "It … it was he who beat my husband to near death just before he went away."

Herwin and Wulf both smiled. "Good for him!"

Katharina smiled timidly. She remembered her secret joy the day Ludwig was found bloodied, bruised, and unconscious in the village latrine. "And where is Heinrich now?"

"He was taken to Villmar, but I fear they'll be bound over to the guard at Runkel today. I would expect a quick trial—"

"And a hanging," Katharina added firmly. "Were they alone?"

Herwin thought carefully. "Well, they came to my home alone, but soon after they were taken, two companions came here."

"Who were they?" asked Katharina.

"The lad Tomas returned from crusade and also Brother Blasius ... now called Alwin, the Templar who is hunted for treason. Do you remember him?"

"Aye," replied Katharina. "He and Heinrich were always close."

Wulf's wife had been quietly spinning in the corner. "There are other companions as well."

"Are you sure?"

"Quite. Wil mentioned his wife."

"Then we've allies somewhere!" exclaimed Katharina hopefully.

"Allies?"

"*Ja*. Others who'll dare help them. If you were they, what would you do?"

Wulf's wife answered, "I'd come to the village to see where they are!"

"Indeed!" cried Katharina. "Have you seen strangers?"

"Nay, we've not been about at all. We've been grieving the moment."

"Well then, Herwin, we needs move through the village—and quickly."

"You need to bury your husband."

For Katharina, that obligation seemed suddenly like an annoying interference. Ludwig had, indeed, been a monster to her for all their married life. Nevertheless, she had spent a sleepless night feeling shame for the unspeakable relief that followed his death. The man had beaten her, humiliated her, and had once kicked her so hard that she lost a daughter in childbirth. It had been her first and only babe. The woman nodded in resignation. "Yes, I know."

With hugs to Herwin and his household, Katharina hurried away from his hut and toward the church, where she hoped to find Father Albert. Her path took her along the Oberbrechen highway and past the sheepfold. She walked briskly, a woman on a mission, but as she passed Arnold's hovel, she paused. *If any would know of the manor's business, it would be Arnold,* she thought. She looked at his closed door and took a deep, steadying breath.

☙

"I said I'd help, but your plan is mad," grumbled Arnold. "Humph! I paid that old Jew two pounds of silver for his story. Now it wonders me if I've wasted m'money."

"Heinrich must have known that you could use the information."

"*Ja, ja.* If I had the document in m'hands, I could work a miracle to be sure. But it is in the prior's chamber, and the man always locks his door!"

Pieter was insistent. "Now hear me again. Our little Friederich has fingers as nimble as a young seamstress. I've seen him pluck coins from a pouch under the nose of a brute, and he does it with a smile!"

Friederich grinned mischievously.

"You said you were told exactly where it was put," blurted Tomas.

Arnold furrowed his brow. "Aye, but perhaps the old Jew lied. He wanted a full mark for *that* bit of added information, but we settled on a shilling."

Pieter shrugged. "Have you been swindled often?"

"Nay. I usually have a nose for it."

"So, why are you worried now?"

"A Jew bettered me once before."

Pieter thought for a moment. "Well, we've really no other way. A bluff won't do. We need the thing in hand. Methinks we'll have to trust him."

Arnold grumbled. "Aye, but even if this madness works, it will only help Heinrich. The charge against Wil is too far spread. The village wants vengeance for Marta, the monks for Lukas and their guard. No one would dare make a deal for it."

"But we're told that the deaths of Lukas and the guard are mere suspicions."

"Aye, but the priest speaks of dreams and visions. Herwin told you right, Tomas. Such words from a priest are not easily challenged. We'd need at least one witness, maybe two to say the contrary. And how, my friends, do we prove the man had no such dreams?"

Pieter was quiet. At last he struck his fist on Arnold's table. "I don't know! I cannot think so quickly anymore!"

Frieda took Arnold's arm. "Sir, when we stir the pot, the rabbit rolls first. Then the turnips rise, then peas, then onions, and then yet more. I say we turn our rabbit and see what fortune it brings."

Arnold nodded thoughtfully. "Well said, fair lady. Well said." He turned to Friederich, then to Pieter. "It is agreed then. Firstly, let us think on the plan for Heinrich. Methinks—"

A rap sounded on the door, and the collaborators froze. Arnold furrowed his brows and stared at his guests. Pieter shook his head. "None of ours," he whispered.

Arnold grabbed a stout stick and approached the door slowly. He then flung it open and stared angrily at the slight form of Katharina standing before him. "You!"

The woman bowed. Arnold stared at her for a moment, then looked about to see if others were watching. "What do you want?"

"I need to talk to you, sir ... about Heinrich."

Arnold's eyes nearly popped. "Yet another!" he growled. "Go away. He killed your husband, and he'll pay the price." He slammed the door and spun around. "The widow! The widow of the man Heinrich killed."

Another knock sounded on the door. This time Arnold flung it open with a loud curse. "I told you ... now go away!" he cried.

Katharina ground her shoes into the dust. "No, *Herr* Arnold. Heinrich did not murder my husband. He killed him in self-defense."

Arnold peered into the woman's beautiful, fiery green eyes. "What is this about?"

"My husband was a beast. I submitted to him, but, as God is my witness, I oft wanted him dead. Now he is, and I want to help Heinrich."

Arnold stared at the woman for another moment, then grabbed her by the arm and quickly yanked her through the doorway. As he slammed his door, he shoved her toward the others. The group was wary and unsure of the woman's true intentions.

"You must believe me!" Katharina pleaded desperately.

"I ... I loved him." She began to weep. "May God forgive me, but I loved him."

Frieda's heart was moved, and she touched the woman lightly on the arm.

"I knew it was a sin," cried Katharina. "But I could not rule my heart. I was true to my husband, but I did love Heinrich so."

The group whispered amongst themselves, then Pieter said, "My dear sister, we do not know you. Heinrich once spoke of a woman for whom he had shaming memories, but he mentioned no name. We cannot trust you now, and you cannot help us. It is best that you bury your husband."

Katharina stood, erect and defiant. "Yes. I understand. You do not trust me. So let me tell you this, and you judge whether I earned *his* trust. Heinrich's greatest love was his children, his second was his Butterfly *Frau*, then his bakery, and then the magical place he called the Magi. His baker's mark honors both *Frau* Emma and his faith. He has a heart for the poor, yet he oft hates himself. He follows duty and no longer even faces the sun. I know this man. Only one who cares would know these things."

Her words moved Pieter, for they rang true of a love long cherished. The old man thought carefully. He looked kindly at the woman, then at Arnold. "*Frau* Katharina, bury your husband. Then, if you truly wish to help, take a walk near the Matins Stone."

"The Matins Stone?"

"Yes. Do you know it?"

"Aye. It is beyond the boundary toward Münster. I've been there twice."

Pieter leaned forward. "Then when your duty is done, take a third walk—alone. Perhaps you may help us after all."

ॐ

Later that evening, after remaining for some time with Arnold, Pieter's group made its way back to camp under cover of darkness. Katharina had already arrived by the time they returned and had endured a blistering interrogation by Alwin, Wilda, Otto, and Helmut. But it was Otto who assured them of her trustworthiness. The young lad had been witness to the woman's frequent beatings. One particular spring day he had followed her into the ferns by the Magi, where he had heard her sob the name of Heinrich over and over.

For the others, however, it was the return of Heinrich's sword that bid her welcome. She had concealed it beneath her summer cloak, and when she presented it to Alwin, the man embraced her.

Pieter shared the events of the day with all those present, and more time was spent carefully reviewing and discussing their ideas. As they prepared to implement the first part of their dubious plan to save Heinrich, the old priest joined a circle of bent knees to pray for the protection of the Almighty in "such a mad scheme as this!"

It had been decided that the night's mission needed to be clean and swift. What would be needed were two lookouts, a warrior, a guide, and a set of nimble fingers. The plan did not call for an old man, a minstrel, a widow, or a witch. So it was Otto, Helmut, Alwin, Tomas, and Friederich who received the special blessings of Pieter, who then begged the heavens to shower mercy upon Heinrich and Wil, who were no doubt suffering the terrors of Runkel's dungeon.

In tears the old priest pleaded and wept, then finished his prayer with a final petition on the behalf of all: "Attend to my cry: for I have been brought low indeed. Deliver me from my persecutors; for they are stronger than I. Lead my soul out of prison, that I may praise Thy name, O Lord."

So with a prayer and an unlikely plan, the brave volunteers bade their comrades farewell and disappeared into the darkness. Except for Friederich and Helmut, the others knew the abbey well, Tomas best of all. Though Alwin had been raised within its walls, it had been many years since he had spent more than a passing moment there. Tomas had been an oblate as well and had lived inside the abbey until just a few years prior. The abbey had changed over the years; it had grown with the addition of new dormitories and workshops, a new complex of buildings for the abbot and his prior, as well as expanded gardens and new orchards.

The five hurried through the forest and crossed the Laubusbach at a ford that would lead them around Weyer. They ran cross-country over the stiff stubble of freshly harvested fields until they came to the Villmar road, which they took downhill to the dimly lit village and its abbey. The night was warm, and the air was scented with the pleasant odor of fresh-cut grain. A brief shower fell, dampening the sound of their padding feet as they hurried through the shadows of sleepy Villmar and to the southern gate of the abbey.

Otto looked upward at the alarm bell standing quietly in its place, and he recalled Wil's story of the year before. The lad began to sweat profusely. The company had agreed they'd enter as pilgrims, not beggars, and they'd greet the guard with a coin, not a stout stick! At Alwin's command, all of them lifted their hoods over their heads and hobbled forward.

Alwin stepped boldly toward the soldier who took his place each night at the bells of compline. It had become the abbot's uncomfortable concession to the world of war. "Your pardon, good sir."

The guard was young and alert. "Who goes there?" He leveled his lance.

"Five pilgrims from Egypt bound for Cologne." Alwin tossed back his hood and took a posture of friendliness.

"Egypt?"

"*Ja*, my brother. And we have visited ourselves to holy relics throughout our journey. I have touched the hem of the Holy Virgin's veil and prayed over the bones of St. Amphibalis. We have all worshiped at the blood of St. George, and this fine lad has climbed the *Scala Santa* in Rome. Ah, good soldier, we are well blessed and happy, but we are sleepy and hungry, too! Here, my friend, a coin touched to the tooth of St. Stephen."

The guard reached toward a silver penny lying dull and tarnished in Alwin's opened palm. He picked it up reverently and kissed it, then dropped it in a pouch at his belt.

"With thanks, pilgrim. Please, knock for the porter."

Alwin rapped loudly on the wooden gate as Tomas sank deeper into his hood. After waiting patiently, he knocked again, and a sleepy porter pulled the heavy door open. "Thanks be to God," he mumbled.

"Your humble brethren beg entrance, brother monk," answered Alwin with a bow.

The porter stepped aside and gave the visitors entrance. Closing the door, he raised a torch to see the faces of his guests and recited sleepily, "He who is hungry is welcome; he who is weary may find rest with us."

Alwin bowed. "We are pilgrims, brother. We come from Egypt and are traveling to our homes in Cologne. We have silver to buy a bit of bread and perhaps some wine."

The porter yawned. "*Ja*, my friend. We've an alms box by the guesthouse, and the poor of this manor are grateful. Our guestmaster is asleep, as is the prior. The abbot is entertaining other guests, so you must forgive us if I tend to you myself."

"We are but humble pilgrims, brother. We need not bother any other."

The porter quietly led the group across the abbey grounds. The moon was up but shrouded in a clouded sky that seemed to grow more oppressive as the night passed. A few smoky torches hung on some walls, but they cast only a poor yellow light into the heavy shadows. The pilgrims walked by the bakery and brewery ... both known by their smells, then passed a barn of some sort and the granary now beginning to fill with oats. Far to their left, in the center of the abbey, stood the dark lines of the main cloister and the towers of its church.

"Your abbey seems large and prosperous, at least by night!" chuckled Alwin.

"It is. And it is growing. Rumors are that we've more lands in Saxony to add to our holdings. Lands there and now some near Toulouse, in France."

"Ah, Toulouse, yes. I've spent some time in that region as a knight. I drew the sword against the Cathari for the glory of the Church."

The porter stopped and turned. "You are a crusader, then?"

Alwin bowed.

"We are given lands taken from those heretics. It must be God's pleasure to have you come to us. Your sword has blessed this place! Now, my lord, I shall serve you a feast!"

Alwin had hoped to ingratiate himself to the young porter, but he had not wanted to draw undue attention. "No, good brother, please, I beg thee. I ... I need not feed my pride with such kindness. I do, however, have a special place in my heart for a good wine. Might you lead us to your cellar? Perhaps allow me to choose the wine you would serve?"

"Indeed, my brother! Indeed! Follow me!"

The porter turned left sharply and hurried toward the imposing silhouette of the main cluster of buildings. The pilgrims' hearts pounded as they drew nearer their goal.

"Brother, it is dark, but methinks fine masons built this place," said Alwin. "In Limoges I once took refuge in an abbey that had grown so that it built a separate chamber for the abbot's secretary and the prior's office."

The porter stopped and pointed to a large new addition that reached into the courtyard. "Well, we've kept as much as possible together, so we all are as one. But the abbot's office and the prior's are now there."

"Oh," said Helmut. "And I suppose your abbot has himself a fine window above to keep an eye on the novices!"

The porter smiled. "*Ja*, 'tis true enough. Abbot Udo is a humble man, but I know he loves the high window. I believe he repents of it secretly, however. At chapter he once said he would have gladly given the better view to the prior, but since the prior's knees are bad, he says he thought it better if he'd suffer the steps instead."

"No doubt," chuckled Alwin. He gave Helmut a covert glance of approval.

As they approached the cloister, the porter said more. "There it is. See, the abbot's office is directly on the corner, so he has two windows. His prior is directly beneath, and sometimes they call to one another through their windows.

They both have the southern wall, so they get most of the day's sun.

"Now, my friends, if you will, follow me quietly through these corridors and down the steps ahead."

In a few moments the porter was standing over the sleeping keeper of keys, Brother Perpetua. Otto nudged Tomas, and the two grinned beneath their hoods. It was as they had hoped. Friederich fixed his eyes on the man's keys.

The porter prodded the sleeping monk. "Brother, wake up!"

The fat fellow snorted and opened one eye. "Eh?"

"We've guests."

"Eh?" Perpetua climbed off his stool and rubbed his eyes. "I ... I was only praying, brother. Now, how can I serve thee?"

"Unlock the door. We need to select a wine for our special guest."

The keeper smiled at the five and reached for a torch. He then fumbled through his keys. Friederich guessed there to be about three dozen. Perpetua chose one and inserted it into a rusted keyhole. With a loud snap, the cellar lock opened. "Aye, it never used to be locked, but the devils prowl about some nights. I see them in the mist. The abbot says we've lost too much to them over time. I'd say he is right about that. The alms box went empty one night near Martinmas some years ago. Once a lord's entourage sacked our cellars and our treasury. Wicked souls, may they be damned to hellfire!"

Alwin feigned interest in the wine, then turned to the porter. "Brother, it occurs to me that you've been away from your post! We are content to make a choice and let this good monk show us our lodging."

Disappointed, the youth agreed. He clasped hands with Alwin and bowed to the others, then disappeared into the night.

"So, brother ..."

"Perpetua."

"Yes. Brother Perpetua, methinks it shall soon be the bells of matins. You'll need leave us for your prayers."

The man grunted. "I've prayed all the night as it is." He looked covetously at the wine barrels set in a long, neat row. "So you are truly a special guest?"

"I am a crusader, sir, on my way home."

It was enough. Perpetua smiled and hurried the others inside the cellar and then closed the door behind them as the bells of midnight prayers rang solemnly over the cloister. He set his torch into a wall-holder, shuffled on heavy legs to a shelf, and reached for several wooden tankards. Chortling like a schoolboy, he beckoned his guests to come closer. "Here, lads. God owes crusaders a special kindness. From where in Christendom would you like to taste wine?" He laughed gleefully.

The pilgrims looked blankly at the round-faced monk and the long row of barrels.

"Well? We've a fine selection of hearty reds from Burgundy. We've a fruity barrel from Alsace and a pale red from the March of Verona. Perhaps you'd prefer something light from Liguria or a heavy port from the Duoro Valley in Portugal?" The man was grinning from ear to ear. "Ah, and the abbot just received a barrel of something very aromatic from the kingdom of Castille."

Alwin smiled broadly. "You've had them all?"

"Indeed!" He squatted on his haunches and leaned over to Friederich. "Boy, I guard the door with my life, and while I'm guarding it, I make sure the taps all work! Ha!" He stood and roared. "I love my calling!"

Chapter Twenty-one

TENSION IN VILLMAR

*T*he pilgrims laughed with the jolly monk and soon followed him up and down the row of barrels. Wisely, Alwin and his companions were carefully pouring most of their "tastes" quietly onto the dirt floor of the cellar, else they would have been staggering like the bleary-eyed Perpetua. Slurring his words and tripping about the cellar, the well-oiled monk was finally coaxed to a bench by the guiding hands of Alwin. "We'll guard the door for you, old friend," said the knight softly.

The monk smiled, then dropped to the floor in a stupor. "We didn't need nimble fingers for this!" snickered Friederich.

Alwin was suddenly serious. "Now, lads, listen. Friederich, take the keys from his belt. Tomas, put out the torch. We'll lock the old fellow in, then get to the prior's office. We've about four hours yet."

In moments, Friederich found the right key and locked Perpetua inside the cellar. The group then hurried up the stone steps and into the arcade, which they followed to the end. Then, turning left, they slunk through the corridor leading them to the abbey's offices, where the porter had said the prior's office now was. Fortunately, a rain was falling, so what few torches were burning in the courtyards were fast being extinguished. The abbey was quiet, save for the patter of summer rain on the earth and on the tile roofs above.

"We didn't ask if it was guarded," whispered Helmut.

Tomas thought for a moment. "It may be. The Templars are under contract as is the lord of Runkel."

Alwin thought carefully. "Tomas, go ahead of us and see. Do you know which door?"

"It'd be down a small corridor that turns to the right, just ahead of us. Then it would be the last door on the left." With that, the lad crept forward.

The other four waited nervously. They feared Perpetua might awaken and begin calling for help. If he did, they'd be found out. "Might he?" whispered Friederich.

"I don't think so, lad," answered Alwin. He hoped he was right.

It seemed a lifetime before Tomas came padding back in the darkness. In a low voice he said, "We've one guard fast asleep. But he's a few doors down from the prior's."

Alwin thought quickly. He pulled his sword quietly from its sheath. "If he stirs, I'll need to finish him. I pray God keeps him in his dreams. Now, Friederich, when you get to the door, you'll need to go through many keys quietly. When you find the right one, open the door, and Helmut will follow you in. Arnold says the Jew vowed he saw the parchment put in a wooden box atop his desk."

Helmut was perspiring and his mouth was dry. "We've no certainty that the key to the office is even on our ring."

The group was quiet. It was logical that it would be there, but it was also possible that the prior would have his own key. No one had given that little detail a thought!

Alwin muttered under his breath, "I should have plied the key keeper!"

"Well, you didn't," said Tomas. "But here we are. I say let's go with what we have."

Helmut was trembling. "But why wouldn't he have locked it in the strongbox?"

Alwin shook his head. "I doubt the prior has his own."

The five squatted quietly, and then Friederich whispered, "Well, we're here. Let's be on with it."

They clasped hands. "For Wil and Heinrich, then,"

whispered Alwin. "Let us go with God."

Otto was placed as a watchman where the group had paused. His duty was to keep an eye on that side of the cloister. Tomas was sent forward, beyond the turn and deeper along the corridor serving the offices. Alwin followed Helmut and Friederich to the corner, where they turned right. He would fix his eye on the sleeping guard whom the two lads sneaked past.

The rain began to fall harder, suddenly in great sheets. Alwin prayed that no thunder would follow. "Keep sleeping, my friend. Keep sleeping."

Friederich was only seven, but he knew what grave consequences both he and his comrades would face if they were discovered. With steely determination, the little lad ran his fingers over the shape of his ring of keys. Some were long, some fat; some had a wide end, some narrow. He ran his forefinger over the keyhole of the prior's door and closed his eyes, imagining its shape. Then, swiftly sorting through the keys once more, he picked one. The lad took a deep breath and lifted it to the hole. He slid it in ever so silently and gave it a twist.

Nothing moved.

Undaunted, the boy tried again, and then again. Suddenly near tears, he closed his eyes and let his fingers run over the whole of the ring once more.

"Hurry!" whispered Helmut. "Please!"

Friederich's eyes stayed closed. He drew a slow breath through his nostrils and felt for the one key that might save them all, the single iron tool that would open the doors of hope. His fingers held fast on one. He could not move them past it. With a smile, he knew. The lad took the squat, short-shafted key and lifted it to the door. He slid it quietly, but confidently, forward. He turned it in its hole.

Click, snap, creak. The door opened!

"Oh, thank You, Jesus!" squeaked Helmut. The two shuffled quickly into the room. It was black as pitch, and the boys strained to see. "The desk should be by the window, Helmut," whispered Friederich.

The trembling boy inched his way forward with arms

outstretched. His knee bumped an unseen stool, which scraped loudly across the stone floor. The boys froze.

In the corridor, Alwin nearly cried out at the sound. It was muffled by the rain, but to his peaked senses, it sounded like the crash of a cymbal! The guard shifted slightly on his seat, and Alwin prepared to pounce. His hands gripped his sword tightly, and he gritted his teeth.

"Go around," urged Friederich quietly.

Helmut moved to one side, then inched forward again. His hands guided him along a table, then past the high back of a chair. Nothing.

"Move farther down the room," urged Friederich.

Helmut crept forward. He felt his heart pounding within his chest, and his breath was short and rapid. A flash of distant lightning lit the room suddenly, and the lad saw the desk just before him. He reached forward. His fingers ran along the well-worn wood of the top, past an inkwell and its quill, past a few dry leafs of parchment and an unseen Book of Hours. They lingered for a moment on the lead seal of a large letter. Had he known, he would have been surprised to be touching a document sealed by the pope.

At last, his hand bumped lightly against a pear-wood box. The lad held his breath and lifted the lid. "I have it!" The boy slowly released his breath.

A low, distant rumble rolled through the abbey. "Hurry, Helmut!"

"I have it!" he answered.

"How do you know it's it?"

"It's the only parchment in there." The deed done, the boys hurried across the dark room, lighted once more by the approaching storm.

The thunder had done what Alwin had feared it might. The guard was now shifting and becoming restless in his sleep. *Hurry, lads!* he pleaded silently.

Wisely, Friederich had kept his fingers on the right key, and he quickly locked the door behind them. Then, like a young cat and its kitten, the pair dashed silently past the guard and rejoined their fellows now gathering around the corner.

"God be praised!" whispered Alwin. "I was thinking that we should get the keys back to the monk. It'll keep suspicion away from us."

All agreed, and in mere moments the cellar door was reopened and the key ring placed neatly on the sleeping monk's belt. "Now, Tomas, lead us out the other gate!"

The five dashed around the cloister and through the abbey's gardens. Like flying ghosts, they bolted through the rain toward the north gate, known by the monks as the lesser gate. It led to a narrow meadow and the docks along the Lahn. The gate was sometimes guarded on the outside, and, just as Tomas had promised, therefore not locked on the inside. The porter, no doubt a sleeping novice, was out of sight. Tomas pulled the door open slowly and looked about for the guard. Seeing no one, he bade his fellows follow, and the five sprinted to safety.

∾

"You've done well!" exclaimed Pieter as Alwin's company presented the fruit of their daring adventure. "You brave scoundrels!" The old man laughed, and the gathered circle cheered as Pieter studied the note by the fire. "By the saints, I believe it says exactly what the Jew said it would!"

Alwin smiled and drew a long drink from a flask of mead. Wilda had returned with a rucksack filled with provisions. She handed the knight a block of cheese.

"Thanks, woman," said Alwin. He fixed his dark eyes on Wilda and the woman blushed.

Pieter read the document once more. "Truly, a gift from a merciful Lord," he cried.

"What does it say?" blurted Friederich.

The old man nodded. "Aye, lad. Hear this, all of you. I hold in m'hand the debt owed to Beniamino the Jew by Lord Heribert of Runkel! Ha, clever heathen! The original sum is for five hundred pounds of silver plus a usurious interest of twenty pounds on the hundred. No doubt the prior thinks he has quite a hold on the lord, but it is we who hold it! The prior cannot collect without it!"

The pilgrims cheered. Tomas stepped forward. "And we'll sell it back to whom … the prior or Lord Heribert?"

Pieter grinned mischievously. "To whoever releases Heinrich."

Frieda blurted, "And what of Wil?"

The group fell silent. "Fair sister," answered Pieter, "we are all still working on that problem. I do not yet know exactly what we'll do. A charge of one murder and suspicions of two others, all foresworn by a priest and supported by a witness, is beyond purchase, even with this. All the manor knows of it. The archbishop even knows of it. Heinrich, on the other hand, could be released at the court's will, or the will of the prior. They could more easily decide the killing was a matter of self-defense or of some nighttime confusion."

"But could we not try to use it for Wil as well?" Frieda pleaded.

Alwin answered kindly. "No. That would overreach its value. Trust me in this. I've seen these kinds of things before. If you ask too much, you get nothing! Now hear me, girl. We've the sly Arnold and our own clever Pieter. We've also the courage of four good lads, the magic of a minstrel, the love of three women, and an angel. And we've my own sword. Add to these our prayers and the mercies of heaven, and you must take heart. We will surely find a way to save Wil as well."

Otto scratched his head and then took a crust of bread from Maria. "So tell me how this plan for Heinrich is to work."

Pieter looked around the ring of faces staring at him. The first light of a new dawn was brightening the sky, and the man knew that time was not their friend. "Actually, we now have the tool but not yet the way. What say you all?"

The pilgrims murmured amongst themselves until Katharina spoke. "Arnold and I can meet with Prior Mattias by terce. I am the grieving widow … he'll see me, and he always sees Arnold, for he's frightened of what things the man knows about his monks." She looked at the pilgrims ringing the small fire and pleaded with them. "I spend my days spinning and weaving. Methinks I am able to weave a web for the prior. I beg you, leave this matter to Arnold and

me. You need to be about the business of Wil."
The group hesitated until Wilda stood by the woman's
side. "She is to be trusted. I know her heart."
Alwin nodded. "Pieter, I, too, believe the woman. With
Arnold, I believe she can make this happen. We need to
trust them both.... I think Heinrich would."
"It is agreed then?" Pieter asked.
The company nodded. The old man took a deep breath
and laid his staff by Solomon. He moved toward Katharina
and faced her squarely, peering deeply into her eyes. Then,
laying his hands on her head, he prayed over her and the
deed to be done, kissed the wooden cross hanging around
his neck, and smiled. The gleam had returned to his eye.
"Go, woman. Go with God. And may the angels be ready!"

৵

It was before the bells of terce when Katharina strode
boldly along Weyer's footpaths and rapped on Arnold's
door. It was flung open, and the nearly crazed man
dragged the startled woman into his home. "Where've
y'been?" he growled. "I near soiled m'drawers at prime. I
heard riders along the road going hard to Villmar. And
where's the others?"
"Not to worry, sir," answered Katharina softly. She lifted
the square parchment from inside her gown. "We have it!"
Arnold gasped. "I ... I can hardly believe it! And it is what
we thought? The Jew did not lie?"
Katharina laughed. "It is exactly what he said."
Arnold grinned and filled two clay goblets with red wine.
He passed one to Katharina. "Then we must find the prior.
He's most likely taking Mass now, but before terce he'll be
walking amongst the workshops."
"Where should we meet him?"
Arnold thought for a moment. "It won't matter. When he
sees me, I'll have his ear. But I doubt you can help. The
monks would want you kept from sight. I think you ought
to remain here."
Katharina frowned. "I think not. I will walk with you to
the abbey, then wait beyond its walls."
"But you've naught to say! I don't need you now!"

The woman looked at the man closely. "I will not inter-fere, but I must come. If you take the parchment inside the cloister, the prior will have you arrested at once. If you leave it here, he could easily send riders to Weyer before we could return. I will keep the parchment on my person. If he needs proof we have it, you can bring him to the portal."

Arnold took a drink. He looked at the woman with new-found respect. "You've reasoned this well."

Katharina blushed.

"So let's be off then!" He finished his wine and laughed. "It feels so much better to do a good thing! Ha! If I had only known before!"

ॐ

The bells of terce echoed over Münster when Pieter finally turned to Frieda. "So, girl. Do you agree?"

The young woman was exhausted, and her face was taut with strain and worry. The group waited. "There is much risk and little certainty in it."

No one answered until Tomas stood. He tossed a bit of kindling into the small fire. "Frieda, we need to act quickly. Wilda's priest says the trial may be on Friday. If that's so, we've only three days. We cannot wait another day to begin a plan."

"We have no other way, Frieda," added Helmut. Otto and the others nodded in agreement.

Maria took Frieda's hand. "You must agree, else we'll not do it."

Frieda knelt before her sister-in-law and took her in her arms. "I am so afraid, Maria. I'm so afraid we'll fail." She looked at her friends. "Pieter, pray for us. I think you are right. We've no other way."

With sighs of relief, the pilgrims gathered beneath Pieter's outstretched arms and received his blessing. Their plan had been painstakingly wrought over heated debate for these many hours. For each of them, having a plan was, itself, a comfort. Hearing Pieter's words pronounced so boldly over them filled them each with fresh courage. When he finished, the priest turned to Tomas and Otto. "Lads, are you sure of your duties?"

"We are," they answered together.

Pieter nodded. He was uneasy but walked quietly away into the deep wood. He found a large beech tree and leaned into its smooth bark with a groan. Solomon joined him, and the two sat for a quarter hour in comfortable silence. "Old friend," the man said to his beloved dog, "I am not so sure of this. These lads will need to sin and sin grievously, and they are prepared to do it with nary a doubt. I do not know if I ought to fear for their souls or admire them!" He tossed a twig away. "When two virtues are in collision, my soul cries out for wisdom. We will soon have truth-telling opposed to justice. *Ach*, it should never come to this."

"You choose the higher virtue, Pieter," said Frieda. The young woman had sought out her friend. "I thought you once told me that."

Pieter nodded. "Well, I oft forget what I once knew." He smiled wearily. "Your counsel is right. In this world of sorrows we don't often have pure choices. We are to pray for wisdom—wisdom to see the higher virtue. Thank you, my dear sister."

Frieda colored with embarrassment. Pieter took her hand and stroked her hair. "You are a beautiful young woman, someday soon to be a young mother. You will be a blessing to your husband and to the little ones who shall clutch your gown. I can see them, happy and bright. One will be like 'is father: spirited and willful, brave ... and a bit prideful!"

Frieda laughed.

"And another will be like you: spirited and wise, brave ... and charitable. As for the rest, a blend of good things, to be sure!"

The young woman was beet red by now, but laughing, and Pieter was glad to see it. The man took both her smooth young hands in his. "Dear Frieda, these next days shall not be days of tepid waters, but rather days of ice or boil. We must all be brave. By compline on Friday, we will have been sorely tested, hammered into yet a finer shape atop the anvil. In the end, whether we fail or whether not, we shall be different ... and we shall have lived life very much alive."

Pieter stared wistfully into the bright forest. He took a deep breath and smiled. "But I believe it shall be a good day. I can feel it in my bones."

❧

According to plan, Katharina faded into the shadows of Villmar's inn as Arnold rapped loudly on the abbey door. The man turned and winked at the woman before a young porter bade him enter. "Thanks be to God."

"Quite," grumbled Arnold. "No kisses, no prayers, and my feet are clean enough, thank you. I'm to see Prior Mattias on urgent business."

Egidius the porter bowed. "You are Arnold of Weyer."

"Of course, y'dolt."

The monk scurried away as Arnold wandered among the gardens of the cloister grounds. He looked at the stone walls now penning him within another world. They were higher than two men and were intended to keep sin and corruption out, as well as to keep the attention of the brethren on things godly.

Of course, honest work was godly to be sure, so within the walls were numerous workshops where lay monks labored to build barrels or hammer tin, to work with iron or dye wool. Both the lay monks and the choir monks shared tasks in the gardens, which, in this July, were lush with the vegetables of the season. Barns were filled with last month's hay and the first bushels of harvested oats. The brewery was always making beer, and the bakery filled its corner of the courtyard with the aroma of heaven. Arnold wandered about all this with a suspicious eye. He had never believed the monks to be sincere. He thought them to be joyless, self-serving hypocrites. His eye fell on the cider press and a row of empty barrels. "In two months, they'll be making cider and selling it for a profit!"

A kindly, rotund little monk waddled toward the man with an offer of cheese and a tankard of beer. "May I serve thee?"

Arnold took the beer and drank a long draught. He swallowed the cheese and glared at the simple man before him.

The monk smiled. "I am Brother Johann, the cantor. Are

you seeking something, my friend?"

"I'm not yer friend, shaveling. But, aye! I'm seeking joy and wisdom ... and long-suffering for the likes of you!" Arnold sneered.

"Ah, well, then you've come to the right place!"

"I doubt that."

"Why?"

"Look about. Not so much as a smile. So much for joy. I'd not dare bother one of your brothers with a good laugh— they wouldn't want to be distracted from their piety!"

The monk grinned.

"If they were wise, they'd not be hiding behind these walls. They've no silver, no women ..."

"My friend, I fear you've much to teach us. See those barrels?"

"Aye."

"In September they are filled with red apples. Most are firm and sweet. By October, we find a few that are soft and brown, their neighbors as well."

"So?"

"So it is the same with us. In good season, the brethren are charitable and selfless. In time, sin corrupts one, then the other. We need our barrel dumped from time to time!"

Arnold grunted. He was planning to do some dumping of his own.

The monk continued. "In thanks for your keen sight, allow me to share this small thing I have learned: when you seek joy, seek it humbly, for you shall not be joyful until your old affections are taken away. When you seek patience, have a care, for you shall not have it until you have been sorely tested. When you seek wisdom, tremble, for first you must be stripped of all you thought was true." The wise monk took Arnold's hand and looked deeply into his soul. "We are not all what you believe us to be."

Arnold spat. "I'm waiting for Mattias. The fool porter went looking for him."

The monk shielded his eyes from the sun and surveyed the grounds. "Ah, there. He is coming toward us. He looks worried." He turned to Arnold. "Well then, good day, brother. May God treat you well."

Arnold ignored the kindly fellow and strutted toward the prior. The two met by a flower garden in the center of the courtyard. Mattias bowed nervously.

"Prior Mattias, I shall come directly to the point. I know a secret, and I have it tucked safely away."

The monk paled. "Follow me," he mumbled. Mattias led Arnold through a labyrinth of gardens, past a small orchard, and into the shade of the cloister. Standing by a windowless wall, he stared down his long nose at the ground, deep in thought. He nodded, then fixed a hard eye on Arnold. "I do not like thee. I think thee to be a wicked man destined for hellfire. Thy soul shall become a smoldering ash that never cools. I have been in this place for more than twenty-five years, and I've known only one other to be as evil as thee. That would be thine very own brother, Baldric. May he suffer in torment always.

"If thou hast robbed my chamber, thou shalt surely hang. Thee and thy nephew and his wicked son. I should summon my guard now."

"Please do. I am weary of this world. But do you think I am such a fool as to keep such a treasure to myself? Hang me, have me tortured if you will, but there are others who would then demand an even higher price."

The monk clenched his hands in fury. "What is it you want? I've not much silver left."

Arnold shrugged, then grinned. "So you've a thought to squeeze Lord Heribert?"

"It is legal to collect a debt."

"You did not buy the debt with your own money."

Mattias's jaw tightened. "I did."

"No, methinks not. I suspect you had a partner."

"I've ... I've no partner," insisted Mattias.

"If you keep lying to me, I shall have to raise my price." Arnold smiled slyly.

The monk began to pace and look nervously about.

"Your partner is Steward Hagan. He stole money from Heribert. With the loss, the poor lord had to borrow from the Jew to pay his debts. Then you and Hagan used Heribert's own money to buy the debt from the Jew! Now the two of you expect to sell it back to Heribert ... or perhaps the abbot ... for your own profit. You, sir monk, sir godly man, are a genius." Arnold smirked.

Mattias was perspiring. White as winter's snow, he stammered and paced about the grass. "What is it that you want?"

Arnold smiled. "Well, what would Hagan pay to not be hanged for this plot?"

"I do not know," muttered the monk.

It was then that Arnold knew. He had thought it to be a good conjecture, but knowing that he had hit the mark made him nearly cry out for joy! His eyes sparkled. "Well, you'll need to speak of it with him, and quickly."

"He is not yet returned from a journey. He is to come on Thursday."

"And he is to hold court on Friday?"

"*Ja.*"

"I see. Well, first, tell me why you do this thing. You put your abbot in a bad place, you have Hagan betray his lord, you betray your own vows. I am interested in such a man as you—you remind me of myself."

Those words made Mattias feel suddenly sick. "I ... I am nothing like thee."

"Oh, but you are!" Arnold grinned a toothless grin. "So tell me."

"You were not the second all your life! I am always to be the prior, never the abbot!"

"Ah, but I was! I was second to Baldric always."

Mattias cursed. "What do you want?"

"I want the baker and his son set free ... and I want to share in one-third of the profit of your little scheme."

Shocked, the prior stared blankly at the man.

"Aye, that is my price."

"No! Never. It cannot be. It would bring too much suspicion on Hagan or even the abbey if we ... if we withdrew the charges."

Arnold turned and walked away. "Have a care, brother, have a care."

"Wait!" cried Mattias. He hurried after the man. "How do I know you even have it? Hagan will want to know that I've seen it."

Arnold kept walking. "How else would I know it is missing? You just had it delivered by the Jew yesterday."

Grinding his teeth, Mattias trotted alongside Arnold. "You ... you might have heard of it from another. You may not have it at all."

Arnold stopped and sighed, feigning boredom at the ridiculous assertion. "Monk, how long have you known me?"

"Most of my life."

"Have I ever bluffed a secret?"

The man shook his head. "But I must see it. It is the only way Hagan will believe this."

Arnold moved toward the portal again. "Then follow me, fool."

The trembling prior followed Arnold through the gate and into the streets of Villmar. Arnold looked amongst the folk milling by the inn. *Where the devil is she?* he wondered. *If she ran off with it, I'll—*

"Hello," came a voice.

The two men whirled about. It was Katharina.

"Move off, wench," growled the prior.

"Good day, then," she answered.

Arnold laughed out loud. "You'd best beg her pardon, Prior, and then look close in the woman's hand."

"What?" Mattias scowled. "I know thee, woman, from Weyer!"

"*Ja*, and I know you as well." She lifted the folded letter from her gown and stepped back one pace. She slowly opened it so that Mattias could read it yet not grab it.

"Stand where you are, monk," sneered Arnold. "Squint if y'must, but read it to yerself and know."

The man's lips muttered the words, and soon his eyes dropped. He nodded. "It is so, then."

"Yes, good fellow, it is so. Woman, return the thing to your gown. He'd not dare reach in there ... at least not here!

"Now, Prior, do this. Talk to the steward and explain your

problem thoroughly. There is no need to send a search for the letter, for you'll not find it. This I swear. You may have me arrested, but I'll not have the letter on my person or in my humble cottage. You'll not see her or the letter again until we've arranged our exchange."

The prior cursed.

"You say Hagan is to arrive in Runkel on Thursday. Good. I shall meet you on the road between Weyer and Villmar an hour after compline prayers. You will come alone. There we shall discuss your decision and, unless you are a fool, the method of our exchange. Remember, Wilhelm and Heinrich of Weyer to be released and one-third of the profits of this letter to me. Agreed?"

The monk glared at Arnold with eyes molten with rage. Barely able to speak, he sputtered, "I shall meet thee then, and may thee burn in hell." With that, the man spun on his heel and stormed into the abbey.

Relieved, Arnold turned to Katharina. "Good woman, well done. You make me proud to hail from Weyer!"

Katharina was troubled. "Why, sir, do you demand a third of the profit? It is too much to ask for that and for both men to be released!"

"Too much? How much is too much? Listen, wench. Do not tell me how to do my business. It is never too much. Do you think they'd ever give all that you ask? No! They'll not give the third, I know that. Do y'think me a fool? But they might give us both men if I yield on the third. If they won't, I would swear on my miserable soul that they'll give us Heinrich at the very least!"

Katharina hung her head. "Alwin said it was not wise to press too hard and—"

"Alwin? The hunted Templar? He is with you? Another blessed secret to my account!"

Katharina quickly paled. "Arnold, if you betray Alwin, I'll deal with the prior myself."

"Ha, ha!" laughed the man. "That'd be rich. Fear not, m'lady. Come! Let's share a pitcher of ale. You've no cause to worry."

Chapter Twenty-two

WISE AS SERPENTS

While Katharina and Arnold were busy in Villmar, Pieter, Tomas, and Otto had made their way carefully toward Weyer once more. It was in the late morning when they entered the village, and many of the folk were preparing their main meal of the day. Not wanting to be recognized, Tomas and Otto remained hidden in the shadows of their hoods as the three picked their way through the sprawling, haphazard collection of hovels and barns.

The day was warm and would soon be hot. Children dashed about in the summer sunshine, no doubt avoiding the many chores of the season as best they could. Housewives gawked curiously at the mysterious trio, and a few old men waved from their seats in the shade. It was a village like countless others—blessed with a few days of joy, burdened with months of sorrow.

"There." Tomas pointed. "She lives in there." Pieter followed Tomas's finger to a poorly maintained hovel in the midst of many others. It was *Frau* Anka's home. She was the widow of a dyer and was the village shrew. Once a friend to Heinrich's wife, Marta, she had spent most of her life consumed with envy. Red faced, stout, easily angered yet fearful, the forty-year-old woman had few friends.

Otto hesitated. "Maybe we should just steal her away."

Pieter understood. It might make things so much simpler. "It was considered. However, Pious will check on her soon before the trial. If she's gone missing, he'll force an oathhelper to swear another testimony."

"Then what if she resists your words?"

"We'll tie her like the sow she is and drag her away!" snapped Tomas.

Otto knocked timidly on the woman's door, and she answered, wiping her hands on her apron. "Eh?" She blew a wisp of gray hair out of her eyes. "Otto? Otto the miller's son?"

"*Ja.* 'Tis me."

"Don't cross this threshold! You've shamed us all. Yer father hated me all these years, and now you come to bring yer curses to my door. Y'failed in yer faith, whelp. I sewed the crosses on yer hearts, and y'failed me."

Tomas removed his hood, and the woman gasped. "Aye, you old hag. 'Tis me. I'll not cower from your foul breath like m'good friend here. Now back away. We're coming in!"

Anka stumbled backward into her modest hovel, and the three followed her inside. No one else was home. Fortuitously, her tenants were delivering hay to the stables in Villmar. "What … what do you want of me?"

Tomas closed the door and answered, "First, food and drink. A loaf of that bread there'll do, and that mead is fine."

The woman obediently handed Tomas the items, and he, in turn, shared with the others as they took seats around the woman's table. Anka fixed a fearful eye on old Pieter. The man had not smiled nor said a single word. He had simply stared at her unwaveringly from the moment she had answered the door. Finally, Pieter turned to the boys. "Aye, 'tis her."

"What? What do you mean?" Anka's face flushed.

"Are you sure, Father?" asked Otto.

The priest nodded.

"What? What is this?"

Pieter stood, walked to Anka, and peered directly into her widening eyes. "Woman, thou art in the grip of sin."

"Eh?"

"'Tis true. I am a priest, one serving the folk through-out all the kingdoms of God. I have led holy processions in Palestine, even once carrying a cross past the Holy Sepulcher."

Anka sat down nervously.

"He is a prophet, of sorts," said Tomas, "and he found Otto and me in need of repentance. He heard our confessions and then had a vision. It is why we are here."

"You have visions?" asked Anka. A tone of respect now melded with her terror.

Pieter humbly bowed.

"*Frau* Anka, you must listen to him," insisted Tomas. "On Holy Week past he returned from the relics in Ulm to lead a procession in Lorraine. He and his followers traveled to the Rhineland, where they prayed in nearly every pilgrim's chapel. He was blessed by the bones of ... of ..."

"Of the apostle Bartholomew," Pieter finished glibly. "They were delivered to the cathedral in Trier for a short time. I was most blessed indeed."

"Tell her, Pieter. Tell her of the journey by the Rhine."

"Oh, I must not boast of such things."

Anka leaned forward. "No, Father, please ... please tell me." She poured herself a tankard of mead and lifted it to her lips with a trembling hand.

Pieter hesitated, then politely asked the woman for a drink before proceeding to spin a long tale of suffering and visions that drew Anka ever closer. "Then, finally, near the city of Worms I saw the Holy Mother bathing."

"Bathing?" Anka was astonished.

Pieter nodded, astonished as well. "*Ja*, my child. The water was to her neck, and a golden glow hovered over her. The river sang with the sounds of a thousand sirens. I saw fish leaping for joy, and then the heavens opened. Two angels bearing a gossamer gown descended to the water and then beneath, guarding the blessed modesty of our Lord's Mother by wrapping her before she was drawn from the river to the clouds above, refreshed and smiling."

Dumbstruck, Anka nearly fell from her stool.

Pieter drained his tankard and continued. "It was then,

on this Pentecost past, that I vowed to purge all Christendom from what vice and wicked deeds my path might cross. I have sent a baron to justice for defiling a holy shrine, and I have sent a bishop to Rome in disgrace for his blasphemy. I could go on."

Anka was speechless. She stared at Pieter with worshipful eyes.

"Which is why he is here, *Frau* Anka."

"Why?"

Tomas lowered his voice. "Hear me, hag. I'll make it plain. With my own ears I heard that snake Pious tell Wil what herb to give his mother."

Anka stiffened. "No! It cannot be! It was Wil who chose the poison!"

Otto shook his head. "No, *Frau*. It was not. I, too, heard the priest tell Wil. I was doing errands for m'papa. I came by the bakery to see what flour needed grinding. Tomas was working in the attic and saw me come. He was watching Pious and Wil below, through a knothole in the floor. I came up slow and quiet, and I heard it too."

Anka stood to her feet. "No, it cannot be. Why did you not say it then?"

"We didn't know it to be poison then, and neither did Wil."

The woman looked at Pieter. The priest bowed. "Good woman, it is true. I found these poor lads yesterday, hiding in the wood near Limburg. As you know, Otto, here, was put out from his father's home. He believes it is for some sin in his life. Both he and Tomas then learned of this Wilhelm fellow's arrest, and they wanted to confess their many sins to save him.

"I listened to their confession and then fell into a deep sleep. It was then that I saw a face of a woman. The face of a woman deceived ... like Eve by the serpent. I then saw the serpent crawling about her feet. It was short and fat; it hissed from behind its squinted eyes. It is the Devil that slides about, emboldened by the ambition of mere men. His evil ways sprout in soil watered by the blood of innocents ... and he must be stopped.

"I did not know what this meant until I described the

woman to these good lads. I said she was aging, but as yet pleasing to the eye, stout as a strong woman should be. And, I said, she had a face that glowed warm and red like a ripe apple.

"Well, I had no sooner said the words when Otto and Tomas both cried out, '*Frau* Anka!' Now that I see thee in the flesh, I know it is true."

The woman was utterly flabbergasted. She collapsed on to her stool. "B … but deceived?"

"*Frau*," stated Pieter sternly, "thou art in the hands of a devil—a serpent named Pious! He has deceived thee, and worse—he has stolen what would have been rightfully thine."

"What do you mean, Father?"

"These lads tell me that Wil had foresworn to thee and to a Father named Albert, that thou wouldst be granted one-fourth of his lands if his mother lived until his return. Is this not true?"

"It is. It is why I am so angry at the boy. He deceived me—"

"Woman, canst thou not see? What did he have to gain? The loss of a mother to save some land? Did he hate his mother so?"

Anka shook her head. "He did not love her, but methinks he did not hate her."

"Look into my eyes, my sister," continued Pieter. "Under God I do so swear to you that Wilhelm of Weyer did not murder his mother."

Tomas was pacing. "Listen! Can y'not see? Who got all the land?"

"Father Pious."

"Aye! Who must Pious fear most?"

"Wil."

"Aye!"

"But Pious had visions." Anka was now wringing her hands. "He said he had dreams and visions of Wil grinding the poison."

"Woman," said Pieter, "I have told ye the truth of Wilhelm. Do with it as thou wish. But be warned. I have come to set the captives free. I have come to seek God's almighty justice for those who would deceive. If thou art part of this deceit, if thou art a tool in the serpent's hand, I shall strike thee down!"

Anka shuddered and began to weep. "I ... I saw nothing of this m'self."

"My dream says thou hast a good recollection of Wil telling thee of Pious's advice that the herb be given. Is it not so?"

Anka trembled. "It ... it may be so. I ... I ... I cannot think clearly now."

"Then thou ought not put thy soul in further jeopardy. Do not bear false witness against the lad. Dost thou hear me, woman?" Pieter's voice was now hard and demanding.

Anka hesitated. She feared Pious's wrath if she did not attend the trial, yet her confidence had been shaken to its very foundation. She nodded mutely.

Tomas leaned close to her. "Otto and me shall be in that court. We shall gladly bear witness to the truth. When the judge sets Wil free, he will turn against you and against Pious. Consider that!"

Anka was now shaking. She looked at Pieter with imploring eyes.

"Fear not, child," said Pieter, now gently. "I've not come to harm thee but to save thee." His tone changed again. "But if I see thee in the court, I shall bring the judgment of all heaven down upon thee. Terrors and visits of the dead shall surely greet thee by night. Boils and oozing sores shall rise with every dawn. I shall summon demons to pluck thy hair at eventide and gore thy belly by day with a pain that has no end. And this, my child, shall be only the beginning. The truth shall be surely avenged, so help me, God."

The poor woman backed away from Pieter and stood in the farthest corner of her hovel. Terrified, she sank to the floor and wrapped her body with her arms. Unable to speak, she only whimpered and nodded. She understood.

Otto had pity. "*Frau*, the priest is only an enemy to deceit. He is a friend to the righteous. Here, here is a gold coin. It is fitting, he says, to reward goodness." The lad plinked the coin on the woman's table. She stared at it from a distance, wide eyed and disbelieving.

Pieter bowed. "My child, thy faith hath saved thee. Live in peace."

ᚦ

By midafternoon, Pieter returned to camp with good news. Anka, it seemed, had been silenced. "I have great hope for your husband, Frieda, though I do worry for my own soul. I am too old and weary to do much more of this." The man was troubled. "We should not need to do such things to defend the truth."

"What things?" asked Benedetto.

Pieter dismissed the question with a wave of his hand. "Have we heard from Katharina and Arnold?"

"Not yet, Pieter," offered Alwin. "But soon, I'm sure."

While Tomas and Otto relayed the day's events, Pieter slowly retreated into the forest with Solomon. Benedetto strummed his lute, and the lads spun more tales to a circle of admiring friends as Frieda and Maria followed after Pieter into the woodland.

It was dusk when the music stopped and a loud "hurrah" was lifted. Katharina had returned! Relieved, the whole company gathered about her in a close circle. She had come with a bundle of her belongings that she had hastily gathered from her cottage. Setting them on the ground, she wiped her brow.

"It was not wise for you to go home," scolded Frieda.

Katharina nodded. "I may never be able to return to my home, so I went back briefly to take the few things I needed."

"What of Arnold?" asked Tomas.

"He said he'd be safe enough in his cottage. He is certain the prior would see no purpose in his arrest, since it would not yield the parchment."

"You are certain no one saw you?" asked Tomas.

"I was very careful. I did speak to Herwin, though. He offered his support if needed and gave me Wil's dagger." She handed it to Frieda.

The band was nervous.

"They will be searching," grumbled Tomas.

Katharina took a swallow of ale. "I am certain of it. They'll scour the manor carefully. We must keep the flames low, as well as our voices."

"And what of the trial?" asked Helmut.

"We're now sure that Steward Hagan will hold court in Runkel on Friday."

"Friday! 'Tis two full days hence!" grumbled Tomas. "It gives the prior two full days to counter our plans." He kicked the dirt. "I cannot bear the wait!"

"Why in Runkel?" asked Benedetto.

Otto answered. "The abbey is under contract with Lord Heribert for all such matters, and his steward is oft the judge in trials."

"The abbey does not wish to be the place of judgment for temporal matters," added Alwin. "They've a church court for sins and for keeping the brethren in place. I know they have flogged a few monks on account of blasphemy and lewdness, and they have whipped a few peasants on account of adultery, but they've never hanged a soul within those walls, nor do they want to bother with thefts and the like."

"So, *Frau* Katharina, do you think our plan can work?" asked Maria.

"I believe it can. Your great-uncle Arnold is a good ally. He's to meet with the prior once more, past compline on Thursday, to settle the final arrangements. Then I am to meet him so that we know what to do. Until then, we must be careful."

Alwin swallowed a long, refreshing draught of ale, then looked at Katharina and chuckled. "If Lord Heribert learns of his own steward's betrayal, or if the abbot learns that his own prior is in league with another, hell will not have fires hot enough!"

The circle laughed. "Then cheers to Arnold! If any could make the fools sweat in their beds, 'tis he!"

The company quickly decided that although the Matins Stone was technically on Lord Rolfhard's land, it was close enough to the abbey's manor to be encroached with ease by the abbey's joint protectors—Heribert and the Templars.

"We should find refuge in the heavy spruce farther south and to the east," urged Wilda.

And so it was agreed. The uneasy pilgrims hurried to gather all their provisions and abandoned their camp. Following the sure feet of Wilda along trails familiar to the woman, they soon arrived at a secluded clearing. Now about a two-hour walk from Weyer, they felt safer, and with Paulus lumbering along with an ample load of summer vegetables, salted joint meats, and fresh ale, the company was eager to build a new fire and enjoy a hearty meal.

Before long, the pilgrims settled into a pleasant chatter. Benedetto sang softly for an hour or so, then lulled his fellows to sleep with a lullaby he oft sang in the warm summer nights of his Italian home. No more could be done. Two days would now need to pass, two days that they yielded with some reserve to the watch of a silent Providence.

≈

The days passed slowly to be sure, but they surely passed, and, at long last, Friday's dawn broke. On the night before, Katharina had taken Alwin to meet with Arnold, and the two had returned safely with news. They huddled with Pieter, and the three reviewed the details of their two plans. Then he, ashen and anxious, looked nervously about his beloved company. The circle of faces staring back at him was tight but determined. *A more brave-hearted band of fellows I have never known,* the man thought. "Katharina, tell them the plan for Heinrich."

Katharina looked about at her new friends. "Well, the good news is that the prior has agreed to release Heinrich."

A happy cry resounded around the ring.

Katharina nodded. "Arnold did well, though he was not able to sway the deal for Wil." She looked at Frieda.

"I did not expect he could," the young woman replied. "God's will be done. We've another plan for that."

Katharina smiled and squeezed Frieda's shoulder affectionately. "We do need you in this one though."

"As you wish."

Katharina faced the others. "Now, Arnold's plan is a bit

more muddled than I would have liked. Listen carefully. I am to meet the prior's personal guard, a large red-headed soldier named Hann, in the courtyard during the trial. Once Heinrich is released, I shall be his hostage until the parchment is passed to the steward's secretary.

"Frieda, you will stand by the drawbridge. The secretary knows to look for a 'blonde damsel under hood' in that place. He will come to you *after* Heinrich is released. When you see Heinrich safely away, give the secretary the parchment. He will confirm its contents, then signal the guard who is by me, so that I can be released."

"And if you are not?" asked Tomas.

The woman shrugged. "Seems that's the muddy part."

Alwin answered, "Then blood will spill!"

Pieter shook his head. "I am still not sure of this. What if Heinrich is not released? What if they have guards spotting for the both of you?"

Frieda answered, "I'll keep hidden until we know for sure. It may be as simple as that."

"Were you seen by anyone near the abbey ... passing officers, pilgrims, monks?" challenged Otto.

Frieda shook her head. "I kept away.... I stayed by the inn. I doubt anyone noticed me."

Wilda disagreed. "Lads, would you have noticed her?"

The boys blushed. Wilda turned a brow up at Alwin. "And you?"

Alwin looked at the ground and shrugged.

"Well, you're all liars," scolded Wilda. "Of course you'd remember her! Look at her! Shapely and young, smooth skinned and fair! What man would forget?" The woman paused. "Nay, listen. I say we should let her be seen near the bridge. She'll catch their eye quick, and they'll soon reckon her to be the one. But I will carry the letter. I'll stay in the shadows and emerge at the proper time."

Pieter groaned. "We've risk here, risk aplenty."

Heads nodded.

Alwin stepped forward and rested his hands on the two swords in his belt. "Heinrich and Wil have no more time. We've no choice but to try as we can, and if we fail, we'll try to save them by force. Helmut, bring Emmanuel. Maria, are you ready, sister?"

Under the knight's instructions, Wilda adjusted the sleeves of the little girl's gown.

"I am, sir."

The weary priest looked at Maria. "And are you sure, my dear?"

She lifted her chin. "*Ja*, Papa Pieter. I am."

Alwin began to pace. Predawn songbirds were now filling the forest with a loud chatter. Mist hung heavy atop the needled ground, and the air was damp and cool. "Now, as for the plan for Wil—everyone knows their part? Otto, Tomas ... are you sure of yourselves? You know exactly what to do and when?"

The lads nodded firmly.

Alwin took a deep breath. "Everyone else knows their part? We know our plans and counterplans?"

"We've spoken of nothing else for two days!" barked Tomas impatiently.

"Pieter?"

The old man had dropped to his knees again to beg the legions of the heavenly host to "forgive this miserable servant and ready thy swords, fill thy quivers full, and prepare a great slaughter of the unjust. *In nomine Patris, et Filii, et Spiritus Sancti.* Amen."

Now ready, the entire company—including Solomon— made a quick descent to the village of Münster and delivered Paulus to its helpful priest for safekeeping. They then hurried along a circuitous route that took them cross-country to the far side of Oberbrechen and through the dangerous holdings of the Templars bordering Villmar's manorlands. It was full light as they turned onto the road that led them north through sleepy Niederbrechen and beyond. Finally, at the bells of terce, the anxious company of eleven joined others now crossing the drawbridge into Runkel's brownstone castle.

The pilgrims funneled across the plank bridge, then emerged on the other side to find their positions according to plan. Wilda, bearing the valued parchment, withdrew to the shadows of a shed, where she climbed atop a cart to keep a sharp eye on the bailey. From here she would direct the movement of her friends as needed.

Katharina had already spotted the prior's monstrous guard. He was a burly young man with long, straight, red hair. He was dressed in chain mail and a sleeveless gray robe. The man regularly looked in the direction of several soldiers standing nearby. The woman did not fail to notice. She swallowed and closed her eyes, then bravely walked forward to present herself as the man's hostage.

Otto and Tomas took their places at the witness stall. Tucked deeply within their hoods, they waited here for the bailiff's announcement of Wil's name. They were understandably anxious. Both were about to perjure themselves in a capital offense. More than that, if they were spotted by Weyer's reeve—who was sure to come—they could be arrested as fugitives from the manor to which they were bound.

Sweating profusely, Benedetto was strolling about to serve as a potential distraction. He seemed always able to turn heads in his direction with a clever rhyme or a bawdy song. The poor little fellow was so nervous, however, that he could barely speak, let alone sing. He was bounced to and fro among the milling folk like a child's toy!

Helmut was hidden in the shadows of a smith's shed. As instructed, he had brought Emmanuel with him. He was not the archer Wil was, but the lad had practiced from time to time on the journey north. In the last two days, he had done little else. He now reckoned his range to the judge's bench and then to the gallows. He licked his lips nervously and looked for Alwin.

Near the entrance to the dungeon, Frieda adjusted Maria's little gown and fixed the flowers in her hair with trembling fingers. She then smoothed the wrinkles from her own gown and wiped the dust from her shoes. She picked up her basket and hung it on her elbow, then nodded to Pieter. The old man drew a deep breath, summoned his waning pluck, and led the two females directly to the jailer. "Good sir," began Pieter, "I am the priest of these two damsels. One is the wife of an accused and the other his sister. Might I beg thy Christian charity and humbly ask their permission to see him one last time on this earth?"

The guard laughed. "I've no time for this. Begone!"

Frieda smiled flirtatiously. She moved closer and lifted the towel from her basket. Underneath was a loaf of bread with a gold coin sticking into it. "A strong man like you must be hungry?"

The jailer gawked at the coin, then looked about. He turned a hard eye on the three standing before him. "Who's yer husband?"

"Wilhelm of Weyer—"

"The yellow-haired devil? He's a hot-tempered, arrogant son of Hades! He bit one of m'guards. He'll swing and so shall his father."

Frieda's jaw clenched. Maria, however, smiled innocently. "Sir," she chirped, "could we see them both?"

The soldier stared at the imp beneath him. He was a giant of a man, dressed in heavy chain mail and holding a lance. The little girl seemed like a tender flower, too delicate to harm—even for a hardened warrior as himself. He chuckled at her sleeves hanging below her unseen hands, and he thought of his own daughter in a village not far away. "Well, I'm not to do this." He took Frieda's bread and searched her basket. He then reached out to search her body for weapons and she recoiled sharply. "Fair enough, wench. Then you stay out. I'll take this little one to them for a quick hug and a good-bye. You two stay here."

Maria smiled and waved to Frieda and Pieter as she disappeared into the dank bowels of Runkel's dungeon. The soldier carried a torch high overhead and cursed at the prisoners now pleading for mercy. The pair turned a corner, and the man handed a guard his torch as he reached for his key. Unlocking the cell door, he nudged Maria inside. "Now, be quick about it."

Heinrich and Wil cried out from the shadows as they recognized little Maria's face in the flickering torchlight. Maria ran to Wil first and wrapped her arm around him. The young man wept for joy as he bent to kiss his sister on the cheek. "Do not be afraid, Wil," Maria whispered into his ear. "We've cause to hope. You must be ready. I love you."

Maria slyly lifted her deformed arm upward. It had been covered with an extra sleeve sewn by Wilda the day before. Inside was Wil's dagger tied by a thin cord to the girl's shortened arm. "Hurry," whispered Maria. "We've a plan, but if it fails, you are to have the blade."

Wil's fingers flew over the easy knot, and the dagger was released to his grip. With Maria drawn close, he quickly hid it within his tunic. "For hope, then," he whispered.

The girl kissed Wil on the cheek and turned to Heinrich, who was kneeling alongside. "Oh, little daughter," he cried softly as he embraced her, "God bless you always."

"Enough now!" commanded the jailer. "Time's up!"

With a whimper, Maria bade her brother and her father a sad farewell. They would now need to wait for whatever mystery unfolded, and they'd need to wait in ignorance, very much alone.

Once outside, Maria followed Pieter to the feet of the imposing gallows, where the two stood quietly holding hands. Solomon sat by his master and whined. Pieter, too, hoped their assignment would never be called upon.

In the meanwhile, Frieda had placed Friederich near the end of the judge's bench, where Lord Heribert's personal clerk would soon be seated. From here, the scamp might hear something of import. If he did, it was he who could scurry between legs the fastest. Frieda, now under hood, then positioned herself in the general vicinity of the bridge, where she'd eventually need to make contact with the secretary.

Alwin was in the greatest peril of all. Numbers of his former Templar brethren were milling about the castle grounds. They were easy to spot in their cross-emblemed white robes. He hoped that his long beard would help disguise him, and he lifted his hood over his head as he sank into the crowd. His purpose was plain. If other plans failed, he was to command a violent consequence. At his signal, Helmut would be ordered to shoot the judge and then the hangman, while Alwin attacked the guard holding Katharina. Others would rush the judge's bench and seek to cause enough confusion for Wil or Heinrich to escape. It would be an unlikely victory.

The bailey was rapidly filling with a heavy-footed parade of peasants plodding about in hopes of taking pleasure in the delights of the floggings and the hangings sure to come. At the bells of terce, the judge and his court finally emerged from their chambers.

"It is to begin," murmured Pieter. "God save us."

Keeping deep within his hood, Alwin studied the bench and the witness stalls. *Where the devil is Pious?* he wondered. He turned his face toward Wilda. The sight of her perched atop the distant cart made his heart beat faster. Tall and willowy, she stood like a triumphant herald angel bravely poised for duty. "Oh, Wilda," he muttered. "If we live the day ..."

An inebriated castle priest belched a loud prayer, and the day's business began. With little delay, Steward Hagan— now acting as Judge Hagan—immediately pronounced several of the accused guilty from prior trials by ordeal. Under the supervision of the court's bailiff, three days before, hot irons had been laid across the opened hands of those charged, and their unhealed blisters were proof enough of guilt. "Twenty-four stripes," he shouted. "One for each tribe of Israel and one for each apostle."

From his post, Tomas thought Hagan looked agitated and distracted. He knew the man would offer little mercy on this day. The young man watched as a long line of others accused passed by the bench with oathhelpers at their sides. They suffered quick judgments on matters of theft, slander, assault, and sundry complaints regarding things such as sawdust in baker's dough and damage by loose swine. A merchant's wife testified against her butcher. "I bought the whole cow, but I caught him eating m'tenderloin!" she cried.

A grumbling line of others followed—some petitioning relief from taxes, others claiming unpaid debts. Hagan stood and pointed a long finger at one poor fellow. "Pay him in a fortnight, else lose thy thumbs!"

Lords and their squint-eyed attorneys presented

sundry complaints regarding boundaries and violations of contracts. With a yawn and a few nods, Hagan settled these matters by favoring the highest bidder. For Hagan, discerning justice was a rather profitable business.

"There!" cried Maria. "Father Pious has arrived." The girl pointed to the round priest rolling off a swaybacked donkey.

"Pious!" Pieter closed his eyes. *Six things does the Lord hate, yea, seven are an abomination: a proud look, a lying tongue, and hands that shed innocent blood. A heart that devises wicked imaginations, feet that are swift to mischief, a false witness that speaks lies, and he that sows discord among brothers.*

The others of the company had seen Pious as well, and everyone was immediately on guard. Tomas and Otto shrank deeper into their hoods as the sweating oaf lumbered toward them. He was grumbling and looking about wildly.

"He's searching for Anka," whispered Tomas.

"Aye," Otto answered. The lad studied the priest and then looked through the crowd at his beloved Father Pieter waiting forlornly at the gallows. Seeing both men clothed in the robes of the Church gave him pause. He knew of things a peasant boy might know: the hand of violence and the hand of mercy. But before him was more. Coming toward him was a priest of Babylon, overstuffed and haughty, boasting wealth and driven by ambition; he was the bearer of false teaching, an abuser of the law, and void of mercy.

By the gallows, however, stooped a priest of Zion, lean and battered, poor and in the service of others, ready to offer grace in the moment of death—not yet resting in his coming reward as a servant of the Light.

Father Pious grabbed a wooden tankard from some hapless wench in the crowd and slaked his thirst. Still searching for Anka, he stood pompously, his hands gripping the folds of his most expensive garment—a slate-gray linen robe embroidered with silver and gold thread. This would be his finest hour, he imagined. *At last, at long last I shall be free of these cursed fools! Ah, the law, the wonders of the law!*

The next to be tried was neither Wil nor Heinrich, but a young knight of Lord Heribert who had changed loyalties in battle and was captured. The questions were brief. Two accusers bore witness against the sullen fellow, and in less than a quarter hour the man was lurching at the end of the hangman's rope above the bowed heads of Pieter and Maria. Pieter prayed for the flailing man as others cheered and laughed. The man would dance in the air for a bit longer before his soul would finally fly free.

A burly, mean-faced fellow was then charged with extorting silver from two merchants—friends of the judge. Hagan did not bother to hear testimony—matters such as these were not confined by strict rules of evidence such as were required in England. Instead, with a bark he ordered the accused to repay all monies taken plus half again as much. "And do it by St. Michael's, or lose your right hand!"

The wool-clad peasants cramming the courtyard were drunk and demanding another hanging. Bloodlust was running high, heated, no doubt, by the scalding July sun above. They, like the judge and his court, were chafing and surly. For Wil and the others waiting their turn, such a mood was not a good thing.

During the proceedings, Alwin had slowly moved closer to Katharina. With his eyes fixed on Hann, the knight ran his fingers along the handles of the two swords hanging on his hips. *If he moves to harm her, he'll feel my steel!*

Three more disputes were judged before the name "Wilhelm of Weyer" was finally called. Scattered about the castle, his anxious comrades stiffened. Helmut nervously lifted an arrow from his quiver and turned a hard eye on the judge. But it was Pious on whom he took aim.

Pieter closed his eyes and prayed until tears flowed into his beard. Maria took his hand in hers and squeezed it lightly. With a calm voice she said, "You said that God is good. I believe you."

The old man smiled and willed himself to accept whatever the hand of Providence might present in the next few moments. Should Wil be found guilty and if no plan might save the lad, it would be he and Maria who would serve next. It would fall to them to stand close to the young man, close enough for him to see them, close enough for him to know that he would not die abandoned by those who loved him.

Chapter Twenty-three

THE ORDEAL

"In the matter of Wilhelm of Weyer," cried the court's bailiff, "where are his accusers?"

Father Pious stepped forward. He bowed and turned toward Wil. It was as though the great boar had spotted a store of gold. His lips shined wet, and his face flushed with satisfaction. He slobbered his words, drooling with anticipation. "I do so accuse him, my lord."

"You are?"

"I am Father Pious, priest of Oberbrechen and Weyer in the lands held by the Abbey of Villmar."

Many in the crowd hissed.

"And who else accuses this man?"

The pilgrims held their breath once more. Their eyes flew about in terror. Would Anka step forward? Would another surprise them?

"I say once more and for the final time, who else accuses this man?"

Silence.

Pious was flustered. He had assumed Anka was milling about, and he called for her. It did not impress the court. Hagan glared at the man with utter contempt. For years, Hagan had heard the complaints leveled against the priest and his ambitious ways. "No other witnesses?"

Angry, Pious shook his head. "It would appear she has not come."

"But you as a priest do so swear to this man's guilt?"

"I do so swear. As God is my judge, I do so swear. The death of his mother by poison can be witnessed by myself and one *Frau* Anka of Weyer."

Hagan looked at Wil. "And you, what say you?"

Wil clenched his jaw and puffed his chest. "I swear under God that I am innocent of these charges."

"Humph," groused the judge. "Does anyone else accuse this man?"

Otto and Tomas stepped from their stall and threw back their hoods. "Sire!"

Annoyed, Hagan growled, "What's this, bailiff?"

Tomas strode forward with Otto on his heels. "Sire, begging pardon. We are witnesses to this *priest's* murder of Wilhelm's mother." Tomas pointed at Pious. "It was *he* who poisoned her, and we so accuse him!"

The crowd and the court gasped. Completely undone, the priest stared speechlessly at the two. "Tomas? Otto? But—"

Hagan pounced. "Do you lads swear under God that it be so?"

"We do so swear."

"But they're only boys!" cried Pious.

The judge narrowed his eyes at the pair. "How old are you?"

Otto swallowed hard. "Sixteen, sir."

"*Ja?* Humph. And you?"

"Eighteen."

"They're lying to you, Hagan. They're—"

"'Hagan'? You dare call me Hagan?" The judge slammed his fists on the table. "I have two witnesses against the priest, and the priest is witness against this other. I—"

"But ... but I accuse him of two more murders as well!" pleaded Pious. "Hear me! You must hear me!"

The crowd began to laugh and jeer. "Hang the priest!" cried one. "Put him on a spit!" cried another.

The bailiff shouted for order, while Hagan consulted his clerks. With his eyes then slanted toward Pious, he raised his hands over the surly crowd. "We have two accused of the same crime. The first has only one accuser, albeit a priest. The other has two accusers. Both of the accused have sworn innocence under God. So we shall let God sort it out. Bailiff, trial by water ordeal at the moat."

The crowd roared its approval. Wil paled, but Pious collapsed, trembling and in terror. It would not do for the robes of a priest to be disgraced, so the man was immediately stripped by the grasping hands of the court's guard. To the mocking laughter of the delighted crowd, his rotund body quivered and shook within the dubious confines of his underlinens as the wretch wept like a babe. A soldier finally kicked him to the ground, and callused hands hauled him across the dusty courtyard.

Wil was roughly handled as well. He was dragged through the mob and placed alongside a now-wailing Pious near the bridge. Both men's wrists were bound behind their backs, and a priest drew near. Wil took a deep breath and searched the crowd for any sign of his companions. He spotted Tomas and Otto being held nearby, for if their charge proved untrue, the court would need to deal with them. He looked past them, desperate to find his wife. At last, his happy eyes fell upon Frieda. "Oh, dear God!" he murmured. The young woman had tossed back her hood and stood under the summer sun, still and calm. Her hair shimmered and her face was steady. She smiled, and at that moment he did not care what waited in the depths of the moat.

Pieter had flailed his way through the annoyed mob by swinging his staff like a man gone mad. Finally, panting, perspiring, and utterly exhausted, the man stumbled close to Wil. "Release your air," he whispered.

Wil turned.

"Release your air … you must sink or be hanged."

Wil understood. In trial by water ordeal, the water would be prayed over and God's will sought by a priest. Then the accused would be thrown into it while tethered to a long rope. The sanctified water would reject sinners by expelling them to the surface. Hence, guilty parties would float, and the innocent would sink. If the judge ruled quickly enough, the innocent man might be rescued before he drowned. It was all in God's hands.

The accused were taken to the bridge, and they looked down into the green scum that painted the waters below. The stagnant moat stank with floating excrement and the carcasses of prior days' meals. All manner of refuse had found its way into this dredge of filth. Oily swirls looped between garbage and rotting fish, and a cloud of stinging flies hovered above. Into this black horror both of the accused would be tossed.

A soldier grabbed each man and led them to the bridge above the water. Wil lifted his shoulders and breathed deeply. He was lean from a long season of suffering. His heart was strong and his soul prepared for whatever his Maker would demand. Beside him wept a bulging, gluttonous man bent in terror. Soft and self-indulged, Pious was a tragic spectacle suffering the mocking taunts of those whose favor he had coveted.

The court's priest turned to Judge Hagan. "It is supposed to be cold water, my lord," he said quietly.

The judge grunted. "'Tis cooler than the air. Go on."

The priest nodded and lifted his hands over each of the accused and cried, "May our omniscient God who did consecrate water for the remission of sins through baptism decree a rightful judgment by His mercy. If thou art guilty of the charge against thee, may the water that received thee in baptism reject thee now. If thou art not guilty, may the waters of thy baptism welcome thee into their depths."

When he finished, the bailiff cried, "Now!" With a shove, each man was pushed off the bridge and fell about the height of two men into the water below. The scum blew away in the great splash, and a rolling swirl of brown water filled the punctures.

The crowd cheered and waited, and the priest prayed over the water, "I beg thee, water, *in nomine Patris, et Filii, et Spiritus Sancti,* to refuse the guilty and send him to thy surface. May nothing be employed against the discernment of truth. May no magic, no charms, nor devils' ways conceal the holy will of our Lord Creator."

None needed to wait very long for the water to pass judgment. Like a giant bubble rising from an abyss, Pious burst from the depths with a loud gasp. He bobbed on the surface for a moment, like a lonely cork, and then desperately tried to sink himself into the water that had rejected him. He choked and sputtered, unable to burrow his body beneath the surface for more than a brief moment. At last, Hagan signaled the guard, and the man was hauled ashore.

Wil, however, hit the water with the vision of his bride in his mind's eye. He calmly blew the air from his lungs and let his body drift peacefully to the bottom. There, in those murky waters, it was still and quiet. He thought of Frieda's gentle touch, of their happy days in San Fruttuoso. He felt dreamy and warm, and it seemed as if time had taken pause until his arms were suddenly hoisted behind him. He was pulled to the surface, and when his face broke into the sunshine, he opened his mouth with a loud gasp.

From atop the walls and the bridge, from either bank of the moat, the simple folk roared their approval. They clapped and applauded, and when Wil was set free, a great cheer filled all Runkel!

Still bound and dripping with the stench of the moat, the young man was led before the court now reassembling by the bench. Hagan spoke with his clerks in low tones, then to his bailiff. The bailiff ordered the pleading Pious be taken away and then pointed to Wil. "Release that man!"

Wil watched with an odd twinge of pity as the priest disappeared into the jail. *What shall come of him?* he wondered. His cords were then severed, and he disappeared into the crowd in search of his wife.

The day's business was not yet finished, however. When Wil had nearly reached Frieda's side, she hastened to meet him and led him into the shadows. "You must wait here," she said insistently. The young woman then took her place near the bridge and searched for the steward's secretary. *There, I see him!* she thought. Indeed, her eyes met the clerk's. He glared at her from under his skullcap and gathered up his black robes and moved closer.

The courtyard was restored to order, and Judge Hagan

prepared for his next case. Pieter and Maria returned to their place at the gallows, while their fellows watched anxiously from places all about the castle grounds. Finally, the name "Heinrich of Weyer" was called by the bailiff. The rumpled man stepped from the shadows with his shoulders straight and his chin up.

The crowd hissed and jeered, but the baker lifted his eye to the bright blue sky above and smiled. His son was spared, and that was all that mattered to him now. He allowed his spirit to soar far beyond the stench of Runkel Castle and the blasphemies rising from its folk.

The faithful band of Heinrich's company once again made ready. With Wil nearby, Frieda cast a quick eye at Friederich positioned near the court's bench. She turned her head subtly to see Wilda slip through the crowd toward her.

Wil moved carefully closer to his wife. He did not trust the secretary nor the few soldiers standing nearby. He slowly removed his dagger from within his tunic. In the shadows of his screen, Helmut fitted his arrow once again. His fingers trembled as he prepared to take aim at the judge.

Katharina stared at Heinrich blankly; she had not seen the baker for years. She looked at the patch covering his eye and fixed her gaze upon the vacant space that had once been filled with a strong arm. Her throat swelled. *So broken,* she thought. *Oh, dear Heinrich, if I could only comfort you.*

"Who accuses this man?" Judge Hagan roared. He tapped his fingers briefly when Yeoman Horst abruptly appeared from nowhere. "I do!" he cried.

Hagan was startled. There was to have been no accuser! He and Prior Mattias had worked this all out. *Who is this fool?* Hagan spat and cursed. *Now, Hann, do your duty!*

Surprised, Hann looked hard at Katharina and squeezed her arm. He dragged her forward, crying, "Hold! Hold fast, sir!" Hagan and the prior had wisely arranged for the unexpected. The soldier plunged through the grumbling crowd with one hand in the air. "Hold, Judge! The man ... the man is innocent!"

Heinrich looked toward the voice and gasped. *Katharina!* Suddenly, nothing else mattered. His heart raced, and warm blood pulsed through his veins. *Katharina!* Countless memories flew through his mind. But when he noticed that she was being dragged along by Hann, he was filled with rage. He wanted to bound across the bailey and embrace his beloved—and he wanted to tear the soldier limb from limb.

Frieda held her breath. Wilda motioned for Helmut to lower his bow. Following orders, Hann shouted loudly. "The abbot withdraws all charges against this man. The deed was committed in self-defense."

"Nay!" cried Horst. "Nay, I am a witness against this man. I—"

Hagan rose angrily and pointed a long, stiff finger at the complaining yeoman. "Bailiff, arrest this mad dolt for disturbing the court's peace!" Horst was abruptly thrown to the ground and dragged away, howling loud protests. Hagan turned a red face to Heinrich. "Release this man!"

The baker was shoved forward by two men-at-arms, his eye still fastened to Katharina's gentle face.

"Go, I say!" roared the bulge-eyed judge.

Confused, the baker nodded and then plunged into the crowded courtyard toward Katharina, who was now being dragged away from the bench and toward the center of the courtyard. The crowd jeered and pelted the man with clods of manure as he thrashed his way forward.

In the meanwhile, Alwin, always the alert knight, recognized the look on Hann's face as the man dragged his hostage back to his position. *When the deal is done, he'll kill her!* He pressed his way forward.

With the release of Heinrich, Hagan's secretary was beside himself. He was pushing through the crowd toward the young blonde woman he assumed bore the letter. At the same time, the two soldiers Wil was watching began to move toward Frieda. The young man was ready.

But it was Wilda who brushed by the secretary in the press of the crowd and squeezed the letter into his hand. "Release the hostage and call off those two," she hissed in his ear. "Else I'll cast a spell on you where you stand."

The secretary froze. He knew of Wilda and had once seen her curse a knight with a spell of madness. He nodded and abruptly waved his accomplices away.

"Now the hostage!" growled Wilda.

The clerk licked his lips nervously. "No need to hex me, witch." He lifted his hand over the crowd so that Hann might see. "See, I've signaled him. Leave me be, woman." He backed slowly away as Wilda and Frieda melted into the crowd.

It was then that little Friederich sprinted from cover and flew past the unsuspecting clerk, snatching the letter from the man's hand. Stunned, the secretary gasped and spun around in disbelief as the scamp dashed away.

Judge Hagan had kept a distracted eye on his secretary. Now fearing some mischief, he rose and stared, unaware of Friederich's theft. He called quietly for some Templars. His suspicious movements caught Wilda's attention, and she looked nervously about. *It is time to go!* the woman thought. She raised her arm to signal her fellows.

Pieter had already led Maria close to the bridge, where he had kept a close eye on the events. Seeing Wilda's hand raised, he squeezed his staff. "Hurry, child! We need make for the bridge and quickly." The old man was tired. His legs bowed limply beneath him. The day had been far too much for him, and he now begged God to just let the two of them fly with angels over the walls of the stinking castle and into the safety of the clean forests by Münster.

With Solomon threatening all in their path, Maria took the old man's hand and helped him hurry forward. She tightened her grip and pulled the perspiring, wobbling priest onto the bridge midst the milling assortment of coughing, lice-ridden peasants. The old man held the girl's hand firmly and followed her into the safety of Runkel's winding streets.

In the meanwhile, Heinrich was still pushing his way through the courtyard in a mad press to rescue Katharina. At last he saw her. She looked so brave to him, so beautiful. Her hair had grayed some, but it still shined under the summer sun. She was slender and graceful, he thought.

But, suddenly, the soldier began to drag her away. It was never intended that she be released. In fact, both she and Frieda were to have been seized.

"No!" cried Heinrich. He bolted forward, but it was Alwin who would strike first. Standing only feet from Hann, the knight had anticipated the betrayal. He had already drawn his sword, so when Hann made his move, Alwin lunged forward and fixed one hand hard on Hann's elbow as he placed the point of his sword at the base of the man's skull.

"Release her or die," Alwin hissed.

Hann froze and cursed. He hesitated, and in that brief pause Heinrich arrived to tear the man's hand from Katharina's arm. "Let her go!" the baker growled. The soldier yielded and stood stiffly as Heinrich abruptly led Katharina on a mad dash for the bridge.

Alwin waited with his sword on Hann's skull until the baker and the woman were lost in the crowd. With a push, he quickly spun about and began a retreat of his own. Hann roared and drew his sword. He took a few steps toward the retreating knight when an arrow landed between his feet. The soldier froze and stared into the ramparts, then into the shadows. Fearing to take another step, the man backed away.

Alwin was nervous. He saw soldiers of the castle guard begin to prowl suspiciously. *Time to get out of here!* He shoved his way through the mob and toward the bridge to which others were now moving. In the slowing press of shuffling folk, he spotted Heinrich and Katharina ahead. The knight pushed harder and finally caught up to the pair. "Heinrich, raise your hood!"

The baker obeyed.

"Now, hurry!" The trio pressed anxiously toward the drawbridge in a growing crush of reeking, unwashed folk. In the courtyard behind them, four Templars on horseback were now barking at the peasants, shouting as they plowed their mounts forward.

At last the three set foot on the wooden planks and took their next desperate steps. Alwin looked anxiously about for the others, and his eyes fell upon Otto's head to one side and Tomas near him. *They've all been signaled.* The trio had nearly reached the far side when the Templars arrived on the bridge behind them. Alwin sank deeply into his hood and cried to Heinrich, "They're going to block it! Hurry! We must hurry!"

Indeed, the man had no sooner said the words when he felt the hot breath of a horse on his neck.

"Move off!" cried a Templar. "Move off or die!"

The shoulder of another's horse bumped Katharina forward, causing her to stumble. Alwin exploited the moment. He, too, feigned tripping and wrapped a securing arm around the woman. Together, they lurched forward, off the bridge, and tumbled onto the shoulder of the far side.

Ignoring them as some bumbling peasants, the Templars spurred their way forward a few more steps, then turned their mounts to face the oncoming crowd. Heinrich lowered his head and rolled between the flanks of their horses, barely breaking through the line before a row of lances was leveled to hold the rest at bay. Moments later he found Alwin and Katharina, and the trio hurried into the lengthening shadows of the village of Runkel, where they stopped. "God be praised!" Alwin cried. "God be praised."

The baker fought for his breath, then looked at Katharina in disbelief. "I ... I cannot believe you are here, standing right here!" The woman lowered her face shyly. She hesitated and then leaned quietly against him. For Heinrich, the moment was one of dreams, of fantasy once shaming. The soft frame within his strong embrace was an unexpected gift from a merciful heaven.

For Katharina, it was as though all time had suddenly stopped. The noise of the village vanished within the sound of her heart's pounding, and she trembled for joy.

Alwin looked about. "We'd best be moving. We cannot stay here for long, though I only saw Otto and Tomas on the bridge."

Heinrich wiped his eye. "Wil, Frieda, Maria, and Pieter were ahead of us ... and Wilda as well. That leaves Friederich, Helmut, and Benedetto."

Katharina looked at the worried knight and at Heinrich. "What happened today was not of things earthly. The angels smiled on us *all*. I do not believe they'd leave any behind. We should believe; it is all we can do."

Heinrich thought for a moment. He looked at the woman, then to the dimming sky. He smiled. It was true; heaven *had* rained mercy upon the brave band of misfits. Indeed, if the man's ears had been able, he would have heard the legions of the unseen singing joyously.

ᠵ

For the next two days, the exhausted pilgrims—*all* the pilgrims—rested comfortably in the forest near Münster. They had shared their adventures over and over and now waited patiently for Wilda to return from Münster with Paulus and any news. They had served one another well— they had lived for something greater than themselves, and in that, they had once more tasted the pleasure of true joy.

News of the day's astonishing events had traveled quickly along the highways and footpaths of the "Golden Ground." After the trial Wilda had returned to Münster, where her priest had informed her of what he had learned. She hurried back to camp to share the news.

"Arnold escaped the village soon after the trial. Actually, he was in hiding during it! He said he had a sense of trouble. Anyway, he came to Münster with news, and I was there to hear him with m'own ears. He has a grave warning for us, but first, Heinrich, you needs know something."

She turned to the baker solemnly. "The poor of Weyer gathered on the village common the morning of the trial. They had not forgotten the kindnesses you showed them so many years before. They armed themselves with hoes and forks and swore to attack the abbey if you were not released. The reeve quickly summoned the garrison, and it seems that a small battle occurred on the Villmar road. Arnold says that four cotters were killed and one soldier."

"That's why the reeve was not at court!" exclaimed Alwin.

The pilgrims shook their heads in disbelief, but Heinrich sat stone faced and overwhelmed. He had, indeed, done his best to help the poor of Weyer, but he didn't think any ever noticed. Katharina laid a tender hand on his. "But now, all, listen carefully. Arnold says that the prior and the steward are enraged. They've ordered a search of every village, every field, and every forest of the manor. They are desperate to capture us all." The group murmured worriedly.

Wilda continued. "Heinrich and Wil, you are officially under warrant as fugitives of the manor. Arnold says the steward intends to have you hanged as runaways. Warrants are also issued for Maria, Katharina, Otto, and Tomas. And he says I shall be sent to Mainz for trial as a witch. I fear for us all, even the minstrel and Helmut ... and Pieter."

The group fell quiet. None spoke for a long time until Tomas stood and looked at his fellows from Weyer. "Wil, Heinrich, Otto, Maria ... Katharina ... we can *never* return," he declared flatly. "Weyer is no longer our home."

Katharina held Heinrich's hand as the man now wrestled inwardly with both rage and sorrow. For two days the two of them had spent the hours gazing into one another's eyes and discussing everything from the days in Emma's gardens to the trial. Heinrich had begged her forgiveness for killing her husband, and he had confessed his shame in his past affections. They had wept and laughed, and they had groaned over shared memories and beamed with new hopes. It had been a time of healing. But with this news from Wilda, the baker could only shake his head. He had supposed it all along, but now it was certain: Weyer was no longer his home; he was no longer Heinrich of Weyer. The thought of it left him dismayed. At last he spoke. "Wilda, is it safe for you to seek out your priest again?"

"I believe so. Arnold has spies who say the abbot has not yet gotten permission to send riders into Lord Rolfhard's land."

"Then, could I ask you to do something? Could you ask your priest to tell Arnold that I've no words to say how thankful I am to him and to those blessed cotters? Tell him I wish I knew a way to show my heart to him and to them."

Friederich had kept a secret for these two days. *Now*, he

thought, *now is the right time!* "Pardon, all. I've other news as well."

The circle turned toward the cheerful imp. "I've this!" In his hand he held a piece of folded parchment. "I snatched it from the secretary in the castle. 'Tis the letter of debt!" he cried.

The group was astonished, and after a moment of utter silence, they roared.

"Well done, lad!" cried Pieter. "I think."

"'Tis no wonder the prior is wild!" cried Tomas. "He lost Heinrich *and* the money!"

Echoing one another's comments, the group laughed and chattered loudly. At last Heinrich stood humbly. "I've no right to speak on this. It was you who risked all to save Wil and me. And I am confounded as to how to thank you. But ... but would it not be good if Wilda could give this letter to Arnold as our thanks. He could use it to save himself and even wrest a profit from it. It would be our wish that he would then share any gain with the poor in Weyer, especially any widows from the battle."

The idea was met with unanimous approval. Wilda smiled. "If it is agreed, I shall take it at once!"

But the woman would not need to deliver it, for her priest suddenly burst into the camp. "Wilda, I've been trying to catch you!" he cried. "No sooner had you left then I learned that Steward Hagan has sent a delegate to Lord Rolfhard with a bag of gold to ask permission for entry on his lands. This means he'll be coming here with soldiers and soon! You must leave before the dawn!" He whirled about and fixed his eyes on Alwin. "Do not tell me, sir, but a rumor is about that you are a deserting Templar. They've wind of it and have issued a warrant for you as well."

Alwin paled. *Someone must have seen me close.*

Alarmed, the pilgrims stared at one another blankly. Where would they go? None spoke. Those of Weyer had not yet fully grasped the fact that they no longer had a home, and they had certainly not even begun to consider where they now belonged. This was not the way to set a new course. Yet a new course needed to be taken, and quickly.

Wil took his wife's hand and looked at the others. "Well, where shall we go?"

Alwin rose and answered. "We should not run about the country like ships without rudders. I say we start at once for England. 'Tis a place where a man can be free. Things are afoot there that seem good to me. We could travel west, across France and to the ports in Normandy, we—"

Pieter shook his head wearily. "Alwin, I fear it is too much to ask of any. They'd need to learn another language, and they know nothing of the laws. It is simply too much, my friend, too much."

"Too much for you or for them?" snapped Alwin.

"No, we do not wish to go to England," answered Wil. "Not now. There must be another place amongst those who speak our tongue?"

"We could go south," blurted Otto. "South to the Emmental. It felt good there."

His idea was greeted with some nods. The Emmental was a pleasant place, to be sure. It had deep green valleys and good folk. "But we'd still be fugitives in a land of lords," grumbled Tomas.

The group murmured anxiously. A few ideas drifted round the circle but none that seemed reasonable. Wil retreated deep into his thoughts as he aimlessly sharpened a stick with his dagger. Lost in pictures of places he had been, his eyes fell suddenly upon the inscription on his blade, and he turned to his father. Both men stared at the words for a moment until the baker muttered, "'Freedom always.'"

Heinrich took the dagger from Wil's hand and held it up almost reverently. He turned to his fellows. "You, Wil, Maria, Frieda, Tomas ... all of you, listen to me. We are free now, even though we are driven from our homes and chased like animals across the land. We are free, and we'll not spend our days hiding from those who would deny us God's gift."

Heinrich laid hold of Karl's cross, which he now carried in his belt once again. He looked squarely at Alwin. "Good friend, we are all fugitives now. You are welcome with us, but go to England if you must. Yet by your own words you say that their king is a tyrant. I've had a belly full of tyranny." The baker looked deeply into Katharina's eyes. "I know a place where the sky is large and the fields are covered with flowers. There the sun shines brightly over freemen who stand firm for what is theirs, who fight shoulder to shoulder against tyrants. It is a place where we can be what we have become. Let us make our way to a new home, to a new beginning, to a new life. Let us make our way to Stedingerland."

The baker's words stirred each heart encircling the fire, and the friends stared at one another for a long moment as the idea washed over them. Then, one by one, the pilgrims rose and clasped hands. "To Stedingerland then!" proclaimed Wil. "To Stedingerland!"

It was a moment that brought cheers and nods—and a few doubts as well, for only Heinrich and Alwin had ever seen the place. So before long, the two were barraged with questions until Heinrich finally raised his arm. "Enough!" he laughed. "You'll need to trust us. We'll tell you all that we know, but now we must hurry."

"*Ja!*" pleaded Münster's priest. "You must be away long before dawn."

"Which way, then?" quizzed Pieter. The old man was enlivened by his flock's decision, but he barely had the strength to stand.

"Along the Lahn to Marburg. I've a friend there, a wealthy merchant who'll give us shelter," said Alwin. "Then we should go overland to Kassel, where we can follow the Fulda River toward the Weser. Then we can follow the Weser north."

"Aye!" exclaimed Helmut. "My home is just east of Bremen."

Heinrich nodded. "Good, perhaps we'll take a rest there. But, lad, once we're in the bishop's realm, we'll need to have a care."

With the matter forthrightly settled, the fugitives prepared to flee. Wil helped Benedetto load Paulus and then called for Pieter. "Your throne, my lord!"

Pieter did not complain. The adventure in Runkel had taken a terrible toll on him, and the past two days of rest had restored only a portion of his strength. "Too much excitement for these old bones," he chuckled.

Wil surveyed his gathering company. "We have everything? Our satchels, our gold, our weapons? Is everything in order?"

The group nodded. Wil took hold of Emmanuel and his quiver. He felt his satchel and secured the dagger in his belt. "Frieda?"

The young woman nodded. She still had her quills and parchments. The priest had even sent her a fresh jar of ink.

Heinrich had counted the company's coins and now gave each traveler seven pennies of his or her own before distributing the balance equally among Wil, Alwin, and himself. As he placed his coins into his satchel, he brushed along his Laubusbach stone, which he promptly lifted to his eye. He stared at it wistfully. Instead of a symbol of his return, it had suddenly become a relic of his past. Dropping it back into his bag, he secured his sword and nodded. "I am ready."

Solomon took his place alongside Paulus and his master as Pieter smiled at Maria. "You must promise me that you'll find some pretty flowers for your hair along the way!"

Maria giggled. "Of course … and for yours, too!"

Heinrich walked to Katharina's side. He took her hand in his and looked deeply into her green eyes. The baker's heart melted. Keeping his own hopes at bay, he said gently, "Woman, you have lost everything. Your husband is dead, your land will be taken by the abbot, and your chattels sold."

Katharina nodded. She gazed upward into Heinrich's kindly face. "Like you, I am saddened to leave the graves of our children behind, but more than that I do not mourn. The land was a curse to me; my chattels were fetters on my soul. I've an ample dowry safe enough with the Templar banks." She squeezed Heinrich's hand softly. "No, dear man, I have not lost everything."

The baker could hardly ask the next question. "Shall … you seek your family elsewhere … or travel with us to Stedingerland?" He waited breathlessly.

Katharina turned her eyes downward. *Dare I be so bold?* she wondered. Her heart fluttered. "If ... you permit me, sir, I should be honored to join your company."

The baker's heart leapt with joy. He wrapped his arm tenderly around the woman. "Permit you? Permit you? Oh, Katharina, come with me, I beg you!" For the man it was as if the world had been made right and good in that one brief moment.

Katharina smiled broadly. Her eyes sparkled, and her cheeks flushed warm and happy. "Then to Stedingerland—together."

In the meanwhile, Alwin sought out Wilda as Wil assembled the others. "And you, Wilda?"

"Are you going to England?" she asked.

The knight shook his head. "No. I belong with these, my brothers and sisters. They need my sword now more than ever."

"As do I."

Alwin released his breath and nodded. "That is good. That is good, indeed." He looked about the heavy shadows now filling the wood and then abruptly tilted his head at the cries of three seabirds sweeping overhead.

"Come, everyone!" shouted Frieda happily as she pointed. "Follow them! Believe me and you'll see."

Chapter Twenty-four

WAYFARERS ONCE MORE

he wayfarers soon found themselves racing beneath the starlit summer sky. Wisely, they had kept off the roads, and they hurried overland according to the cries of the birds above. *It is a strange night,* Pieter thought. *A blessed night, one touched by heaven's magic.* The birds seemed to be leading them northwest over rolling hills and past the dim torchlights of Lord Rolfhard's hamlets that were scattered about the darkness like little golden coins. By daybreak the column passed Weilburg and came to the Lahn highway, where it paused to rest behind a screen of silvery willows.

"The highway's not safe, Wil," said Heinrich.

The young man nodded. "I agree."

Frieda pointed to the gulls sitting in the treetops above. "Should we ask them?"

Wil shrugged. "They are seabirds, no doubt flying to the sea. We are traveling toward the sea as well. That does not mean they are angels guiding us!"

Helmut and Tomas giggled, but Maria stepped forward. "You weren't with us when we were lost by the Rhine!" she quipped. "I believe they are sent to help us."

A conversation ensued that bantered about all matters of the inexplicable. Friederich spoke of whispering trees and Otto of a fog that healed the sick. Wilda remained silent, though her mind was filled with memories of her life as a witch. She shuddered as she considered the dark side of such things. Others spoke of enchanted waters and devils' springs. Some mocked; most believed.

Pieter took a long draught of beer and listened carefully. He scratched Solomon's ears and smiled. Finally, all faces turned toward him. "What say you, Pieter?" asked Heinrich.

The old priest shrugged and thought for a long moment. "Well, I've had a long journey, my children, one often limited to the measurements of my senses. I have tasted fine food and touched the rough faces of mountains. I have smelled the fragrance of the rose and listened to the songbirds. I have seen the wonders of what God has made. I have grown in knowledge, and my mind has considered the great doctrines of Holy Scripture.

"But I fear that I have oft been confined to that which my senses bring to me. My knowledge of things seen has held me captive. I have failed to go beyond what seems reasonable to my mind. So I say this: what we measure by our sight is truth in part, but we do, indeed, see through the glass darkly. Truth also dwells in the great Unknown.

"My beloved, study to show thyselves approved. Use your minds well and do not be deceived by fools and their fantasies. But also, be still and know that He is God. It is good to increase in knowledge and to test things by reason, but I believe we must listen to the silence so much more; it is the way of faith."

Above, the birds suddenly cried out, and all eyes turned upward to watch them lift from their perches. The pilgrims said nothing as their three winged companions swooped into a great arc around them and flapped their way eastward.

Alwin rose. "We should move. We cannot stay by this road much longer, for it is already beginning to fill. I say we keep to this side of the Lahn until we reach Marburg. It should take us about three days."

It was quickly agreed, and the company began on their way. They first traveled eastward, walking overland within sight of the sluggish Lahn and the highway paralleling its green waters. They looked longingly at the wagons rolling so easily along the road and wished for all the world that they might have the liberty to do the same. But at the sight of every company of knights roaring past, they were content to trudge behind the cover of the softwoods lining the narrow meadows of the river. Behind them the long, low ridges of lower Thurungia were gradually sinking lower. Ahead waited the lumpy mountains of the duchy's heartland.

It was on the feast of Lammas, Thursday, the first day of August, when Wil led his brave band across the bridge at Marburg and through the growing town's gates. The column of thirteen souls and two kindly beasts made their way quickly through a throng of revelers toward the home of Alwin's friend. The town was built on a conical mountain atop which was perched a menacing redstone castle. Brick-paved streets wound their way upward to the fortress like narrow serpents coiled around a stump. Lining the narrow streets were well-built houses and heavy-timbered shops that leaned over the passersby like curious onlookers.

"Seems like a wealthy town," said Benedetto.

"Aye," answered Alwin. "Its lord is clever and ruthless, but the folk are hardworking and honest, as I recall. My friend is a salt merchant and has made a small fortune with a contract from Ulm. He does a good business with the Templars as well. I escorted him and his silver to Paris some years past, and I once guarded a wagon of his salt from Ulm to Strasbourg."

Heinrich grumbled. He knew more about salt than he cared to remember. "How much farther?"

"Soon."

The wayfarers struggling up the town's steep hills were soon hot and perspiring. The summer sun beat upon them, and the buildings rising close by every side blocked any breeze. Paulus was heavily frothed with sweat and had slipped twice, dumping Pieter to the ground. The townsfolk howled as the spindly fellow bounced on the bricks with a wheeze and an oath.

"*Ach,* stupid beast!" grumbled the priest as he fell a third time. He pulled himself up on his staff and shook his head. Aching, he bowed to the laughing crowd. "Ha! Fit as a young stag!" he cried as he beat his chest facetiously. He turned to his smiling companions and wiped his face. "God be praised! I could've shattered both m'hips!"

At last, as the column turned a corner, Alwin pointed to a three-storied house at the end of the street. "There!" he cried happily. "The one of brick and stone."

The knight ran to the door and rapped on it loudly. In a few moments, an usher answered, received Alwin's introduction, and then disappeared within. Shortly after, a well-dressed man appeared and greeted the knight with a large smile. "Old friend! Brother Blasius!" he cried. "I would not have known you. Come! Come in, all of you! Hans!" he shouted to a servant. "Have the groomsman take the donkey to the stable. Jon, bring pitchers of beer, and hurry!"

Within the half hour, the happy company was properly introduced and resting comfortably within the confines of the merchant's home. "You've come on the right day!" The merchant laughed. "I've guests in the hall making ready for their Lammas feast, but we've room for more."

"Ah, good Godfrey!" answered Alwin. "Any day in your company is a good day indeed."

Godfrey chuckled and then changed his tone. He leaned forward slowly. "Tell me, old friend, tell me the stories of you are lies."

Alwin paled. He should have known that the news of his desertion would have traveled from France to Marburg by now. In hushed tones he proceeded to tell the man the truth of his recent past.

The others sat quietly, listening a little but mostly marveling at Godfrey's clothing. The man wore an ankle-length, sleeveless, blue silk robe atop a white silk shirt. Atop his head sat a fancy red hat, complete with a large plume. A scarlet sash was wrapped around his waist and fastened by a large silver clasp. Each of his fingers bore a golden ring, and around his neck hung a golden chain.

The merchant took Alwin's hand. "I knew it, man," he

said. "Fear not. You're safe here. My guests know nothing. You shall be 'Alwin,' knight errant." He turned to the others. "Now, it seems quick baths might be in order? I'd rather smell my fare than all of you!" He laughed. Godfrey clapped and summoned his fuller. "Man, pour baths for each of these and hurry. I've rosewater for the damsels and some good lye soap for the foul brutes they travel with! And scrub their garments."

The travelers bathed hastily, and their clothing was washed and returned to them well wrung but still damp. They were then escorted to the lord's hall, where a table had been set for them near the others already eating. Ushers ran forward with freshly filled platters of the season's bounty riding precariously atop their flattened palms. Trays of cheese and fresh vegetables, as well as roasted chicken, boiled hare, stuffed peacock, numbers of sausages, and baskets of bread were quickly delivered to the table. Red wine and beer flowed generously.

Solomon was allowed to romp about the rush-strewn floor with the lord's hounds. He eagerly gobbled the many secret offerings of the children and dashed about for bones tossed by others. It was a wonderful Lammas, the best any had remembered.

The day brought back memories of times past for Heinrich and Katharina. Sitting alongside one another, they spoke in low tones of feast days gone by. Katharina giggled and groaned when Heinrich teased her about May Days, and he grumbled loudly when she recalled his poor efforts in bladder ball. "And once you wrestled Richard by the reeve's own table. His wife was drunk and sleeping on the ground. He yelled from across the common, but it was too late! The both of you knocked the table atop the poor woman and spilt cherry preserves all over her face!"

"And then the bees came!" Heinrich roared. The two laughed and looked fondly at one another. Their faces glowed in the warmth of their happy hearts, and beneath the table they held one another's hands.

At the end of the meal, Benedetto stepped forward to offer his thanks with a song. To the delight of all, the minstrel stood atop a stout stool and strummed his lute happily. Singing songs of his beloved homeland, he wooed all into a dreamy mood. Then, staring wistfully at the timber beams of the ceiling above, the man took a deep breath. He opened his mouth to sing, but it was as if another whispered the words.

I'll know a place where all is bright, where all is good, and
    all is right.
I'll know a time when all is done, when all is ready
    beneath the sun.
I'll know a song that I will sing, that I will offer, that I
    will bring.
I'll know a reason for why I came, for why I am, and
    why my name.

The man stopped and let his words trail away. Surprised by the lyrics, he stared blankly at Pieter and then bowed his head.

The diners clapped and praised the fellow, pleading for more. The minstrel politely declined and quietly went to his seat. A wandering discussion soon followed. A loud contest of ideas began, which quickly drew Pieter to its center. He listened carefully as Godfrey's other guests shouted at one another about the ideas of St. Anselm and Abelard. The discussion grew heated and soon wandered to the political legacy of Bernard of Clairvaux, the logic of Aristotle, and the works of the Scot, Richard of St. Victor.

"A dreamer!" shouted one. "A mystic of a time now past. A toast, I say. A toast to the true scholars, the children of Aristotle!"

Pieter bristled. *A time now past? Past what?* he wondered. *Past the nudgings of the Spirit, past the "peace that surpasses all understanding?"* He could keep silent no longer. "Keep your blasted Aristotle! I'll take the Scot and his 'reasonable mysticism'!"

A diner slammed his fist on the table. "Give me the Greek and his logic, and I'll change the world!"

Pieter rose. He took a goblet of wine in his hand and

drank slowly. Calmed, he said, "My lords, there should be no war between faith and reason. Our faith is reasonable, though it does not stand or fall upon logic. After all, it stands on grace, and that, sirs, is not logical at all."

The diners fell quiet.

Pieter went on. "But if the two become opposed in the life of a man, it is faith that shall always rule reason—"

"Nay!" shouted a diner. "Reason shall prevail, and faith must find a home in it!"

Others agreed.

Pieter, however, shook his head. "No. Reason shall not prevail because it *cannot* prevail. I say this because of two *logical* points!" He smiled. "First, reason is a mere faculty of the intellect, while faith springs from the heart. It is the *heart* of man that ultimately rules his mind.

"Second, unlike the intellect, faith has no bounds; it is a gift of the Infinite. The intellect cannot grasp truth because truth always enlarges itself just beyond our grasp."

A voice grumbled, "And why would that be?"

"Because truth does not wish to be fully known," answered Heinrich from his seat. All eyes turned toward the burly man with surprise, not the least of which was Pieter!

The priest smiled. "*Ja!* 'Tis so!"

"No!" roared a merchant. The man stood and rested his hands in the folds of his robe. He looked down his long nose at the faces now turned toward him. "No, I say." He looked squarely at Pieter. "You are a churchman, and no force on earth would more severely oppose the scholars than your Holy Church." Murmurs of assent rippled around the table. The man went on. "My nephew is a student at university. He will be a doctor of philosophy in time. On Easter past, he shared with us the marvels of the ancients. The crusaders have brought back the works of Aristotle and Ptolemy, Socrates and Plato. In their writings we are discovering another way of thinking. Now, he says, the students are beginning to reject the dictates of others, even their professors. They are beginning to reason with their *own* minds, and in time, he says, that will change everything.

"When a man can think on his own, he becomes a new man indeed. He becomes a free agent, unwilling to lose himself in some vague order of others. No, he will stand apart. This, sirs, is what is happening, and I for one welcome it! We will no longer be mindless, cowering sheep led to slaughter by the Church! No, sirs. We are freemen, free to think, free to serve that which is reasonable, and free to reject that which is not!"

The diners rose, applauding. Godfrey, however, was anxious. "My dear guests," he said slowly, "have a care. The world is what it is. The Holy Church will not be cast aside so easily. It will surely answer, and it shall do so with sincere zeal."

Frustrated, Pieter interrupted. "You need not cast away faith to find your freedom!" His voice was nearly desperate. "No, sirs, no! You boast of your fine minds, yet you do not understand. Faith *is* the way of freedom."

"The Church is a place of bondage!" shouted one. Others agreed loudly.

"Listen!" cried Pieter. "I did not say that Rome is the way to freedom. I said that faith is the way. If not checked, your scholars will simply lead us into a new tyranny. Yes, yes, use your minds freely, but do not be so foolish as to deny the mysteries—for that is where truth also abides."

"And who should 'check' the scholars, old man? You and your—" A loud, rapid knocking at the front door interrupted the man's speech. Godfrey rose and asked all for silence. He ordered an usher to the door. The man returned, ashen faced. He whispered into Godfrey's ear. The merchant nodded and licked his lips nervously, then summoned another servant to his side. The three huddled anxiously as Wil and his fellows began to shift in their seats.

Godfrey summoned Alwin. Drawing him close, he said, "Two Templars are at my door with some men-at-arms. My servant says they demand to speak with me."

"About what?" blurted Alwin.

"They did not say, but you must leave." Godfrey's face was tight and pale. "Please, my friend. Take your companions and follow my servant to the rear. Disappear into the town. They'll surely search my home and the stable, and that should take some time."

Alwin squeezed the man's hand and motioned to Wil. No words were needed. The company rose quickly and hurried behind the servant toward the rear of the house as Godfrey offered an explanation to his perplexed guests. "Rest easy, all of you. We've some soldiers at the door who are searching for these others."

Godfrey stiffened and spoke sternly. "Now listen. We here are all men of business. We need one another. I ask you to trust me." He looked at the table's vacated places and knew he could deny little. Fists were now pounding on his door. "Please, I will tell them our guests left an hour ago. I need you to keep silent on this."

The door burst open, and six knights charged into the house, shouting. Godfrey bowed as his guests stood. "Welcome. How can we serve you?"

A Templar spat. He looked at the empty places. "Where are they?" he roared. "We're told of a one-eyed man and an old priest with a knight and a company of youths. A peddler claims he saw them here!"

Godfrey nodded. "Indeed, sir. Indeed they were. I thought them to be pilgrims in need."

The knight kicked at a hound. "Where are they?" he growled.

"Ah, good sir. They left us, oh, perhaps an hour ago or more."

Another soldier looked at the perspiring guests suspiciously. He looked at the plates, still partly filled with food. "Why would they leave their food behind?"

Godfrey faltered. The Templar stuck his finger in a sausage. "Still warm!" he cried. "Search the house!"

Wil, Heinrich, Alwin, and the others ran desperately across the merchant's rear courtyard and into his small stable. There they feverishly gathered their provisions and dragged Paulus into the alleyway. Behind them they could hear shouts and breaking glass. "Hurry!" cried Wil. "Hurry!"

The desperate company followed the merchant's servant down the winding descent of the town's streets until he pointed them to Marburg's eastern wall. "There, through that gate. Godspeed!" he cried.

The pilgrims flew from the town and dashed across an open field toward the cover of a wooded slope. Maria dragged Paulus, and Wil and Tomas carried Pieter until they all crashed headlong into a thicket. Tripping and collapsing into their cover, the company abruptly spun about to see if they were being followed.

"Can you see?" asked Frieda. "Wil, can you see?"

Wil studied every horse, rider, cart, and peasant leaving the town gate. He turned his face to the roadway, to the riverbanks, and he stared at the many folks feasting outside the walls. "No. I don't see them."

Heinrich counted everyone, then checked their provisions. "We should have left Paulus behind. It was foolish."

"No!" snapped Maria. She wrapped her arm around the donkey's long face. "No. They might have killed him. And ... and Pieter needs him."

Heinrich nodded. "Well, 'tis a miracle we were not seen running with him. If they had been on the walls, they would have seen us for sure."

"Godfrey must have delayed them," said Alwin. "He's like a fox when he needs to be."

Frieda thought she heard the cry of gulls. She looked up. "Wil, we must keep moving."

ò

The company stumbled northwestward all that day. With anxious eyes cast behind them, they pressed deep into the twilight darkness. No longer following the Lahn, they traveled on the starlit highway leading to Kassel. The next day they moved off the roadway and paralleled it at a safe distance, keeping a sharp eye on those passing by. The road was crowded with summer traffic—peddlers, pilgrims, clerics, caravans, and men-at-arms—but they did not see the white robes of Templars all that day or the next.

They continued their journey through a widening landscape decorated with yellow and purple wildflowers sprinkled generously in the clearings between stands of beech and spruce. It was here that Maria pranced happily once more. She gathered enough summer blooms to decorate the hair of the three women and then presented a ringlet of vines for Pieter's white head.

The column crossed the Eder River at Fritzlar and then began a rolling march through a knotty landscape that delivered the travelers to the outskirts of Kassel.

"They have not trailed us, Alwin," offered Heinrich. "We've seen nothing of them for almost a week. They would have no way of knowing which way we went from Marburg."

The knight knew the discipline of the Templar Order, and he was still anxious. "I don't know," he murmured. "I just don't know."

Wil ordered the night's camp be set, and soon the fugitives were resting uncomfortably around a small fire. "My beloved," Pieter began slowly. He coughed weakly. "I know a cloister near these parts. I think you ought to leave me there. I am now a danger to you all. I slow you. My time is nearly come."

Maria began to sob softly. She snuggled against the bony man's frame like a kitten nestling into a safe place.

"No," stated Wil flatly. "Pieter, we are safe enough here. They are not following us any longer. We need you, Pieter. We still need you."

Pieter took a shallow breath. He did not have the energy to argue. The last five days had been grueling, and he wanted nothing other than to sleep. He nodded and closed his eyes. Soon, midst the gentle chatter of the others, he fell to sleep. Lying in the firelight with a slight smile on his face, the old man was quickly carried to pleasant places on the wings of dreams.

Morning broke with a fresh August breeze. It was quickly decided that the group would not enter Kassel but would spend the day quietly at rest. The women were to tend to Pieter and to put their provisions in some order, while the men and boys would scout the highway. Alwin believed that the Templars were either close behind—in which case they might be seen entering Kassel's gates that very day, or they were ahead—in which case it would be good to let them go farther. "But if they've gone ahead," the knight said, "we'll need to keep a sharp eye for their return. They are not easily fooled."

"As I've said, they have no idea where we went from Marburg!" protested Heinrich. "We could have run in any direction. Even Godfrey does not know our plan."

Alwin shrugged. "I feel better about it now than a few days ago, but I know them. They've the instincts of master huntsmen."

Wil agreed. "Stedingerland will wait for us. Each league makes us safer, but we are not safe. I think we are right to do this slowly."

The day quickly passed without any sight of the dreaded Templars, and night fell lightly on a company now beginning to relax. Conversations became lighthearted, even jovial. Pieter had slept throughout the day and was now surprisingly refreshed. He ate a small supper and began to recount tales of his youth.

Wilda and Alwin walked slowly away from the camp toward a nearby clearing where they stared dreamily into the starry canopy above. They spoke of many things and as their hands brushed, the touch felt warm to them both. Alwin looked into Wilda's face uneasily. "Wilda, is it true that you are Heinrich's cousin?"

"Did he tell you that?"

Alwin nodded.

"It is so. My mother was his aunt, his father's sister."

"And who was your father?"

"I do not know. My mother was raped by a pack of wicked shepherds."

"Gunnars," said Alwin sadly. "They were my kin."

Wilda's face fell, and she did not answer at first. She shifted subtly away from the man. "I … I thought that was a rumor."

Alwin shook his head. "No, dear Wilda. It is true. Heinrich and I have spoken of the feud of our fathers. It was some of my kin who raped your mother … and someone of Heinrich's who killed my father."

Wilda wrung her hands. "It may be that we have the same father then!"

Alwin's throat swelled. He had grown to love this woman, but the knowledge of their pasts could ruin it all. "Nay, 'tis not so. Neither my father nor his brothers were involved in the attack. Yet surely our house has paid for its many sins against your kin."

Wilda turned her back on the handsome knight and walked a few paces away. She had begun to love this man. "I know not what to say. 'Tis a horrible thing that was done to my mother—it ruined her life ... and mine."

Unable to restrain his heart any longer, Alwin strode toward the woman and turned her face to his. Holding her shoulders firmly, he asked, "Can you find it within to forget the sorrow? You must, if you can ... for I love you, Wilda."

Wilda buried her face in the man's heaving chest. Weeping, she could not answer.

పం

The next day delivered the quiet company past numbers of mills sprinkled along the woody banks of the Fulda River. The meadows had widened, but the slopes on either side of the river rose steeply. The column kept to the forests as much as possible, making the walking rather difficult for that day and the next. Finally, they came within view of the newly built gatehouse of the walled town of Münden, and they paused to decide whether they should venture within or not.

"We need beer or mead, Heinrich," offered Katharina. The woman had kept a careful count of their shrinking provisions. It seemed they had left some items in Marburg after all. "And we're low on meat. We've salt enough and a few wheels of cheese. But the bread is gone, and I've only a little grain for *Mus*."

"I say we ferry across in separate groups," said Tomas. "Heinrich, methinks you are a risk, what with your one arm and patch. Can we not add a sleeve to your tunic like we did with Maria? If any is searching at all, it'd be for a *one*-armed man."

The idea was met with approval.

"*Ja*," answered Katharina. "Indeed I can. We'll tear cloth from a sack."

"Good!" said Alwin. "Good indeed. We'll cross in three groups and meet back here by the bells of nones. Like in Basel, each group should buy a set thing."

It was agreed. Over the next two hours, three groups crossed the Fulda at intervals and warily entered the town of Münden through its south gate. The inscription above them was troubling. It was worn and in a difficult script. Pieter squinted. "I believe it says, 'They faded away, but their ghost lives on, an everlasting reminder of our duty.' Dialect perhaps?"

Maria shuddered as she passed beneath the strange words. She pulled hard on Paulus's lead and looked anxiously at Pieter.

The town was fairly large, though not nearly so large as Marburg. It was protected by massive stone walls and many high towers that overlooked the three rivers that converged just beyond its northern gate. Coming from the southwest flowed the Fulda and from the southeast, the Werra. Together, these two rivers joined to flow north as the River Weser.

Inside, the town was much like every other town of its time: crowded by narrow, crooked streets and filled with a varied collection of houses, workshops, sheds, barns, coops, and churches. The streets were clogged with groaning two-wheeled carts, oxen, and swaybacked palfreys. The air was filled with the stench of urine and manure, made all the more pungent in the summer heat.

Pieter's group included Maria, Katharina, and Otto, as well as the two animals. The four were assigned the task of buying salted pork and cheese. It was at the butcher's shop that Maria became frightened once more.

"Strangers, eh?" asked the butcher. He was a large, menacing character wearing a skullcap and leather apron.

"Pilgrims, my son," answered Pieter.

The mole-faced man bent low and stared into Maria's face. He was toothless and his breath was horrid. The girl recoiled. "Ha! Ha! My deary. Best be on yer best whilst here!

Are you one of them crusaders come home?"

"I said we are pilgrims," snapped Pieter. "Now sell us some pork!"

The man picked his nose and smiled wickedly. "Hmm." He stared at Maria a bit longer. "See there, little girl?" he pointed to a tower under construction at the town's edge.

Maria nodded shyly.

"Well, if you look up about six rods or so ... near the top of the scaffold, you'll see the face of a child in the stone."

Maria was puzzled and all eyes strained.

"No, y'fools. You'll not see it from here! You needs get close."

"Why is it there?" asked Otto.

The butcher looked the lad over. "You, boy. You've the look of one of them crusaders."

Otto spat. "Can y'not answer m'question?"

The butcher grinned. "A child was put in the wall just months past. A little blond one, like her ... only it was a boy, a real screamer."

Pieter stiffened.

The butcher carved a ham from a hanging swine. "*Ja*, I can still hear him. The priest said it'd keep the ghosts away."

"What?" barked Pieter. Solomon bared his teeth.

"The lord of the town captured four lads who was lost. He says they was in the crusade, but they said not. I don't think it mattered much. They were strangers here. He locked three up in the jail over there." He pointed to a squat stone building. "Aye, we've had some bad time with spirits coming from the river mists more than ever. Two priests died at Easter; a midwife was slain by a dragon born from a strumpet. Aye, we've had a bad time of it. So the lord says we ought quiet the spirits. He locked the three away and let 'em starve. They never said much. Just went quietly. We buried them where they lay in the jail, though some say they hear them groaning at night.

"But the boy in the wall was different. He cursed the priest with a blasphemy and spat upon the altar. So he was mortared into the wall—alive. Now we see his face in the wall, and the lord's lady claims his ghost prowls the great hall."

Pieter was dumbstruck. He looked at his companions in astonishment and then turned a hard eye on the butcher. "Keep thy meat, y'wicked devil. I pray the God of Abraham will release the demons of the Pit to raise the rivers high enough to swallow you and this evil place!" He shook his staff with whitened knuckles. "A curse on thee! A curse on thee and thine!"

Otto spat at the butcher and kicked over his table. A gathering crowd murmured as the butcher shouted for the guard. Solomon barked wildly and kept the man at bay, while a cursing Pieter led Maria in a hasty retreat across the market square.

"Run, Papa Pieter," the girl squealed. "I don't want to be put in that jail!" She leaned forward with all her might to drag Paulus through the streets.

The four did their best to vanish in the alleys, but Otto looked back and saw a deputy being pointed in their direction. "Quick, we needs get out of the town!"

"Where? We can't go back through the main gate!"

Otto thought hard. Pieter answered. "Over there. We can get through the far gate and hide. The guards won't be looking for us yet."

With that, the four hurried through winding alleyways until they came to the town's north gate. All was calm and quiet. "Perhaps they'll just let it be," grumbled Pieter.

"Perhaps," answered Katharina. "But we should get out of this place."

The group composed themselves and walked slowly through the gate, past two sleeping guards and toward a stand of massive trees near the water's edge. Poor Pieter's legs were wobbling again. The surge of anger had sapped another week's worth of strength, to be sure. Solomon leaned lightly against him, instinctively serving as something of a prop for his master.

In the meanwhile, Wil's group—including Frieda, Benedetto, and Helmut—had watched the whole event from a measured distance. Moments after the deputy arrived at the butcher's stall, Wil made a dash to intercept him. "Sir, it seems m'grandpapa has made some trouble again."

"Grandpapa? He dresses like a priest."

"Aye, you understand then."

The guard and the butcher looked at one another. "Oh," answered the soldier. "He's mad. Well, this man's suffered some loss."

"How much?"

The butcher looked over his table. "The sausages are covered with dirt."

"So?"

"Humph. Well, I was slapped and lost some buyers in the shouting."

Wil nodded. "Here. Take three pennies. It ought to be enough. Did he buy his meat?"

The butcher shook his head.

"Then I'll buy what we need. Just send the guard away."

The butcher agreed, and soon Wil's group was searching for the old man and his companions. "They would not have gone back through the main gate," muttered Helmut. "They're either hiding or out another side."

Wil agreed and looked about the town. "Helmut, go find the others and send them out the north gate. They're probably seeking cover along the riverbanks. Tell them to look for us there."

Chapter Twenty-five

CHANGES BY THE KISS

his place tempts me to return to my old ways like nothing else has yet done!" cried Wilda as Pieter told the butcher's story. It was past vespers, and the group had found one another in a stand of trees beyond the town's walls. They now sat quietly by a small fire in the welcome coolness of evening.

The sky was still blue, though darkening a little with the passing of the day. No one had come to bother them, and it seemed all was in order.

"We still have need of a few things before we leave on the morrow," said Wil. He looked pointedly at Pieter. "We were interrupted at the market." The group laughed softly.

"But for tonight we rest here. We've food enough and drink. Methinks the town has no interest in us now."

With enough daylight remaining to enjoy a brief walk, the wayfarers broke into small groups and scattered along the riverbanks to talk or sleep or cast the net for small fish. Katharina grew melancholy as she walked alone along the bank and watched the walls of the wicked town. Recalling the butcher's tale, she moaned, "Oh, dear children, what did they do to you?"

Seeing her roaming about the tall grass, Heinrich joined her and took her hand. "Are you well?"

Katharina leaned into him. "This world is so cruel,

Heinrich. Oh, I wish it could all be as Emma's garden once was."

The baker nodded sadly. He spotted a cluster of red poppies and walked away briefly to pick them. "Here, my Katharina. They are nearly as lovely as you."

My Katharina! she thought. *He said "my" Katharina.* The woman blushed and lifted the flowers to her nose.

"They're not so fragrant as a rose," Heinrich said.

She lowered her eyes shyly. "I've not held so wondrous a flower in all my days," she answered.

Benedetto's voice was heard chirping from the camp, and the pair turned to see him standing at the fork of the rivers' junction. He was waving for others to join him.

"Shall we see?" asked Heinrich.

Katharina nodded, and they walked briskly toward the group now encircling the minstrel and some object lying on the ground. "Look, see!" Benedetto was pointing to a flat stone bearing a weathered inscription. Tomas brushed some mud away and spat on it to make the etched words easier for Pieter to read. As the old man squinted, Frieda and Wil read it in unison.

Wo Werra und Fulda küssen, Sie Ihren Namen hüssen mussen.
Und hier erstehd durch diessen Küss—der Weser Flüss.

Where the Werra and the Fulda kiss, their names they must renounce.
And here, through this kiss, arises the River Weser.

The group stared at the old inscription and then looked at the scene around them. Indeed, here two rivers lost themselves into another. Heinrich stared at the Fulda to his left. He remembered it as sluggish and weary, running quietly through softwood meadows. But here, at his feet, it became excited; here it now churned and rolled as it lost itself in the first currents of the Weser. He turned to his right and watched the Werra flowing to its own end. It had traveled a great distance as well, only to leave itself behind in this place and become something entirely new.

The baker walked away from the others, staring at the Weser running quickly northward. He reflected on his life and turned his eye toward the sky of early evening. Katharina joined him, and together they spoke of things past and things to come, of the converging of journeys, and of their quest for freedom. Heinrich took Katharina's hand in his. It felt warm and tender, soft yet strong. He faltered for words, but she smiled. In the quiet calm of her smile the man felt peace. As he faced her, the unfulfilled longings of so many wasted years overwhelmed him with a bittersweet sorrow.

"Katharina, I ... I should like you to be my wife."

Utterly surprised, the woman trembled and blushed. Her world had been one of beatings and neglect, of sadness and mute suffering. She had not dared hope for better except during those times when she had wandered by the Laubusbach, so very alone. Still stunned by the man's words, she answered slowly and happily. "My dear Heinrich, it would be my honor to serve you as your wife." The woman began to cry, and the baker pulled her to his chest.

"Here in this place?" he asked.

Katharina nodded.

Heinrich stretched a grateful hand to heaven with a shout of joy. At the sound, his fellows looked his way. "Come! Come all!" he cried. "Pieter, come quickly!"

The curious group hurried to join the beaming couple, and as they drew near, Heinrich reached out to Wil. "Lad, I am to marry, now, in this place."

Wil was startled. He nodded bravely, but he wasn't so sure. He felt an odd sense of anger rise within, an anger he had not felt for these many weeks past. He turned as Frieda and Maria rejoiced, congratulating the happy pair. In moments, the couple was swarmed by their excited band of fellows, and Pieter tried a little dance.

"Pieter, will you bless us in this?" asked Heinrich.

"Indeed. It is lawful and right. It is my honor."

The baker noticed Wil's reluctance, and he took the lad aside. "Son, is something weighing on you?"

The young man looked at his feet. It was a hard moment

for him. He had not forgiven his father fully; he did not know if he would ever be able to do that. But he loved him and had come to respect him. Remembering his father charging across the field to defend him had exposed the heart of the man to him as no mere words could convey. Hearing his confessions had moved him yet more.

Wil took a deep breath as Frieda came to his side. "I wish you happiness, Father, but ... but ..."

"Say it, Wil," urged Frieda.

The young man set his jaw. "It seems wrong that you left Mother alone for all those years, and now she lies in her grave, while you are here, alive and happy. It does not feel right to me ... so this is not easy."

Heinrich nodded. He looked at Katharina, then at the others. He stared into the green trees across the waters before answering. "*Ja*, I ... I feel the weight of that as well."

"What would you have him do, Wil?" asked Frieda.

A long silence followed as others gathered close. Wil struggled with himself until he answered in a resolute yet kind tone. He looked squarely into his father's face. "I would have him live life free from any pride of his own goodness ... yet also free from the shame of all sins confessed." He looked to Pieter, and the old priest smiled approvingly. The young man had learned much on his journey, and his teacher's heart was warmed. Wil turned to his father again. "It is what I would have for myself as well."

Astonished, Heinrich stared at his son and marveled. He was inspired by the lad's unexpected wisdom and compelled by the selfless virtue of his character. The baker bowed his head and humbly thanked his son.

Over the next half hour, all hands busily prepared for the surprise wedding. Maria and Wilda raced about the riverbanks, picking flowers, and they soon adorned the bride-to-be with a wonderful ringlet for her head. Frieda braided the woman's hair and brushed her gown clean and smooth. The three then continued to fuss over the blushing Katharina with the spirit of care uniquely granted to their gender. Soon the woman was ready.

"Oh!" Maria clapped in delight. "You are beautiful."

Katharina lowered her face in the twilight. The first star of the night appeared in the east, and Maria pointed to it. "Luck!" she cried. "Katharina, make a wish!"

The woman looked at the star and smiled as she remembered the Christmas star of so many years before. She took Maria's hand in one of hers, then Frieda's in the other. Together they followed Wilda to meet Pieter, who was now standing at the three rivers.

The groom had picked the brush and twigs from his leggings and adjusted his belt. He laid his sword atop his satchel and had Otto wrap his sleeve tight to the stump of his left arm. He wiped his boots clean, then ran his fingers through his beard and hair. He adjusted his patch and chuckled. "Well, Benedetto, I'm not the handsome knight of your ballads, am I?"

The minstrel shook his head. "*Non, signore.*"

Alwin and the lads all roared. "No, indeed! The poor bride is getting a man with a few missing parts!"

"Are we ready?" asked Pieter.

The company quickly formed a ring around the bride, the groom, and the priest. Pieter raised his hands over the couple and prayed. He then asked Frieda to recite 1 Corinthians 13—in German—and she did so, much to the delight of all.

Heinrich listened to the words of the Holy Scripture and smiled warmly. *Love bears all things, hopes for all things, endures all things....* He looked into Katharina's face, one aged a little, but yet beautiful to the man. She was gentle and soft, wise and kind. She had become well seasoned by life and had remained strong and humble. *I do not deserve this good moment,* he thought. A tear formed beneath his eye, and as Frieda finished, it ran down his cheek and disappeared into his beard.

Katharina beamed. She looked at the thick-chested man before her and was filled with joy. The baker had aged as well. His rebellious, shoulder-length hair gave him the look of a lion, but she knew his heart was soft as warm butter. She was proud of his newfound defiance, drawn by his humility, and secured by his courage.

The couple exchanged simple vows—Heinrich promising love and protection; Katharina, obedience and respect. Pieter then cried happily to the heavens, "Lord, Your hand of mercy be upon them, Your goodness rain upon them, and give them peace. Amen." He removed his beloved Irish cross from within his robe and kissed it fondly. "It is rough because our Lord suffered on His." He then lifted it over his head and presented it to the bride. "Dear woman, I give this to you with my blessings for you both." With that Pieter hung the necklace over Katharina's neck and prayed over the two of them again.

Happily, Benedetto strummed his lute. "Now, dear Katharina, I am inspired by such a love as yours and Heinrich's and must sing for you a song, which I am sure conveys his true thoughts of you."

Come winter and summer,
Come springtime and fall.
I'll stand by you always
And love you in all.

Come seasons of pleasure,
Come seasons of pain.
I'll love you for always,
In sunshine or rain.

Come kiss me and hold me,
Come love me and more.
I'll be with you always,
Be we rich or poor.

Katharina wiped her eyes as the baker colored with embarrassment. He smiled and reached a foot forward. He tread lightly—even tenderly—upon the woman's foot to claim her as his, then reached for her. Katharina's green eyes glistened softly in the failing light, moistened by tears of joy, and she fell into her husband's embrace with a happy cry.

❧

The bride and groom went their way to spend tender time

with one another apart from their fellows. The camp was soon quiet, and Benedetto sang softly under the stars.

> Find me a treasure that's only for me,
> That tells to the world what I want to be.
> Not rubies nor emeralds nor glory nor fame,
> But only the splendor of my destined name.

The minstrel then set his lute aside. "This place has something good about it. There, inside those walls is evil, but here I feel the good. Listen! Listen to the music of the water running by us. Can you not hear the rivers singing?"

Tomas grunted in disgust, but Maria answered, "I do, Benedetto. I do. They are telling us tales of their journey—"

"And hopes for the one that lies ahead," interrupted Frieda.

Pieter leaned forward and stoked the fire with a small stick. He was feeling more rested again. His eyes twinkled in the firelight, and he played with Solomon briefly. Benedetto strummed his lute.

> What thing is that which spins within the potter's careful
>   touch?
> I wonder if it has a special name,
> For goblets are not platters, nor cups be bowls or
>   such;
> The potter knows each one is not the same.
> He moulds, He shapes, He forms, He wipes, and
>   makes them on His wheel,
> And means for them to be His precious things.
> And with a name He claims their worth; their purpose
>   He reveals
> So we enjoy the blessings that they bring.

"Where did you learn that?" asked Pieter.

"Oh, I am not sure. But when we learned of these rivers' names changing, it came back to me. I think it was a rhyme some pilgrim must have taught me back in Fiesch."

The group quietly lounged by the small fire, whispering

about things past and things to be. A few were still anxious about the Templars, but most were enjoying the night sounds of August. Listening to the minstrel's song, however, gave Otto an idea. The lad stood and spoke. "Listen, all of you.

"Here these rivers change their names. They ... they are no longer what they were but have become something new. Methinks they are like us!"

A murmur circled the ring, and Frieda chimed, "*Ja!* Then we ought—"

"Aye! We should take new names too!" cried Otto.

The idea immediately inspired the pilgrims, and they discussed the idea loudly.

Pieter interrupted. "Brothers and sisters, a name is something to be treasured. In the Holy Scriptures, names were given with great purpose and forethought. A name has the power to tell much about you. Otto, are you still Otto of Weyer?"

"No!"

"Tomas ... is Tomas the Schwarz enough for you?"

"No!"

Pieter nodded. "Well then, Otto, you may have a good idea. Here in this place, you might help one another find a rightful name, one you can take with you to your new home. I can think of no better time."

With excitement it was agreed, and for the next hour they bandied about names both silly and serious. Another hour's conversation ensued and then another's. Long after Münden's bells of matins chimed, Otto finally stood. "I have decided."

The group fell silent.

"I am to be known as Otto Traveler. It is this journey that has changed me."

The group approved.

Tomas stood next. "I ... I should like to be known as Tomas *Retten* ... Thomas the Saved. I was once saved from a shearing shed, then from the dungeon at Dragonara ... and finally from the way of darkness." He looked at Pieter.

Helmut was content to keep his name as Helmut for the time being. "I'm not ready yet," he said.

"Nor I," said Wilda.

"And what of you, Benedetto?" asked Frieda with a knowing grin.

"*Si*, I have a new name." The man was blushing. "Maria gave it to me. I ... I hope I am worthy of it. I put it in my own tongue. I am to be called Benedetto *Cantore degli Angeli*."

The group stared. Maria clapped and said, "It means 'Singer of the Angels'!"

Now the circle cheered.

"A good name, Benedetto!" cried Tomas.

The beaming minstrel smiled and sat down.

Alwin stood. He had pondered the matter quietly. "I was once Alwin of Gunnar, then Alwin the oblate, then Brother Blasius, the Templar. I am content to remain as Alwin."

"Nay!" blurted Wil. "'Tis not enough. I think you should be Alwin Stoutheart."

The ring cheered and the knight grew embarrassed. "I ... I think it a boastful name...."

"But true enough!" cried Pieter.

Alwin shook his head and then offered shyly, "Perhaps, Alwin *Volker* ... Alwin the protector of the folk?"

"Aye!" sounded a chorus of voices.

It was Friederich who took his turn next. He smiled mischievously. "I am to be Friederich Nimblefingers!"

"Friederich Nimblefingers?" roared the circle.

The fellow puffed his chest. "*Ja*." He wiggled his fingers in the firelight. "They've served us all well. 'Tis what I do best."

Pieter chuckled. "But, lad, your fingers are only a part of you!"

Friederich stiffened. "But what they do pleases me."

The priest nodded. "Well said, my boy, well said. Then Nimblefingers it is!"

Wil and Frieda had been whispering together for some time. At last, Wil took his turn. The group fell silent and waited as the young man stood. "I am unsure of all I have become or all that I may be. So I am content to be known as Wilhelm *Freimann* ... Wilhelm the freeman. My wife shall be known by Freimann as well. As a freeman I'll live, and as a freeman I'll die!"

The group roared its approval.

Maria stood. "And until I marry, I shall be Maria of Heinrich."

Frieda took her hand and squeezed it. "A good name, my dear sister. A good name indeed."

Now all faces turned toward the priest. He drew Solomon to his side and pulled himself up slowly on his staff. Standing on his badly bowed legs and stroking his beard, he looked about the circle. "So it has come to me. I think it too late for a change."

The group protested loudly.

"I have been Pieter the Broken for many years. You all know the story of m'cracked hips! It has been a good name, methinks, but I confess it is one that is not so true. I fear I have not been a broken man at all, but rather a willful one, stubbornly disposed toward a stiff neck.

"But perhaps I overstate the point. This have I learned: *who* we are is not how we look, from whence we've come, or what we have. We are not what we do, nor even what we think. Nay, in the end, who we are is what we love."

The company fell silent until Maria finally chirped, "Well, Papa Pieter, tell us what you love."

Pieter sighed. "Oh, my dear *Mädel*, what a question!" He sat and tossed some sticks into the fire. "I have loved many things. Some I should have loved and some I shouldn't. Sometimes I love God more than anything else, but I do confess those times are not as often as I'd like. It is good that His love for me does not depend on my love for Him!"

"So what's your name, then?" blurted Friederich impatiently.

Pieter smiled. "Well, I suppose I *should* call m'self 'Pieter, lover of God.'"

The circle wasn't sure it was such a good name. It was met with a volley of grumbles.

Pieter looked about the disappointed faces and shrugged. "Well, as I said, it is only true in part anyway."

"A name like that is too heavenly," grumbled Alwin. "Try again."

Pieter laughed. "I was not serious! Actually, we followers of the Christ are called by Him as his sons. *That* is our true selves! Hmm. As I think of it, perhaps we should all be naming ourselves 'Godson'!"

Alwin nodded. "More truth could not be told. If we could only grasp all that name means, we'd face the world differently."

The pilgrims murmured for a few moments until Wil stood up. "It seems you've found something here, Pieter. It ought to be as God's sons that we go forward, whether as Travelers or Rettens, Volkers, Angel Singers, Freimanns, or even Nimblefingers! I think we all should add 'Godson' to the middle of our names!"

Pieter scratched his head. "Well, if you think so. 'Tis a bit odd."

"And so are we!" roared Otto.

"There it is then," cried Tomas. I am Tomas Godson Retten."

"And I am Otto Godson Traveler!"

"Friederich Godson Nimblefingers."

Wil stood. "And we three shall do the same." He turned to Benedetto. "And you?"

The minstrel beamed. "In my tongue, my name will sound like magic! I am now to be Benedetto *Figli di Deo Cantore degli Angeli!*"

The company shouted its approval.

"Make a song of it!" cried Wilda.

"*Si, donna.* In time I surely will!"

Wil turned to Pieter. "And you?"

Pieter smiled broadly. "What a wondrous night. Aye, my beloved, yes, I do have a new name for m'self." He looked at the faces eagerly awaiting his announcement. "I see you all, and I see amongst you the faces of others. I see Karl and Georg, Gertrude, Anna, and the Jons. I see Heinz and Manfred … and oh, so many others. Dear ones, I loved them as I love you now." He wiped his eyes and petted Solomon for a quiet moment.

"Yes, I have a new name for myself." He lifted his face proudly. "I should like to pass to my eternal rest forever known as Pieter Godson *von Kinder*—Pieter, God's son, of the children."

~

At the bells of prime, Wil assembled his company. "We did not get all the provisions we needed. I want Nimblefingers, Traveler, and the Saved to take some silver into Münden and buy what we need." The company smiled.

Friederich, Otto, and Tomas eagerly stepped forward. They were handed some coins and given specific instructions as to what to purchase, then sent on their way with a warning. "Do not dally, and do not cause a scene. Have a care in that place," said Alwin.

The trio nodded solemnly and turned toward the town as the others ate a modest first meal of boiled mush and cheese. Frieda uncorked a clay bottle of red wine and pointed to Heinrich and Katharina. "They're coming," she exclaimed happily.

Heinrich and his bride ambled into the camp holding hands like young lovers. Midst a few jibes, they were given a portion of the meal along with a disclosure of the prior night's namings.

"Freimann?" exclaimed Heinrich. "Wil and Frieda Godson Freimann?" He thought for a moment and then shrugged. "Well, 'tis new to me, but I think I like it." He shook Wil's hand. "So, *Herr* Freimann, then."

Maria tugged on the baker's sleeve. "And I said I would be Maria of Heinrich."

A large lump filled the man's throat as he looked down at the girl's wide, hopeful eyes. He knelt in front of her and took her by the hand. He kissed her on the cheek. "Oh, dear daughter, you are indeed mine, and I shall love you always."

Maria jumped into his embrace. "I love you, too, Papa."

Katharina handed the wine to Heinrich. "So drink to your daughter's long life."

The baker tilted his head back and poured the warm drink into his throat. "Ah," he said, wiping his sleeve over his beard. "'Tis good!" He handed the bottle to Katharina, who took a more delicate drink, and she, in turn, passed it to the others, who prepared to toast the newlyweds. "*Gesundheit und Glück!*" shouted Helmut. "Health and happiness!"

When the applauding was done, Frieda asked, "So what of *your* name?"

Katharina turned toward her new husband. "Are you still Heinrich of Weyer?"

The baker looked surprised. "No, I … I suppose not." It was hard for him to say the words. Weyer had been his only true home; it was where he had always belonged. "Well, it seems I have become a baker without a bakery and a man without a home. Now I am not sure who I am!" He laughed awkwardly.

Katharina took his hand as the group told more of the prior night's discussions. The woman finally asked, "Then tell me, husband, what do you love?"

"You."

The company clapped.

"Thank you, sir," Katharina said as she curtsied. "Besides me, what do you love?"

"My children."

"And?"

"My freedom."

"And?"

Heinrich thought for a long moment. "God?"

Alwin interrupted. "You love truth, my friend. It is truth that has pursued you and set you free. It is truth that now guides those you love. It even hangs on your hip!"

Heinrich looked at his sword thoughtfully. "Aye. 'Tis so. It is truth that has shaped me."

"Then call yourself 'Heinrich Truthman,'" blurted Frieda.

"Nay, just Heinrich Godson Baker is good enough. A baker is what he is," chimed Helmut.

"No, a baker is what he *does*," answered Wil.

Pieter joined the conversation. "I remember when you were called simply 'Friend.'"

Heinrich nodded. "Aye, Pieter. It was a dark time for me." He fell quiet and turned his thoughts to Emma and the sunshine that lit her gardens. He tilted his head toward the pink light of the sky and the sun now rising over the mountains. He remembered how she pointed him always upward, beyond himself, and to the "eye of God."

"Truth is beyond me, and I have too oft failed it to claim it as my own, Frieda. And Wil, I've no bread to bake nor ovens to heat. Nay, lads, I fear these names won't do." He thought a moment longer, remembering Emma's words exactly. *The sun and the moon are like the eyes of truth; sunshine is hope, and moonlight is mercy.* The man looked at Katharina and then took her hand. "I would like to be called Heinrich Godson *Lieberlicht*... Heinrich, Lover of light."

Katharina smiled broadly. She took his hand. "'Tis wonderful, husband. And I, of course, do gladly take your name."

It was agreed, and the man repeated his new name over and over. He looked once more at the sun now in full orb above the horizon. He drew a deep breath into his lungs and looked at the white clouds floating in the blue sky overhead. "It is good to be free," he murmured. "So very good indeed."

The matter settled, all finished their meal, packed their bags, and waited quietly for the return of their comrades. Wil took his wife for a walk along the riverbank, where the pair paused to study a pool of water filled with slippery-looking black creatures. "Leeches!" exclaimed Frieda.

Wil stooped at the water's edge and stared into the curling mass of wiggling worms. He shuddered. "I'd not want to stumble into this at night!"

Alwin joined them. "The town makes a business of them. I heard in the market yesterday that they have leech pools all along the banks. They sell them all over the empire and beyond."

Wil tossed a pebble into the pool and watched the creatures writhe about. "They'd suck a man dry in an hour!"

"Indeed," added Pieter as he approached. "Or less. As a student, I once left a fevered patient lying in her bed with a full dozen attached to each arm. I went for a stout beer and forgot the poor wretch. *Ach, mein Gott,* when I came back, she was white as snow and barely breathing!"

"And?"

"Well, her fever was gone, and after a few days rest, she bought a fine silver brooch for my hat!"

The four cut their laughter short when they heard the cries. They whirled about to see Otto, Tomas, and Friederich dashing toward them. "We've trouble," muttered Alwin.

The boys charged into camp, panting. They shared their chilling news between great gulps of air. "Templars!" wheezed Otto. "Templars."

Friederich cried over Otto's voice, "Six knights on six mounts bearing six flags! They're searching for us!"

"How many Templars?" roared Alwin.

"Two, sir."

"The others?"

"One flag is from Runkel," said Tomas. "I know it well. The others I'm not so sure of."

"They've found us!" exclaimed Helmut. "And we're trapped here!"

"Everyone, listen to me," commanded Wil. "Gather everything. Tomas, where were they?"

"We saw them entering the south gate. They had dismounted and were talking to the guards."

"They'll be questioning the constable or his deputies," muttered Alwin. "That means we've a little time. No one would remember a one-armed man ... not with Heinrich's added sleeve ..."

The baker quickly unfurled the false sleeve.

"We'll need cross the Werra at the bridge, just over there," said Wil. "It's our only way. But we can't get to it without being spotted by guards on the wall."

"We're on the town's north side. The soldiers on these walls haven't learned of us yet," blurted Alwin.

"Then load Paulus and let's be off at once!" barked Wil. He pointed to this bag and that, and quickly studied the campsite for any satchels or provisions left behind. He secured his dagger, bow, and quiver, adjusted his side bag, and checked his wife. The young man then sent his company forward in six pairs at intervals behind Pieter, who led alone with Paulus and Solomon.

Pieter pulled his hood over his head, placed his staff confidently into the ground, and walked as upright as he could. Behind, the twelve waited, and when Pieter set his foot upon the wooden bridge, they began to make their way as well.

Alwin and Wilda followed next. Perspiring under his hood, the knight held Wilda's hand, and they passed casually beneath the tall, parapeted walls of Münden. They prayed fervently with each step, expecting at any moment to hear the dreaded shout of a sentry. "Do not run, Alwin," urged Wilda anxiously. She could feel the tightness in the man's grip, the tension in his legs. She licked her dry lips.

The knight did not answer. He squeezed the woman's hand all the more. Closer and closer the pair drew until their eyes fell upon the toll-taker standing by a gate on the far side of the bridge. "Oh, God above," moaned Alwin, "I don't want to stop for any man at all."

The pair arrived at the tollgate and waited for the guard to collect coins from those ahead. Alwin reached into his satchel and retrieved two pennies. "It should be enough," he whispered.

When the guard came to the couple, he paused. He ordered Alwin to throw back his hood. "Why d'ye wear it on a hot day as this?"

Alwin's mouth was parched, and he faltered. It was Wilda who spoke. "He's a pilgrim under vow. He's not to let the sun light his hair for three months, sir."

The guard grunted. "Humph. Two coins, then, and be on yer way."

Alwin dropped the silver into the man's hand and avoided the fellow's suspicious eyes. He turned his face toward the roadway ahead and hurried along, greatly relieved.

The others followed in turn and without incident. Soon they gathered together a half league north of Münden and made their way into a thicket off the side of the road. Friederich and Tomas were immediately sent back to spy the highway and the bridge as Wil ordered the rest of the company to sink deep into the heavy forest.

It was after the bells of sext when the spies returned. "We saw only one rider," panted Tomas. "No Templars were on the road, and none were by the bridge."

"One rider?"

"Aye. He dashed over the bridge and down the highway. In about an hour he came back."

"I thought as much," said Alwin. "I tell you, Wil, we must hurry away. I've said it before; they've an unearthly sense about them. I know ... I was one of them!"

As though on cue, the whole of the company suddenly looked up at the sound of seabirds crying overhead. "They're telling us to hurry," said Maria calmly. "Listen to them."

Indeed, the birds' shrieks were crisp and demanding. Wil was in no mood for either mystics or doubters. "Birds or not, we need to hurry away." With that, the thirteen scrambled to the roadway and rushed northward. Above, three seagulls swooped and soared ahead of the hurrying column, crying loudly. The day was hot and steamy. The Weser, flowing to the travelers' left, ran hard, but the trees to their right stood limp like exhausted giants parched by sun. Their leaves were curled and silvery, their branches drooping like weary arms. For once, the forest did not look inviting.

Chapter Twenty-six

THE BEES OF RENWICK

"Are we wise to keep on the highway, Wil?" quizzed Pieter from his perch atop Paulus.

The lad considered the question. "We have a lead on them. We can make better time on the road than in that brush."

Alwin wasn't so sure. "Wil, once they think we've left Münden, they'll charge down this road again. They'll know we eluded them, but they also know we're on foot and easy to catch."

"How long for them to search the town?" asked Otto. The boy was red faced and sweating profusely. He was thirsty like the others.

"It can't be known," answered Alwin. "If the toll-taker is questioned, he may speak of an old priest or a man with a patch. Perhaps they know of the donkey."

"Wil," called Tomas from the rear of the column, "if we go to the wood, they might pass us by. We'd see them and know they're ahead."

Frieda agreed. She looked at Wil without saying a word. The young man looked up to see the seabirds suddenly swing wildly to the east. He pressed his column forward against the protests of those now pointing to the birds. "I'll not be obeying three gulls!" he cried.

Alwin stopped. He fell to the ground and placed his ear to the road. "They're coming!" he shouted as he leapt to his feet. "We've only moments!"

With a shout, Wil sent his panicked company scrambling across the shoulder of the road and into the forest. They crashed through brush and over fallen logs, dragging the braying Paulus behind. Pieter dismounted and stumbled with the others until they were about a bowshot away from the road. They had barely settled when thundering hooves raced past.

Alwin closed his eyes and listened. His well-trained ears could count the horses. "Six," he said quietly. "Six horses ... four heavy chargers, two Arabians. It is the search."

"How did they find us?" whimpered Benedetto. "From Marburg to here!"

"They haven't caught us," blurted Otto.

"Not yet," grumbled Tomas.

"Not ever," snapped Wil. "If they chase us to Stedingerland, they'll still not have us."

"If they bring their swords into that place," said Heinrich ominously, "they'll not be going home."

The sounds of the horsemen faded quickly, and the company began moving again. They now needed to make their way through difficult underbrush and thickets of saplings. It was a difficult journey, made easier only by the occasional discovery of a welcome spring. It was agreed that they would consider buying passage on a boat sailing for Bremen. No one knew where one might be found, but it was a reasonable idea, one that brought the weary Pieter much hope.

They journeyed for the next day under a heavy gray sky that released a few brief showers that did little more than dampen the ground. The rain did bring a cool breeze, however, a harbinger of the coming autumn. Finally, they found themselves at the edge of a planted field and staring ahead at a small Benedictine monastery.

"What say you?" asked Wil.

Heinrich looked about. The road was quiet in the late evening. They had not seen the Templars for two days. "Do you think it is safe?"

Alwin nodded. "Pieter could use some good food and a good night's sleep."

The group stared ahead at the cloister about a furlong away. It was neat and inviting. They could see vegetable gardens and orchards, a swine yard and a flower garden by a small bake house. Their thoughts quickly turned to fresh bread and stew.

"Oh please, Wil," begged Frieda.

It was enough. The young man agreed reluctantly, and soon the column was marching across the field. They arrived at the low wall surrounding the cloister and were greeted by a monk dressed in his black robe and scapular. His sandals were dusty and his tonsured head uncovered. The brother bowed. "Thanks be to God," he said.

Pieter returned the same. "Brother, my fellows are in need of rest and some food. We've silver for your alms box."

"How many of you are there?"

"We are thirteen."

The monk nodded.

"Have you welcomed any Templars?" asked Alwin.

"No, my son. Not lately."

The monk beckoned the wayfarers onto the cloister grounds, where several of the brethren scurried about for food. Before long, the pilgrims were sitting alone in the refectory and enjoying a plentiful feast. The monastery was a fledgling community under the priorship of a larger monastery in Höxter to the north. Run by a deacon, it was a settlement of twenty devoted to their scriptorium.

Those serving were happy to share the bounty of their harvest with Wil's company, though they offered little conversation. And after their meal, they directed their guests to a small shed that served as a modest guesthouse. Here the pilgrims were invited to spend the night.

In the morning, the deacon presented Pieter with a generous gift of baked bread, salted pork, and a rather poor beer brewed in their new brewery. Midst smiles and humble bows, the pilgrims and the monks parted company, and a new day of travel was begun.

The pilgrims left the cloister and stood along the highway once again. A raven cried overhead and flapped its wings lazily as it flew in a wide circle. Frieda and Maria smiled with Pieter, and soon the column began its march. They passed only a few other travelers and were relieved to spend the morning without incident. By midafternoon, however, the seabirds had returned, agitated and loud. Crying from the branches of a river willow, they alternated flight paths leading directly away from the Weser and into the heavy forest to the east. Back and forth they flew, one after the other. Their cries became scolding, and they swooped low.

"Why won't you believe what you see?" scolded Frieda. "Listen to them! Watch them! We must follow."

Wil was hesitant.

Pieter finally commented from his seat atop Paulus, "Lad, could it hurt to move into the wood for a bit? We could use a rest, methinks."

Wil spat, then stopped. Alwin and Heinrich both nodded, and the young man yielded. "We'll go a short distance, then rest a bit. We'll soon see what's about."

The pilgrims turned away from the road and struggled up a steep slope into a forest of old trees. On they climbed as though drawn ever deeper into the shaded woodland. They finally spotted a clearing not far ahead. "There." Wil pointed. "Up there."

When they arrived, they found a pleasant glade of short grass and wildflowers atop the ridge. A little farther to the east lay a narrow creek bed that paralleled the highway. It was lined with such ancient trees as to block almost all the light from the forest floor. "See there, Wil?" Heinrich pointed. "It is clear of brush, and quiet. We've even fresh water in the stream. Why not follow it instead of the highway?"

Wil nodded. It seemed reasonable enough. The others agreed and took their rest marveling at the world sur-rounding them. The forest here was not like those near their villages. The woodsman's axe had never rung in this place ... not ever. Beautiful giant oaks stood proudly and boasted wide-spreading, muscular limbs. Like the skin of wise old men, their bark was etched with deep crevices. Maria spotted one with a large hole in its trunk. With a squeal she dashed away and climbed into the woody fortress. She peeked her face out from inside. "Beware!" she cried with a laugh. "I am the tree queen!"

To another side was a grove of white birch. Their bark was blotchy and shaggy, and their leaves cascaded from limbs weeping toward the earth. Nearby, huge beech trees rose to the heavens, their gray bark smooth and cool to the touch. To one side was a stand of spruce. To another, an endless host of pillared trunks stood like the straight-backed sentries of the realm of fairies.

The earth of the creek bed was soft and spongy, so when the march began again, it was easy on tired legs. For the next hours the wayfarers walked cheerfully along the easy path, enjoying the splendid sights of the woodland. Their ears were filled with the lively song of countless birds; the place was dreamlike and enchanting. It had become a very good day indeed.

The first night in the heavy forest was spent comfortably, though in the light mist of the next morning, Friederich swore that he heard spirits whispering nearby. The lad pressed the point with such passion that even Pieter began to wonder.

"We need to make our way to the highway again," said Heinrich. "We might soon find a boat sailing northward. We've coins enough for passage."

"According to the monks," Alwin said, "the Corvey cloister near Höxter ships its goods to Bremen. It's about a three-day journey. I say we go there and then find a vessel."

It was a plan that was quickly approved by all, and after a quick breakfast the company began their journey again. By late morning the air turned cooler, and breezes suddenly rustled the leaves. Friederich stopped.

"Wait!" he cried. "Listen."

The group paused and listened to the wind rattle the stale leaves of mid-August. "They're telling us of something, but I don't know what." The boy was anxious.

"Move on," groused Wil sarcastically. "They're telling us that rain is coming!"

For the next few hours, the column snaked its way

between virgin stands of timber that towered overhead and kept the darkening sky from view. By midafternoon, however, thunder clapped above the pilgrims' green shelter.

"Come on!" shouted Wil over the din. "You've all heard that before."

The earth trembled, and flashes of lightning sent bright bursts of light between the branches above. Oddly, it did not rain, and the unusual event gave everyone cause to wonder. The sky raged in such a way that it seemed the world might be coming to its end. But in the waning hours of the day, the strange storm passed, and the forest quickly brightened with slanted sunbeams that pierced the canopy like great golden lances.

Maria was walking beside Pieter and Paulus, stopping from time to time to play with Solomon. Singing to herself, she pranced toward small patches of tiny woodland flowers. She gathered a familiar bouquet and presented it to Tomas, whom she thought seemed melancholy. The lad thanked her and she danced away, gathering others as the day wore into evening.

The forest was growing dim, lit in dull streaks by the setting sun. The birds were settling in their branches, and the squirrels had stopped scampering about. Wil searched for a flat spot to spend the night but stopped when he heard Maria call to him.

"Wil, look."

The young man followed her finger as she pointed, and they all strained to see an oddly shaped object lit by a dusted shaft of waning light.

"Follow me," said Wil. He turned slightly and led the column to a pole standing a mere rod away from another one. Curious, the company gathered around them each as Pieter dismounted and walked slowly forward. The poles were positioned to form a gateway of sorts. They were the first of two rows that ran parallel to each other along a narrowing path that disappeared into the forest ahead.

Each pole was carved with symbols that Pieter quickly recognized. "Look, an altar with two cherubim—the Ark of the Covenant. It means a place where God is present. And on this one, a doorpost and lintel—God's protection in the Passover."

Intrigued, Pieter hurried ahead and studied more carvings. "There, see. Three nails—the symbol of Christ's suffering. And here, a human foot—the sign of humility and human servitude."

"How so?" asked Otto.

"We walk through the dust of the earth," answered Pieter. He led Wil's column deeper into a darkening wood. The farther they went, the narrower the path became until the travelers began to feel cramped by the trees now rising close on either side. Pieter's attention was fixed on the symbols. He strained to see them. "There is the ox, the sign of strength, patience, and sacrifice. There the Trinity's trefoil, and there, ha! The beehive of St. Chrysostom! He was an eloquent preacher in the early church. It is said that when he was born, a swarm of bees flew from his mouth!"

On one pole he found the double-blade axe of St. Cyprian; on another, the swastika; on another, the stork of the annunciation; on yet another, the winged lion. He finally came to a carving of his beloved Celtic cross. "I am astonished. Who ever made these knows much about the faith." He looked about at his fellows, who were growing more concerned about their whereabouts. They had walked into the bowels of a darkening wood where the trees now tilted over them. They felt as though they were being drawn into a haunting snare.

Solomon suddenly lifted his snout. He whined and blinked, then raised his nose yet higher.

"Someone is watching," whispered Maria.

Friederich nodded. "I know."

The company stood perfectly still. They peered into a forest now nearly blackened by the setting of the sun. Wil looked about anxiously. "We needs make a fire—now. Otto and Helmut, gather tinder. Friederich and Tomas, find some small logs. Alwin, find your flint."

"*Ja.*" The knight fumbled through his side bag, while others reached carefully to either margin of the path, feeling for kindling and broken sticks. In a few moments, a tiny flame was growing in a small pile of dead leaves and twigs.

A deep voice sounded from behind. "Who goes there?"

The company chilled. None spoke, and none moved save Solomon, who curled his lips and snarled. The pilgrims peered into the darkness.

"I say, who goes?" The voice was low and menacing and moving closer.

Alwin and Heinrich drew their swords, Wil his dagger. Maria and the women felt their way to the center of their comrades as Pieter held his dog close.

"We are armed," said Wil threateningly. "Show yourself."

Another voice roared from ahead. "Armed? If you could see, you'd laugh at yourselves."

The pilgrims strained to see into the inky curtain surrounding them. Their fire crackled a bit, casting a little yellow light at their feet.

"Now, put your swords away," ordered the first voice. A small, barely flickering torch rose from the ground, lifted by an unseen hand. It moved through the air as though it were floating on its own. It rocked toward the terrified pilgrims in long, sweeping arcs until it rose to expose the face of a man. The trembling company could barely see more than patches of the man's face, but judging by the height of the torch, they knew they were being confronted by a giant.

The second man now drew close with a flickering faggot of his own. He, too, appeared to be a giant. "Do as my brother says. Put your swords away."

With one giant in front and one in the rear, the trapped travelers had nowhere to escape except into the coal-black mysteries of the forest. They sheathed their swords, and Alwin said bravely, "We have put our weapons away, sirs. Now, can you help us? We are pilgrims."

"Ah, so it is you," came the strange answer.

The company murmured.

"Have you been following us?" asked Wil.

"No."

"Then how do you know us?"

"Our birds led you here. It seems castaways and pilgrims are want to follow them."

Maria gasped. "Then you are good?"

"Ha! Ha!" roared both giants. "We do not know the answer to that! But we mean you no harm. Come. You must follow us."

Wil and Heinrich whispered with Alwin, and, with some reluctance, they agreed that they should obey. No sooner had they taken their first steps, however, when other torches rose from some cover on either side of the path.

"All is well," roared one of the giants to his fellows. "We've a band of pilgrims."

"To the village, then," came the answer. It was an unseen man, seemingly giving orders to others. Heinrich thought his voice sounded odd.

The column marched between the giants cautiously, following a smooth, spongy trail for what seemed to be a great distance. The lines of torchbearers following them on either side were unnerving but had not threatened them.

Finally the giant in the fore halted. "Now y'must wait," he said. His voice was deep and resonant—as a giant's should be—but no longer fearsome. Maria thought it was almost kindly.

Poor Benedetto, however, shook uncontrollably. He wanted to burst out in tears, but Frieda wrapped her arm gently around him. "Don't worry. We are with you, Singer of the Angels!"

Ahead, another figure greeted the giant, and the company was again instructed to follow. They carefully descended into a short ravine and transversed it for another half hour until Solomon stopped and lifted his nose.

"Aye, hound," boomed the giant in the rear. "'Tis a village y'smell!"

Within moments, the column was ushered around a corner and, to the pilgrims' great surprise, into a welcoming hamlet glowing yellow in the firelight of several hearths. A lone man beckoned them to come to the village center, where a large bonfire was being stoked. To Wil's keen eye, it appeared that the man was a priest or monk. The giants nudged the company forward. As the bonfire rose, the pilgrims turned to face the giants, and they gasped.

"Welcome," one said as he bowed. Standing nearly twice the height of a tall man, he bent low and smiled. But more than that, he was also white as a ghost—as was the other, whom he introduced as his twin.

"Albinos," whispered Pieter. "I've ne'er seen one ... and here are two!"

The village cleric approached. "Welcome, pilgrims. Come, sit, eat, and drink. You are our guests tonight." He eyed Pieter and his staff, then Benedetto and his lute. The man grinned. "So, we've a priest and a balladeer! Wonderful! You two have much in common: you both make things up!" He laughed loudly.

Confused, Wil and his fellows obediently followed the young churchman to a group of benches set closer to the fire. As the pilgrims sat, he introduced himself. "The villagers call me Oswald—God's protection. I was once an anchorite in the wastelands of Estonia but am now called to serve those in need. Actually, I am really Friar Oswald, 'friar' being the new name for we monks who mingle with the world that needs us. I have been led by God to serve the good folk of this village where no other priest will come."

"Where are we?" asked Wil.

"Ah, forgive my lack of courtesy." He raised his arms. "Welcome, travelers, to Renwick. It means 'where the ravens dwell.'"

The pilgrims shifted uneasily and looked up into the darkness of the trees. Wilda leaned close to Alwin and shuddered.

Oswald sensed the concern. "Brothers and sisters, do you fear the ravens? And why not? Some say they blind sinners and carry the souls of the damned to hell. They are accused of being harbingers of evil and destined to feed on the carrion of Armageddon. They are despised, unwanted, feared by the ignorant, who send their pretty falcons to chase them from the sky.

"They gather here in our trees, and they care for us. We

know who they really are; we understand them to be our reminders of divine care in places of solitude. They have fed saints in the wilderness, saints such as Paul the Hermit and even Benedict. Yes, they are unclean, as are we all, yet God used them to feed Elijah by the brook of Cherith. Yes, they are often despised, as are we, but they are well cared for. 'Consider the ravens, for they neither sow nor reap, which have neither storehouse nor barn; and God feeds them.'

"So, my new friends, fear the ravens if you wish, but you may soon learn that they are grateful, affectionate, hopeful, and brave—not unlike you, methinks." He smiled.

Pieter studied the friar as he spoke. About thirty, he thought. Unusually wise. The man wore a slightly tattered gray robe and sandals. His head was shaven in the tonsure; his face was full and kindly, enlivened by bright brown eyes shining beneath thick, arching brows.

Numbers of figures began to drift from the shadows, and the pilgrims shuffled closer to one another. "Have no fear, any of you," Oswald said as he smiled. "These are your brothers and sisters in the Lord. Some we have found; others have come to us by following our birds."

"Your birds led them?" asked Frieda.

"*Ja*, sister. Our ravens bring those that are close by, but we've other birds that venture farther. We've a few small flocks of gulls, some free falcons, a few hawks, and one eagle. The seabirds seem to prefer flying in groups of three, the others in pairs or alone. They cover great distances, and whenever they come home crying loudly, it seems someone is always following!"

"They are of God then?" Friederich asked open mouthed.

"I believe it to be so. But some say it is simply that those in grave need search the sky for signs like mad fools, and when they see our birds, they follow."

Wil eyed the villagers slowly moving closer to their fire. He grew wary.

"Now," Friar Oswald continued, "you must meet my friends." The man wrapped an arm around the first young man who came near. Like the others he was shy, but when asked by Oswald, he withdrew his hood. The pilgrims shifted on their feet.

"You must see past what you see, my dear guests. Look past the deformities and into the man's eyes. See the warmth of a gentle heart."

Maria walked to the young man and took his hand in hers. She looked up and smiled. Indeed, the poor wretch was badly disfigured. His face was extraordinarily broad and his eyes spread unnaturally. His nose was flat and turned upward, stretching his nostrils wide. His jaw was recessed and his ears misshapen. His shoulders were severely uneven. When he spoke, however, his voice was clear and kindly.

"Good Sabbath evening, little maiden," he said softly.

"And to you, good sir," answered Maria with a slight curtsy.

Oswald smiled and motioned for the others. Emboldened by the little girl's kindness, they emerged from the shadows. They removed their hoods and stood before their guests, exposed for what they were. In various degrees, many were disfigured like the young man. They included a nervous huddle of dwarves, two hunchbacks, several suffering microcephaly, one called Spider-legs, two ferals, and others. A woman approached with a gift of bread and handed it to Tomas. The lad backed away slightly. Her face was covered in bumps as were her arms. She stooped and smiled gently, then reached a handful of twisted fingers toward the lad's head and patted him lightly.

Conjoined twins made their way forward and presented Wil with a basket of mushrooms. "For you, young squire," they said in unison.

Wil gawked. They were connected at the hip yet walked in perfect step with one another.

More came from the shadows to bow and curtsy. A few began to dance around the guests, singing nonsense to the air. Oswald quickly silenced them and addressed the company.

"We have found one another, and together we have built a village. We have woodsmen and a tinker, a potter, a silversmith, a saddler, a cobbler, and more. We raise crops on land we were given by the monks in Corvey. We have a swine yard and raise sheep. We've much to boast. The villagers elsewhere call this place 'Abscheindorf'— village of discards! Can you imagine that? What fools! Discards? Indeed not! But now, my friends, come, follow me."

The pilgrims listened to all of this in amazement. They stared at the villagers uncomfortably and walked closely together as the friar led them deeper into the village. The misshapen bodies of the folk were eerie to see in the yellow glow of the fires. It was true that the villagers seemed friendly enough, but some of the pilgrims could not help but shudder whenever they drew too close. "Two score or more," mumbled Helmut. "It is like a night terror."

"Actually, young sir, we are three score and four; by morning perhaps three score and five. Our dyer's wife is to bear a child at any moment."

"These people are married?" challenged Otto.

"Indeed, my son. They love as we love, they touch, they laugh, they eat and drink. They are very much like you."

Finally the company arrived at a nicely built timber house. It was sturdy and well thatched. A low fire crackled in the hearth at the center of its long room, and straw was heaped about for bedding.

"Till the morning then," said Oswald.

Still dazed, Wil's company found their beds quietly. They said little but lay atop their straw wide eyed and anxious. It proved to be a long night for all of them except Maria.

Morning came with a happy cry from some young villager with gamboling eyes and a cleft palette. Seeing his smiling face in the first light of the new day gave the startled pilgrims pause, but they soon laughed with him as they followed him to the chapel for morning prayers.

The column walked briskly behind the cheerful lad, but none could avoid casting their eyes warily at the many blackbirds crowding the treetops above. The birds called to one another loudly, as if engaging in a morning's conversation. They leapt from branch to branch, sometimes fluttering briefly upward or down. They preened and fluffed their feathers, content to be as much a part of Renwick as the long line of wool-clad folk now funneling to church beneath them.

The chapel was a simple log building set in a small clearing just beyond the village edge. It was the pathway to it, however, that caught the attention of all. It was covered in a heavy blanket of pine needles, making it soft and spongy. It was about two rods wide, its margins marked by round, rope-wrapped beehives. In the early morning mist, the hives appeared to be vacant. Curious, Otto leaned his ear to one and quickly retreated.

"They're buzzing about inside!"

Their escort laughed. "Friends. They'd be our friends. Friar says they fly far for us. He says they find flowers in the meadows by the river and make honey for us."

Pieter marveled. The double row of hives extended the entire length of the path—perhaps forty paces—and were spaced about two rods apart from one another.

"I count twenty," he said slowly. His finger trembled as he counted them again. "Yes, yes, twenty. I'm sure of it."

Frieda took the priest's hand and let him lean on her as they walked forward. "*Ja*, Pieter. I count twenty as well. And look there! Other paths join the church from the right and the left. They, too, are lined with hives!" Indeed, the chapel was positioned in the very center of an intersection of paths that formed the shape of a cross.

As they neared the doorway, Friar Oswald greeted his guests. "Brother, you like our apiary?"

Pieter nodded. "'Tis a marvel."

"We sell honey far and wide. The river meadows are filled with flowers, and the glades in our forests have the same. To the east the mountains are cut by fertile valleys, and the bees swarm about those as well. But they are here for other reasons, too." He smiled. "Now please join us."

Friar Oswald walked through the small sanctuary, now filled to nearly overflowing with his beloved folk standing quietly before the simple altar. He read from the psalms, then a chapter from the Gospels. He turned to Pieter and invited the old man to pray. Pieter agreed and walked gingerly to the fore. A wave of giggles rolled through the folk, and the old man grinned. When he did so, his snaggletooth earned a few more chortles. *They think I'm the one who's strange!* Pieter was delighted.

He raised his arms over the congregation. Seeing these broken outcasts now on bended knee and happily lifting their faces toward heaven moved the old man. A sudden wave of emotion washed over him and he began to weep. Oh, what the world might learn from these! "Brothers and sisters!" He choked on his words. "Brothers and sisters, rejoice! Rejoice I say, for 'blessed are the poor in spirit; theirs is the kingdom of heaven. Blessed are the meek, for they shall possess the land. Blessed are they that mourn; blessed are they that hunger; blessed are the merciful and the clean of heart. Blessed are the peacemakers and those that suffer persecution for justice's sake, for theirs is the kingdom of heaven.' Amen."

The friar thanked Pieter with a bow, then continued the morning service. As it was Monday—the day of the week that the Church remembered the angels—Oswald proceeded to read passages from Genesis 32, from the first chapter of Luke, and Matthew 4. To the astonishment of his guests, he read in Latin and then translated into German.

"And," he added, "they are sent to care for us, to teach us." He read from Hebrews, the first chapter, fourteenth verse. "'Are they not all ministering spirits, sent forth to minister for them who shall be heirs of salvation?'" The congregation clapped like happy children. They liked Mondays best of all.

Friar Oswald read a few more Scripture passages and then served as their priest, taking the Mass on their behalf. Finally, he dismissed his flock from the chapel with an admonishment to "fill the day with honest work."

As the villagers scurried on their way, Oswald joined his guests. "You see, my new friends, these folk are not what others think them to be. They are earnest and honest; they serve one another selflessly. They work hard and without complaint. They are a community of brothers and sisters, drawn together in their common brokenness. From here, they serve a world that fears them—maybe even hates them. They are the church, dear pilgrims."

"And why are they so hated?" asked Otto.

Oswald smiled and looked carefully at the lad. "What is it you see when you look at them?"

Shamefaced, the boy looked downward.

Oswald laid a hand on Otto's shoulder. "What that world fails to admit, my son, is that these poor creatures are like them, only inside out. Consider the great halls of the lords. They are filled with handsome knights and fair ladies, men and women pleasing to the eye. Yet on the inside—where their hearts reside—they are bent and twisted, misshapen and even revolting to the eye, like my beloved here in Renwick. Look around you now, Otto, and see them as looking glasses into your own soul. It is a good remedy for pride." He smiled.

Oswald escorted the company out of the chapel and along the path. The group chattered quietly until the monk paused by a beehive. "Now, as for these hives. Father Pieter, you are a man of many years. Tell me, sir, what better picture of what the church should be could nature possibly offer?"

Pieter smiled and leaned heavily on his staff. "None better than these, brother."

Oswald nodded. "Indeed. None better at all. See the little bees, how they rise from their beds to fly about the world, partaking of its beauty while serving it well. It is these buzzing creatures that pass the seed of life from bloom to bloom; they fill the orchards with fruit. They spend their days sprinkled amongst the color of God's creation; they draw from the very essence of beauty. From it they make the honey that nourishes both others and themselves with the sweet taste of God's goodness.

"Watch them. They toil without complaint, each knowing his task and serving the other. They fly and return, only to fly out again. They harvest happily and sleep well. They work together for the benefit of all, and they do so without malice, greed, or pride.

"This is why we placed their hives here, along what we call our *Via Crucis*, the Way of the Cross."

The group watched the bees fly from their hives, lightly lifting to the air as others landed heavily, their legs covered with a bounty of pollen. These climbed awkwardly into the small openings leading to their city within and, in a short time, would spring into the air once more.

Oswald led the pilgrims to his own simple hut. It was a timber cottage with a well-thatched roof. He ducked into his doorway and returned in a moment with a clay bowl in which sat a dripping chunk of honeycomb. He smiled at the faces staring hopefully at the bowl. "Ha, ha! Yes, it is for you, and I've more to share." He laughed. "But first, if you'll indulge me, I've one more thing to say." He lifted the honeycomb from the bowl and beckoned all to come close. "See here," he said as he pointed to the cells of the comb. "Study it and learn. *Res ipsa loquitur* ... the thing speaks for itself."

The pilgrims leaned close and stared blankly at the honeycomb. Most wished the friar would stop talking and just pass the honey to eat! Pieter, however, was intrigued. His eyes scanned the wax chambers.

Sensing their impatience, Oswald chuckled. "Forgive me. I oft speak too much! So here," he said as he passed the bowl to Maria. "Share this one and I'll get more inside." The friar retrieved several wax combs and a sharp knife. Soon the pilgrims were sucking sweet honey into mouths dripping with delight!

"I love this!" squealed Maria. Her chin was smeared with sticky honey as she licked her fingers clean. "Pieter, it's all over your beard!"

The company roared. Pieter's scraggly beard was matted with globs of honey, and flies were now swarming toward him. Laughing, a clubfooted little girl delivered a small bucket of water, and the old man quickly washed his beard clean.

When the group had settled once again, Friar Oswald begged their pardon. "Now, if you'll indulge these last thoughts." He took a badly gnawed honeycomb from Otto and held it up for all to see. "I hear how the scholars are now rushing to fix the matters of heaven and earth to the ideas of men's minds. I hear they seek knowledge as the way of truth."

Oswald pointed to the comb. "*Deus et natua non faciunt frusta* ... God and nature do not work together in vain. See here. See the cells of the bees." He pointed to the little hexagons. "The wax walls of these cells are like the words of man's knowledge. They grow in number with time, and as they do, our world enlarges.

"But the hive is far more than its cells; it is not merely walls of wax. It is in the emptiness of the waiting cell where the true wonder lies. It is the airy place that will soon fill with sweetness that will nourish many.

"Even so, truth is not confined to things known. Rather, it also dwells in the spaces between the words, in the silence of the cells ... in the mystery.

"To be sure, as the worker bees enlarge the hive, they add more wax around more air. Likewise, as we increase in knowledge, we, too, add more mystery.

"So, as you dwell among men of knowledge beware: they that deny the place of mystery will not taste the honey of the silent places."

Pieter took a deep breath and closed his eyes. He reached forward and took hold of Friar Oswald's hand. "Truth never dies," he said slowly. "*Deo gratias.*"

"Now, enough of my preaching!" laughed the friar. "Please, rest here this day and the morrow if you wish. Mingle as you like and watch the work of our little hive."

The company thanked Oswald profusely for the honey and his hospitality, then gradually dispersed throughout Renwick. With each passing hour the pilgrims felt more at home than the one before. Maria quickly found a friend. A little girl had spotted her deformed arm during Mass and presented herself. "My name is Katerina," she said. She held out both her arms. They were both shortened to the elbow, like Maria's, and badly misshapen. "Papa called me a devil child. But I followed the birds here!" she cried joyfully. The two soon disappeared to play.

Pieter was too weak to walk about very much. He sought

his favorite chair—the wide trunk of an old tree. There he sat atop the soft forest floor and leaned back to rest with Solomon lying on his legs. Heinrich joined him, and the two men watched their comrades move about the village. The pair sat in quiet companionship, saying little more than necessary until Heinrich noticed the friar speaking with two panting dwarves. "Something's afoot, Pieter."

Oswald nodded to the men and then walked toward Pieter and the baker. "You need to stay until the morrow," he said.

"And why, brother?" asked Pieter.

"It seems you've been followed."

"You are certain?"

"Our sentries spotted a group of six riders approaching from the south. They were studying the trail like hunters following prey, and they were seen studying the sky."

Heinrich cursed. "How? How on earth do they find us?"

The friar smiled. "Our birds, sir. They are following the three birds."

Heinrich shook his head. "The birds? Why would they?"

"Well, perhaps they reckoned that you might be following them. I wouldn't know."

"Then they'll follow them here!"

"Not likely," smiled Oswald. "Not likely at all."

Wil had drawn near to listen. "Two giants and village dwarves cannot stop six knights!"

"No, young sir, probably not. Though the fright of seeing them could send an army the other way! I've seen that once already."

"That's your plan?"

"Oh no ... no, indeed not. I have no plan."

"Then—"

"The birds flew off at dawn. Three of them, to be exact. Seabirds that look very much like those you followed." He smiled. "They flew straight into the sun."

Frieda joined the group. "But ..."

Friar Oswald shrugged. "I don't know. Perhaps the gulls are following a fresh wind. If so, it is to your good fortune. We have spies watching the knights. Two have returned to report that the fools are galloping wildly to the east." He laughed. "We've others still spying on them. If they change course, we'll soon know."

Pieter took a deep breath. He was quickly learning to love this strange place. "So, Wil, my lad, have no care for it today. If the Templars abandon the birds, they'll either turn north and be far ahead of us, or they'll come back this way, in which case we'll have plenty of warning."

Wil looked about uneasily. He turned to his father, then to Oswald. "You've good sentries?"

"The best."

Frieda took his arm. "Wil, methinks we should stay the day and even the morrow."

Wil turned his eye to the village and spotted Benedetto playing his lute for a breathless group of children. He watched the happy fellow dancing and singing. "Look at our minstrel," muttered Wil, shaking his head. "Very well. Then on the morrow next we leave."

Chapter Twenty-seven

THE ANGELS SING

Heinrich and Pieter were relieved and Oswald as well.

"Good," the friar said. "I shall see to it that you are well fed as long as you remain with us. I ask only that you help as you can." He pointed to Benedetto. "God be praised. We've craftsmen and farmers, woodsmen and the like, but we've no music in our village. It is music that heals and restores; it is music that stirs the spirit. Music is the language of the heart, and we need it desperately! Look! Look how the children smile.

"Our children are not all odd, you know. I have married dwarves whose union has born children that tower over them. Our hunchback married an armless spinster, and they've three *kinder* who are sound." He smiled contentedly as he watched the folk milling about.

"Our village keeps growing. We've our own births, as I said, but others keep coming. Here we are free. We are free from evil men because we are unwanted, and we are left alone because our ugliness repulses them. We live here in our deep forest protected by the legends and myths that frighten others. Look about you. I could tell you stories of these poor souls that would turn your bellies sour. Yet here they belong, and here they serve the purposes for which they were born."

The friar invited the group to follow him about the village, where he pointed to the many workshops. "Ah, here is old Wilmot, our silversmith. His name means 'beloved heart,' and so he is. He is half mad and half sane, but his hands are deft at hammering fine shapes into silver cups or bracelets. He buys silver in Höxter from merchants coming out of Franconia, and he sells his wares in the market there. He makes a handsome profit but shares what he has as is needed.

"And there, Traugott—God's Truth—the harness maker." Oswald chuckled. "When he's not preaching my homilies to the deaf, he fashions all manner of saddlery. See, how his back tilts him to one side? His right hand almost touches the ground. Some say he was stood in hard wind as a baby! He buys excellent leather from the dealers out of Bremen and now has a contract with the knights of the archbishop!"

"And who carved your poles?" asked Pieter as he sat down on a barrel to receive a tankard of beer.

"Ah yes. That'd be Wendell. He's a wise old pilgrim from Hamburg. A bit angry, I must confess, what with his terrible past. But he is clever with his art and amazing with his chisels. His shop is just yonder."

The friar led his guests into Wendell's workshop. The man looked up from a small wooden desk. By the sight of him, most would think him mad as a one-armed juggler. Drool ran from the corner of his mouth, and he snorted and lurched.

"Hello," said Pieter warmly. "I wanted to meet the man who carved such amazing things on the poles."

Wendell put down his quill and stared at Pieter. "Aye?" The man's head ticked to one side.

Pieter nodded. "Aye, sir. It is wonderful work. You've a fine gift."

Wendell said nothing but turned his face back to his quill. He continued scratching a design onto a small piece of poor parchment. His hand was remarkably steady, and his eyes quickly fastened themselves to his work.

"He's been commissioned to make a seal for some farmers in the north. They've their own government of sorts, though I doubt for very long."

"The Stedingers?" blurted Heinrich.

Friar Oswald raised a brow. "You know of them?"

"Indeed! We are traveling to Stedingerland!"

"I see. Well, I've not been there, but I met one of their merchants on the Easter just past. Somehow he knew of Wendell's work and paid him handsomely for a design. Seems they're hiring several others as well, and they plan to pick one soon. They want a seal for themselves. I'm not sure it is a good idea, though. They've had troubles enough, and a seal will seem defiant. They've fought with the archbishop's armies over the years, and I hear that he is frustrated with them. Apparently they've made a rich land out of marshes, and now the bishop's knights lust for it."

Frieda looked over Wendell's shoulder. The man grunted and then showed the young woman his work. Frieda's artistic eye scanned the ink drawing. It was a circle in which was drawn Christ on the cross. Frieda thought the Christ figure looked unusual—it expressed an artistic liberty that could be subject to misinterpretation. She was about to speak when the friar called them to the next shop.

The pilgrims spent the rest of that day and the day following in the pleasurable company of the villagers. Heinrich spent several hours in the bakery, delighted to help the baker in kneading dough and paddling loaves into the ovens. Others went from hut to hut and shop to shop, some helping carry firewood, others weaving reeds for baskets, one scraping hides, and another carrying thatch to a roof.

The village herbalist—an ancient, bald-headed woman named Herta—had watched Pieter's feeble efforts about the footpaths. She presented him with a potion of hawthorn berries and asparagus.

"Yer heart fails ye," she said bluntly. A deaf woman, she spoke clearly though in an odd pitch. "Drink this, and take this pouch for yer journey." Pieter nodded and received the gift with a bow. The two smiled at one another like two old veterans of many battles.

Later, the guests were treated to a summer feast of woodland fare: venison, hare, mushrooms, and boiled greens. To this was added honey-laced bread, lentils and peas, bowls of early kraut, and turnips. Beer was not plentiful, though mead surely was, and the company was more than content to slake their thirst with the sweet taste of the honey drink. The night passed easily, and the next day was pleasant.

It was late on Wednesday evening when the village scouts returned to give their report to the friar. "They've followed the birds far to the east," said one of the dwarves as he removed his rucksack. "We saw them yesterday about noontime. They had just finished a rest in the valley by Schönhagen. Then we followed them southeast for several hours until the birds turned straight east again, toward the long ridge beyond Escherdorf. From there they came to the highway leading northeast. We stayed on the ridge and watched them hurry along that road until it was too dark to see. We waited this morning to see if they'd double back, but they never came … nor did the birds."

"Well done!" cried Oswald. "Now feed yourselves well and spend the morrow at rest!"

Wil extended his hand to grasp those of the scouts. "Many thanks to you," he said respectfully.

The four men nodded and then hurried away for a good meal and a song with Benedetto.

"We'll leave at prime," announced Wil.

His company nodded and soon made their way to their beds, save Benedetto, who spent some time walking about the village with Solomon. Renwick was pleasant by day and peaceful by night, and the moon set midst a few harmless snorts and snores of those resting in deep slumber. Then, as on countless predawn days gone before, the cocks crowed loudly just before the rising of the sun. At the sound, the village began to stir, and soon the summer hearth fires scattered about the footpaths glowed with fresh tinder. Sleepy housewives lugged kettles to the spits, and before long, water for morning mush bubbled and steamed.

Heinrich stepped into the gray dawn, yawning. Others slowly climbed from their beds. They had enjoyed three nights of good sleep under a sound roof. Stretching and belching, they assembled out-of-doors as the sun cast its first light into the woodland. They smelled the burning fires and walked toward their provisions, which were arranged near the tethered Paulus. They dug through their satchels and retrieved salted pork, some cheese, and a few flasks of mead.

Friar Oswald arrived with a small delegation of villagers. They presented the company with fresh-baked bread and a wealth of good wishes. The monk took Wil aside and gave him a strange bundle that was quickly placed deep within a basket on Paulus's flank. Gifts were then presented to the others. Traugott stepped forward and proudly presented Heinrich with a new eye patch. It was made of soft sheep-skin, kneaded and pounded so that it had the feel of fine velvet.

The baker held it in his hand and marveled. "I ... I have no words, sir."

Traugott beamed, then pointed to the design he had neatly embossed. "What you cannot see, God sees," he said.

Heinrich held his new patch out for the others. On it was etched the triangle of the Trinity surrounding an opened eye. "It is wonderful, Traugott. I thank you from my heart."

The leather worker turned to Maria. "And for you, dear sister." He held out a small headband, also of softened sheepskin. "Wear it over your golden hair, and in it you may put the many flowers you pick."

Maria squealed with delight and let the leaning man place his band over her head. She kissed him on the cheek and curtsied.

To the surprise of the rest, others stepped forward and presented more gifts. Katharina was given a colorful scarf from the weaver, Wilda a tin brooch, Alwin a silver clasp for his long hair. Frieda was presented with a draw-string pouch to be tied on her belt. Friederich and Otto were presented slings from two of the village boys, and Tomas was handed a dagger from the smith. The blade was crude but sharp.

"A freeman needs the tools to keep his freedom," the

smith said. He looked at the lad with a crooked smile that brought both admiration and pity to Tomas's heart.

Tomas received the gift from the man humbly. "I ... I thank you, good sir. The lords fear freemen with a good blade."

The smith nodded and Friar Oswald interrupted. "They are fools. *Quemadmoeum gladis nemeinum occidit, occidentis telum est.*"

Wil translated: "'A sword is never a killer; it is a tool in a killer's hand.' Well said, Friar." The young man smiled and drew his own dagger. He had no sooner done so when another stepped forward to present him with a fine deer-skin sheath.

"To keep it clean," the giver said. Wil bowed.

Delighted with their gifts, Wil and his fellows tore into their breakfast with vigor! All, that is, save the minstrel.

Benedetto stood apart from the others. Finally, Maria looked at him curiously. "Why are you not eating?"

The group stopped chewing and looked at the fellow.

"*Non, bambina,* I have something to say."

Wil rose, as did the others, and they formed a circle around their friend. The man rocked on his feet and pulled nervously on his pointy black beard. He fumbled for words for a few moments and then cast his eyes toward a cluster of dirty-faced children staring at him from one side. They smiled and waved. Benedetto looked at them kindly. *So many pitiful creatures,* he thought. *Oh, how I do love them.* Emboldened, he turned back to his comrades.

"Dear friends." He cleared his throat and prepared to deliver that which he had rehearsed through the night. "We have journeyed together through kingdoms and sorrows. I have sung to princes in castles and paupers along the wayside. In my mind I see those we have lost. I sing to Karl and Georg when I'm alone." A large lump suddenly filled his throat, and he paused. "*Si,* 'tis true. And to others as well."

He looked at Maria. "Dear sister, you and I sang with the angels in Arona."

Maria ran forward and hugged the little man. "I

remember, Benedetto. Your song is what kept me close in the fever."

The minstrel took her by the hand and kissed her lightly on the cheek. Now facing the others, he continued. "I have said little along the way. I am a timid man, some might say a coward. Yes, I believe sometimes I am, and I am not proud of that. I am neither keen of mind nor quick witted. I am not well suited for the world we know. No, I am what I am."

He looked directly at Pieter. "My old friend, you have taught me much."

Pieter leaned weakly on his staff. The priest's face was drawn and pale, and his legs trembled slightly. He had rested well these past days, but he was failing and he knew it—they all knew it. "As you have me," he answered faintly.

Benedetto took a deep breath. "Father Pieter said we are what we love." He pointed his finger at the huddle of village children inching closer. "There, my friends. There is what I love. In these past two days I have sung to them, and their hearts were joined to mine. See them. They are so pure, so forgiving. They are harmless and giving. I should like to serve them and this village.

"I am a minstrel," he added with a sudden ring of boldness. "And I am called to sing the songs of angels for the likes of these."

The village children and the pilgrims stared at the good fellow, speechless and waiting for more.

"Wil, dear Frieda, my sweet Maria ... all of you, God bless you as you claim your freedom in Stedingerland. I can feel the rightness in it. But as for me, here I shall remain."

The glad-hearted children of Renwick cried out for joy and rushed the man with outstretched arms. The pilgrims stood and gawked, shocked at the man's decision. Friar Oswald had been standing at some distance and, upon hearing the announcement, fell to his knees and rejoiced.

Benedetto was nearly swept away by the tide of homespun that now swallowed him in its midst. Happy cries and clapping hands drew yet others, and soon heads popped from workshops and barns. A stream of folk gathered and shared the news. In moments, they were shouting their thanks to the blushing fellow.

Pieter sat down, dumbstruck. "Oh, my little Benedetto! May God bless you always."

The others looked at one another and then at the happy scene. "It is what he wants," declared Alwin. "We needs give him our blessing."

The pilgrims agreed and soon joined the villagers in well-wishing. It was a merry time—a happy time for most, a bittersweet moment for some.

At last Friar Oswald lifted his hands and asked for silence. "*Mirabile dictu* ... I never cease to be amazed! Welcome, Benedetto!"

"His name is Benedetto Figli di Deo Cantore degli Angeli," cried Frieda. "He is Benedetto, son of God, singer of the angels."

The friar grinned from ear to ear. "What a name! What a wondrous name! And so he is, and so shall he be."

It was a summer's hour before the minstrel finally withdrew himself from the happy village folk to stand before his comrades one last time. As the villagers kept a respectful distance, Benedetto embraced his old friends one by one. He assured them each of his eternal affection, of his gratitude, and of his hopes for their safekeeping. He moved slowly from Tomas to Helmut, to Alwin, Wilda, Katharina, and to Otto. He held Heinrich tightly, then Frieda, Wil, and weeping Friederich. When he came to Maria, he fell to his knees, hugged her, and kissed her head. She handed him a small bouquet of hastily gathered flowers. They were tiny— like the two of them—and pure.

Benedetto held them to his nose and breathed deeply. He tucked them within his shirt and rose to face Pieter. The two fixed a gentle stare upon one another. They had been comrades along their difficult crusade of tears; together they had redeemed their suffering, and they now faced the time that both knew would surely come.

"Dear minstrel," whispered Pieter, "I shall not be long upon this earth. Know that my journey has been made lighter by your song and your lute. You have blessed those who have suffered at your side, and I have been proud to call you 'friend.'"

Benedetto could not speak. He had words that he wished to say, but he could not utter one. He wrapped his arms around the man—his blessed priest, his own wise monk—and held him close. "I ... I will see you in the clouds sometime. There we shall sing together for always."

Pieter laid his hands on the man's head and prayed for him quietly. "May God be with you, minstrel of heaven. And may His Spirit kindle great joy in your song. Delight in the Lord your God, my brother, and may His face smile upon you."

The column looked on sadly and then obeyed Wil's quiet commands to assemble. They had been resupplied generously by the village folk and were well fed and rested. They were ready. But Maria dashed toward Benedetto one last time.

"Sing for us, Benedetto. Sing for us before we leave you." Her voice was pleading, her cheeks stained with tears.

The minstrel nodded. He touched the little girl under her chin, then lifted his lute to his chest, and smiled weakly as his fellows encircled him. Benedetto strummed his strings and sang through a verse he had sung long ago.

Fare thee well, my dearest friends.
Fare thee well.
God's breezes gently drift you toward your farther
    shore.
Fare thee well, my good friends.
Fare thee well.
May God's blessings be upon you evermore.
Fare thee well....

He had barely finished, however, when Maria and then the others joined the song, repeating the verse again and again. They sang to their beloved minstrel and even to their new friends of Renwick, who were watching sadly from behind. Finally, awash in tears yet filled with hope, the brave choir was joined by Benedetto to finish their song as their hearts had always been—together.

இ

It was a somber group of pilgrims that departed Renwick. They said little to one another for most of that day and the next. On the evening of their second day, they emerged from the woodland to stare once again at the River Weser flowing calmly at their feet. The river was not very wide, but it looked deep and virile. The light of the setting sun slanted across it, giving the water a silky sheen that dappled in its currents and danced along its eddies.

Pieter stepped to the water's edge and planted his staff firmly at his side. He drew a deep breath and looked from south to north. He bent over slowly and cupped some water into his hand and let it run over the nape of his neck. *This is good*, he said to himself. *This river runs with purpose. It has served its calling well since the day its Maker etched its place with His finger.*

He turned and faced his flock. "This is your river of promise, dear ones. To its currents you have been led, and it will lead you to your destined end."

The company made its way to a small ferryboat rocking lightly some bowshot away. They climbed aboard the flat-bottomed craft and were rowed to the west bank of the river, where they walked quickly to the busy town of Höxter. Here they spent the night in an inn filled with quarrelsome travelers and left the next morning for the large monastery of Corvey built along the river a short distance downstream.

The imperial abbey of Corvey was a large community of Benedictines founded nearly four hundred years earlier. For centuries, its missionaries had received their blessings within the pastel blocks of its chapter house before being sent across all Christendom: to the Slavs in Prague, to the wintry desolation of Burka in Sweden, to the flat marshes of Schleswig, and beyond. The brethren here had thrived, benefiting greatly from the trade routes that fed Höxter from all directions.

Pieter dismounted Paulus carefully and stood beneath the twin towers of the cloister's church. Marveling at the size of the busy monastery, he leaned lightly against

Heinrich for support and waited as Wil solicited information from the porter. "It will be good to float on a flat deck
instead of bouncing on that beast!" said Pieter with a half
smile.

Heinrich chuckled. "Soon, old man, soon you'll be resting in the sun of Stedingerland."

"There," said Wil as he returned. He pointed beyond the
cloister walls. "Down the steps is the dock. The porter says
the boats leave at the bells of prime, sext, and vespers.
We've about two hours' wait."

"The fee?" asked Alwin.

"Four pennies each to Bremen."

The group shrugged. It seemed a small price to pay to
relieve their sore feet. So they soon found a place of lush
grass and deep shade to rest as the time passed. "How long
a journey from here?" asked Wilda.

"With stops, it should be seven days to Bremen," answered
Wil.

"Stops?" asked Tomas.

"Aye. They fear to sail by night."

"So you mean we have seven days before we have to walk
again?" exclaimed Friederich with a happy smile.

The group laughed and clapped. It was good news, and
for the next hour, a discussion ensued regarding the
plans for this final leg of their journey. After a heated
argument, it was agreed that, despite Helmut's protests,
they would escort him to his home before continuing their
own journey.

"But you'll be so close to Stedingerland! You could hire a
ferry in Bremen and be there within the day."

Heinrich nodded. "*Ja*, lad. But we are not going to
abandon you until we see you home safely!" The others
agreed.

"But Pieter should not travel more than necessary,"
lamented Helmut. "Look at him. He is weary and growing
weaker each day. Leave me in Bremen, and just travel on
directly. I can find m'home easy enough."

Pieter shook his head. "God's final gift to me is to see that
all my remaining sheep have found their homes. My heart

is at peace for Benedetto, but to bid you farewell without the same would take my joy away."

Helmut fell quiet. Finally he nodded, and the matter was settled.

The August morning was warm. The sky was pale blue and dotted with puffy white clouds. Birds flew above, but to Frieda's great disappointment, no trio of seabirds could be seen.

"I don't see them either," whispered Maria.

"They're taking the Templars to Poland," said Katharina with a confident smile. The group nodded, albeit anxiously. Thoughts of the six knights had not been far from any of their minds.

Heinrich had finished an accounting of their money and now lay on his back with his head resting on his hand. He stared upward. Katharina joined him and snuggled by his side in the cool grass. "What are you thinking of, husband?" she asked.

The man did not answer at first. He just stared vacantly at the sky. "I am thinking of Karl," he finally said sadly. "I think of him always, but especially when the world is still. I miss him more than I can say."

The woman rested her hand lightly on his heart and said nothing. Together, the couple lay quietly for the next hour, each lost in thoughts of times past. For Katharina the time was one of soul rest. Her spirit was refreshed by the silence and in the gentle rise and fall of her husband's chest.

Meanwhile, Frieda had found a comfortable seat between some shallow roots of a large tree some distance from the others. She was busy writing again, and, seeing her, Otto and Tomas finally insisted on an explanation.

"You've kept the secret long enough, Frieda," complained Otto.

The young woman put down her quill and blew lightly across the fresh ink. "I suppose I have," she answered. She pointed to the parchment. "I did not want others to know of this before, because I did not want any to be aware of my listening."

"What?" Tomas wrinkled his nose.

"I have been collecting what we have been learning for these many months from Pieter, Heinrich, Alwin, and others. They've shared great wisdom, and I thought it would be a good thing to write down what we've heard so that my children and my children's children might learn from this hard journey."

Tomas looked over her shoulder. "You've written much."

Frieda nodded. "I'll need to put it to better order another time."

"So you've chronicled the journey?"

"Well, not so much the events as the truths."

Otto stared thoughtfully at the parchment. "You've done a good thing. Sometime when we're old, you must read it to me."

Frieda smiled. "Indeed, I surely shall."

It was within a half hour of the bells of sext when Wil assembled his company. He led them quickly to the docks and paid their passage on a stout riverboat. The shallow-keeled craft was built like most of the others seen gliding on the Weser. It was about seven rods in length and made of long, overlapping oak planks fastened together with iron nails. One short mast carried a square sail, and four long oars lay waiting for the crew. Caulked with animal hair, it leaked a little—a condition that gave considerable pause to Maria and Friederich as they stepped gingerly aboard. There were a few squares of decking to sit on, but the rest of the interior was simply heavy spruce beams and knees suspended over a ribbed floor. The boat was loaded with crates and barrels filled with sundry wares: grain, leather goods, salt, ells of cloth, and kegs of beer.

Soon four oarsmen and a captain—of sorts—were grunting and pushing their way around the awkwardly placed passengers and their braying donkey. The river's current was not swift, but it was adequate to carry the company northward at a reasonable speed. "Twelve leagues a day," boasted the captain to his passengers as he directed his oarsmen.

One of the river men shook his head and looked at Frieda.

"Nay," he whispered. "More like eight. If we've wind or hard rains, maybe more, but in August, never ten."

The Weser was full of sweeping bends, and its waters felt cool and refreshing to the touch. For the next hours, the pilgrims floated happily through a flattening landscape. Rolling green mountains fell away as broad meadows and fields of grain appeared on either side. The sky seemed larger than ever, and the evening sun cast a glorious pink light across the rippled water. By the end of the first day, Wil's company found themselves enjoying the ride and were sorry to disembark for the night.

The following day was as pleasant as the first. They sailed around a knobby hill where a small castle overlooked a wide valley. From here the boat rode the current to the town of Hameln, where they again stopped to spend the night in an inn at the market square near the sandstone church of St. Boniface.

Pieter reveled in the river journey. Lying on a soft bale of wool, the man felt the sunshine on his face as he listened to the happy chatter of his flock. Arriving in Hameln, he walked slowly through its streets until he found the church, which he entered to pray. He had asked none to follow; he wanted to pray alone. When he emerged from the sanctuary, he felt as though he had been touched by the Spirit of God. To the eyes of his waiting companions, his face had become radiant and his beard shone luminescent in the moonlight. The priest leaned forward to lay a kind hand on Solomon. He said nothing, but an air of peace had so settled upon the man that all felt comforted to be in his presence.

The dawn brought a brisk walk to the dock, where the wayfarers loaded themselves again into the boat. The oarsmen pulled them into the currents that turned the bow slowly northward. The journey continued past meadows of milk cows and pastures of sheep, past sturdy villages, and then to Minden and its Cistercian monastery, where they spent the night.

The next day they sailed to Verden. Along the way, Pieter summoned his strength to offer a song or two. Crowing with what strength he had, he earned a few good-natured barbs from the oarsmen. The man was weak and even feeble, but his spirit soared as he lifted his quaking voice under the summer sun. Laughing, his companions joined in, and soon they were singing tavern songs and the ballads of Benedetto.

The land near Verden was flat and open, making the horizon appear as a long arc in the hazy distance. The town was known for Charlemagne's slaughter of some five thousand Saxons near its center. Now it was welcoming and busy, and, at Pieter's request, the company found the redbrick cathedral towering high above the Weser's banks. The company entered the cathedral's western portal, descended its three stone steps, and stood in the rear of the massive basilica to gape.

The sanctuary was stunning to the peasants. Tall, massive columns of stone rose magnificently to an arched ceiling high above.

"I feel the presence of God here," said Wilda softly. She slowly walked toward the altar. Alwin followed and took her hand. She turned to face him and her belly fluttered. To her, he looked like the prince she had always dreamed of. Strong, broad shouldered, handsome, and kind, the man was all she had ever wanted. He stood proud but not haughty. His blond hair hung defiantly at his shoulders, yet he had a servant's heart. A long-sword hung at his side, but he was gentle. His boots and leggings were dusty, his green robe well worn. The man was seasoned and fit, truly the defender of the helpless and destitute. Alone with her knight, the woman leaned into his sure embrace.

"Oh, my dear Wilda," said Alwin softly, "I do love you so."

"Aye, as I do you," she answered. "You are the hero of my dreams, dear knight, and I could love no other as I love you."

Wilda waited breathlessly.

Then there, before the altar in Verden's glorious cathedral, Alwin kissed her on the cheek and surprised her as he knelt to one knee. "Woman, I pledge thee this: I desire to marry no other, and it is you I would take as my beloved wife, to cherish and defend always."

His voice was strong and sure, and as he stood to embrace her, his grip was firm and comforting. With a happy whimper, Wilda wrapped her arms around the man's waist and lifted her face. "My dear Alwin, *ja,* truly, I shall be your wife." With that, the two lovers kissed—and the choirs of heaven sang!

Chapter Twenty-eight

CROWNS ALONG THE SHORES OF PROMISE

orning came, and the travelers were once again aboard their sturdy craft. The air was damp and made the river smell all the more as rivers do: a hint of fish and standing mud. The Weser was more sluggish in this place and somewhat narrow. The captain grumbled about the dark silt banks that rose unseen from the riverbed and caused crafts such as his to ground. With a sharp eye, he tested the depths with a large pole.

Seabirds now abounded above, and many villages dotted the countryside beyond the Weser's grassy banks. Rain showers began around noontime and continued for all that day. Despite their woolens, the pilgrims were soon soaked, and Pieter was badly chilled.

The night was spent before an ample hearth in a riverside inn, but by morning it was clear to all that Pieter was failing rapidly. The poor man awoke gray and ashen. He trembled and staggered from the inn in the sure hands of Alwin and Wil and was carried to the boat, where he was laid limply atop his bale and covered with a heavy blanket.

"He is in a grave way," whispered Frieda. "His eyes betray him; he shall leave us soon ... very soon." Tears formed in her eyes. She looked at the man and at Maria, who was now lying close to him. "She is desperate for him," Frieda added. "She loves him so."

Wil could not speak. A large lump swelled within his throat, and he looked away.

࿇

The walls of Bremen finally loomed large and menacing over the riverboat's bow. "There," announced the captain. "The Rome of the northland!"

Indeed, Bremen was a powerful, wealthy diocesan city, endowed with its privileges from Charlemagne himself nearly four hundred years prior. From here the archbishop ruled his vast see, which encompassed the northern reaches of the German empire, the Baltic region, and Scandinavia.

Wil studied the scene alongside Helmut. "No bridge to join the two banks?"

Helmut shook his head. "My father says they've been planning one for years."

The pair stared forward at the busy docks of the Weser's east bank.

"Do they sail to the sea from here?" asked Wil.

"Not easily," the captain answered. "The bishop is demanding better ways to get by the silt beds. Some flat-bottomed barges get through at high tide and trade with the ports at seaside.

"Now, get your people ready. We'll dock soon," barked the captain.

In about an hour, the riverboat's oarsmen skillfully navigated their craft alongside a badly warped fishing boat and tossed their ropes to the dock men. With a few heaves and a gentle bump, the vessel came to rest in Bremen on Wednesday, the twenty-first day of August.

The pilgrims immediately disembarked into the city's streets now beginning to glow in lantern light. Bremen's wealth had attracted the best and the worst elements of the German empire as well as all manner of men from beyond. Like all cities, its air reeked of manure and human waste and was choked with the smoke of thousands of hearths burning within its cramped neighborhoods.

Alwin was glad to hide under the cover of eventide. He lifted his hood over his head and watched a small troop of the archbishop's army march past. The men were armed with long halberds and swords. One carried a crossbow—an instrument supposedly illegal for use against Christians. They wore heavily padded leather vests and pot helmets over chain mail hoods.

"Ready for combat," Alwin whispered to Heinrich. "The place feels tense."

It was quickly agreed that the company would not spend the night in Bremen but rather in the relative safety of the countryside. They gathered themselves close together and positioned Pieter carefully atop Paulus. The man said nothing as they lashed his legs securely to the beast's back, but he managed to chuckle at the antics of a bumbling beggar nearby. Heinrich took a position to one side, Tomas to the other, and the two steadied the failing man. Maria was placed with Frieda and the other women in front of Paulus and behind Wil and Helmut. Otto, Friederich, and Alwin took their places in the rear. With all in order, Wil led them quickly through the city's streets and out its eastern gate.

Once beyond the walls, Helmut directed Wil northeastward along a flat, quiet roadway for about three leagues. Then, under an endless canopy of dazzling stars, the company made camp. The wayfarers were comfortable but were troubled on several counts. Foremost to all was Pieter. The man had been lain atop a soft bed of grass, and his head was now lying across Maria's little lap. The girl stroked his hair and hummed lightly. They had given him more of the remedy of Renwick's herbalist, and it had seemed to calm him. He had slept well for most of the river journey, and the past few days had been spent quietly, almost dreamily.

"Would that he might cross with us to Stedingerland," Heinrich said worriedly. *Stedingerland*, he thought. *What awaits us there? Will Cornelis welcome us, or will he fear my return? Will I put them in peril once again, or has enough time now passed?*

Melancholy hung heavily over the pilgrims, as did fear. They had seen no hint of the Templars since Renwick, but the reputation of these warrior-monks was such that the company remained uneasy. It would not have surprised most of them if the six riders had fallen upon them in their sleep. They looked about the growing darkness with unease. Sensing their nagging fears, Alwin spoke. "I see dread on your faces. I know you still fear the Templars, but I have prayed hard on the matter. Can you not feel the shield of an unseen hand about us?"

A few heads nodded.

"Indeed. We ought not let fear rule us. I believe with all my heart that the riders are long since gone away. I can feel us being drawn into a strong current of another's will. I truly doubt that six riders will be able to draw us away. It is the end of it; let it leave your minds." The company murmured, then an ease warmed them. Soon they drifted to their beds, where they closed their eyes in peace.

Early morning songbirds awakened the wayfarers, and Helmut and Wil conversed softly over a morning fare of bread and wine. "My father is from Wümme in the lands of Lord Ohrsbach. It's about one day's easy journey. As you can see, the land is flat here—flat like pan-bread."

Wil looked through the mist. The morning's light brought a very different landscape from what any of them had expected. Wide grasslands spread before them as well as the stubble of harvested fields. The soil was sandy, and the trees were a mixture of pines and hardwoods.

"Well, it ought to make a smooth ride for Pieter," Wil said.

The day passed without incident, and it was soon after the bells of vespers that the company rounded a bend and Helmut pointed gleefully. "There!" he cried. "My village!" Wil's column followed the happy lad as he dashed along a neat grid of streets and byways, past the village church, its bakery, a row of shops, some stables, and a fishpond. At last, they stopped.

Panting, Helmut smiled. "I am home." He turned to Wil and to his fellows with wet eyes. "I am home!" he cried. "God be praised! He has brought me home."

The lad sprinted away from his comrades to the door of his father's large redbrick house. He rapped loudly on the heavy oak, and in moments the door was opened by a servant who cried happily at the sight of the young man and quickly pulled him inside.

Wil led the company to the doorway, where they waited respectfully. They could hear Helmut's mother weeping joyfully and the booming voice of his father. Wil smiled at Frieda, and the whole group laughed as they heard Helmut's mother scold him for his tangled hair and unkempt garb.

Then, beaming, the happy lad burst from the doorway and cried for his fellows. Pieter was lifted from Paulus and helped into the hall, where they were all greeted with great enthusiasm. Helmut introduced his father as Horst Emilson von Billungsmarch. "I am a trader of whatever one might buy," he laughed. He extended his hand to each of the men and then bowed to the women. "My wife, Margot, and I owe you more than what this world might offer. You have brought back to us our only true treasure … our Helmut."

Servants were immediately ordered to carry Pieter to a soft bed. Others were sent outside to remove Paulus to the stable, and Solomon was invited to play about the house with the merchant's hounds.

"Now," announced Horst, "you all may remain here as long as you like. I will summon the surgeon and a priest for the old fellow."

Wil spoke for the others as he expressed his gratitude and insisted they would not remain very long. "Our friend, Father Pieter, will soon die. It is his wish that he would see us to our final home."

Horst lifted his finger. "Please, young sir, I should like to hear all about it at the table. You look hungry, and, I must confess, you smell bad."

The group giggled.

"Indeed," blurted Margot. "Look at you, Helmut!"

Horst ordered his cook to prepare a light supper, while he sent the company to the rear of the house where a bewildered washwoman had been ordered to draw water for eleven baths. After some griping and guffaws, the pilgrims faced the town's barber, who clipped and trimmed the guests with great skill. Now gathered along Horst's table, they gawked at one another in surprise. Heinrich and Alwin had kept their beards, but they had been shortened to look less "barbaric." Both the men's and the lads' hair was trimmed neatly, though left the length that a freeman's should be.

The women let the barber cut the ends of their hair and braid it. The wives and the betrothed Wilda were told that the coming fashion for them was to plait the hair, then pile it atop their heads. And so they did. Maria's hair was plaited neatly into two long braids and decorated with red silk ribbons. They hung neatly over her shoulders.

Now facing one another, the company marveled. "You look handsome, Heinrich!" Katharina said, laughing.

The man blushed. "You always were beautiful, wife, only now even more so."

Wil stared at his lovely young bride sitting on her wooden chair upright and proud. She looked suddenly very much like the daughter of nobility that she was. He smiled at her and his heart raced.

"Now," began Horst as he took his place at the table's head. He turned toward his son and laid a hand on his shoulder. "Now, God's blessing to my table, God's blessing to my guests. *Deo gratias!*" he cried. "You have brought my son back from the dead. God be with you always."

The diners lifted their goblets and toasted Horst, Margot, and Helmut loudly. When the hurrahs had ended, another voice drifted from the doorway. "*Omnia vincit amor!* Love conquers all!" It was Pieter.

Wil's company turned and welcomed their dear friend to the table. The pale priest leaned heavily on his staff as Solomon followed faithfully. The diners fell quiet, and a few began to sniffle. "Do not weep for me, my beloved. For another lost sheep has found his home. It is a night to rejoice."

He was escorted gently to a seat, where a bowl of stew was set before him. "Many thanks, m'lady." He lifted his face and stared at his fellows with a broad, though quaking, grin. "You look different! You look civilized!" He chuckled and shook his head. "Who could have imagined it? Now, all of you, please, eat and be merry. This old fool will sip a bit and return to his bed."

The rest of that evening was spent in long conversation. The pilgrims shared their stories of bravery and fear, of failure and victory—of shame and redemption. Horst and Margot sat speechlessly, alternating between tears and laughter, amazement and disbelief. They looked at their son proudly and at his fellows with respect. In sum it was a tale of adventure and mystery they would never forget.

⁊

Morning broke brightly over Wümme. It seemed to Maria that the birds were singing louder than usual and that the sky was quickly turning a wondrous shade of blue. She ran to Pieter's room and found the man sleeping with Solomon curled at his feet. His breathing was uneven, however, and he felt cool to her touch.

"Papa Pieter?" she said softly. Her throat was swollen and her chin quivered. "Papa?"

Pieter lay perfectly still.

"Papa?" A tone of desperation laced the word.

The man moved. His eyes fluttered open, and he turned his head weakly toward the child. "Ah, my angel," he whispered. "Am I now in heaven?"

Maria touched his cheek. Relieved, she shook her head. "No, Papa."

"But soon?" The man's tone was hopeful and oddly reassuring to the girl.

She nodded as tears began to drip along her smooth cheek. "I think so."

Pieter drew a long, quivering breath. He released it slowly. "My dear," he said, "forgive me for this final failure. That I am not able to do more ..."

Maria leaned against the old man, sobbing. "Oh, Papa," she whimpered, "it is not a failure. Have no shame in this. I will love you always."

Pieter closed his eyes and nodded. "And I you, child."

Frieda entered the room and saw Maria sprawled over the man's breast. With a start, she hurried to the side of the bed and laid her hand on Pieter's brow. *Cold,* she thought. *So cold.* She leaned close to his face and felt his breath slowly drifting by her skin. *Not much time.*

The company had hoped to press on that very day, but after they finished their generous morning's meal, dark clouds suddenly loomed in the east and thunder rumbled toward them. To take Pieter through heavy weather was unthinkable. So Friday passed with the company doing little other than waiting about Wümme for the storm that never came. "All gas, naught to pass," grumbled Alwin. "If it's not to rain, it ought not threaten!"

Horst had hired the surgeon to spend the whole day with Pieter, and he filled the alms box so that the priest might remain close by as well. The two hovered over the man's bed, probing and praying, applying compresses and laying on hands.

At the bells of prime on the next day, however, Pieter climbed from his bed and weakly grabbed hold of Wil's tunic. "Help me to the garden," he pleaded. The young man led his elder through the cool morning air to a flat rock in the center of a small vegetable patch. "Ah, many thanks, my son." He sucked a quivering breath through his nose. "Now, lad, I beg you, nay, I *implore* you. If there is any good in you, please set me loose from the cursed surgeon and his partner the priest. They are death's porters—one for the body, the other for the soul!" He shook his head. "By the saints, whether in tempest or by calm, I should very much like us to be on the roadway once again."

Wil smiled and nodded.

"Eh?"

"*Ja,* Pieter, so we shall."

Relieved, Pieter nodded and turned his eyes toward the wide horizon. In the purpled morning sky, the last star of the night could be seen falling in the west. "Good," he said in a whisper. "Now, look there." He pointed to the star. "We shall follow it, my son. See how it sinks into the horizon? *Ja,* lad, it is filling your new home with its light."

Wil smiled and looked at his friend sitting slump shouldered and frail beside him. He wrapped an arm around the feeble fellow. Fighting the lump filling his throat, he said tenderly, "I love you, Pieter. Thank you for all you've done for us. May ... may heaven give you rest." He sniffled and wiped his eyes. "I ... I do have one more thing to ask of you."

"Aye, lad?" Pieter brightened a little.

Wil stood and fought for the words. His chin quivered as he said, "Please ... please tell Karl I love him ... I miss him so—"

Pieter moaned faintly, pulled himself to his feet, only to fall forward into Wil's heaving chest. "Oh, my son. Aye, aye ... a thousand times aye."

The two faced one another, neither speaking, neither moving. And in that brief envelopment of master and student, that embrace of comrades, that enfolding of Christian brothers, they shared the warm juncture of past and future, if only for a fleeting time.

At last, Pieter reached for his staff and held it in his two hands. "Do you remember, Wil?"

"I do."

Pieter smiled and sat down once more. "Ah, good Georg. He found this for me along the way. He chose it for me, and with it I did shepherd my little flock as best I could. I pray God forgives my failings, for they were many." He sighed and then looked evenly at Wil. He kissed his staff, prayed silently over it, and then presented it to his young friend. "Serve them well, my son. For the task now falls to you. 'To whom much is given, much is expected.' Lead them by serving them. It is the way of wisdom."

The priest released his staff into Wil's strong grip slowly, even reluctantly. He fixed his eyes on the trusted crook, and when he abandoned his touch, he sighed. "Your sufferings have set you free, lad. But hear this, too: to live freely, learn to live for something greater than yourself."

He struggled to stand and laid both of his hands on Wil's shoulders. "Draw from the past, my son; it is a deep well of wisdom. Keep an eye on the future, for there lies hope. But do not fail to live for today, for it is what binds wisdom and hope together."

❧

After the morning's meal, Horst called Wil and the other men to his office, where he delivered a series of instructions. "You've a journey of two and a half days. Follow the roadway northwest from here for about a full day. You'll come to an intersection of roads by a large brick millhouse, and there you will bear straight westward.

"That road will take you almost to the Weser. At a pilgrims' chappelle, it turns directly south toward Bremen and to the ferries to Stedingerland."

Alwin shook his head. "We wish to cross at a ford. The city is dangerous for us."

"Well, I warn you, you need have a care if you do. I am not sure which is more perilous, the provost of Bremen or the shifting silt of the Weser."

"We will ford at low tide," answered Wil.

The merchant furrowed his brow but yielded. "I am told the place to cross is directly west of the road's bend. It is a place called Blumenthal, the valley of flowers."

A chill ran up Heinrich's spine. *Blumenthal! Oh, Emma,* he thought.

"Now, this," continued Horst. He handed Wil a bag heavy with gold. "You'll not say no. Share it as need requires. It is enough to buy a good start for you all."

Astonished, the pilgrims stared at the leather pouch. "But—"

"But nothing. I'll replace it with higher rates for the bishop!" The man laughed. "It is not a matter of discussion. And here. I've this as well." Horst handed each of the men, including Tomas, a square letter with a wax seal affixed to it. "It was good that the storm threatened yesterday, for my lawyer had a thought ... for once! We hired Lord Ohrsbach's secretary to make passports for each of you. They declare you as freemen, by name. If any should challenge you, it will serve in court."

The pilgrims could not speak. They stared at the letters in disbelief. Horst looked at Friederich and continued. "Little fellow, I took the liberty to name you as the son of Alwin."

The boy grinned at the surprised knight. Horst then laid a hand on Otto's shoulder. "And you, stoutheart. You'd be of age soon enough, but I've given you to Alwin as well."

Otto looked at the kindly knight with a face laced by bittersweet. His heart was still heavy for his own father in faraway Weyer. "It is my honor." The two clasped hands.

Horst turned to Heinrich. "I have taken the liberty of naming Maria as your daughter. I hope that is acceptable."

"More than acceptable, sir, it is delightful!" Heinrich smiled broadly and draped his thick arm around Maria's shoulder. "You're mine, dear girl. 'Tis the law of the land!"

Pleased, Horst addressed the women. "I assigned wives as they should be, and Wilda, I recorded you as the wife of Alwin and the mother of Friederich and Otto."

The woman blushed as Alwin laughed happily. "So be it!" he cried.

The men embraced the merchant one by one. They could not find the words to thank him.

"Of course you've no words to thank me!" he roared and laid his arm around Helmut. "And I've no words to thank you! So the score is even! Now, follow me."

Horst led his guests outside, where Paulus stood heavily laden with fresh provisions. "I hope he can swim!" he cried. "Here." He pointed to a sturdy canvas litter. "We need four strong arms to carry Father Pieter. He's in no shape to ride the donkey."

Wil agreed that the idea was a good one. He shook Horst's hand. "Again, sir, our thanks to you. It is now time." He called for his company to assemble, and one by one each pilgrim embraced Helmut for the final time. It was a painful farewell for them all. From the jetty of Genoa to this place in the northland, he had been a faithful friend—and they had been his.

Alwin and Otto lifted Pieter onto his canvas, and four strong hands lifted the weary priest. Then, with a final wave and chorus of thanks, the travelers disappeared onto the roadway once again.

చ

For the rest of that Saturday, the pilgrims walked briskly, stopping briefly from time to time so that Pieter's litter bearers might rest. Every able hand helped as the day wore on, and by night they were all ready for sleep. Solomon did not stray more than a few rods from his master's side. He did not sleep, though his eyes were dull in the firelight and his head drooped. Somehow he knew.

On Sunday the column passed the millhouse, turned due westward, and followed the path of the sun. The pilgrims met a few other travelers, including a small caravan traveling from Stettin, and from time to time a villager would emerge from nowhere to share a bit of news. It was a comfortable, warm day and quiet, as Sabbaths ought to be.

On Monday, sometime before noon, the band arrived at the chappelle and the bend of the road of which Horst had spoken. Alwin prayed at the feet of a little crucifix, and Pieter asked to be lifted from his litter to do the same. Together the former monks raised prayers to God that were not so different; their spirits were kindred and similarly burdened for the welfare of others.

When they had finished, Pieter summoned Otto to come close. "My dear lad," he began, "you are a stout heart and as resolute a fellow as I have e'er known." He pulled his satchel awkwardly off his shoulder. "I fear there is naught inside but a few crusts and some silver, but it has hung on m'shoulder for more leagues than I dare consider. I should like you to have it."

Otto's chin dropped, and he received the gift with a trembling hand. "Oh, Pieter, Father Pieter, I ... I ..."

"Fill it with the bounty of your liberty, lad." Pieter smiled.

Otto embraced the old man lightly. "I shall treasure it always."

Pieter was then laid upon his litter again, and Wil directed his column away from the roadway and led them due west across the flat countryside. The company traveled slowly through small stands of pine and scattered hardwoods for much of the afternoon, eventually noticing a subtle descent, which they followed until they spotted something glistening between a thin row of trees in the distance.

"There!" cried Tomas. "I see the river through the trees!"

A loud hurrah was lifted. It was the Weser!

The sun of late day lit a host of tiny white wildflowers that were sprinkled generously atop the green field waiting just ahead. Awed, the company lifted their faces past the white-tipped meadow and to the tree line beyond. Their eyes fixed on a ribbon of silver threaded between the shadowed trunks, and they quickly pressed on.

To liberty, rejoiced Heinrich. *To freedom's home!* The pilgrims hurried through the wide field of shin-deep grass and stalky flowers until, at last, they slipped through the tree line only to be held in place by the sheer wonder of the enchanting scene now opened before them.

Unable to speak, the blessed wayfarers now gazed upon Blumenthal, the splendid valley of their river of promise, which welcomed them with such a flourish of heaven's greeting as would dwarf the homecoming of the greatest kings of time! The light of day had faded softly as the sun sank respectfully toward the distant horizon. A few puffed clouds edged the yellow ball. Slanting shafts of golden light were cast across a fresh carpet of vivid wildflowers standing pure and precious before the dumbstruck travelers. The dappled colors of the creation sprawled as far as the eye could see, divided only by the water's silver strand. It was a presentation of the Master's palette, a masterpiece of gentle brilliance that heralded the very presence of its Maker's glory.

Wil ran to Pieter and, with Heinrich's help, stood the priest up to behold the world as it should be. Pieter stared silently for a long moment. His eyes moistened and his throat swelled. "Fields of gossamer touched by the rainbow," he whispered weakly. "Dear God, You have brought us to the portal of paradise."

The man began to sag in his fellows' grip. He tossed his head weakly toward a stout oak to which he was quickly carried and seated against its sturdy trunk. Solomon slumped close by, then laid a forlorn chin on the man's lap. Pieter rested a loving hand atop his companion's head. "My good and faithful friend," he whispered.

Looking across the river, the failing man pointed a

trembling finger and asked faintly, "Is it there? Is that Stedingerland?"

Heinrich knelt by Pieter's side and laid a soft hand on the man's shoulder. "*Ja*, Pieter, it is there, just beyond the river."

The priest smiled, then looked quietly into the distance for a long while. His lambs gathered close to either side, and the whole of the company stared wistfully at the panorama before them.

In time, Heinrich retrieved Karl's cross from his belt. "Pieter, I shall plant this in free soil."

Pieter nodded. "Good. He would have it so." He lifted his feeble hand upward to touch the apple wood lightly. "Dear friend, would I be too bold to ask you to set it at my grave?"

The baker's throat swelled. He turned a wet eye to Wil and nodded. "Indeed. I surely shall. Karl would have liked it to be so."

Pieter sighed contentedly and closed his eyes. He then awakened with a start and stared into the distance again. His breathing began to falter before he pointed his finger once more. "You all do see it, don't you?" he asked weakly. "Maria, Wil ...?"

"*Ja*," his fellows answered in unison.

The good man nodded, then stared into the shadowed lands far beyond the Weser. "Then your day is come ..." His eyes lost their light, then fluttered and closed. "You are home," he whispered faintly. He took a difficult breath and muttered something indiscernible.

"What, Papa?" asked Maria as she clutched his arm. "What did you say?"

Pieter stirred as his troubled flock leaned close by either side. He opened his eyes and gazed ahead once more, then lifted his timeworn face toward heaven. There he sat silently as the sun sank peacefully in the west. Frieda led the others in some quiet songs, and Pieter's breathing became shallow.

At last, the old fellow's eyes rolled slightly, and his head tilted to one side. In a faint whisper he murmured, "What ... hidden harbor ... greets the fleet of stars ... that cross the night ... and ... where do shadows gather ... after they have lost their li ..." Pieter Godson von Kinder's voice trailed away, and his chest released its final breath. He slumped into his beloved Maria's arms, and his soul flew to his Maker's breast.

Solomon whined and Maria whimpered. Great groans of sorrow rippled through the grieving company. Their Pieter—their Papa Pieter—was gone from them. It could not be, yet it was; and it was very much to bear.

For the next hour, the mourners suffered their loss with sobs and anguished cries. Death remained as it always had been: that certain shadow that follows every life, that ruthless foe that bites the tender places and shows mercy to none.

In time, Wil and Alwin laid the good man prostrate on the soft, bloom-spotted grass and folded his cold hands over his heart as Heinrich stood to speak. He wiped his eye and cleared his throat.

"Pieter Godson von Kinder was my friend," he said with a loving smile. "He taught me much of things that are and of things that shall surely be." The pilgrims shuffled close and listened carefully as the simple baker proceeded to bless them with something of a homily on the resurrection to come. His words were soft and comforting, and he finished by saying, "For in the rising of the Christ we find our only hope against this curse. In that, and in that alone, is our final triumph. Take heart, my brothers and sisters, though we grieve this night, we *shall* see him again."

Then, under the gauzy light of the rising moon, Pieter's body was carefully carried to the shores of the lapping Weser to be bathed. His mourners stared heavenward, as if hoping to somehow see his white beard amidst the silver of the night's sky. Frieda said that he would have loved the way the stars were shining down on the river. "They are making the water sparkle clean and bright," she said. "He is smiling on us; he is at peace. I can feel his joy all around."

Pieter's body was carried back to the camp, and Wil walked slowly to Paulus in order to retrieve the bundle that had been discreetly handed to him by Friar Oswald in Renwick. It was another gift from Traugott—a fine deer-hide shroud, one fit for a prince. Wil unfurled the shroud, then handed his wife a ball of leather cord and a heavy needle.

Frieda nodded and quietly gathered the women together. In less than an hour, Pieter's body was sewn within the deerskin and then laid in the center of the camp, where the company fell slowly to sleep until distant birds signaled the coming of dawn.

෨

It was Tuesday, the twenty-seventh of August in the year 1213. Heinrich rose first and added a few small logs to the red ashes of the night's fire. He looked at Pieter's shroud lying stiff and straight atop the earth.

"Father?"

Heinrich turned. "Aye, lad?"

Wil stretched his open hand toward the man. "Let all things be forgiven ... let all things be made new. You have brought us safely to a new land, and I thank you for it."

The baker squeezed his son's hand hard and answered, "We have brought each other here, both guided in ways I cannot explain." He looked deeply into his son's eyes, now enlivened by the rising flames. "May God bless you richly as you take hold of what is now yours." He released his son's hand and retrieved Karl's cross from his belt. He kissed it and held it to his breast. "I pray that none of us forgets the sufferings or the joys of our journey." Heinrich's throat swelled, and he could no longer speak.

Katharina slipped to the baker's side as Frieda joined Wil. Maria emerged from the darkness to lean against Heinrich. Together, the five stood silently as the first light of the new day streaked pink across the bluing sky.

The light breezes of the early morning teased their hair and brushed warm against their faces like the breath of angels. The quiet group watched their fellows rise, and when all had gathered, Wil spoke. "We'll not eat here," he said firmly. "Today, we eat our first meal as freemen!" He looked at Pieter's shroud and then smiled at Maria. The stitching had been filled with flowers in the night. He lifted his sister into his arms. "And we take him with us. He shall rest in free soil."

In a quarter hour, the brave company was standing in proper order as Wil inspected each of his comrades. With Solomon at his side, he planted his staff firmly into the rich soil of Blumenthal and walked up and down the small column with pride. Tomas, Otto, Alwin, and Heinrich each held a corner of Pieter's litter—Heinrich and Otto in the fore. Wil paused to look at each of them. *Brave men all,* he thought. *And Friederich, too.* He turned to face Maria and the women. *Dear sister, dear wife, brave Wilda, and good Katharina...*

"May God bless us all on this good day and for many to come," he proclaimed. He walked past Maria and rubbed Paulus's ears with a contented smile. Then, taking his place in the fore of his beloved company, he pointed westward.

With cries of jubilance, the pilgrims advanced, measuring their steps lightly atop the yielding petals of the valley floor, drawn deeper into color and to light as the sun rose higher behind them. Splashed to either side was the brilliance of this new day's dawn, set to glory by the fluttering of butterflies now dancing atop the morning mist and the gift of wildflowers spread far and wide. Above, the sky was filled with songbirds, and ahead the lightly riffled waters of the Weser lay easy and warm, peacefully waiting to receive this tithing of free brethren.

Drawing deeply of the sweet, fragrant air, Wil paused at the water's edge and took Otto's place with Pieter's litter. He held the rail handle firmly in his left hand; to his side stood Heinrich holding the litter with his right. The pair looked at one another, then turned their heads southward as their memories suddenly carried them across green forests and wending fields of grain. They were swept far, far away, through narrow valleys and into the magnificent desolation of the highest places. They closed their eyes to smell the wood smoke of a hundred campfires, to hear the laughter and the tears of those much loved.

It was in that moment that their fellows began to sing the

"Crusaders' Hymn," that gentle song of so many lost along the way, that melody of innocence and purity that had graced the hearts of all who had lifted it to their lips. "Fair are the meadows, fairer still the woodland...."

Heinrich listened and looked to the heavens, where he imagined Karl joined in chorus with Pieter and Emma, with Lukas and Ingelbert. It was as though he could see them floating with the angels at that very moment, in that very place. He let a tear fall from his eye as Katharina stepped to his side.

Wil looked at his father knowingly. He had seen the same vision and was comforted. He took a deep, resolute breath and planted his sturdy staff firmly into the pebbled bed of the River Weser. Frieda approached to lay a hand softly on his elbow, and he turned his shining eyes toward hers. "It is time," he said.

Wil faced his father once more. "We ought to take our first steps together."

The baker nodded humbly. "Together it shall be."

Then, rendering their thanks to heaven, Wilhelm Godson Freimann and Heinrich Godson Lieberlicht squared their shoulders toward Stedingerland and smiled as their fellows made ready behind them. It was time to claim that which they had been given, to lay hold of the prize hard won. With seabirds soaring high above, the two stepped bravely into the kindly currents of their appointed destinies. The warm waters of the Weser welcomed them gladly, and with a triumphant shout they splashed through the clear river of liberty as freemen, well forged on the anvil of suffering and prepared by truth to serve others in the gardens of the sun.

THE END

THE CHRONICLES OF FRIEDA

*E*go, Frieda Westphaliensis, *uxor Wilhelmi Freimanni, anno Domini 1213,* in order *gloriam Dei,* the *auctori* of all things, *nunc* chronicle the wisdom that has been offered by many along this journey of the souls. May these things be shared in the memory of my beloved brothers and sisters of crusade.

My ears have been blessed by my beloved friend Pieter, for whom my heart does yet ache. It has also been my great honor to learn from dear Heinrich, the father of my husband; from *Signore* Salito of Arona; from Sebastiani, the brave soldier of Domodossola; from the Waldensians Jean and Philip; and from Friar Oswald of Renwick.

My quill has been further blessed with the words of others I have never known such as *Frau* Emma of Weyer, Brother Lukas of Villmar Abbey, Sister Anoush of Rome, and Father Wilfrid of Zell. To these and to all who have passed the Bread of Life across the generations, I give my thanks.

Now, in the name of our Lord, I do present this humble portion of my gain to the child in my womb, to others yet unborn, and to their children and to their children's children unto the end of time.

Amen.

ॐ

Be these things considered:

Some of us shall find our end in shadows, others near the heavens. What matters is that we delight in whatever journey we are granted.

Nothing on earth rules with authority unless it rules according to God's Law of Love.

Strong faith and strong opinions rarely share the same heart.

If we are to lead men, we must know this: even an unredeemed heart bears the mark of his Maker's image. It is good to find that stamp in both friend and foe.

For those fearing death, let it be said that our heavenly Father would no more leave us alone in that dark valley than He would in any other.

The good farmer wanders over a fallow field and says, "I have hope." When he plunges his plough into the earth, he is saying, "I believe." He spreads his seed and says, "I trust." When the warm sun and the gentle rain nudge tender blades through the hard ground, he smiles and says, "I knew." And when the harvest is yielded and his storehouse is full, he is thankful, for he has been blessed.

Every lamb needs a ewe to lean upon. We all need more than a touch from the clouds.

Where love is, hope is.

God is not a hard taskmaster; we are stiff-necked students.

I believe in order to understand.

We are truly free when He fills us with the faith to do nothing and the wisdom to know when.

Notice your youth. Taste what of it you can and capture it in your mind, for such memories shall be your most prized treasure.

Here is a rub: the very thing that gives such value to our past is that which steals it away. For 'tis only when the present fades to a memory that it becomes so very precious. Yet in such fading it does leave us. Oh, what a double-edged sword is this thing called "Time."

Behind every belief is a premise; behind every premise lies a desire. Decisions are more often made by the will than the mind. We choose what to believe from our heart, not from reason. If one wants to change a man's mind, one must first change his heart.

There are two kinds of anger, and they should be discerned. The first is the good anger of God. It is outraged at evil and ignited to defend the innocent; its target is the Evil One. The second is the rage of arrogance, the fruit of hard hearts defending their vanities; it is the child of disappointment and the grandchild of pride.

Preachers need to know that brevity is oft a good substitute for ability!

God can do miracles as and when He wishes, and it is a wise man who seeks them. But they are not for our taking. Our task is to act on what is before us in plain view. Our faith ought not to presume on God.

We must face this troubled world as it is, not as we would hope it to be.

Our Father above forgives His children always—and not because it is deserved on their account. If forgiveness could be earned, it would not be forgiveness at all, but rather a bartered exchange.

Beware the sinister code that demands us to be right rather than forgiven. We are never truly right, for there is a quality of either error or pride that stains all we do. Hence, we are wise to live aware of our unending need for forgiveness.

Self-reliance is a merciless tyrant. It blinds the eyes, its appetite is never quenched, and it never rests.

If we choose to trust ourselves alone, we shall surely spend our days in the grip of a dragon.

We are allowed to suffer sadness, sickness, poverty, pain, or even failings, for these He mysteriously redeems as paths to His mercies and, hence, to Him.

Simplicity may bring joy, but two ways of simplicity exist. The first way is the simplicity of blindness, and it is never a virtue. The second way understands that simple truths do, indeed, govern the world. But they are only understood on the far side of complexity.

It is important that we look beyond the steps of our own little journey.

Perhaps there is never a time for treachery, but cunning has its place!

Our miseries are but the heavy labors of a worthy Gardener, working and kneading God's soil into our hard, barren hearts. He has planted vineyards of sweet grapes within each of His children. Indeed, we stand upon Holy Ground that is well worked into each of our hearts.

Sad is the man who is blind to the order, beauty, and goodness that lie amidst the confusion of the world. The earth may groan for a time, waiting for its redemption, but it groans in hope. For wherever there is evil, there is always a reminder of good. We see both tears and smiles, clouds and sunshine, death and birth, sickness and healing, hunger and plenty. For every night there is a day.

Our sufferings seem to be that which do most surely draw us closer to Him. And in that closeness we will find love, not madness; hope, not despair.

We are changed in our sufferings. Like a thirsty tree in drought, our roots grow deeper into the source of our life. The confusions and miseries in this world are but tools in God's workbox—tools to incline us toward Him and the mysterious joy that awaits our meeting.

Our God is the known and the unknown, together and the same. He is the source of sunlight and shadows, smiles and tears. It is the heart of God that is our haven, the mighty keep of all joy and all pain, all triumphs and all failures.

Mystery is our destined boundary. We may choose to stand before either the mysteries of fear or the mysteries of hope.

We ought to observe a simple flower and consider the heart that might design such a thing. Even the edges are laced with delicate color so that another's eye might look and be glad.

Can we not see that the God of the storm yet tends the beauty of a wildflower?

The flower is our symbol of the presence of God, and the cross is a symbol of His love. By them we know these two things: that God is there and that He cares. Know these and we need to know little else.

Beware of falsely religious men. They destroy all that is within their grasp.

Knowing who hates you can teach you much about yourself.

Where Truth is present, light is present.

Color is the fruit of light.

Beware of virtues, for they easily become objects of arrogance.

Things are not always as they seem, for sometimes they are so much better.

Sunshine is hope; moonlight is mercy. The sun is but a sign like its sister the moon. They both urge us to look past our world to the sure things above.

God's gifts are for those humble enough to abandon themselves.

True humility draws a man's face upward, not downward.

What our eyes see, our tongues taste, our noses smell, our ears hear, and our fingers touch do much to call upon the spirit within us.

Freedom, like hope, is a birthright from God.

Truth is what remains when all else fails.

Wounded people serve others well, for our God is a God of scars.

A man has a right to keep what is his so long as none in his view are starving.

Fixing the eyes on failure is like staring into a chasm, for it draws us to disaster.

God's mercy is not His only gift ... it is just the beginning of gifts. He offers us so much more than forgiveness; He offers us the whole of His love.

Faith is not proven by things attained but by walking in love.

Guilt sprouts where shame is planted. Hope grows where trust is sown.

Suffering is the path to faith and the doorway to compassion.

Greed is oft found in proportion to gain.

The promises of a priest will do more to prompt alms than the face of a hungry child.

Someday, when our strength wanes and our virtues fail, when we long for hope, we must turn our eyes upward and find the other way.

The sun always shines; it is only hidden by the clouds.

Where the light is brightest, the shadows are darkest.

We must not let our regrets rule us, else they become who we are.

The sight of heaven makes all of life easier.

Live life wisely, and have a care for the passing of time. For our world is like a garden and we like roses. Our blooms open and spread over others fading nearby. In time, new buds shall surely come, and they will bloom fresh and fragrant near our own withering petals. It is the cycle of life—the way it ought to be ... and it is good.

Ours is an astonishing journey. Indeed, goodness and mercy have followed us, and the swords of heaven's legions go before.

To have a handle on trouble, we must first name it.

Preachers and balladeers have much in common: they both make things up!

God and nature do not work together in vain. He gives us this earth as a glimpse of His greater glory; it is a reminder that He is present in all things, and from that we can draw hope.

Repentance follows forgiveness, and that is the very essence of redemption.

Order and love are not always friends.

The conscience is reached by love.

We are never too far gone for grace to find us, nor too close for us to need it.

Do not be so proud as to carry shame.

The past is oft a good place to remember but not a good place to dwell.

See the host and his diners seated before a table spread with a bounty of good things. This is a fitting image of the kingdom of God.

All men are either poets or merchants. Poets see beauty for what it is; merchants see it for what it does.

Any of us can become the ugliest face of our idols. If we

worship wealth, we become greedy. If we worship power, we become tyrants.

Men may call us bound or free, foolish or wise, brave or cowardly, even saintly or wicked, but it is heaven that has already declared who we truly are.

We must believe in the Word and learn to want what it offers. For, in the end, we will live as we have learned to want.

Some only pretend to be forgiven, for they pretend they are sinners.

Many fear their reputation, but few their conscience. Yet have a care. The conscience can be a tyrant as well. It is not always a proper master.

There should be no war between faith and reason. Our faith is reasonable, though it does not stand or fall upon logic. After all, it stands on grace, and that is not logical at all.

We are not called to know all things, but to trust the One who does.

Unlike the intellect, faith has no bounds; it is a gift of the Infinite.

In this world of sorrows we do not often have pure choices. So when two virtues are in collision, we are to pray for the wisdom to choose the higher.

When we seek joy, we ought to seek it humbly, for we shall not be joyful until our old affections are taken away. When we seek patience, we must do so carefully, for we shall not have it until ours has been greatly tested. When we seek wisdom, we should tremble, for first we must be stripped of all that we thought was true.

Who we are is not how we look, from whence we've come, or what we have. We are not what we do, nor even what we think. Nay, in the end, who we are is what we love.

It is good that God's love for us does not depend on our love for Him.

The wax walls of the honeycomb are like the words of man's knowledge. But the hive is far more than walls of wax. It is in the emptiness of the waiting cell where the true wonder lies. It is the airy place that will soon fill with sweetness.

Even so, truth is not confined to things known. Rather, it also dwells in the spaces between the words, in the silence of the cells, in the mystery. To be sure, as the worker bees enlarge the hive, they add more wax around more air. Likewise, as we increase in knowledge, we, too, add more mystery.

Lead by serving; it is the way of wisdom.

We followers of the Christ are called His sons and daughters. That, above all else, is our true selves.

To live free, live for something greater than yourself.

Draw from the past, for it is a deep well of wisdom. Keep an eye on the future, for there is hope. But do not fail to live for today, for it is what binds wisdom and hope together.

Ad Amairem Dei Gloriam

Readers' Guide

For Personal Reflection
or Group Discussion

READERS' GUIDE

hat is the current condition of your life? Do you struggle with close personal relationships? Are you controlled by negative emotions or destructive behavior patterns? Do you feel as though you don't belong or even wonder why you were born? Are you terrified by the future and what it holds? If any of these issues plagues your daily existence, there is good news! The Bible says, "You did not receive the spirit of bondage again to fear, but you received the Spirit of adoption by whom we cry out, 'Abba, Father.' The Spirit Himself bears witness with our spirit that we are children of God, and if children, then heirs—heirs of God and joint heirs with Christ, if indeed we suffer with Him, that we may also be glorified together" (Rom. 8:15–17 NKJV).

This truth is beautifully illustrated by the continuing story of Heinrich of Weyer. Having gained newfound freedom of spirit in Christ, our hero faces new sorrows and trials as he continues his journey. His resolve and determination are tested, but as he grows in greater understanding of the truth of God's love, he experiences renewed joy as well. Maria, conceived in sin, yet tender of spirit and beautifully made in the image of her Creator, becomes the child of Heinrich's heart—his own in every way that matters. In a surprising twist of fate, he is reunited with his longtime friend Blasius, son of the dreaded Gunnars. Through the power of forgiveness, Heinrich seeks to be restored to relationship with his son Wil. Every step of the way, God is calling him out of his old ways, desiring to make him whole, righteous, and one with his heavenly Father.

The apostle Paul wrote, "If anyone is in Christ, he is a new creation; the old has gone, the new has come!" (2 Cor. 5:17). Yet adoption is not always a smooth transition. Like Heinrich, we must decide where we belong. Do we return to the old way—with its pain, suffering, and bondage? To the sin that is comfortable and easy in its familiarity? Or do we pursue the promise of life in Christ, which alone brings joy, honor, and liberty? True freedom is experienced to the extent we are enabled to leave behind forever those things that hinder and enslave us. We must be willing to say to ourselves, "Forgetting what is behind and straining toward what is ahead, I press on toward the goal to win the prize for which God has called me heavenward in Christ Jesus" (Phil. 3:13–14). Such is the heart of a true pilgrim.

Chapter 1

1. Despite their miraculous escape from the slave ship, the crusaders suffer additional losses. As they bury their dead, Pieter paraphrases Psalm 34: "I will bless the Lord at all times; His praise shall be always in my mouth." Why is it necessary to praise Him at all times? Why is this often so difficult, particularly in tragic situations? What effect does praise have on our circumstances?

2. Heinrich chooses to set aside his grief in order to help the surviving crusaders. How does he exemplify the role of a servant? What does Pieter mean when he says, "Our God is a God of scars. Wounded people serve others well"? In what ways has suffering or loss in your own life affected your ability to relate to others?

Chapter 2

3. Why are the children afraid to return home? Are their fears reasonable? What does Pieter's message convey about the true meaning of success? In your own life, have you defined success and accomplishment according to the

world's standard or the standard of faith? In what ways can even the most simple, unremarkable life achieve great things in the kingdom of God?

4. How does Heinrich respond to Pieter's question about where he truly belongs? Given Heinrich's new freedom of spirit, why does he still find his identity in his old, bound, miserable existence? How is this similar to the behavior of the Israelites in the Old Testament? Have you ever found it easier to return to "things familiar" than to trust God in a new and better place?

5. When the crusaders are rejected and despised by the people of Genoa, Pieter is challenged by one of the children who asks him, "Should we forgive them, Father?" How does Pieter's response reveal the changes in his heart and attitudes? What lesson has he learned about forgiveness and judgment?

Chapter 3

6. Like a young Robin Hood, Paul devises a plan to plunder the wealthy of Genoa before leaving for Rome. What is most disturbing about this situation? Are the children justified in stealing what should have been offered to them?

Chapter 4

7. Psalm 23 says, "The LORD is my shepherd, I shall not be in want. He makes me lie down in green pastures, he leads me beside quiet waters, he restores my soul…. Even though I walk through the valley of the shadow of death, I will fear no evil, for you are with me." How does this psalm illustrate the refuge the weary children find at San Fruttuoso? What does this Scripture reveal about God's compassion, provision, and love for us in the midst of trials and suffering?

8. Wil struggles mightily with his anger toward his father—

some of which is perhaps understandable, but much is the fruit of seeds planted by his mother and others. Why does he find it so hard to forgive his father? Should he have a deeper compassion for the imperfections of others, given his own recent failings? What significant truth does Frieda share with Wil about the power of forgiveness?

Chapter 5

9. Pieter is outraged to find that Maria has been "sold" to the neighboring lord's home as a servant. Is his anger justified? How has Maria fared under the lord's care? Are there times in our lives when God can use difficult or even "wrong" circumstances to bless us? How is this truth illustrated by the story of Joseph, as told in Genesis chapters 37, 39–45?

Chapter 6

10. Heinrich struggles with the choices he has made in life and doubts his worthiness of God's mercy. How does Brother Stefano challenge Heinrich to think beyond the confines of simple forgiveness? Do you ever find it hard to understand how God can forgive the mistakes you've made? How does considering God's perfect and unfailing love—rather than whether or not you "deserve" forgiveness—change your perspective?

11. Does it seem ironic that while Wil refuses to forgive his father, he worries over his own betrayal of his sister, Maria? Is it true that "men want justice … except for themselves, in which case they want mercy"? What is the inherent consequence of living with this type of attitude?

Chapter 7

12. Heinrich rescues Tomas and pays a hefty price for his freedom. Given Tomas's defection and hostility toward Heinrich and Wil, is he really deserving of the help he is

given? How is this similar to the redemption Jesus offers each one of us?

13. What does Wil's reaction to Tomas reveal about his character? Why does he have such trouble offering and receiving grace? Is it possible for grace to be earned? How does pride cause us to miss out on many of God's greatest gifts?

Chapter 8

14. When Wil asks for Maria's forgiveness, she gives it freely and joyfully. What does Maria mean when she says she "saw a bit of heaven"? How might seeing heaven change your outlook on earthly matters? Why is the hope of heaven usually not enough to influence us in the same way?

15. Proverbs 31:30 says, "Charm is deceptive, and beauty is fleeting; but a woman who fears the LORD is to be praised." How does this Scripture reflect on Lucia and the painful lesson Wil learned of her true character? How does Frieda—who is beautiful in her own right—demonstrate qualities of higher virtue and worth?

Chapter 9

16. Heinrich is very disturbed to learn that his wife was unfaithful to him and consequently gave birth to Maria. What extra measure of angst is due to the likelihood that Pious is Maria's biological father? Is it easy to understand Heinrich's desire to have the truth of Pious's treachery known publicly? What is more important from God's point of view—that Heinrich be vindicated or that Maria be spared the shame and rejection of her illegitimacy?

17. Pieter tells Heinrich, "Sometimes we need to guard against our conscience. It is not always a proper master." Is this surprising advice? Is the conscience always a true

moral compass according to God's standards? If not, what consequences might result from choosing the conscience as a guide, rather than the Word of God or the leading of the Holy Spirit?

Chapter 10

18. When the pilgrims return to the site of Georg's grave, Heinrich reaches out to Maria and finally declares that she is his daughter and that he shall be her father. How is this moment significant for both of them? Does God define the role of a father as simply biology or something greater? In what way are we all "illegitimate" like Maria? How would we respond if God failed to extend His acceptance and love to any one of us? How can this lesson be applied to those who face similar real-life situations today?

Chapter 11

19. Heinrich briefly encounters his old friend Blasius after witnessing a battle between the Templars and another band of knights. How do the Templars treat Blasius, whom they capture and accuse of betrayal? Would a true traitor be worthy of such treatment? Why is a difference in opinion so threatening to the establishment of the Roman Church and its soldiers?

20. Heinrich, Pieter, Tomas, and the others attempt to rescue Blasius and in the process set the entire town of Burgdorf on fire. Are their efforts heroic or merely destructive? Is the price paid in lives and property worth the life of one man? Is it possible that God is using the pilgrims to bring judgment on the city? What past biblical events suggest that might be a possibility?

Chapter 12

21. How do the events at Burgdorf bring about a turning

point in Tomas's life? Given his typical hostility and disregard for others, why is he moved to such grief over the destruction he helped set in motion? What is significant about Wil's offered forgiveness and friendship?

22. Blasius—or Alwin—reveals the events that led to his capture by the Templars. What caused him to become disillusioned with the "holy war" he was fighting? Is there truth to the saying that "the conscience is reached by love"? Is there ever an appropriate time for the use of force, and if so, when?

Chapter 13

23. Death and destruction follow the pilgrims to the town of Olten. Are they somehow to blame for the disaster that follows them? Should they surrender (as Alwin attempts to do) in hopes of sparing others, or are they justified in fleeing for their lives? Would the powers that pursue them really be satisfied with their surrender?

24. Dorothea is a remarkable woman of kindness, strength, and bravery. What distinguishes her from other wealthy and influential citizens the pilgrims have encountered on their journey? Is the courage that she displays in the face of evil for naught? What is the inevitable consequence of her generosity? (See Matt. 25:34–46; Mark 9:36–37, 41.)

Chapter 14

25. When the pilgrims are trapped in the town of Olten, many circumstances conspire to open the door for their escape. How does each member of their company manage to escape unscathed? Is this sufficient evidence of God's protection and intervention in their lives? Is there really such a thing as coincidence?

Chapter 15

26. Rudolf is welcomed home by the open arms and joyful

hearts of his family without one suggestion of any supposed "failure" on crusade. What sets this family apart
from so many others—even that of Heinrich and Marta?
What role does faith, expressed as a simple, trusting relationship with the Creator, play in their lives?

Chapter 16

27. Is it surprising that discrimination against Jews was
rampant even in the thirteenth century? What seeds are
sown that will germinate in Germany hundreds of years
later? Is there ever any "new" face on an old evil?

Chapter 17

28. When the pilgrims arrive in Weyer, some of those
returning are overcome with emotion and rejoice to see the
familiar sights of home. Is Weyer really worthy of such kind
regard? Are Heinrich's hopes realistic or is he choosing to
ignore the truth? What is he really responding to?

29. Many people define themselves based on what others
say or think about them, but Pieter wisely tells the company that "what they *say* we are and who we *really* are is
oft not the same at all." How might this be true in your own
life? Whose is the one opinion we ought to believe? What
does God say about us in His Word?

30. When Otto returns to his home, he is berated and beaten
by his father. Is it possible to justify or explain his father's
behavior? Why does he become the scapegoat for the entire
town? What does this situation reveal about human nature?

Chapter 18

31. Wil and Heinrich return to Weyer only to walk right
into the cunning snare Pious has laid for them. What hope
is there when men in powerful positions deliberately seek
to destroy those in their care? Does the truth always win,
or are there times when evil prevails?

32. What does Pieter mean when he says, "It is good to be free of my mind sometimes. We are not called to know all things, but to trust in the One who does"? How might our lives be different if we truly allowed God to bear our burdens—rather than trying to control everything ourselves? Are we even capable of that task?

Chapter 19

33. Heinrich and Wil are captured and thrown in prison. Is it ironic that they encounter a Jew, Beniamino, who offers to help them? How often does God answer our prayers in the manner we expect? How might we miss His help and deliverance if we allow ourselves to become blinded by our own prejudices and expectations?

Chapter 20

34. How has Arnold changed, and what has caused him to reevaluate the condition of his life? Does he fully understand why his family's fortune has been so decimated? What fruit has the "code" of his forefathers borne? What motive might God have to allow a man to lose everything?

35. Arnold, Katharina, Herwin, and others join with the pilgrims in their desperate plan to rescue Wil and Heinrich. Is their involvement merely coincidence, or is some unseen hand directing their steps? How do the unresolved issues of many years begin to come to a head? What does this reveal about God's timing?

Chapter 21

36. Pieter—so often beset by his own weakness of character—struggles with the choice before him. He is unsure whether seeking justice for Heinrich and Wil is a worthy reason to manipulate Anka and to involve others in the deception. What is Frieda's counsel? Why is wisdom so

critical in such situations? Is the "higher virtue" always plainly obvious?

37. Arnold once more calls upon his faithful trade of blackmailing. How is the monk trapped by his own actions? How would bringing everything out in the open—particularly when sin is involved—negate the power of those secrets? How does the monk react when Arnold tells him he reminds him of himself? Is Arnold right?

Chapter 22

38. Pieter, Tomas, and Otto terrify *Frau* Anka, using spiritual blackmail to convince her to stay away from the trial. Has Pieter chosen rightly? How is their behavior similar to that of Pious? Would God approve of their motives if not their methods? Are good intentions ever enough to justify our choices?

39. Pious arrives at the trial fully expecting his plans to be fulfilled. Of all abominations that God hates, is Pious innocent of any? Is Pious truly evil or merely pathetic? Is he more worthy of Heinrich's hatred or his pity? Why?

Chapter 23

40. Pious's plan is completely undone, and he abruptly finds himself facing his own trial by ordeal. How are his years of excess and greed—and true character—exposed? How does this scene symbolize the eternal judgment we all must face? Despite the archaic methods, is justice well served?

41. After being awarded their freedom, Wil and Heinrich, along with the others, learn they must flee for their lives. How does Heinrich react to the realization that Weyer will never again be his home? Is it surprising that the band of pilgrims decides to journey to Stedingerland in hope of settling there as freemen? How does this development lend

new purpose and meaning to Heinrich's long journey and suffering?

Chapter 24

42. When the pilgrims arrive at Godfrey's home, they are welcomed with warm hospitality. Once in the dining hall, the many guests debate the virtues of faith versus reason, most siding with the "new way of thinking." How is this mind-set similar to the philosophy of the world today? What danger lies in relying too heavily on the intellect?

43. One man declares that the Roman Church is a place of bondage. Is this true? Pieter responds that faith is the way to freedom—not the Church. Why do so many people have trouble distinguishing between real faith and the form of religion? Do you know someone who puts his trust in the identity of the church rather than a relationship with Jesus?

Chapter 25

44. When the pilgrims reach the town of Münden, they decide to take new names for themselves. What does this act symbolize from a spiritual standpoint? What does the meaning of a name convey about a person and his or her identity?

Chapter 26

45. Stumbling upon the village of Renwick, the company discovers a strange assortment of men, women, and children who have been rejected by society. What does Friar Oswald mean when he says that they are like the rest of the world, only inside out? Might this explain why their deformities and imperfections make others uncomfortable?

46. Friar Oswald presents a bevy of beehives as an analogy for the church—as it was intended to function. What similarities exist between the productive hives and a healthy,

thriving body of believers? In what ways do many churches fall short of these standards?

Chapter 27

47. Benedetto decides to remain behind in the village of Renwick. Why does he feel so comfortable there? What special purpose does he serve for the people? What is Benedetto's own handicap? Might this weakness explain why he finally feels that he has found the place where he belongs?

Chapter 28

48. When the pilgrims reach the city of Bremen, Pieter bequeaths his staff to Wil. What is significant about this moment? After so much suffering and change, is Wil ably prepared to shepherd the tiny flock? What is important about leading by becoming a servant? How did Jesus demonstrate this principle during His time on earth?

49. Helmut's father, Horst, blesses and cares for the weary pilgrims and provides them with passports of free status before they depart for Stedingerland. How is God's great mercy evident as new families are created out of broken, disowned, and rejected people? Is this an example of how He can turn all things for good for those who love Him?

50. Like Moses leading the Israelites, Pieter dies before he enters the promised land. Has Pieter's life evidenced the work of the Holy Spirit? What special blessing does the Lord give him before he passes on? Is he now free to go because Heinrich has finally embraced freedom?

GLOSSARY

The Medieval Clock

Medieval time was divided into twelve hours of available daylight. Therefore, a summer's hour would have been longer than a winter's. The corresponding times below, typically called the seven canonical hours, are approximate to the modern method.

Matins: midnight
Prime: daybreak (6 A.M.)
Terce: third hour of light
  (9 A.M.)
Sext: sixth hour of light
  (noon)
Nones: ninth hour of light
  (3 P.M.)
Vespers: twelfth hour of light
  (6 P.M.)
Compline: twilight darkness

The Medieval Calendar

The Seasons

Winter: Michaelmas to the Epiphany. A time of sowing wheat and rye.
Spring: the Epiphany to Easter. A time of sowing spring crops (oats, peas, beans, barley, vegetables).
Summer: Easter to Lammas. A time of tending crops.
Autumn: Lammas to Michaelmas. A time of harvest.
Note: The medieval fiscal year began and ended on Michaelmas.

Holy Days and Feast Days

- Feast of Circumcision / Feast of Fools, January 1: celebration of circumcision of Jesus / a secular feast marked by uproarious behavior honoring those normally of low standing.
- The Epiphany /The Feast of Three Kings, January 6: celebration of the three wise men's visit of Jesus.
- The Baptism of our Lord: the Sunday after the Epiphany.
- Lent: begins 40 days before Easter, not counting Sundays. A time to deny oneself in order to meditate upon the sufferings of Christ.
- Palm Sunday.
- Holy Thursday, Good Friday, Holy Saturday.
- Easter Sunday.
- May Day, May 1: not a holy day, but celebrated throughout much of Christendom as a time of renewal.
- Ascension Day: 40 days after Easter, usually early to mid-May. Celebrates the ascension of Christ into heaven.
- Pentecost: 50 days after Easter, usually late May or early June. Celebrates the coming of the Holy Spirit.

- Midsummer's Day: not a holy day, but rather a celebration of the summer solstice, June 21.
- Lammas, August 1: beginning of harvest.
- Assumption of the Virgin, August 15: celebrates Mary's assumption into heaven.
- St. Michael's Day (Michaelmas), September 25: celebrates the archangel.
- All Hallows' Eve, October 31: a vigil that anticipates All Saints' Day.
- All Saint's Day (Hallowmas), November 1: the honoring of all saints, known and unknown.
- All Souls' Day, November 2: commemoration of all the faithful now departed.
- Martinmas, November 12: celebrates St. Martin of Tours, who spared a freezing beggar by sharing his cloak.
- Season of Advent: begins 4th Sunday before Christmas and lasts through December 24. It is the anticipation of the birth of Christ.
- The Twelve Days of Christmas: Christmas Day to the Epiphany.
- Christmas Day: December 25.
- St. Stephen's Day, December 26: to honor the martyr.
- St. John the Evangelist's Day, December 27: to honor the disciple.

Miscellaneous Terms

abbess: the female superior of a nunnery.

abbey: an autonomous monastery ruled by an abbot.

abbot: the title given to the superior of an autonomous monks' community.

alles klar: German for "all is well."

almoner: an official appointed to distribute alms to the poor.

arpent: a unit of land roughly equivalent to an acre.

assart: the clearing of woodland.

avanti: Italian for "keep moving."

Ave Maria: Latin referring to a prayer to Mary.

bailey: the inner courtyard of castle.

bailiff: the chief officer of a manor, typically supervising general administration and law enforcement.

balk: an unploughed strip of land serving as a boundary.

bambini: Italian for "children."

benefice: a grant of land or other wealth.

bienvenues: French for "welcome."

bitte: German for "please" and "you're welcome."

bloody flux: dysentery.

bon: French for "good."

bowshot: a unit of measurement equivalent to approximately 150 yards.

Bube: German for "little boy."

castellan: the governor of a castle.

cellarer: a monk charged with providing food stocks for the kitchener.

cerebritis: inflammation of the brain.

chain mail: body armor made of small, interlocking steel rings.

chalice: the cup holding the wine of the Eucharist.

chapter: the daily convening of a religious order for purposes of discipline and administration.

chapter house: the building attached to a monastery facilitating the chapter.

chin cough: whooping cough.

cives: Latin referring to the aristocracy.

cloister: a place of religious seclusion; also a protected courtyard within a monastery.

commotion: concussion.

confiteor: the formal expression of repentance.

congestive chill: accumulation of blood in the vessels.

corruption: infection.

cottager: a bound person of the poorest station.

creels: the gaps in the parapets atop a castle's ramparts.

croft: a small yard adjacent to a peasant's cottage, normally used to grow vegetables.

demesne: the land of a manor managed exclusively for the lord.

dowry: originally a gift of property granted by a man to his bride as security for her old age or widowhood.

ell: a unit of measurement equivalent to 4 feet.

flail: a hinged stick used for threshing wheat; also a weapon consisting of a long rod with a swinging appendage on a hinge.

forester: a manorial officer managing the lord's woodland, usually under the supervision of the woodward.

frater: Latin for "brother."

Frau: German for "wife," "Mrs.," or "woman."

furlong: a unit of measurement equivalent to 220 yards.

glaive: a weapon with a blade attached to a shaft.

glebe: a parcel of land owned by the Church for the benefit of a parish.

Gloria Dei: Latin for "praise God."

gratia: Latin for "grace."

grippe: influenza.

halberd: a lance-like weapon.

hauberk: a heavy, sometimes quilted protective garment usually made of leather.

Hausfrau: German for "housewife."

hayward: an official charged with supervising the management of the fields.

hectare: a unit of land measurement roughly equivalent to 2 1/2 acres.

herbarium: the building in a monastery where herbs were stored.

heriot: death tax.

Herr: German for "husband," "Mr.," or "man."

hide: a unit of land equaling about 120 acres.

hogshead: a unit of volume equivalent to 2 barrels.

holding: typically, heritable land granted to a vassal.

Holy See: the seat of papal authority.

Ich bin: German for "I am."

In nomine Patris, et Filii, et Spiritus Sancti: Latin for "in the name of the Father, the Son, and the Holy Spirit."

ja: German for "yes."

Junge: German for "boy."

Kind/Kinder: German for "child/children."

king's evil: swelling of neck glands.

kitchener: the monastery's food overseer.

lago: Italian for "lake."

league: a unit of measurement equivalent to 3 miles.

list: the area of castle grounds located beyond the walls.

Mädel/Mädchen: German for "maiden/young girl."

manor: the land of a lord consisting of his demesne and tenant's holdings.

manumission: the fee required to buy freedom from the lord; also the act by which freedom is granted.

mark: a unit of weight or money equaling roughly 8 ounces of silver.

matrona: Italian for "mother" or "woman."

mead: a fermented beverage made from honey and water.

mein Gott/mein Gott in Himmel: German for "my God/my God in heaven."

merchet: a tax paid for the privilege of marriage.

merlon: the solid segments in the gapped parapets atop a castle's ramparts.

milites: Latin referring to the military class.

milk leg: inflammation of the leg.

monastery: a religious house organized under the authority of the Holy See.

morbus: disease.

mormal: gangrene.

mortal sin: according to the Roman Church, a sin so heinous as to rupture the state of grace between a Christian and God.

Mus: German for "mush," a dish of boiled grains.

Mutti: German for "mommy" or "mama."

novice: a new member of a religious community undergoing an apprenticeship of sorts and not yet fully committed by vows.

nunnery: a religious house for nuns; a convent.

oath-helper: a person who pledges his or her word in support of an accused.

oblate: a child given to a monastery for upbringing.

ordeal: a method of trial by which the accused was given a physical test to determine guilt.

Ordnung: German for "order."

paten: the dish on which the bread of the Eucharist is placed.

pater: Latin for "father."

Pater Noster: Latin referring to the Lord's Prayer.

Pfennig: German for "penny."

plenary indulgence: according to the Roman Church, the remitting of temporal punishment due for sins already forgiven by God.

portcullis: the iron grate dropped along vertical grooves to defend a gate.

postulant: a candidate for membership in a religious order.

pottage: a brothy soup, usually of vegetables and grains.

poultice: an herb-soaked compress.

pound: an accounting measurement of money equaling 20 shillings, or 240 pennies; a pound of silver.

prior: the official ranked just below an abbot; sometimes the superior of a community under the jurisdiction of a distant abbey.

putrid fever: diphtheria.

pyx: the box in which the Eucharist is kept.

quinsey: tonsillitis.

reeve: a village chief, usually elected by village elders.

refectory: the dining hall of a monastery.

rod: a measurement equivalent to 6 feet.

routier: mercenary.

scapular: a long smock worn over the front and back of a monk's habit.

scriptorium: the building in a monastery where books were maintained and copied.

scrofulous: skin disease.

scutage: a tax paid by a freeman in lieu of military service obligations to his lord.

see: the seat of ecclesiastical authority, i.e., bishop.

serf: a bound person of little means.

shilling: an accounting measurement of money valued at 12 pennies.

signora: Italian for "lady" or "Mrs."

signore: Italian for "gentleman" or "Mr."

Spiritus Sanctus: Latin for "Holy Spirit."

St. Anthony's Fire: skin infection.

St. Vitus' Dance: nervous twitches.

steward: a chief overseer of a manor, typically including legal and financial matters.

Stube: German for "parlor."

tithing: a unit of 10 persons.

tonsure: the shaving of the crown of the head to signify Christ's crown of thorns; received as part of religious vows.

trebuchet: a catapult.

trencher: a flat board used as a plate.

tunic: a garment worn as an overshirt, typically hooded, sleeved, and belted outside the leggings.

vassal: a freeman who held land from a lord in exchange for his oath of fealty, usually obligated to perform military service.

Vati/Vater: German for "daddy/father."

vattene: Italian for "hurry along" or "leave."

vellein: a bound person of some means owing labor to his lord and subject to certain taxes.

venial sin: according to the Roman Church, a sin that interferes with a Christian's fellowship with God, though not serious enough to violate the state of grace.

vielen dank: German for "many thanks."

virgate: 1/4 of a hide; considered the minimum amount of land necessary to support one peasant family for one year.

Volk: German for "people."

wattle-and-daub: construction material consisting of woven sticks and clay.

whitlow: boils.

winter fever: pneumonia.

woodward: a manorial overseer of the lord's woodland.

wunderbar: German for "wonderful."

yeoman: a free farmer of modest means.